Too True

BLAKE MORRISON

Granta Books
London

Granta Publications, 2/3 Hanover Yard, London N1 8BE

First published in Great Britain by
Granta Books 1998

A CIP catalogue record for this book is
available from the British Library.

1 3 5 7 9 10 8 6 4 2

ISBN 1 86207 162 4

Typeset by M Rules
Printed and bound in Great Britain by
Mackays of Chatham PLC

Contents

Acknowledgments

Most of the following selection of stories and pieces were published in the past three years, but a few date further back. Two of them – 'Bicycle Thieves' and 'The Quiet One' – are more stories than they are pieces: they start from events that happened to me, but end somewhere else. The rest are features, profiles, interviews, columns and reviews, most first published in the *Independent on Sunday*, others in *Granta*, the *Guardian*, the *Observer*, *GQ* and the *New York Times*. Several have been cut, added to or rewritten in places, not to disguise their ephemerality (which would be impossible) but in the hope of making them truer or more accurate than they succeeded in being first time round.

'Field of Dreams' appeared previously in *Saturday's Boys* edited by Harry Lansdown and Alex Spillius (1990), and 'The Woman on the Doorstep' in *Mind Readings*, which I edited with Sara Dunn and Michèle Roberts (1996). 'Two Wheels Good' was broadcast as part of a BBC Radio Four series *Better Than Sex*. The text of 'The Great Divide' formed the basis for a BBC2 documentary in 1997.

I'm especially grateful, for their editorial skill and encouragement, to Frances Coady, Ian Jack and Jan Dalley. Others

I'd like to thank for their help in various ways are: Liz Jobey, Peter Wilby, Richard Williams, Rosie Boycott, Barbara Gunnell, Sabine Durrant, Beaty Rubens, Richard Askwith, Laurence Earle, James Atlas, Gill Fletcher and Emma Tobias.

Too True

It was a phrase my father liked to use. Whenever something required rueful acknowledgment or cheerful assent, 'too true' would be his response. Horrible weather today: too true. Wonderful news about X's recovery from illness: too true. Anyone feel like going down the pub? Too true. I loved hearing my father say the phrase because it was spare and self-rhyming – oxymoronic, too, though I didn't yet know the word. I'd been told (hadn't he told me himself?) that I should always strive for truth, so how could anything possibly be *too* true? The phrase suggested that truth wasn't the high point or ultimate goal but a state of compromise: some things were untrue, and others too true; truth lay sensibly in between. There were dizzying philosophical implications here, if I'd had a mind for them. More useful was the thought that if my parents sometimes lied to me, which I'd begun to realize they must do, it didn't necessarily make them bad people. My father spoke of 'white lies', fibs told in the service of a higher good. I supposed there might also be black truths, honesties that sprang from (or resulted in) cruelty, wickedness or malice. The lesson was to try to tell truths, not too-truths.

The literature I began to read in my teens – the poetry of

Owen, Sassoon, Eliot and Yeats, the fiction of Lawrence, Joyce, Woolf and Steinbeck, the plays of Ionesco and Beckett – was a challenge to that belief. It didn't offer the customary moral justification for truth-telling, but something fiercer. Fierce, or some variation on it, was a word that kept coming up with these writers: it wasn't enough to be truthful, one had to be *ferociously, uncompromisingly, recklessly* so, in defiance of state tyranny or stale convention and at the risk of one's own freedom and sanity. Most of these writers were modernists, and I understood that the often fragmented and disconcerting methods of modernism – whether cubism or imagism or expressionism, whether Eliot in *The Waste Land*, Stravinsky in the *Rite of Spring* or Picasso in 'Guernica' – were all part of a search for deeper wisdoms or sharper insights. Whether art from earlier periods had the same aspiration I wasn't sure. And even the artists in this period offered very different truths. But most, one way or another, had run into trouble, and, being a teenager, I liked the idea of that. My father, I dimly perceived, had provided a phrase to explain why certain books excited me: not because they were true, but because they were *too* true.

It wasn't only imaginative literature that excited me in this way. At some point in my teens, my parents started taking the *Sunday Times* (to add to the *Daily Mail* and *Sunday Express*). The *Sunday Times*, under Harry Evans's editorship, was in its heyday. Its Insight team created new standards in investigative journalism, and there were several famous exposés, including the thalidomide scandal. (My mother had once delivered a horribly deformed thalidomide baby; the issue felt close to home.) It seemed natural to pore over the colour photographs of atrocities from the Vietnam war much as I had done over Wilfred Owen's poems; or, after reading about it in the *Sunday Times*, to get hold of Thor Heyerdahl's bestselling account of the Kon-Tiki expedition, which I found as compelling as I had *Robinson Crusoe* and *Treasure Island*. No one had told me then that journalism is vulgar, ephemeral, the obverse of art. At best, it seemed to me the same, telling stories that excite and disclosing truths too close for comfort (sometimes too deep for tears as well). Whether fiction or non-fiction didn't seem to matter.

Later, when I read English literature at university and then worked as a literary journalist, I was made to understand that it does matter, greatly. On one side, the novelists I studied, or whose interviews I read, proclaimed their disdain for the lowly grubbers and hacks from (as it then was) Fleet Street. On the other side, the journalists who profiled and wrote news stories about these novelists constantly questioned their artistic integrity: it was alleged that they had plagiarized, or used 'real people' as characters, or shamelessly enriched themselves. (It intrigues me that stories about publishers' advances should still command so many column inches – why should a journalist on £40,000 a year find it outrageous when a novelist receives £100,000 for perhaps five years' work?) Beneath the fighting and backbiting lay an old enmity, a disagreement over which side has the better claim to be telling the truth: novelists, with the subjectivity and imaginative authority of fiction, or journalists, with the objectivity and verifiability of fact.

Literature versus journalism. Fiction versus non-fiction. The picture remains one of mutual antagonism. But as a teenager I thought the categories fluid, and I still think that's nearer the truth. Many novelists, dramatists and poets (from Defoe, Whitman and Dickens to Tom Stoppard, Michael Frayn and Brian Moore) have worked in journalism before flying free of its nets. A few have confessed to learning useful tricks there. Most continue to write for newspapers from time to time. Equally, journalists commonly refer to the articles they write as 'stories', and the best journalism borrows many devices from traditional fiction. A few tabloids fly higher and

more daringly still, into the realms of magical realism. Even
the more scrupulous broadsheets are commonly approached
with scepticism. 'Never believe what you read in the papers'
goes the old adage, which Malcolm Muggeridge amended
when advising a young colleague 'Never believe what you
write in the papers'. Every media studies graduate knows that
reality is constructed. One can imagine a sturdy pragmatist
disputing this, like Dr Johnson taking issue with the philosophy of Berkeley by kicking a stone: the Gulf war *did* happen;
Princess Di *was* killed in a car crash; I refute Baudrillard thus.
But even the pragmatist can't deny that when the media report
events there must always be a line, an angle, a spin. In effect,
a construction. Or story.

We grow up on stories. From infancy onwards, they're a
means of intellectual understanding and emotional recognition, a way of making sense of the world. At some point
during childhood we become aware that many stories are
made up, are fairy-tales. To hear the phrase 'It's only a story'
is one of childhood's crushing moments, like learning Father
Christmas doesn't exist. But children persist with fantasy long
after the dawn of disenchantment. Adults do, too. To believe
in stories is an essential human need. When Defoe wrote
Robinson Crusoe, he helped invent the novel, but he also hoped
that readers would believe his story was true. He posed, as
many novelists have since, not as its author but as its editor,
and presented it as 'a just history of fact; neither is there any
appearance of fiction in it'. Here is an early definition of fiction: the pretence of being 'a just history of fact'.

In this century, as the realist tradition has lost its monopoly,
much fiction has advertised its unbelievability. Magical realism, fantasy, science fiction, neo-fabulism, metafiction,
'surfiction', postmodernism, the *nouveau roman*: these are
forms that let you know 'This isn't strictly – or even
remotely – true'. Non-realist fiction is no less concerned with

reality: often it assumes the form it does (allegory, fable, satire) in order to say the unsayable, or avoid censorship, or get at truths in ways that realism (and journalism) can't. But it isn't interested in making readers think that the events described took place, that the people portrayed exist. The eighteenth- and nineteenth-century realist novel did sometimes work this trick. There were those who fell for the delusion – just as some, in this century, have fallen for *Coronation Street*, confused by where acting ends and life begins. Modern novelists don't expect to be taken literally. They don't want to be taken literally. It was a great shock to Western readers when *The Satanic Verses* was taken literally, and treated as heresy, since Salman Rushdie had called it a novel. The fatwa is a reminder of how dangerous fiction can be (to the author above all) when taken as tract or fact, when misread (or not read) by parties who find it politically useful to take offence. It's a danger other writers still face in the Third World, and that used to exist in Russia and Eastern Europe, too. But in Europe and the US now, fiction has a special licence: it's a protected area where no one need come to any harm. The contemporary reader is sophisticated and understands this. It's never forgotten that novels are made up.

But many readers, including those who enjoy fiction, do have a craving to believe. The growing interest in what's been called 'narrative non-fiction' is part of this need for authenticity, sincerity, credibility – the re-suspension of disbelief. It's arguable that writers and publishers have half-created this need, not merely met the demand. There was a time when autobiographical tales would be dressed up as novels; today the label 'non-fiction' makes sounder commercial sense. The memoir, a form which used to suggest genteel belleletrism, now promises danger and controversy. It's democratic, too, no longer the preserve of famous politicians or novelists looking back in old age but open to the 'ordinary' and unknown, as

Jung Chang, Nick Hornby and Frank McCourt were when they wrote (respectively) *Wild Swans, Fever Pitch* and *Angela's Ashes*. As Robert Winder pointed out in an analysis of the rise of the memoir for the magazine *Granta*, 'bookshops now groan with confessions: criminals and addicts, abuse victims and sports fans, war heroes and domestic saints (or sinners) queue up to get their lives off their chests.' Once, young writers wishing to make a mark would automatically choose fiction. Now, if it's essentially their own story they're telling, they may prefer to tell it as fact. And the editors of publishing houses would probably encourage them to do so: chances are it's more profitable to market a memoir of growing up abused in Darlington than a first novel on the same subject.

Beyond this commercial exploitation of the genre, the rise of narrative non-fiction does say something about the *Zeitgeist.* The memoir is the chosen form of a culture of intimacy, where what used to be secret has come out in the open and voices that used to be silent make themselves heard. There's a veneration of first-person truth-telling – and fiction, because it tells lies and/or does not allow for a simple conflation of author and narrator, has lost some of the prestige it enjoyed in the 1980s. It's no coincidence that two of the most successful books in recent years – Alan Clark's *Diaries* and Alan Bennett's *Writing Home* – have assumed that overtly candid, first-person form, the diary. The bestselling paperback of 1997 was also a diary, Bridget Jones's: it may have been both fictional and pseudonymous, but its trick was to use a discourse that's informal, self-communing and seemingly artless. Perhaps there's a feeling now that novels can't get our attention, having lost their power to surprise and shock. Or perhaps it's that we're more suspicious of the made-up than we used to be, and (temporarily) more inured to it – that we're guilty of what Doris Lessing has called 'a reluctance of the imagination'. Whatever the reason, narrative non-fiction –

with its personal testimony, its guarantee that *this actually happened* – has arrived to fill a gap.

Some would say it arrived more than twenty years ago. In 1975 Tom Wolfe produced his anthology of 'The New Journalism', and it was, he claimed, ten years before that when he first discovered 'it was possible to write accurate non-fiction with techniques usually associated with novels and short stories'. Others in the 1960s had made the same discovery: Truman Capote in *In Cold Blood*, Joan Didion, Norman Mailer, George Plimpton, Hunter Thompson. Wolfe mentions several distinguished forerunners: Boswell, Dickens's *Sketches by Boz*, Henry Mayhew's *London Labour and the London Poor*, John Reed's *Ten Days That Shook the World*, George Orwell's *Down and Out in Paris and London*, John Hersey's *Hiroshima*. Even at their most subjective, however, the New Journalists and their predecessors had a documentary purpose and often made use of the third person. The present wave of narrative non-fiction is more inward, 'I'-fixated, even solipsistic. The American critic James Wolcott has called the genre 'the erotics of neurotics'. The British novelist and literary editor Robert McCrum sees it as the modern equivalent of the war memoir: with their tales from the operating room or Freudian couch, the generation of writers born after 1945 have only inner battles to relate. They are, everyone says, 'confessional'.

Confessionalism has always been a disreputable genre. It depends on the sort of intimacy between writer and reader which, as Angela Carter once noted, constitutes 'the narrative mode of a good deal of downmarket women's magazine fiction'. It is the art of the diary, the home movie, the e-mail. Its venue is the confessional box, or the therapist's couch, or the bedroom. It is privacy for public consumption, something picked up by a hidden camera or tape recorder. It has that bottom drawer feel, the 'could do better' of the school report, as if something more estimable might have been achieved. It is, at its best, reality writing itself, but its practitioners may be made to feel that they're not 'real' writers, since they've broken the rule that only by imaginatively transforming and transcending personal material can a writer achieve universality. They stand accused of narcissistically pouring out their stories, rather than shaping them – of being authors who have more problems than they have talent. They are arraigned for breaching decency, for being tasteless, self-important and exhibitionist. They may even be suspected of laziness. One of *The Late Show*'s brightest critics, asked why there was such a vogue for memoirs, replied that they were simply easier to write. And this is a well-founded suspicion: fiction and poetry are hard to perfect; most journals do better to stay private.

Yet truth-telling is a quality we esteem in authors, especially when it can't be found in politicians, which is most of the time. And there are periods – this seems to be one – when there's a need for authenticity, a need to rest near a beating heart. Some books, in any period, demand to be fiction: if J. G. Ballard had written *Crash* as some version of autobiography, our interest in the issues he raises (cars, speed, celebrity, eroticism) would have turned to prurience instead. But other kinds of book compel us by getting down off their plinths and declaring their modest stature – by being small stories, not tall stories. There is nothing so exhilarating as reading fiction that has been thrown free of the author's life, that is driven entirely by invented characters and events. But the traditional disclaimer of novels, that the characters and events described bear no resemblance to living or actual ones, can look like cowardice if we suspect these are just passages from the author's life thinly disguised. Why wear a fancy dress if you look better with your clothes off? Let's be honest. Candour can be very sexy.

The American poet Robert Lowell discovered this, back in

the 1960s and 1970s, with books such as *Life Studies* and *The Dolphin*, which incorporated slices of autobiography (and, more controversially, letters from his estranged wife Elizabeth Hardwick). Lowell was credited with founding a 'confessional' school of poetry, along with Sylvia Plath and Anne Sexton. But the genre goes much further back, to Saint Augustine, whose *Confessions* repented both of childhood misdemeanours (such as stealing pears from an orchard) and of adult sins of the flesh (the year being 397, not 1997, the details were in short supply). Saint Augustine didn't think he was exposing himself unduly, since the all-seeing God whom he addressed knew the intimate truth about him already. But he hoped that by recounting his godless behaviour he might make other miserable sinners better people – that the error of his way would lead others to choose the path of righteousness. Some such do-gooding motive used to lie behind most confessional literature, including Jean Jacques Rousseau's (on sex and love) and Thomas De Quincey's (on addiction to opium): the revelation of the self is supposed to bring moral elevation to others. These days, the emphasis isn't moral but psychotherapeutic. With luck, one's own murky tale will help those with similar experiences, who might otherwise suffer in silence, thinking they're the only one – putting the book down, they will feel vindicated, validated, less pathological than they'd assumed.

In the US, the new literature of self-revelation is perceived as a female form, the result of women finding their identities and voices. Kathryn Harrison's *The Kiss* (about incest), Elizabeth Wurzel's *Prozac Nation*, Mary Karr's *The Liar's Club*, Sallie Tisdale's *Talk Dirty to Me* (addiction to pornography) Caroline Knapp's *Drinking: A Love Story* and Jill Ciment's *Half a Life* (teenage delinquency) are prime examples. Behind them lie Maya Angelou's autobiographical volumes, the slogan 'The personal is political', and the influence of women's groups in the 1970s and 1980s. In Britain, female confessionalism has been common enough in newspaper columns but (aside from Fiona Shaw's *Out of Me*, Jenny Diski's *Skating to Antarctica*, Andrea Ashworth's *Once in a House on Fire* and one or two others) rarer in book form. Instead, the talk here has been of a new generation of men 'in touch with their feelings' who expose these feelings to an almost indecent degree.

Causing discomfort doesn't make a writer good, but good writing can often cause discomfort. Christopher Ricks once published a book called *Keats and Embarrassment*, about the blushfulness of Keats's poetry, and with confessional writing embarrassment is inescapable. We can feel awkward reading it in public, not because it's samizdat or (like porn, say) sub-literary, but because we feel somehow exposed by it – as if by reading it any stranger sitting nearby would be able to read us. It may be we feel that the author has said things that would have been better left unsaid. But it may also be that he or she has disclosed awkward information about ourselves. Confessionalism is the art of the mirror, but the face in the glass can be ours as well as the author's, an image we recognize but would rather not see.

As this suggests, candour is a delicate business. To say 'I'm not perfect, and I know you're not either' may be to stretch out a friendly hand, or merely presumptuous. When the exchange doesn't come off, the writer will feel grubby and the reader bullied. The famous 'cleansing' process of catharsis is known by another name: 'washing your dirty linen in public'. Confessionalism has to know when to hold back. Honesty has to be worked at. 'A little sincerity is a dangerous thing,' said Wilde, 'and a great deal of it is absolutely fatal.' Writers who confess merely in order to make themselves feel better are likely to leave their audiences feeling worse. It takes special charm in a writer to make us look into our own hearts, or history, to see if there's something comparable there. It takes art. Without art, confessionalism is masturbation. Only with art does it become empathy.

Many recent narrative non-fictions own up to weakness by telling tales of grief, breakdown, abuse, illness, depression and addiction. Almost all of them end on an upbeat note. Almost by definition, there has to be a happy ending: such 'crisis memoirs' can be written only when the authors have put some distance between themselves and the material. This is emotion recollected in tranquillity, or on tranquillizers – memoirs composed not on an alcohol- or drug-induced high but during recovery. They may seem to come straight from the heart, but they wouldn't exist had the authors not repossessed their minds. Their 'I' isn't blind with turmoil and emotion, but rather the 'I' of the storm, calm amid chaos, or else the 'I' of the needle, precise and sharp. To write about the self's hot flushes, you have to be cold and detached.

It's important to emphasize this, because confessionalism is usually thought of as transparent and messy, a spontaneous overflow of powerful feeling. Perhaps the confessions heard during the *Oprah Winfrey Show*, or on radio phone-ins, or from garrulous cab drivers, are little more than a damburst of emotion. But even they depend on the telling of stories and the projection of a self. Confessional writers who want to offer their readers more than a cheap thrill must first create a trustworthy persona. Candour doesn't write itself straight from the heart; it's a device, requiring artfulness; to succeed, all trace of disingenuousness and self-delusion must be purged. Honesty is a *policy*, not an involuntary emission of naked ego. Sincerity is a trick, like any other. The process of being 'truthful' as a writer is not unlike that of constructing a narrative voice in fiction.

It's no coincidence that one of the great narrative non-fiction books of the last twenty years, Tobias Wolff's *This Boy's Life*, reads at times like a novel. It certainly begins like one, as a truck dramatically plunges over a cliff. Even when the narrator breaks the spell and explains that this all happened long ago, his isn't the calm, reflective voice of a man tidying up his early years but of somebody plunged back inside the adventure of being ten:

> It was 1955 and we were driving from Florida to Utah, to get away from a man my mother was afraid of and to get rich on uranium. We were going to change our luck.

Tobias Wolff doesn't pretend he still is ten: we glimpse the frame of an adult perspective. But nor does he pretend he has it all worked out, and that is part of the attraction. Like Salinger in *The Catcher in the Rye*, Wolff creates a voice we can trust.

One reason we trust both these narrators is that, far from pouring everything out, they're highly selective, have a sense of story, can be depended on to avoid the extraneous and clichéd. As Holden Caulfield famously puts it:

> I'm not going to tell you my whole goddam autobiography or anything. I'll just tell you about this madman stuff that happened to me around last Christmas just before I got pretty run-down and had to come out here and take it easy.

The Catcher in the Rye is a novel written like a confession. *This Boy's Life* is a confession written like a novel. The differences between the two genres are real, but can also be much exaggerated. Both depend on the art of storytelling. And both depend on the construction (or reinvention) of a character who has become almost redundant in modern literature: the reliable narrator.

All fiction, it's been said, tends towards autobiography: think of Proust or Dickens. Yet most novelists, in interviews with journalists, are reluctant to surrender their autobiography, fearing that if they do their life will become *the* story, the ur-text, and the novels be read as a pale reflection or sub-plot. Recently, a number of novelists have turned to non-fiction not so much to write conventional autobiography as to brood over the real-life sources of their art. Kathryn Harrison, having written on the theme of incest in her novel *Thicker Than Water*, came back to it again, non-fictionally, in *The Kiss*, as if this were the 'honest' way to tell her story, though some of the passages are almost identical. Philip Roth did something similar in *Patrimony* when he wrote about his father, Herman, having previously fictionalized him in various guises. What impelled Roth was a wish to pay tribute, his father having recently died; what impelled Harrison (whose father was alive to read her memoir) was more adversarial, even parricidal, as well as cathartic – the need to lay a family ghost. Both writers grasped that we read a story differently if we believe it to be true. In this country Jenny Diski has had the same insight: her *Skating to Antarctica* revisits in person, autobiographically, a number of episodes from her novels. Whether we can trust her in non-fictional mode is doubtful: the very title of her book suggests something fantastical. Can we trust Philip Roth, either? Can he even trust himself? A couple of years before *Patrimony*, he published *The Facts*, subtitled 'a novelist's autobiography', which sprang, he said, from his 'exhaustion with masks, disguises, distortions, lies'. Its preface, cast as a letter to his fictional alter ego Nathan Zuckerman, explains how

> . . . in its uncompelling, unferocious way, the non-
> fictional approach has brought me closer to how
> experience actually *felt* than has turning the flame up

under my life and smelting stories out of all I've
known . . . [A] book that faithfully conforms to the
facts, a distillation of the facts that leaves off with the
imaginative fury, can unlock meanings that
fictionalizing has obscured, distended, or even inverted
and can drive home some sharp emotional nails.

It's a wonderful rationale for non-fiction. But Zuckerman, at
the end of the book, answers back, accusing Roth of '*de*-imagining a life's work' and arguing that 'the facts are much more
refractory and unmanageable and inconclusive, and can actually kill the very sort of inquiry that imagination opens up.'

A danger of the current fashion for caring-sharing non-fiction is we'll forget that epiphanies of recognition are part of
fiction, too. The 'Yes, I know that feeling!' echo or rhyme
which we get from good writing doesn't depend on the author
personally having had the experience described or from the
reader having had it either. What authenticates isn't fact but
art. Ian McEwan's *A Child in Time* begins with a brilliant
description of a father losing his child in a supermarket.
Whether McEwan himself, as a father, went through a similar
ordeal is irrelevant; whether his readers have is also irrelevant;
it's the power of the writing that makes the experience familiar and identifiable with. Richard Ford's *Independence Day*
includes a stunning episode during which the hero, Frank
Bascombe, is party to an accident involving the teenage son he
had by his now estranged wife. As it happens, Richard Ford
does not have children. It doesn't matter. The scene works by
plausibly imagining. Ford himself was never there but he
makes us feel that we were. We believe in his invented truth.

Yet autobiographical facts inevitably make a difference to
how we read. If it were discovered tomorrow that
Wordsworth had grown up in Sussex, not the Lake District,
The Prelude would be no less magnificent, but it wouldn't be

the same poem: the understanding between Wordsworth and his readers that it's autobiographically truthful would have been violated. Non-fiction always implies some such understanding. When Harold Brodkey wrote a piece for the *New Yorker* that began 'I have Aids', readers were moved; they'd not have been moved if it had turned out Brodkey was making this up, though they knew him to be a writer of fiction. There have been other interesting non-fictional books about illness and death in recent years: Joseph Heller's *No Laughing Matter*, Tim Lott's *The Scent of Dried Roses*, Ben Watt's *Patient*, Jean Dominique Bauby's *The Diving-bell and the Butterfly*. The claims they make on us depend on our conviction that their ordeals really did happen as described. There have been columns of this kind, too – Oscar Moore on having Aids, Ruth Picardie and John Diamond on having cancer. Perhaps illness and death are special cases, requiring solemn observation of category lines. Certainly there'd be a sense of outrage if these writers had secretly been enjoying good health.

Away from hospital, it's possible to be more playful. When Paul Theroux published a book with the title *My Other Life*, he called it a novel, just as he had his earlier *My Secret History*. But the main character is a novelist called Paul Theroux, whose background bears a striking resemblance to that of the real Paul Theroux, also a novelist. Other characters in the book include Anthony Burgess and Queen Elizabeth II, as well as some whose real-life lineaments are recognizable but whose names have been changed. Whether any, some or all of the events described (they include an extraordinary conversation with the Queen) actually happened or not, Theroux isn't telling. Or rather he is telling, story-telling, asking us to enjoy his book for its own sake without worrying overmuch whether it's true. This isn't something every reader will feel able to do. Thomas Hardy once said that there was an 'infinite mischief' in 'the mixing of fact and fiction in unknown proportions'.

Theroux is being mischievous when he writes in his preface: 'As for the other I, the Paul Theroux who looks like me – he is just a fellow wearing a mask. It is the writer's privilege to keep some façades intact and use his own face in the masquerade. It was the only area in which I took no liberties. The man is fiction, but the mask is real.' This preface is signed 'PT', which could be a confession of authorship but might stand for 'prick-tease' or even 'postmodern trick'. It is a tricksy preface, yet the texture of the stories themselves is old-fashioned, intimate, dependable. They seem honest. Even if they're not honest, they're true.

'All the best stories are true' ran the logo to a non-fiction award a few years ago. The slogan is seductive, but it's equally arguable that all the best stories (Aesop, Homer, Chaucer, Shakespeare, Grimm, Tolstoy) are made up. Great fiction, by carrying readers along with it, by informing and enticing and absorbing them, creates its own truth – truth that may be truer than the truest memoirs. Some memoirs of public life are notorious for their economy with recorded fact. Memoirs of private life (and most recent narrative non-fiction is of this kind) aren't easily checkable in that way, yet are assumed to have reliable narrators. A little wariness seems appropriate, since memoirs depend on memories, which are often false. When an author recalls in exhaustive detail a scene from thirty years ago we may wonder if it happened exactly that way.

If we don't wonder, it's because the narrator has convinced us of his honesty. The narrator may be an invention, made real merely through words set down in a certain order on the page. But if he bears the same name as the author, in effect seems to *be* the author, the reader will be more inclined to trust him. This is the special contract which non-fiction offers, and once it has been established the reader will feel uneasy if something appears to be made up. As Janet Malcolm puts it in her book *The Journalist and the Murderer*, a novelist is master of his own house and may do what he likes with it; he may even tear it down if he is so inclined. . . . But the writer of non-fiction is only a renter, who must abide by the conditions of his lease, which stipulates that he leave the house – and its name is Actuality – as he found it . . .

I speak about the limitation on a non-fiction writer's scope for invention as if it were a burden, when, in fact, it is what makes his work so much less arduous. Where the novelist has to start from scratch and endure the terrible labour of constructing a world, the non-fiction writer gets his world ready-made . . . The reader extends a kind of credit to the writer of non-fiction which he doesn't extend to the writer of fiction . . .

Janet Malcolm may exaggerate when she says that we read non-fiction 'in a more lenient spirit than a work of imaginative literature', but perhaps it's true that we don't look for the same architectural subtleties. The overwhelmingly important thing is the content, or felt life; 'style', in certain contexts at least (the description of a death, for example), may be resented as indecent and will certainly raise questions (as an equivalent description of a death in fiction wouldn't) about the author's motivation and possible culpability. None the less, overtly or otherwise, good non-fiction does inevitably employ many of the devices of fiction: narrative, characterization, suspense, surprise, and a sense of beginning-middle-end. The truth must be there, but it may come refracted rather than straight and it won't be the whole truth. Setting down words on paper can enable an author to say things which he or she wouldn't have the courage to speak aloud, in person. Nevertheless, the disclosure of the self is firmly in the author's control.

In other words, selectivity and detachment are as much a part of confessionalism as other forms of writing. However

frank the tone, what's revealed in a final draft will often be
more self-dramatizing than it is self-revealing: the author
pares his or her fingernails while seeming to let it all hang out.
Susan Sontag has said 'Some people are their lives, others
merely inhabit them', and if you're in the latter camp, as many
writers are, there's a distance that enables you to dissect yourself without it hurting. The most non-fictional of passages
can feel, as they're being written, like fiction: what the reader
finds shockingly intimate may have seemed to the author
strangely impersonal. In *As If*, a book about children, childhood and the Bulger case, I describe having an erection when
a small child (gender unspecified) sits in my lap. Naïvely,
perhaps, I was shocked that people were shocked by the passage; there was no controversy when a Martin Amis character
describes the same experience in *The Information*. One scene
may be invented, and the other not, but presumably the
phenomenon itself isn't an invention: both narrators are dis-
comfited by it – erections may produce children, but children
aren't supposed to produce erections – and it's the discomfi-
ture which both authors explore. In *My Father and Myself*, J. R.
Ackerley speaks of 'this life I am prowling about in [as if] it
were someone else's and I its historian'. It's a good description
of how memoir and autobiography operate.

   In the end, the difference between fiction and non-fiction is
not so much a matter of lies versus truth, but of reading
habits. When we think a story hasn't been invented, there's an
extra frisson in reading it – a frisson which an author can
exploit. To be brutal, it sometimes helps not to make things
up. I think it helped me when I wrote a book called *And When
Did You Last See Your Father?*, about my father's death from
cancer. Writing a novel based on the experience – a narrator-
son a bit like me, a father based on my father – seemed, in the
end, inappropriate, so I tried to stick to the facts, even though
this risked upsetting relations and friends. 'Sticking to the

facts' didn't preclude me changing one or two names, however, including the name of a woman with whom my father had had a long relationship: the relationship, and my attempts to understand it, went into the book, but the woman acquired a new name to be saved from prying. There were other liberties taken: a scene in a tea shop, described as taking place on the day I went to register my father's death, happened months later, in a different part of the country, while I was writing the book. Being truthful, I sensed, meant being true to the book's form, its themes and structure, as well as to the facts.

Some critics have argued that non-fiction encourages sloppier reading habits, inimical to the stringency and intensity of imaginative literature. Others have complained that the novel has had to resort to faction, or doc-fic, in order to survive. Certainly many successful 'literary' novels of recent years – for example, Pat Barker's First World War trilogy, Thomas Keneally's *Schindler's Ark*, Michael Ondaatje's *The English Patient* and Seamus Deane's seemingly autobiographical *Reading in the Dark* – depend on 'real' historical events and characters. But there is nothing new about novelists doing this: Defoe and George Eliot did it, too. Nor is there anything new in predictions of the death of the novel because of competition from other forms: each autumn, round the time of the Booker Prize, dire prophecies fill the columns and airwaves. Thankfully, the novel is far too robust to be forced out of business, least of all by non-fiction. This isn't a fight to the death. It isn't even a contest. Writers can be competitive animals, but in the end the only struggle is against themselves (to find the right words, to complete the book that needed to be written), not against other writers or genres.

The problem with fiction is being able to shrug it off: 'Why should I care about this stuff? It's all made up.' The problem with non-fiction is being unable to shrug it off, even if you'd prefer to: 'Do we have to be told this? I'd really rather not know.' But in the end, both novels and memoirs have to be judged for their interest *as stories*. And for that what counts isn't honesty but narrative skill.

1
Lost
Childhoods

Bicycle Thieves

Late June, scorched grass and sprinklers, the sky as if scuffed and beaten. Too hot to work, too lazy to think, I've knocked off early to play tennis. I'm sitting on the edge of the bed, putting on my trainers, when my son crashes in, a raspberry lolly bleeding in his hands, huge breaths and distraught between them, dragging the words from a well:

'My bike . . . they took . . . I left . . . when I came out . . . my bike . . .'

'Don't cry, don't cry, we'll sort it out,' I say, pulling his wet head to me. 'What is it, what's happened?'

'The bike. It was outside the shop. I was buying a Twister. Two boys took it.'

'What about the chainlock? I've told you.'

'But I was only a minute.'

'Did you see them?'

'No, two little kids said. But I saw them outside before.'

'How old?'

'Bit bigger than me. Twelve or thirteen. The little kids pointed where they'd gone.'

'Good. We'll go and have a look.'

We jump in the car. It would have taken him ten minutes to

run back. Five minutes more have passed. They're quarter of an hour away at least.

The shop is at the edge of a small estate. HAPPY SHOPPER it says over the window, which is covered by a metal grille. This is one of the better estates: an estate people try to move into, not out of. You can tell because the shop has only a grille, not metal shutters or wooden boards. Behind his sloping rack of sweets, the Asian owner is upset.

'Sorry, no, I didn't see. I served the boy, yes. It's happened before. You have to lock your bikes. I try to tell them.'

'I've tried to tell him too. But it was only a minute. You didn't notice any boys outside?'

'No. Only two schoolchildren at a time in here. That's my rule. It keeps down incidents. But outside . . .'

I duck out again, angry at these bullying great kids who've taken my son's bike, and also excited. We pause by the shuttered off-licence next door, CHEERS, long past its last closing time.

'Which way did they go?' I ask.

'The kids said here,' he says, pointing to a walkway between lock-up garages. We follow down, glancing to left and right, in case the bike has been abandoned. At the end is a metal barrier, a pedestrian crossing over the road, and, beyond, the Ferrier Estate. I've read about the Ferrier: named after an opera singer, Kathleen Ferrier; sixties planning dream gone sour; rhymes with terrier, not Perrier. Wasn't there an article once, about the Drain Children here, kids living underground among sewage pipes? I've heard the stories: about murders, rapes and stabbings; about crack-dealers ripping each other off; about the dangers of parking. You get the same jokes and stories about other estates. But I'm new to this bit of southeast London. I didn't realize the Ferrier was so close. I've not been paying attention.

We cross over, and follow the dust-groove of a path across

the grass. It runs by a high metal fence, like tennis court mesh, but the concrete square beyond the wire has no markings – a compound of nothing. Where the high fence ends, a lower wood-slat fence begins, with a sign saying ANTI-VANDAL PAINT. A big-windowed building, some sort of institution, sits peeling beyond – a school, with spiked railings to keep the pupils in by day and out by night. We head on over the grass to where the first block of flats looms up on our left, like a docked cruise liner.

'I think those are the kids who saw,' says my son.

A boy and a girl, black, about six. They're holding a small plastic holey bat each, like a pair of waffles, the sort you're supposed to use with spongy-light balls. When they strike their yellow tennis ball the bats flop limply and the ball dies. Seeing us, they stop the game, curious, waiting.

'You saw his bike being stolen?'

'Yeh.'

'It was two boys?'

'Yeh.'

'Do you know them? Did you see where they went?'

'Up there. Past the yellow block, the next one, that begins with number twenty. One of them lives at number twelve.'

'So you know him?'

'No, but he lives there.'

'Do you know his name?'

'Andy, yeh, innit.'

The boy has done all the talking but now the girl says:

'We're visiting. From Wandsworth. We don't live here.'

She picks up the ball and whacks her bendy racket at it: 'Come on, Stephen.'

'Thanks,' I say, not knowing which of their answers, if any, are true. A stolen bike: in my day, that would have been something, and if a boy and his father were out looking, you'd want to help, you'd join in the hunt, you'd . . . And yet they'd not been unhelpful. The spareness, the wariness: I recognize it from my own kids; it's how the young are taught to be with strangers. So we were looking for a bike; so they had seen the bike being stolen? It didn't mean they should trust us, co-operate, go out of their way. How they'd been was as unobstructive as anyone could be without running risks. To answer when strangers ask you questions – this is plenty, this is more than enough.

We press on, under the unfiltered sun, past the first block and into the square beyond, over concrete slabs with weeds growing through. The square is like a giant courtyard, the four cruise liners (each with five decks) round the sides, a fenced-off adventure playground in the middle – slides, climbing frames, ravine bridges, twirls of metal. Among the dozen or so boys here – shaven-headed, bare-chested, earringed – two are riding bikes. As we move towards the playground for a better look, I try to remember what the bike was like – silver wheels, hairy grey saddle, black foam bits (like the sort used to insulate copper pipes) over the handlebars. My son hangs against the wire like a prisoner. Then he says, 'Nah, not mine.'

'Are you sure?' I ask, wondering if he – his father's son – merely fears the confrontation. These bikes all look the same to me. High above, men in vests lean from balconies, watching, waiting. I'm glad, really, that I don't have to challenge these bikes' owners, or putative owners. I'm glad I'm not black or Asian, not Jamaican or Pakistani or Tanzanian or Vietnamese or Somali, much riskier here – to judge from the stories I've heard – than being a middle-class white.

We pass on to the next square: no sign of a bike. Beyond, there's a light-blue map-board saying FERRIER ESTATE, and I try to get my bearings. There are some names here, faint and faintly foreign – Pinto, Gallus, Dando, Romero, Telemann – but most have been defaced, as if it were wartime and the signpost had been blanked out to confuse the enemy.

The estate's much bigger than I thought. A railway runs through it, dividing east from west. A four-wheel drive nought-to-sixties in five seconds down the abbreviated street.

It's hot, and my son is lagging. 'Keep up,' I say, noticing the kicked-in front gates, the flaky window frames, the front doors grinning broad and toothless where letter boxes must once have neatly gleamed. 'Keep up,' I say again, wondering how conspicuous we look, how much like strangers. We're in the second square now, and for a moment lean against the wall, cupped by its shadow. Like all the other walls here, it's battle-ship grey and ribbed in texture, like a roll of Plasticine. Searching for deeper shade, we sit in a gully of broken steps. Around us pigeons purr and tick over, scanning the concrete, something stuck in the back of their throat; the balconies above us are covered in chicken-wire to stop them sitting and shitting there. A tyre-less old Ford sits on its arches. That fall-out of glass must have been its windows once. Under the sun, the shards are like ice: I want to gather a handful and wipe them across our faces. Up ahead, the windows and vents are painted yellow, not blue, which means the next block on our left must be the one the little boy meant, if the first door is number twenty, which it is. We get up. We move on. 'Stay near me, pretend we're not looking,' I say, as if we're stalking a murderer, not a kid who may or may not have stolen a bike. The numbers run down to twelve: a front yard with a rusting washing machine, a barbecue, a baby's car-seat, a toddler's scooter, a plastic patrol car, a box of empties. No bike. I hadn't expected it, out in the open. If I were bolder, I'd knock at the door. But I couldn't do that on the say-so of two six-year-olds. And what would the use be, even if I had the nerve, even if the doors, everywhere on chains, were opened wide? No answering kid would shop himself; no parent would shop him either.

We walk on, to the next square, painted red. The sun seems

hotter here. Beyond there's a tall chimney, like a factory chimney except that there's no factory. We go closer, drawn by the furniture dumped in the yard behind it. But this is a boiler-house, and there's no sign of a bike. 'What Must I Do To Be Saved?' asks an advert posted on what looks like a bus shelter, but, windows intact, turns out to be a lift lobby. We search the brambled slope of the railway embankment. We search the next square and the squares beyond: green, purple, brown, pink, navy-blue. I'm getting the hang of the estate now, its fierce symmetries and sudden departures: the ground floor yards and then, above, the decks of glass and metal, some with ensigns of washing, some with the foghorn of a satellite dish. It's like a gaudy chessboard, a square of squares, vertical squares of glass, horizontal squares of stone, different shades and different colours. But just when I seem to have worked it out, I'm lost again, away from the thronging squares on a patch of broken concrete, the only sign of life a dog snarling from behind a wooden fence and then a second dog, snappish, running towards us.

'Fuck off,' I say, ready to boot it. Rather than harass us, it sniffs at the fence confining the bigger dog, driving it to new fits of frenzy. We move away.

'I don't think we're going to find it ourselves,' I say. 'I think we should go home and call the police.'

The sun presses down again, unforgivingly hot, as if this were a foreign country we'd slipped into from some hole in the map. Under the glare, the flats look sinister, like a new Stonehenge: bad blood in the shadow of the obelisk. An ice-cream van ting-tangs an ancient pop song. On the path, disposed of, a disposable nappy. Did the child who was its wearer, toddling in these canyons, drop it here? No, some adult has tried to roll it up, to fold its odour in on itself, though not, in this heat, successfully. Far from any rubbish chute, it seems an odd place for a nappy to have strayed, though I've known odder. One summer when my son was small, we parked in a rush at Stansted Airport and left the passenger window open half an inch. By the time we came back two weeks later, someone had posted a nappy through. It sat there on the passenger seat, a welcome-home banner, a friendly gesture to remind us, in case the holiday had over-excited us, that now we were back in Britain.

No sign of a bike. Disappointed and relieved, we soodle homewards, back to square one, hoping to find and quiz some more the kids who'd seen the other kids, but finding only their tennis ball, its yellow fuzz marking the spot, the spoor of their limp game.

'It's all right,' I say to my son, as we reach the car. 'It'll turn up.'

'As if,' he says.

Back home, I phone the police, who take down details, and promise to send an officer round, 'when an officer becomes available'.

'When will that be?'

'That I can't say, sir.'

This is what being middle-aged means: not avoiding the police, but needing them to come round and feeling pissed off when they don't. My son is pale still and bleared by his earlier weeping. But it isn't some ultimate shaking grief: he knows how the world works, that possessions can't any longer (or not for long) be possessed. Boys steal bikes – and car radios, and anything not nailed down in shops – as casually as they once stole apples. Those are the good boys. The bad ones take the cars as well as the radios. The worse ones take the cars, then set fire to them, if they haven't crashed them first. Once, if something went, there was the thought, consoling to the liberal-minded, the guiltily affluent, that someone less well off must have needed it: that car, or bike, would be riding around somewhere, under different colours. Now the old motives –

need, greed – can't be relied on: as often as not, stolen possessions might pass, not to a different owner, but into oblivion, wrecked or set alight.

Easy-come, easy-go, cheering himself up with Weetabix, my son seems resigned now – more resigned than I am, still angry at the world I've brought him into, which has now carried off his favourite thing. I tell him not to worry, that it wasn't his fault, that there are other bikes, that we'll buy him a new one, which he'd have needed soon enough anyway. We're sitting in the kitchen, under the old fifties built-in cupboards we've never bothered to tear out, and I think of how the scene might have played itself out then: one of those epiphanies of childhood, bringing with it the end of innocence and a lesson in the epistemology of loss: the boy dries his tears and, harder, wiser, learns henceforward how to watch out for himself, how to mourn, how to stand up. But these are the nineties. It's only a bike, for Christ's sake. There are queues for them every day at Argos. Things get broken or go missing, and you replace them. What more is there to say?

Later, alone, I drive back through the hot night to number twelve and park. Small children pass in and out through the open door into the front yard. A teenager tinkers with his motorbike. The man of the house comes out with a can of Kestrel and leans against his wall. I duck down behind my newspaper till he goes back into the flickering neon square beyond the net curtains. I sit for an hour, until the ebb and flow of small children has ceased. But there is no twelve-year-old returning on his – or someone else's – bike. I drive back home, still tracking the estate, certain it's there. My car was stolen once, outside a flat I had in Greenwich, and afterwards, convinced it was just kids taking a quick way home after the pub, I drove round the streets of south-east London, in a friend's car, madly exhilarated for hours, on the case like

Sherlock Holmes or Maigret, only belatedly getting out the *A–Z* and seeing what a small patch I'd covered. But a bike . . . it could not have gone far.

Later still I lie awake in bed and hear sirens and more sirens. The estate seems close now, scarcely beyond the bottom of the garden. I half-doze and imagine blue lights surrounding the estate, police cars and fire engines and ambulances, and a solitary boy on a stolen bike at the centre of their arc lights: 'There's no hope, kid. Step down from the saddle and walk towards us with your hands up.' But the sirens are speeding all over the city and suburbs, to diverse domestic incidents, the humdrum nightly toll, stabbings and smashed windows and stolen VCRs. It's up to me to solve this smaller crime. I get up and begin putting my clothes on. As I reach for my trainers, my wife wakes.

'Where are you going?'

'To look for the bike.'

'You're mad. It's three in the morning. It's only a bike. We can get it back on insurance.'

'It's the principle. Plus I feel sorry for him.'

'He's OK about it. I've talked to him. It's you that's the problem. Anyway, they didn't hurt him, did they, they didn't beat him up? It could have been a lot worse.'

'He's my son. It was his bike. I should try my best to get it back for him. My father would have, for me.'

'Jesus, you have tried. He knows you've tried. Come back to bed. Leave it to the police. Didn't they say they'd be round?'

'When an officer becomes available,' I say, starting to undress. 'Meaning never.'

But an officer stands on the doorstep the following morning. I go through the incident again. I show him the 'owner's manual' for the bike, a four-page leaflet. I confirm that, no, the bike hadn't been engraved or tagged with an ID number.

I describe the conversation with the kids, and mention the address they gave.

'Number twelve? Ah, yes, a family known to us, I think I'm right in saying. We'll pay them a little visit, though I don't hold out much hope.'

'Well, you never know . . .'

'There's a trade in stolen bikes, you see. The boys don't rob them for themselves: they sell them on. We've had a tip-off they're being shifted to second-hand shops up north. You really have to get your bike coded or make your boy use a lock.'

'He does, usually. But it was only a minute . . .'

The days pass and the police don't ring back and slowly I stop scrutinizing every child's bike I pass: I'm not going to run into it; it's not going to run into me. But I acquire the habit of leaving work half an hour early and parking near number twelve on my way home. They're always about somewhere, in this hot weather: him with his chest hair spooling over the top of his vest; her with the black-sheen cycling shorts, and the figure she's already getting back now the baby's eight months; and the older kids – Michael, Leah and baby Charlene: yes, I've heard them shouted at so often in reproach, I've learned their names. All of them small, though, no twelve- or thirteen-year-old bicycle thief. Where's he? It can't be Michael, who's no older than nine. Nor the lurky biker, seventeen at least, who turns up on Tuesday nights and Thursdays, for a quick tea and fiddle with his Yamaha, and who must be a younger brother to one of the parents. Why did the police say they knew about number twelve? They seem a harmless lot; there'll be rent arrears and unpaid bills, but nothing big. They watch telly inside, and sit in the yard when the sun comes round, and take the kids off to school, and drive off in the blue Bedford to Safeway, and that's about it. They don't look to have the energy for crime.

Sometimes, as well as parking there, I get out and walk, not in search of the bike, not for exercise, just to get the feel of the estate. It seems less scary now. I notice things I didn't before. There are flats whose fronts are pretty with hollyhocks and hanging baskets, though round the back they've gone to hell. In The Wat Tyler pub, the rotor blades of huge fans sweep the ceiling. I buy myself a Guinness while Otis Redding, deep from the speakers, is just sitting on the dock of the bay. A man in shorts goes past, a rose tattooed on the back of his thigh. CHARLTON ATHLETIC and AC MILAN compete as graffiti, as if Milan were as local as Charlton – and tonight, in this heat, it feels as if it is. When the sun eases off round eight and there's a pink glow over the roofs, the estate seems almost happy, relaxed. For a moment I see it as the architect who designed it must have – wide spaces, protected acres, light-blessed windows, walkways like Venetian bridges, streets in the sky. The westward panes shine like scattered jewels. I know the local papers say this is a sink estate, and sinking. I know I have a score to settle. But in this moment of orange sunset the estate feels like a good place to be.

Another week passes. Now I stop off at the estate in the morning, on my way to work as well as on the way back. I get my kids off to their schools, and there's still time to be round at number twelve to see Leah and Michael trooping down to theirs – reception class in her case, middle school in his, or so I deduce, watching them go in at different times and by different entrances. Once, I keep an eye on Charlene, unbeknown to her mother, not trusting the pushchair to stay where she has left it just inside the playground, the compound of the peeling barracks. These mothers, don't they read the papers, haven't they learnt there are some funny people about? I nearly say something as she comes out with Michael and Leah past the classroom window with its pasted cut-out dragons and Indian deities and smiling suns. She wears black leggings and a white embroidered blouse. She has a long nose and a no-crap manner. She could pass for pretty. She *is* pretty. The same this evening, in her cut-off denim shorts and yellow floptop, her bare legs slender though mulberried with varicose veins. It's hot still, even at eight, even with the engine running and the air-conditioner. The dog days whine. Tonight it's a family barbecue: he's leaning over a rack of briquettes, turning sausages and chicken wings with his tongs. She hands him a Kestrel, and he stands there gripping it like a torch. All over London men are standing or walking with similar torches, tubes to light up with, to take the dark away. The kids pedal in and out the yard. I should be home with my own kids, for our own barbecue, but for the moment they've become anonymous and it's this surrogate family that obsesses me instead. I hang on here at a safe distance, feeling conspicuous, a voyeur. This isn't Saab country, yet here I sit twice daily in my red 900i. It's as well there are trees, and cars left by commuters at the station, and the indolence of a London estate in mid-July.

But I'm not inconspicuous enough. One evening, strolling between the decks, I'm stopped by a woman of sixty or so, overweight, wearing glasses and wheeling a shopping bag full of fliers. She speaks with a Scottish accent, not clipped, more of a roll.

'Do you live here?' she asks.

'No,' I say. 'I'm just walking through.'

She relaxes. 'I guessed you were a stranger.'

'How?'

'I sit on the tenants' asociation, I meet most of the new people coming in, I thought you looked lost.'

I'm tempted to tell her a bike's been lost and that is why I'm here. But I sense she'd become suspicious, would think I was another outsider with a grudge against the estate.

'I'm not lost, just out for a walk,' I say.

'You missed a funny thing the other week. There was a

cockerel right there,' she says, pointing across to one of the squares. 'No one knew how it got there, but it was flapping around, and someone called the police, and two policemen came to remove it, and they didn't know how to catch it, they can't have training in that, I suppose, and I don't know what happened in the end, whether they nabbed it, but everybody had a laugh about it afterwards, and that's the kind of thing people never say about this place, the doors are shut and people are scared but there is a sort of spirit sometimes. Anyway, I better be going now, these leaflets.'

She wheels her trolley off, like a golf caddy. I feel I've been given my club membership, my permit, that I'm accepted here. But I don't forget – the dead stares of others I pass don't allow me to – that it's an illusion. I'm a stranger, a skulker, here in search of a missing bike.

One night I come much later than usual, a bit drunk, after a party. The estate is dark and silent. I park in the usual spot, between the rusting Bedford and the Escort with beaded seats. I step out on to the walkway, and light – from the moon, or streetlamps, I can't tell – catches silver in the yard of number twelve. My heart misses a beat. I hesitate in my stride, then adjust it like a hurdler, an extra step in it before I reach the gate. I stare in as I pass and the bike's there, high above the plastic patrol car and the lowly scooter, black and gleaming, like a timing device. I walk by, wondering if it's chained to something or if in the heat of the moment, the aftermath of a barbecue – which stirs and glows in a gust – it's simply been forgotten. I turn after the last house, like a busby at the end of his beat, and cursor back along the line I've made, once more past the gate. No chain that I can see, no lock, no tether; it must be a mistake, the kind of mistake most kids have learnt not to make, that their parents wouldn't make either, a mistake made tonight only through distraction or exhaustion, a bike for a ten-year-old shining brightly. I walk back to the car, and sit there for a while, and scan the line of flats for signs of life: not a bleep, not a chimmer. I wonder if I dare do what I want to, and feel a surge of elation, that once-in-a-decade certainty of being in the right. Tracy Chapman, on Jazz FM, dies with the ignition. I get out and listen. I ooze across the grass on my soft heels and need not even open the gate, only reach over to where the bike is leaning against the low wall and tilt it away to upright. I pause and listen again, holding it there, my stomach muscles tensing as I raise it off the ground, one hand under the saddle, the other squeezing the mudguard and front wheel, no chain noise, no scraping against the wall, the thing hanging mid-air now as I draw it back and up towards my face like a giant pair of spectacles, one wheel revolving slowly as I lift it higher, raising it to my lips, over the summit of the wall, safely and in silence over the summit and down on the pavement, gently down, still not a noise. A last pause before I carry it up the walkway, not daring to put it down yet in case it squeaks but walking in tandem with it. Then ten yards on I set it down at last, my wrist muscles tight and pinging, and I lift my leg over and clamber on, forcing the right pedal down as I do, wobbly for a second, far too small for it, my knees absurdly winging out each side. Inside I'm a silent scream of triumph and reparation, the scales tipping back to middle, the world put to rights again. I'd do tricks if I could – no hands, see – but I spin over to the shadows by the railway embankment, look round to see all's clear, then leave the bike under the darkness of the fence while I go back for the car. All quiet at number twelve, no lynch mob, no torchlights of outrage: I drive the Saab the hundred yards up to the sprawl of spokes, swing the big mouth of the boot open and lift the bike in, doubling back the front wheel to squeeze the whole frame in free of the catch. Boot locked, doors locked, I drive back through the spotlights and security glare of street after street, preparing my story should the police stop me and demand to see the contents of my boot: easy enough, 'my son's bike, officer', which is true. Then I'm home, and stow the bike in the garage, and climb the stairs, saying nothing to anyone, saving my surprise for later.

I lie awake, listening for sirens, resisting the temptation to wake my son, thinking back to my own childhood and its deferred gratifications, the surprises my father once prepared for me. I remember the extravagant secrecy of his Christmas presents – the huge train set in the attic, which he must have worked at for weeks, joining the tracks, ensuring the points worked, painting fields and sticking down bushes, and all the while me banned from the attic because, he said, he was redecorating, the ban lifted only on Christmas morning. Then the next Christmas, the pedal car in the garage, my *old* pedal car, which I'd nearly outgrown but into which he'd had the engine of a moped fitted, so I could learn to steer and brake and accelerate, so I could bat around the outside of the house like Stirling Moss. For my father, the surprise had been more important than the giving. I grew up expecting surprises. Now I'd prepared one myself. I get up and scribble a note and leave it by his bed: A SURPRISE FOR YOU IN THE GARAGE.

In the event, though, I wake before him, and have to rouse him to make him read the words on the note. He's confused, and doesn't understand why I wrote the message, and why I can't just tell him now what the surprise is, rather than making him trail downstairs. He dresses. We go below together. I turn the garage light on, waiting for triumph to light in his eyes as it has in mine.

'There,' I say, 'Your bike.'

He goes over to look, takes hold of the handlebars.

'It's second-hand, Dad.'

'Well, third-hand, I suppose. But at least you've got it back. Everything's OK again.'

'But it's not my bike.'

'Well it may be a bit more scratched than it was but . . .'

'No, it's not mine. It's a different make. It's a Raleigh, and it's got a fur saddle.'

'But couldn't they have . . .'

'It's not mine, honest, mine had a big scratch here,' he says, pointing at the frame. He pauses, straightens up, and turns to look at me. 'What, did you nick it, then?' He seems suddenly indignant, even triumphant, relishing my discomfort. 'Dad, you mean you've stolen some poor kid's bike?'

He goes off to school, I drive to work, stowing the bike in my boot while I work out what to do. I could go to the door of number twelve, and try to explain, but who'd believe me *before* beating me up? I could go to the police, but they might charge me – 'It's an offence, stealing and taking the law in your own hands: this was police business, sir.' I could try to leave the bike in the night, just as I'd stolen it in the night, but won't they be looking out, extra vigilant? And if they aren't looking out, who can guarantee the bike won't be gone before they wake? I could hide the bike, and write a note telling where to find it, an anonymous tip-off, but how could I get the note delivered safely? The post takes too long, a courier would have my name and address, leaving the note myself means going to the door. I could do nothing, and keep the bike, but even if my son consented to ride it (which he won't, if only on aesthetic grounds), would it be worth the shame and guilt?

I try to work, but can't. I feel stupid, criminal, a failure. Now two bikes have been stolen instead of one. Seeking to cure my son's misery, I've made another child miserable. Setting the world to rights, I've added to its sum of little wrongs. I think of my father again, and of how pathetic a father I look beside him – he who gave, I who can't even repossess; he who seemed so certain of what was right, I who don't know what to do.

What I do is this: drive to the estate, get the bike out of the boot, and wheel it over the quiet grass, in sight of Leah and Michael's school. It's 3.20 pm, coming-out time, and I wait till I see them walking my way with their mother and Charlene. I turn and wheel the bike around the corner, ahead of me and them, then leave it in the middle of the path, sprawled there like an accident. It's risky, I know. They might choose a different route. They might not recognize this bike as the bike gone from their yard. It might be nicked in the two minutes before they reach it. But I remember the trap my father laid the night we lost the hamster: lumps of cheese placed across the wash-house floor, then up a ramp and abundant in the bottom of a deep cake-tin, tempting the hamster below. It couldn't work, and yet it did. And this will, too, if there's any light at the end of the world, if a man's to be allowed one small act of reparation, a bike returned as if from heaven.

Barnardo Before and After

A rimy morning in 1874. Thomas Barnes, photographer, leans against a wall and coughs. He has had a bad cold for months. These damp mornings do it, the yellow Stepney fog and hanging rain. He hopes the brick will warm his back. Across from him, at the edge of the yard, the Doctor fusses with the urchins, knowing what he wants, unable to get it yet: will they stand like this, can the boy on the end come in closer, would they straighten up and keep their eyes fixed right ahead? Thomas yawns and coughs. He'd like to make a start. Most poses he arranges for himself, but this one the Doctor considers special. The five boys were nabbed from the streets last night and he wants them to stand together with the beadle, Edward Fitzgerald. It's to be a group photograph, evocative, suggesting a street scene rather than this yard. The boys have never seen a camera before and, though the Doctor has explained about photography, they look suspiciously at the lens. They will not keep still, they will not stand straight (Edward least of all), they are slow to obey the Doctor's orders. Black clouds threaten distant roofs. Thomas would like to make a start.

The Doctor moves the boys to show them sitting on a heap

of earth and bricks. It looks more promising: Thomas could make something of a pose like that, with adjustments. Only Edward is missing, having slipped off for a snifter though he said he needed to relieve himself. Leave him out, thinks Thomas, who doesn't like him. But here he is again, reeking of porter if the Doctor only knew. He takes his place with his lantern. 'Could we do something at night with that lantern?' the Doctor asked the other week. The way the light falls out of it, the rays streaming across the faces of waifs and strays: it would be powerful, it could help the Mission. Thomas had to explain: you cannot take street photographs at night. The Doctor protested: surely, in this day and age, with the advances of science . . . In the end Thomas had promised to look into it. Maybe an arc light. Maybe an extra-large flash of magnesium. He will have to try.

He has come here for four years now, with his son Herbert and an assistant, Roderick Johnstone. They give the Mission a part of every day, except Thursday and Saturday, when his own studio, in the Mile End Road, must be manned full-time. He worries that the association will damage business, but so far, on the contrary, it has helped. On display in the studio window is a photograph called 'Lost': a boy of ten or so sitting on the ground, bare feet, bowed back, clothes torn so you see his skin through the rents, chin resting on his drawn-up knees. Customers sometimes ask about the work. They're puzzled. Portraits, weddings, family groups: they can see the point of those. But the little urchins and orphans, sad though their plight is, doesn't it lower his spirits – the lice, the stench, the vermin? He never knows what to say, where to begin. He mutters about the interest, the challenge, and even, with some ladies, allows himself to say 'Christian' and 'charitable', words that will impress. But why he does what he does is not something easily explained. It is to do with the darkroom. It is do with seeing faces swim up into focus out of nothing. It is to do with rescuing permanence from time.

'Thomas!' The Doctor's call. He unpeels himself from the wall and wanders across. Coughing, he stands above the lens, and tries to see things as the camera will. The pose is unpromising but not irretrievable. If the boy bottom right would move between the legs of the boy behind him – like that, yes, but resting his head to one side, cradled. And if Edward would step back a bit to his right (we don't want the bloody beadle centre stage), and raise his lantern – no, not dangling like a dead rat, but high, high, as if he were search-ing. The boy in the middle, top of the heap, makes a perfect apex. He has fresh cheeks, brushed-back hair, a white scarf. A face to remember, though Thomas, if he's honest, isn't good at remembering faces. He's seen too many. Hundreds, maybe thousands now, all of them gone into nothing. He stoops and lowers his head under the black curtain, the hood of the lens.

'I think that should do, Doctor. If you're content.'

'Yes, I'm content.'

Thomas fetches the plate. He prepares each plate ahead, pouring collodion over the centre, tipping his hand to let the liquid run evenly over the surface, just like his good lady on Shrove Tuesdays with the batter for pancakes in a pan. After years of practice, he knows the process perfectly: the liquid draining off at one corner; the gun cotton congealing on the plate; the plunge into a bath of silver nitrate; the two-minute wait; the glass plate stored, ready for use, in the dark slide. Readiness is all, he likes to say. Not that the Doctor is inter-ested. Thomas has explained the work to him, not just the glass plates but the darkroom after, the paper coated with white of egg and all the rest: dishes, wooden draining board, brush of sable, zinc washing trough, travelling lamps, head-rests, eye-rests, a pair of scales. The Doctor understands enough to have invested the necessary guineas. But as for engaging him, it's like talking to a wall.

He slides the plate in the back of the camera, behind the bellows, bends under the velvet cape, peers through the dead black, focuses, and asks the boys to keep still. Ready? They must not move until he says. He straightens up again. He takes the cap off the lens, and – one, two – starts to count. That boy with the neck-scarf: you'd never guess from his open face how cramped his life has been. Not that Thomas knows his circumstances, or wants to, exactly. Once or twice in the early days, he went out with the Doctor, to see what these children's homes were like. Never again. It's not as if his own house is grand at all, but Stratford, two miles away, isn't Stepney. Eighteen, nineteen. Such long exposure-times. Such long exposure to his own times. Is this what's making him ill? He tries hard not to feel anything, to close out all beyond the shutter. But then some soft-haired street Arab tilts his head to one side, or some girl with a flowerpot on her head smiles for no reason, and he can feel his eyes water. The other week, a real asthma attack. A boy of four, his sister of eighteen months. He made them pose like parent and child. Silent, bewildered, they looked out in appeal below their hats. The stripes of the boy's cotton apron. The silver nails in the soles of the little girl's shoes. He felt himself getting wheezier, took the photograph while he could, then subsided into an hour of coughing. It could have been the clothes they were wearing, the dust on them, cat's hair, rat's hair, lice, lath and plaster. But faces, too, affect a man, a parent especially. You don't want to know, but you do know. Those children will be better off now, with the Doctor. But still, that take-me-home look. If his wife had been there, she'd have made him fetch them home.

Thirty-one, thirty-two. A strange job for a man to end up in: as the Doctor's eye and propaganda tool. Even their names are confusable – Thomas Barnes, Thomas Barnardo – though his name, being shorter, fits inside the Doctor's, which is apt, his being the lesser part. There are those who think the Doctor *is* him, that he's nothing but a pseudonym or synonym. It isn't true: if they doubt his corporeality, let them stand against this wall and hear his cough. But he knows what they mean. The Doctor takes over, bullies, is ruthless in furthering his ends. Those anonymous letters in the newspaper, defending his good name and works. Edward says the Doctor wrote them himself. So what, if it helps? The Before-and-After photographs take liberties, too. This shot today with the five boys is an invention. To deceive in the service of good, to lie to be truthful: Thomas has no trouble with this. He sniffs and looks at his watch. Let vicars meddle with morals. His own conscience is the lens.

Forty-four, forty-five. 'That's enough, boys, thank you.' The boys separate and loll, while Edward disappears for another swig. Soon the Doctor will take the boys inside. They are big lads, twelve years old, thirteen, but Thomas feels sorry for them, imagining them tonight in the dormitory, under clean bedclothes and a high ceiling, rescued but afraid. The Doctor says you can take a child and start afresh, driving all the past from its mind. Thomas is not so sure: he still remembers every nail in his father's workshop, though they moved to Stratford when he was ten. But you have to hope. The Doctor has hope, faith and charity, which is why Thomas goes on working for him, despite the bullying, despite the meagre fees. The Lord knows, a man or two in the East End can't do much to heal the world. But the Doctor is trying, and Thomas Barnes wishes to help his mission in the only way he knows: by pointing his camera straight ahead.

Almost nothing is known about Thomas Barnes. Histories of Victorian photography rarely mention him. The archive at the Barnardo's head office in Barkingside is informative about the children he photographed, but not about the man himself. The cost of his work is recorded in the annual accounts, but his value to Barnardo's in particular, and nineteenth-century social reform generally, cannot be calculated. Sitting in the archive at Barkingside, riffling through the old albums, I have a vision of Thomas Barnes at work: his lens, his hacking cough, the day of the famous photograph with the beadle, Edward Fitzgerald (who shared a name with the man who wrote *The Rubáiyát of Omar Khayyám*). Working back from the photos, I see it clearly, as if it were the negative, or a story happening inside out. But I know I'm fabricating most of the detail. I console myself that Barnes, too, was a fabricator, and that it didn't stop him being truthful. He didn't consider himself as an artist, either, but some of his photographs deserve to be considered art.

They look so desperate, the children in his photographs. Emma Cook, hands clutched nervously, eyes like a frightened hamster's. John Washington, black and in a bowler hat, like a Deep South crooner. Basil Hope, scrunched in terror in a corner, refusing to face the lens. Many are dressed in rags – bare feet, torn britches, buttonless coats – but a few wear improbable fancy hats and fine fur coats. Here's a boy with half a leg. Here's another with a squint. Here are two sisters in feathers, furs and hats, dressed up to the nines by kindly neighbours and cradling long-haired dollies in their laps. Saddest is Thomas Marks, his legs amputated so high he seems to float, stumpless, on his navel, no visible means of support.

There are half a million photos in the archive at Barnardo's – half a million moments of sad time. To the archivist, John Kirkham, here is the country's 'most evocative visual image library', and he's pleased that, a hundred and fifty years on from the birth of Thomas Barnardo, it's more open to the public than it used to be. Everyone knows the Victorian street scenes, the shots of nervous toddler-evacuees during the Second World War, and the children waving goodbye as they set sail for the Colonies. But there's so much more: the three hundred cine films, for example (most 16mm), the snaps from the mid-1940s of children wearing goggles in front of a sunlamp, and the photos which show the work Barnardo's has been doing in recent years – with the homeless, with young offenders, with drug addicts, with Aids sufferers, and with the handicapped. Such images deserve to be better known.

All the same, the large mounted sheets of the first generation of children taken in by Barnardo – row after serried row of them – are the most compelling images in the archive, and it's hard to look at them and not cry. True, there isn't the dreadful retrospective foreboding that surrounds photos of under-age First World War volunteers or Jewish children circa 1943 waiting for the train to Auschwitz: for these Barnardo's children, whatever the ordeals to come, the worst was probably over. But the bewilderment of the subjects is deeply painful. There they are, trying to look dignified, impassive, holding it for the camera (and in those days of long exposure they had to hold it for half a minute or longer), the shadow of their tragic histories seeping through. In the days before these shots were taken they'd have left the streets where they'd been sleeping rough – or left their parents, if they had them – to be prepared for a new life, 'a fresh start', in a home that didn't feel like home: deloused, inspected, measured, lectured, reclothed, one strange new experience after another, culminating in this one, the camera. No wonder they look bewildered. And perhaps their bewilderment is a mirror image of ours, that this could have happened in London not so long ago – worse, that to different children in different clothes, it might be happening still.

From the beginning, photographs were an essential part of Thomas Barnardo's mission to rescue destitute children from London's East End. The work began in 1870, and four years later the sum of £252 13s 9d was spent on 'Apparatus and

Chemicals for a new Photographing Department, and Salary of Photographer and Assistant.' *Night and Day*, the name Barnardo gave to his house magazine, also summarized his working methods. By night, lantern in hand like a poacher, he would go out and catch his children, retrieving them from the gutters, roofs and doorsteps where they slept. By day, on their formal admission, his photographer Thomas Barnes would catch them all over again, posing them in his studio or, more usually, in the yard outside Stepney Boys' Home. Barnardo sometimes used sketches, too, including one called 'Born of a Dream' – an allegory of the origins of his mission, himself asleep in an armchair, a drowning child above his head. But the photographs far outnumbered the drawings.

Their primary function was, as he put it, 'to obtain and retain an exact likeness, which being attached to a faithful record in our History Book of each individual case, shall enable us in future to trace every child's career, and bring to remembrance minute circumstances, which, without a photograph, would be impossible.' Each photograph appeared on the child's file, along with details of age, height and background. The art was still in its infancy, then, and though Dr Barnardo was not alone in using the camera like this, as a means of record and surveillance – prisons, lunatic asylums and the police force (also in its infancy) were equally quick to exploit its potential – he was the most committed and comprehensive. Between 1874 and 1905, Thomas Barnes and his successor Roderick Johnstone took some 55,000 photographs of the children in Barnardo homes.

But Barnardo used his photographs for propaganda, too. Early on, he learnt the fund-raising potential of Before-and-After shots: the child on admission, filthy, ragged, listless; the child after redemption, scrubbed, shiny and gainfully employed – who would not give generously to support such miraculous transformations, to help crude clay metamorphose

into precious porcelain? These Before-and-After photographs
(a bit like modern adverts for washing powder) were popular
with the Victorian middle class, and Barnardo sold them in
packs of twenty for five shillings. They got him useful publicity. And they made him money, to be ploughed back into his
missionary work.

More than this, the photographs expressed Barnardo's
essential philosophy: that once children came into his care,
they could put the past behind them and make 'a fresh start'.
Being snapped was an initiation ceremony in which the child
shed its old identity and took on a new one, never to look
back. It's this philosophy, more than any other, that now seems
most unpalatable about Dr Barnardo. For it's an axiom of
modern childcare that children who've been adopted or fos-
tered need to *know* about their past, not repress it. These days
children coming into local authority care are encouraged to
create 'Life Story Books', to understand who their parents
were, and to see photographs of what 'Before' really looked
like. A fresh start doesn't mean, as Barnardo thought it must,
an empty page.

It isn't only in recent years that questions have been raised
about Barnardo's methods. From the first shutter-click, there
were doubts. One of the most famous photographs is of three
black children called Williams peering naked and wide-eyed
from under a blanket. Dr Barnardo left several accounts of
how it came about. He had been brought by a concerned
landlady to a 'dirty, dark and close-smelling room' and there
discovered the 'three woolly black heads' (here is the
language of Empire, circa 1875) lying under a heap of sacks.
Nearby sat their mother: weary, and with tears pouring down
her cheeks, she told how she had come to be widowed – her
husband, a freed West Indian slave and sailor, had died at sea
after diving overboard to save one of his crew-mates from a

shark (Dr Barnardo's stories were always highly dramatic).
He goes on:

> . . . the next morning we carried them in a cab, and in
> the studio of our photographer laid them and their
> sacks down in a heap, much as they had been the day
> before in their mother's dingy room; and thus, in a few
> brief seconds, preserved for future years a picture of
> the state in which we found them.

In other words, this 'faithful' picture was contrived. It wasn't
the only one. Typically, 'Before' shots were taken, not on the
street, but in a studio mock-up of a street, with props: painted
slum backdrops, orange crates, barrels, light from the tall
north window falling across the children's naked feet. 'After'
shots were taken on the same day as 'Before' shots – a wash, a
smile, a change of clothes were enough to show how the rags
of the past had been discarded and a fallen soul redeemed.
There were other ruses. Children found separately about the
East End were photographed in groups looking picturesquely
deprived. One said to be a 'waif taken from the streets' had in
fact been brought in by her loving but uncoping mother. The
poignant match girl, Katie Smith, with broken comb, dish-
cloth and a 'box of lights', had been supplied with these by
Barnardo himself. Another boy, Samuel Reed, had his clothes
ripped by a penknife so that he could more convincingly fit
the caption 'Rescue the Perishing'.

Or so it was alleged. The charges were brought by a rival
Baptist minister, the Revd George Reynolds, who had lost
many of his parishioners to Barnardo's religious mission.
Reynolds had the support of the COS, the Charity
Organization Society (prominent members of which disap-
proved of Barnardo) and even of Barnardo's former beadle,
Edward Fitzgerald, who before losing his job for 'drunkenness

and immorality' had famously been photographed, lantern in hand, with five boys culled from a night's search. People had it in for Barnardo: he was difficult, an autocrat, and bigots said he was creating a dependency culture. Barnardo vigorously disputed the charges, claiming that out of 1,300 photographs a mere nine had been 'representative' rather than real. In the *East London Observer* and *Tower Hamlets Independent* he was staunchly defended by someone signing himself 'A Clerical Junius'. But it seems these letters, too, were fakes, having been written by Barnardo himself, or dictated to one of his staff.

The claims and counter-claims led to a 38-day arbitration case, in effect a trial, which focused also on his right to the title 'Doctor' (he hadn't qualified in medicine when he began using it), ill-treatment of children, mismanagement and immoral relations (with girls in his care and with a former landlady). Most of the charges were trumped-up and malicious, and in the end the tribunal largely exonerated Barnardo, though not before he had suffered adverse publicity. Gillian Wagner tells the story well in her biography of 1979. Among the witnesses Barnardo called was Mrs Williams, mother of the three children under their sack, whose defence of his methods and moving account of her tragic life certainly helped his case.

In 1876, he rode out the crisis, but 120 years on doubts about his probity still muddy the water for his successors working in Barkingside. Barnardo always worried about his image, and ensured that most photographs showed him as gentle, genial and bespectacled, surrounded by family or children. In reality, he seems to have been much tougher and more florid, a dandy in a boater, a rogue and maverick, not at all a pillar of the Victorian establishment, let alone an emblem of solemn charity. It's another Barnardo image problem. To rescue his reputation as a child rescuer means acknowledging that in pursuit of truth he sometimes resorted to fiction.

Certainly he was economical with the facts. Fearing he'd be seen as an obscure adventurer, Barnardo played down his Dublin origins, and encouraged colourful legends of the Barnardo family being of high Spanish or Russian descent. He embroidered his early career, too, making it seem as if he had begun his work with children in London four years earlier than he did and creating the impression that his East End Juvenile Mission had begun life, like the Christ it served, in a humble donkey shed, not a rented house. The two great stories of his mission's beginnings – being led by young Jim Jarvis to a 'lay' of eleven boys in the gutter of a domed roof, and of himself leading a dinner party of Lord Shaftesbury and friends to a lay of seventy-three boys lying under a tarpaulin in Billingsgate – seem to have some basis in fact, but exactly how much is doubtful. He told implausible evangelical tales of deathbed conversions. He kept comically vague financial accounts: one entry for 1875 reads, 'Amount embezzled by defaulting cashier (since dead) £189'. By his own admission he kidnapped children and shipped them overseas without their parents' knowledge or consent. Towards the end of his life he'd relax in his study after a hard day preaching temperance by pouring himself a stiff drink.

A modern audience can more easily accept than Victorians did that this espouser of saintly public causes was himself no saint; indeed, Barnardo's self-contradictions make him, if anything, more endearing. But in 1877, the assault on his reputation threatened his whole mission: if the public lost faith in his integrity, he'd no longer be able to raise funds. This is why he was so sensitive to the charge of producing 'artistic fiction': if the photographs couldn't be trusted, how could he hope to be? Even before the trial he issued a sorry-leaflet with every pack of photographs, desperately explaining why some of them had been reconstructed after the event. There is some specious talk of bad weather and photographers' days off. More plausibly, he explains that between their being found in the 'filthiest rags' and their formal admission, the children had sometimes been dressed up by well-meaning neighbours and relations, 'and thus a child seen for months previously in a lodging-house, almost naked, . . . suddenly appears in the unusual garb of a respectable labourer's child. . . . A photograph of it as it now appears would indeed present a false view of the circumstances of the case. . . .' The mussing and messing were to make the photographs *more* accurate, not less. Borrowed clothes, a pair of scissors, a smear of soot from the wall: they did the trick.

Because Barnardo had to defend himself from other charges of deception, it was hard for him to declare, without apology, that the truest art is sometimes the most feigning. Now, looking through the thousands of faces in the Barnardo archive, we should have no trouble with his argument that 'not one single case of portraiture in our published list is without its real representative in hundreds of street children to be found on every hand'. On one of the glass plates a Barnardo photographer has written so that it looks like graffiti on a wall: DIRT, DISEASE AND DEATH LURK HERE. Was it Thomas Barnes himself, losing his cool for once? Or a younger assistant, whose idealism had not yet been eroded by habit? Whichever, the graffiti isn't so much deceit as a cry of protest. Like Barnardo, the anonymous scribbler practised sleight of hand in order to expose the truth.

The photographs Barnardo took of his foundlings were intended for his use, not theirs. Most died unaware that the photographs existed. The archive in which they were kept was a locked strongbox, not a family album. Even today, many former Barnardo's boys and girls have no photograph of their younger selves to look back on, the organization's strict record-keeping having faltered after 1939, when admissions were no longer centralized from Stepney. In an age when images are intimately bound up with identity – when the camera and camcorder give children a sense of who they are and where they've come from – Barnardo kids are doubly disadvantaged; no family, and no family photographs either.

Take the case of Gerd Lubszynksi, whose story is an unusual one even by unusual standards. Now in his late sixties, he lives with his wife Betty in a happily cluttered end-of-terrace house in Chingford, half a mile from the Walthamstow dog track. Both were Barnardo's children, and, being of the generation they are, spent their formative years in large country houses. Like other evacuees, they remember the wartime years with affection. The nearest thing to a siren they'd hear would be the cry of a peacock. It was – and is – very different in Chingford.

I've barely sat down among the utility furniture (Gerd, who trained as a cabinet-maker, worked for a furniture firm for ten years after the war, and the influence shows), when he hands me a photograph. It's a picture of a dozen or so German boys on their arrival in England, at the Boys' Garden City, in 1939. Gerd was eleven and had been sent from Berlin – a rare case of a child coming from abroad to Barnardo's rather than vice versa. Gerd got to London with the help of the Quakers, leaving behind his father, who was Jewish and later died in a concentration camp, and his mother, who was not Jewish and survived the war and came to England in 1947, only to die of cancer shortly afterwards. Gerd says it wasn't too much of a wrench leaving home – he got on well at Stanley House ('Lord Derby's place'), showed willing, learned English, lost his German accent (there's not a trace of it now), and fitted in. He brought no photographs with him, and had no contact with his parents by letter. But he was adaptable.

He certainly looks happy enough in the photograph. So do the other boys – in their shorts and long trousers, ties and

leather shoes, they're the antithesis of East End urchins. Six
months after this photograph, they dispersed to different
Barnardo homes. Gerd has had no contact with them since,
though he can still remember their surnames from the photograph: Muller, Mann, Klost, Hencken. He'd hoped to come
across one or two of them at a Barnardo's reunion a couple of
years ago. Perhaps he'll have more luck in the future.

Couldn't Barnardo's put him in touch with these old boys
anyway? It's difficult, he explains: the places they went to have
long since closed down, and even if they were contacted they
might not want their privacy infringed. Until this year, when
Barnardo's adopted a more open-access policy, it could be difficult to get information even about one's own family. Betty,
who came into Barnardo's at three when her mother died,
only recently learnt the full truth about her father, who the
files say was 'of good character' but 'suffering the after-effects'
of the First World War: disability, rather than indifference,
had made him hand his daughter over to Barnardo's, and it
matters to her to have discovered that.

What Gerd and Betty possess of their past remains pitifully
small: a few bits of paper, the odd photograph, nothing more.
It is as if, for Gerd, lacking any family photos, this shot of him
and his refugee friends is the key. He's not the complaining or
anguishing sort. But if he could just meet those faces again,
some vital bit of his past might be restored.

An After Care department has existed from Barnardo's since
the early days. But whereas once it helped its old boys and
girls to find houses and jobs, now it helps them solve puzzles
about their past. Here is the other great archive at
Barkingside. In the bad old days, the 'fresh start' principle
meant that children who did dare to ask about their family history would be told not to be nosy and ungrateful: '*We're* your
family now.' Now it's recognized that children, when they're

grown-up, want to know about Before. Since January 1995, all ex-Barnardo's children are entitled to look at their files. As yet only a small sample group have done so. The files need sensitive handling, and it will all take time: there are 1,200 enquiries each month, and a waiting list of a year. But everyone's pleased a start has been made.

Everyone but the lawyers. Legally, open access is a minefield, since under 1987 legislation (which in any case isn't retrospective and doesn't cover voluntary organizations) clients are entitled only to information about themselves. At Barnardo's, 'third party' information - about other individuals, or from other agencies – is therefore edited out in advance of a visit, and the visit is carefully supervised. Apart from birth certificates, admissions cards and photographs, no documents can be removed and taken home. The files can be a shock - they weren't intended to be read by clients, and it's upsetting to see words like 'imbecile', 'worthless' or 'depraved' used about your parents even if you can't remember them – which is why After Care also offers counselling. It would like to offer more, but legal constraints, and the lingering ethos of paternalism, prevent it doing so.

For Sydney Bracken, as for Betty Lubszynski, discovering the truth about his origins has been a long and arduous battle. Now fifty, he was admitted to Barnardo's as an eighteen-month-old baby, in 1946. The files show that his mother visited him at Barnardo's only once, on November 15th 1946, when his diarrhoea and vomiting were giving concern to staff. He never saw her again. Later, when he was old enough to understand, he was told that both she and his father had been killed in the war. Other carers told him other stories but he found the original explanation the easiest to live with. Why else were there no Christmas or birthday cards? Why, unlike most Barnardo boys, was he never visited by relations?

At fourteen, he was called in by the head of the home and

told that his mother wasn't well – so would he write her a letter? Desperate to impress her – if he impressed her enough, maybe she'd have him back – he told her he was training as a printer and of his hopes of being a ball boy at Wimbledon. The letter, it seems, was never sent. Some time later, Sydney was told that his mother had died six months previously. It had been easier thinking she'd died in the war. He also learnt, seeing his birth certificate for the first time when he left Barnardo's, that he was Sydney, not (as he and everyone else had written it till then) Sidney.

Not surprisingly, Bracken as an adolescent was a bit of a handful. He got smart at making money out of mates, selling them roll-ups or lending money at interest when the ice-cream van came round on Wednesdays – not a very nice person, a bit of a mafia boss, he now thinks. At a Barnardo's reunion a few years ago, various grown men came up and recalled his acts of villainy. It was news to his wife, who in twenty-odd years of marriage had never seen this side of him. But then she hadn't known about his Barnardo's past at all, when she first went out with him. Not wanting sympathy, needing to be judged for himself, he hated telling anyone he'd been a BB, and it was only when she'd agreed to marry him that he thought he'd better come clean.

A few years ago, Sydney Bracken saw a television programme on the 'children of empire' (the Barnardo's children sent to the colonies) which touched on the concealment of personal histories. He drove from Wiltshire to Barkingside the next day and demanded to see his files. The After Care department co-operated as far as it could and slowly the truth about his past emerged. He discovered that his mother had got pregnant by another man while her husband was away during the war, and that was why, on his return, he went into Barnardo's. He discovered he had several stepbrothers and stepsisters, and met them. He discovered he had one brother –

and turned up at his house and sat by his swimming pool. He also turned up at his father's house, but learned that he'd died two years earlier. There were some awkward moments among these renewed acquaintances (only one older stepbrother could remember 'the baby that mother had been looking after for a friend') but one stepsister in particular, living in Australia, he got on with famously, and still does. Slowly he put the bits of the jigsaw together.

Two months ago, Sydney saw his file in full for the first time. There were some fascinating items in it: a cutting from the *Hammersmith Gazette* for April 29th 1946, which carries a colourful report of the sentencing of his stepfather, who had gone looking for his (Sydney's) father with an iron bar and knife, to twelve months' probation for 'threatening behaviour'; and memos which show the efforts which Barnardo's later made to persuade the stepfather to allow the son to meet his dying mother. Sidney hoped to have these memos to show me, but they can't be removed from his file in Barkingside. It makes him angry: 'everyone mentioned in them is dead, and I'm fifty, so why can't I have them?' For years he has campaigned for open access, and now it's here it's still not truly open. Kate Roach, deputy of the After Care department, admits that it's 'very uncomfortable possessing information which clients don't. It's all about power, and they feel here we are still telling them what they can and can't do. Migrants to Australia and New Zealand can read everything we have in their files because the law there allows it. But we have to work within the British law.' Sydney, who disputes Barnardo's interpretation of the law (citing a European ruling from Strasburg), admits for his part that many files contain unpalatable reading: to learn that you're the progeny of incest, or that your mother was a prostitute, can knock you off balance. But better to be told the truth than to live among lies and secrets.

Sydney Bracken has seen or had summarized for him most

of what's known about his past. But until he possesses the actual documents, it's as if he is being denied his own history, and he feels bitter about this: whose life is it, anyway? Ironically, because Barnardo's was so comprehensive in its record-keeping, there's often a remarkable amount of information about its old boys and girls. But the fresh start principle dies hard. The brave thing for Barnardo's to do now would be to throw its files wide open – the kind of pioneering, humane act its founder, however pre-Freudian his beliefs, would surely have approved had he been living now.

The photographs which Thomas Barnes took in the late nineteenth century rapidly fixed the notion of Barnardo's in the national consciousness. It's a notion that has changed very little since. We look at the images and words come rushing to our lips: *orphans, urchins, strays, waifs, bastards, vagabonds*. But these are old words, old images. For an organization which wants to show that it has entered the modern world, the richness of its archive is a mixed blessing. Six out of ten adults, asked what they think Barnardo's does, say that it runs homes for children. But those homes were run down after 1945 and the last of them closed in the 1970s. These days the bulk of Barnardo's work is preventive, and not with individual children but (in the hope of keeping them together) with families. Drawing on a budget of £76.5 million, and with 150 projects involving 22,000 clients, it tackles homelessness, poverty, disability and much more through its community centres, day centres, family centres and training centres. And yet Barnardo's in the 1990s seems curiously *de*-centred, since other agencies do this work as well. Devoid of its homes, its boarding schools for the underclass, Barnardo's lacks a unique selling point to seduce the public. It has its heritage – indeed, it is planning to open a Heritage Centre – but this longevity works against it. Even the liberal-minded Polly Toynbee has said that Barnardo's is past its sell-by date, existing just to exist. It has always done well for legacies, but these have begun to go down. As for donations, it is now ranked fifteenth among British charities, behind Save the Children, Oxfam and the NSPCC.

Unthinkable though it is, some people inside Barnardo's would like to lose their founder's name altogether. He isn't the asset he was, now that the twinkling philanthropist has begun to be presented as a meddling dunderhead – a patriarch who ran harsh institutions and pioneered child emigration, segregating brothers and sisters and distributing his charges ('planting my seeds' as he put it) about the colonies. Loyal followers point out that the good Doctor was less sold on children's homes than is popularly imagined, that he preferred – and virtually invented – fostering and adoption. But now that some of his former charges have come forward to complain of mistreatment, the idea of him as 'the father of nobody's children' is being turned on its head. The charge these days is that he was a father (or good father) to no one.

In 1988, Dr Barnardo's tried to cure its image problem by becoming plain Barnardo's – a less paternalistic name. Some of the former boys and girls were outraged by this doctoring of the Doctor: they were far too young to have known him personally (he died in 1906), but they had grown up with his title and saw it as part of their identity. At the same time, the Barnardo's logo was changed, too: the old motif had shown two children holding hands inside a tight circle; the new motif added a third child and liberated them from the circle – now the kids could run free, their joined hands raised in joy. But these modulations don't seem to have had much effect. There's still the notion that Barnardo's means children's homes – which in turn suggests dormitories, disciplinarianism and discredited forms of childcare.

Those who work for Barnardo's various schemes are trying

to combat this prejudice. In Norwood, South London, two doors down from a house once occupied by a famous contemporary of Dr Barnardo, Arthur Conan Doyle, lives the Cleevedon Project, designed to help sixteen- to eighteen-year-olds. Its leader, Shirley Oxley – young, black and energetic – is the first to admit that 'we don't fit in with what most people think Barnardo's means, which is babies'. When kindly souls ring up to say they'll take a child for Christmas, she has to ask how they feel about teenagers. Few of those in her care are orphans.

Referred by local authorities, the kids come from children's homes or foster care. Many arrive confused and distressed, their previous placements having broken down. The aim of the project is to prepare them for independence at eighteen. Each has his or her own care plan. Each has his or her own bedsit. Working closely with a member of staff, they learn about cooking, diet, health, hygiene, how to use an iron or washing machine. There are three Cleevedon houses (with room for up to six kids and two overnight staff), as well as bedsits out in the community. The seventeen full-time members of staff don't have to be Christian (to ask them if they are at interview would be discriminatory), but are expected to sympathize with Barnardo values. Placements come from all ethnic groups.

Shirley's office is big, with deep-blue carpets and deep-blue sofas and chairs. Potted plants vie with African masks and Nelson Mandela posters. It's quiet here during the day, when the kids are at college and on Youth Training Schemes – or are supposed to be. Shirley is very positive about her charges, and regards every one of them as a success: they don't need to get to university (though at least one has); just to have survived local authority care is an achievement. But she won't deny there are problems. Objects have been known to disappear – everything from fax machines to cutlery. The fire brigade has been known to put out blazes, not all of them caused by culinary incompetence. Anger, she says, is the biggest problem – along with frustration, confusion and lack of self-esteem.

Some of these kids are only just getting to grips with who they are and where they've come from when, bang, they reach eighteen and it's time to leave. Others leave earlier, because – though Shirley's too nice to put it like this – they're uncontrollable. In by midnight and no overnight visitors is the usual house rule, more liberal than the homes they've come from but for some not liberal enough.

Upstairs, Shirley tries to show me an occupied room, but the girl in it isn't dressed yet: she feels ill, she says, and has taken a Lemsip; Shirley recommends a visit to the doctor. We pass on to the one unoccupied room: bed, table, cooker, fridge, television – spartan but not unclean. Demand for places is growing. Cleevedon will soon be opening a fourth home. Referrals come from all over the country now, not just London.

Is there anything specifically Barnardo-ish about Cleevedon? With its impact objectives and equal opportunity policy and mission statements, it has the feel of a local authority project. But would the work get done if Barnardo's didn't do it? The social services are under-resourced and over-stretched. The pendulum which swung away from private charities in 1945 is now, post-welfare state, swinging back. What Cleevedon offers – a home for youngsters who don't have one, care, discipline, preparation for adult life – is perfectly consistent with what Barnado began 120 years ago, and just as needed now as it was then. But the problem is to find an image expressing what Cleevedon does and is. Not easy, even on a video. Impossible on a photograph.

Next to the photographic archive back in Barkingside is a studio. John Kirkham was a photographer here once, but now that running the archive takes all his time most of the work is done by his assistant, Paul. Paul describes some kids who 'were in just the other day, doing a shoot for the shops'. Barnardo's high-street retail business now makes over £3 million annually, and the results of this shoot, computer-enhanced, were intended as a possible frieze. The kids laughed a lot, danced, were dressed up in bright clothes. They weren't 'project kids' but 'model kids' – volunteers found through staff and friends. Of course, photographs are still taken of 'project kids', on site, and these 'model kids' hadn't been hired from an agency. Anyway, this is 1995, not 1874, when artistic licence is better understood. If people think these happy, smiling faces are Barnardo's faces, and donate good money as a result, who's complaining? Surely the founder wouldn't be – a man who had to fight all his life to raise money and who brilliantly exploited the camera to do so.

What is different these days is that smiling faces, rather than ragged clothes, are the way for Barnardo's to raise money: the need is to be positive. It's true that Don McCullin took some photographs for the 150th birthday of Barnardo which show that East End deprivation and poverty still go on. But you won't find any sign of them in the house magazine, *Barnardo's Today*, nor in the mail-order catalogue *At Home* (all gardening and bourgeois bric-a-brac). These in-house shots are all cheery beams. There is no Before, only After. And this breeds a complacency, ouside Barnardo's if not within, that the social problems surrounding children have been largely cured.

Driving home from Barkingside, I pull up at some lights and a posse of ten- and twelve-year-olds descend on me – truants they must be, because it's early afternoon. They have the faces of the boys in the photographs I've been looking at – torn clothes, cropped hair, plenty of soap in their buckets but little, it seems, back home. In 1874, no schools to go to, they'd have been matchsellers in Drury Lane or mudlarks trawling the Thames for coal and copper. But this is 1995 and they're washing windscreens.

The lights change and I drive on, thinking of Thomas Barnes again, his session over, his glass plate safe inside its slide. He is taking down his stand, folding the hood away, packing up the camera, making to leave. It's quite some walk to his studio in Mile End Road, but already in his head he's in the darkroom, rescuing lost children, bringing their faces into focus, their features swimming up at him from the murk. He's never managed to explain the excitement he feels, but it is there whenever he lifts a dripping print from the dish: each time a miracle, each miracle different from the last. He would describe it if he could but he's not a man for words. Before and after. Truth and fiction. Darkness and redemption. Images swirl in his head. Thinking of them makes him walk faster. He's coughing yellow stuff and the heavy bag is cutting into his shoulder. But he has grounds to feel contented. A good day's work.

Field of Dreams

How they kept football from me for so long I don't know, but I was almost eleven before I discovered it – or should I say it discovered me. I remember the moment clearly. It was a Sunday morning in autumn and my father and I were sitting in adjoining armchairs in the dining room of our one-time rectory in Yorkshire, sunlight pouring in through the windows and over our shoulders. He had the *Sunday Times*, I the *Sunday Express*, and as I turned to the back page my eye fell on a photograph and match report. In an instant the wicked secret was out and I was doomed – another of the century's lost boys destined to squander the best years of his life failing to make the grade as a professional or simply supporting the wrong team.

Until that moment in the sunlight my only sporting interest had been motor racing: at Oulton Park and Aintree and Silverstone I'd seen Graham Hill and Jack Brabham, Roy Salvadori and Stirling Moss, Bruce McLaren and Innes Ireland battle it out in Formula One races; at home with Dinky toys, I'd recreate these races in the backyard or round the legs of my father's billiard table. It wasn't much of a participation sport for a boy, and despite the success of Nigel

Mansell and Damon Hill it's hard to imagine a child of the 1980s or 1990s finding anything exciting about a noisy, polluting, past-you-in-a-flash car race. But these were the years when the British dominated the sport, drivers as well as manufacturers, and the 1959 championship – with Jack Brabham pushing his car over the line in the final race to wrest victory from Stirling Moss and Tony Brooks – had all the last-gasp enthralment of the 1988–9 soccer season, when Arsenal took the title from Liverpool with Michael Thomas's goal.

There were other dramas, too – like the system we devised for smuggling two large families into the Oulton Park paddock on a single ticket (slip it out to the next person through the slats of a wooden fence), or the extraordinary practice (when the last race was over) of being allowed to drive round the circuit in your family saloon.

Then on that day in 1961 I picked up the family paper and, looking for motor-racing news, saw instead a muddy goalmouth, a bulging net, and what the poet Vernon Scannell once called 'the blurred anguish of goalkeepers'. I pored over the match reports and league tables like someone trying to get to grips with a foreign language. And straight away, the grip was on me. Only once since, after that European Cup Final in the Heysel Stadium, when I thought I could never bear to play or watch the game again, has it promised to set me free.

My sons, children of the 1980s, had the soccer virus by the time they started primary school. Surely I must have known about football before I was eleven? But there were just eighteen children at our village primary school, and football was not played there at all, not even in the playground.

At home it was no better. My father had never played football, only rugby, and as one of two GPs in an under-resourced practice was confined to home, on call, most weekends; when he wasn't, it was Oulton Park we'd go to, not a football ground. My cousins from Manchester, the only children I saw outside school, were all mad about car racing, too. Isolated as I was, the rich kid in the rectory, it wasn't so surprising that football hadn't impinged on my world. Like sex later, it was something my parents probably preferred me not to know about.

Yet eighteen miles away was the town of Burnley, not only my birthplace (in the district hospital) but home to one of the two great football teams of the day. By now, the point of my initiation, their greatest moment, when they won the 1959–60 championship, had already passed. But I was not to know that, and nor were any of the sports journalists who covered their games that autumn. Burnley were riding high, and even if they hadn't been it would never have occurred to me to support Leeds United, though the place we lived in was right on the Yorkshire–Lancashire border, almost as close to Elland Road as to Turf Moor. Who were Leeds United? Just some team languishing in a lower division. Whereas Burnley, as the autumn of 1961 gave way to the spring of 1962, looked on target for the double, and could boast a team of English, Irish and Scottish internationals: Blacklaw, Angus, Elder, Adamson, Cummings, Miller, Connelly, McIlroy, Pointer, Harris.

It was an exciting season but a sad one. The scrapbook I began, when I look at it more closely, reveals some odd gaps, and stops abruptly on March 3rd, at which point Burnley were four points clear of Ipswich and five clear of Tottenham, with games in hand over both of them. (In the Second Division Liverpool made the pace ahead of Leyton Orient and Plymouth Argyle.) Thereafter, Burnley's progress was too agonizing to record, and I have suppressed all memory of it apart from a rare win over lowly Blackpool: inexorably, Ipswich caught us and the games in hand were blown away.

But there was still the FA Cup, the very reason, some commentators said (as they always do), for the team's faltering in the league. Here my scrapbook details are much fuller: 6–1 over QPR; then Leyton Orient, 1–0 in a replay; Everton, 3–1; Sheffield United 1–0; and finally in the semi-finals a 2–1 win over Fulham, again after a replay. This left the final against Spurs, the Old Enemy, who came to Turf Moor for a league match just fourteen days before and drew 2–2. There were four goals again at Wembley, but this time it all turned to dust. Jimmy Greaves scored after three minutes; Burnley's equalizer early in the second half came from Robson, who somehow squeezed it in the narrow gap that Brown was guarding at one post – anything but a classic. This goal was cancelled out by the burly Smith just one minute later.

Then came a disputed penalty ten minutes from time: Blacklaw lost the ball to two challenging Spurs players (surely a foul), Cummings stepped in to breast away a shot by Merwin (never handball, ref) and the referee pointed to the spot. The decision was agony enough, but nothing compared to the slow-motion trauma of the penalty itself: tubby Adam Blacklaw dropping on one knee to his right as Danny Blanchflower stepped up and rolled the ball gently to his left. At the final whistle I did the only thing a boy could do in the circumstances: took my ball out on the front lawn and re-enacted the entire game, with certain crucial adjustments to the scoreline. This was the principle I'd learnt with my Dinky toys round the billiard table: a world of isolated make-believe, where the action replay, yet to be invented on television, ensured that your favourites could never lose. But to a grow-ing boy there were shades of the prison house about these fantasy games: I wanted to play football myself, and that seemed to mean having somebody to play it with.

For the moment this possibility was remote. My younger sister soon tired of being put in goal and my long-suffering aunt Sheila, who came to stay every school holiday and who one summer allowed me to amass a century against her on the

back lawn, would not extend her tolerance of cricket to football. As for the three boys of my age at primary school –
Simon, Stephen, and Jeffrey – they were so uninterested in
football they used to satirize my obsession with it. In desper-
ation I started going to a youth club in Kelbrook, three miles
away, where there was five-a-side every Friday evening and
where the intention was to form a fully fledged eleven-a-side
village boys' team. My grave offence to tribal loyalties somehow got back to Simon, Stephen and Jeffrey, who took the piss
relentlessly – 'Morrie, Morrie, football mad' – and eventually
stopped talking to me altogether. Their persecution programme only strengthened my faith: I was now a martyr to
football, a sufferer in the cause.

Forced to play alone, I began the process of transforming
some rough and gale-swept ground in the paddock behind
our house into a stadium of dreams. My father helped me
clear the ground of stones, weeds, broken glass. We constructed goal posts from rusty old metal tubing and put some
strawberry nets behind them. (To my dad's fury I left the nets
there the whole winter until grass and weed began to grow
through and they fell apart in our hands.) The touchlines
were ribbon-scatters of sawdust, standard local league practice
in those days. But one afternoon I discovered an old line-
marker and some lime bags in an outhouse, from the days
when the house had had a tennis court. Clearing the cob-
webs, I slowly grasped how the contraption worked: you
poured lime into the heavy metal base, added water, stirred
the sloppy mass with a stick until you had the right consis-
tency, dropped the wheel into the metal slots that held it, and
then went squeaking off down the side of the pitch.

In Kevin Costner's 1989 film *Field of Dreams*, an American
on a farm hears the corn telling him to construct a baseball
field at the back of his house. I had the same sense of mystery
and religious calling myself, though for this Yorkshire field of

dreams it was that line-marker which provided all the magic. The touchlines and penalty areas and centre circle would be a pale, indistinguishable yellow when I marked them out on the wet grass in the morning; by lunchtime, as the day dried out, they'd come up a brilliant white. I surveyed them from the main stand – a large earth mound running down one side of the field, separating it from our garden. It was a short pitch, thirty yards at most, and a bumpy one, narrower at one end than the other and with a ridge running across the edge of the penalty areas. But as far as I was concerned – little Lord Fauntleroy on his earth mound, chairman, groundsman, manager, referee and twenty-two players rolled into one – these were the green expanses of Turf Moor or even Wembley.

I lacked only opponents, but these weren't hard to imagine, any more than it was hard to provide Ken Wolstenholme's commentary as I raced up and down. My favourite move was to pass back to myself in goal (there was no law against passing back to goalkeepers in those days), then punt the ball high in the air and sprint up to the centre circle to head forward; a further rush, a volley on the edge of the area and with luck the ball might hit the roof of the net without bringing down the wonky crossbar. (Why was it always so much more exciting to hit the roof of the net, though all the manuals said that a low shot stood more chance of beating the keeper? Why is that sort of goal still so much more spectacular to see?) A line of elms and chestnuts ran down the side of the pitch opposite the grandstand, a kop that roared and swayed in the wind: if I timed it right there's be a gust of wind at just the moment the strawberry net was bulging – the ecstatic crowd, or even Ken Wolstenholme moved to high excitement by what he'd just seen.

It was all very well but I'd have to put in some proper games of football – with real opponents – if I was ever going to be signed up by Burnley. Then one spring evening as I was dashing about the pitch and muttering Wolstenholmeisms to myself, Simon and Stephen were suddenly there at the field gate. I slunk over to them, shamefaced, caught in the act, only to find that they'd decided they liked football and, more to the point, had resolved to persecute Jeffrey instead. Things looked up after that, for me if not for Jeffrey; we started to play football at break and even managed to con the soppy new teacher at the primary school into letting us have a match during lesson time.

The Kelbrook team got off the ground, too, if only for two matches, one of which exposed me for the first time to violence (unthinkable in our school for a boy to be beaten up by another boy) and the other to the word 'fuck'. It was in the bath afterwards, I remember, that I half-innocently asked my mother what it meant and knew from her fumbling evasiveness that it possessed a power I would want to test out again. Football and fucking (whatever that was) were, I intuitively grasped, a long way from my mother's aspirations for me, which among other things included learning to play the piano. I dutifully went to piano lessons at the house of Mrs Brown, in Earby, until I arrived one Wednesday afternoon in the middle of live television coverage (rare in those days) of an England World Cup qualifying match. To have the football on television turned off and to be forced to practise the piano instead put paid to my faltering interest in that instrument. I have never been musical since.

Later, I moved on to a grammar school in Skipton and at last found boys even more manacled to football than myself. Undeterred that rugby, not soccer, was the official school sport, we would get to the playing fields early on games afternoons so we could use the oval ball as a round one (even heading in) before the games master arrived. And though soccer was in theory banned from the playground, the staff were happy to turn a blind eye to our break-time mauling.

There was a chalked goal on one wall, while to score at the other end you had to get the ball between the drainpipe and the ventilation-grate. Mostly we played with a tennis ball but if there wasn't one to be had we'd make do with a small stone instead. (Out walking today, I still find myself trying to steer small stones through gateposts or other imaginary goals.) For a time we even got away with using a Frido. That all ended the morning I sent a wayward shot towards a doorway at exactly the moment that Wally Evans, the notoriously fierce physics master, came whistling through it on his way to assembly. Like the Blanchflower penalty, I see it all now in horrible slow motion: his unexpected emergence; the Frido smacking him on his bald patch and leaving a neat imprint of mud dots across his forehead; his terrifyingly loud demand 'Who kicked that?'; me shuffling over in terror and contrition as he began to wipe the muddy print off with his handker-chief; an almost audible general sigh of relief that punishment went no further than confiscation of the ball and detention for all those of us who'd been playing. For half a term there was no playground football at all. Then the tennis ball games resumed.

Playing regular rugby for the school would have made it difficult to pursue a soccer career, of course, but whether through design or lack of skill I rose no higher than captaincy of the rarely called-upon third XV, where I played stand-off (lots of kicking, not much service to the three-quarters) and took all the penalties. This left nearly all my Saturdays free to go to Burnley and, later, to play for a team in Colne; only once was I caught out, when I had to bunk off from a third XV game in order to play in a crucial cup match at Lancaster, which we won 5–3 in a swirling gale that allowed me, for the only time in my career, to score direct from a corner.

Sundays were reserved for the highly successful Barnoldswick Park Rovers Minors side, which I joined at fifteen, just after the start of a season which ended with a long unbeaten run and the league title. I didn't think of myself as much of a player but both schoolyard practice and the solitary hours I spent at home modelling myself on Burnley midfield genius Gordon Harris did mean that I was highly trained and motivated. And there was one spectacular goal which helped me make my mark, at least as far as the local paper was concerned ('Left-winger Laurence Stocker raced away down the right wing before putting across a bullet-like centre. Blake Morrison, who had followed up field, came running in to head the ball into the corner of the net with the entire Hellifield defence left stranded'). I still don't know if I meant it or just couldn't get out of the way.

The team went on winning the following season, and soon there were rumours of scouts coming to Barlick in order to watch us: Liverpool, Leeds United, Burnley, Bury and Blackburn were all said to be 'taking an interest' and Preston manager Jimmy Milne himself turned up for one game. Finally an invitation came for six of us to go to Preston for trials. The local paper made much of the fact that I was among them, a grammar school boy and doctor's son, but we all knew that it was the other grammar school boy among the six, Seehan Grace, two or three years younger than most of us and a star sprinter, whom Preston must be after. None the less, after two lots of trials, three of us were offered schoolboy forms.

It seems amazing now that we were so blasé as to refuse, but we were taking the advice of our mentors – Park Rovers stalwarts like Neville Thwaites and Teddy Bamber as well as Seehan Grace's dad, who ran the Barlick carpet shop and knew the score better than we did. Their view was that schoolboy forms wouldn't mean much – no more than a couple of games a season in the B-team. And though I was tempted to give it a go just to see what the level of competition was like, I didn't want to break rank. Preston, in any case, were not Burnley. O-levels were looming, I'd begun to get interested in girls and poetry, and deep down I knew I'd neither the skill nor bottle to make a soccer career.

Still, I went on playing. Langroyd, the Colne adult side I played for on Saturdays, had a lousy sloping pitch and were no great shakes, but I was enough of a fantasist to persuade myself that the stocky young apprentice engineers and flabby, middle-aged millworkers who made up the rest of the team were in the same league as Gordon Harris and Ray Pointer.

We had a fantasist for a manager, too. Ernie, who had been a good player in his day and still sometimes turned out if we were one short, lived in a grim terrace in Earby with an out-size wife and mentally handicapped teenage daughter. Football was his escape from the pressures at home, and he was even more obsessed with it than I was. Unfortunately, he was also a cheat, and had a habit of drafting in star players for one-off appearances in cup matches even if this meant forging their signing-on forms. He got away with it most of the time but there were two notable occasions when his cheating caught up with us. The first was a summer five-a-side tourna-ment, when the Langroyd A-team were progressing steadily towards the final until, in the semi, 1–0 up with two minutes to go, one of our players went down injured. We didn't have a substitute and didn't reckon we needed one either but Ernie, taking no risks, illegally sent on someone from our B-team, an offence immediately spotted by a rival team manager, who reported it and got us disqualified.

Easier to forgive, in some ways, was Ernie's ploy when we found ourselves 1–0 down at half-time in a crucial quarter-final cup match in Skelmersdale: Langroyd had been beaten in the semi-final the previous year, and we were determined to triumph this time. The game should never have started on the waterlogged pitch, and the rain continued to bucket down.

Skelmersdale got a squelchy early goal and there was worse to come when our centre half was sent off after twenty minutes for taking a wild kick at a niggly opposition forward. In the dressing room at the interval Ernie told us – and none of us disputed it – that since we'd hardly got out of our own penalty area there was no chance of our winning; the best thing would be for a succession of players to go down injured and be taken off, forcing the referee to recognize the error of his ways in not having called the game off. I couldn't bring myself to be one of the imposters, but there were a couple of players who made a brilliant job of shamming serious injury and when the second of these had been helped off, after seventy-two minutes, leaving us with eight men, the referee decided to abandon the match – the pitch, he said, with no exaggeration, was now unplayable. Judging by the whistling from the Skelmersdale stand, the small crowd had clearly got Ernie's number: we were even booed as we left the ground for the team coach at the end. But Skelmersdale had the last laugh, invoking some arcane league rule that if a game had been abandoned after seventy minutes the authorities had the right to allow the result to stand. Ernie was phoneless and it fell to me to ring the appeals committee to learn the result of their hearing, and to drive down to Ernie to break the bad news. I remember him, in his cramped front room full of ironing and football trophies, his nylon shirt covered in sweat, indignantly planning our next move. But there was none we could make: Langroyd were out of the cup, and my last season with them before I left for university was all but over.

My interest in Burnley was all but over, too. I had gone on watching them throughout the 1960s, but they were in steady decline and my memories of the period are random and fragmented. I saw newly promoted Liverpool come over to Turf Moor and win 3–0, with Ian St John thumping one goal straight up into the roof of the net from about two yards; I remember an Aston Villa defender squaring up to Willie Irvine (or was it another of Burnley's flash-in-the-pan forwards of that era?) then nutting him full in the face: we howled for his blood, a linesman had spotted it, and off he went. Clearest of all – I remember it as yesterday – was the most spectacular own goal ever seen at Turf Moor, scored for Leeds United (just up from the Second Division) by Alex Elder, who won the ball near his own corner flag, brought it forward a yard or two into a gusting wind, then, without looking, lofted it back to Adam Blacklaw. But Blacklaw had advanced towards the edge of the penalty area, and would have had no chance anyway with Elder's overhit lob, which swung into the far top corner. The only goal in a 1–0 defeat by Leeds: things were never the same after that.

There were still the odd moments of glory, but not many. The last programme I have is against Arsenal – from September 13th 1969, two weeks before I left for university. Arsenal that day had Bob Wilson in goal, plus Frank McLintock, Bobby Gould and George Graham; the Burnley team was Peter Mellor, John Angus, Les Latcham, Brian O'Neil, Dave Merrington, Sammy Todd, Dave Thomas, Ralph Coates, Frank Casper, Martin Dobson and Steve Kindon. It was still a classy outfit – or should have been with Dobson, O'Neil and Coates there – but only Angus was left from the Cup Final side seven years earlier and the inexorable slide had begun. Two seasons later, in 1971, Burnley were relegated. They quickly climbed back up again, but only for two seasons, and then cascaded down until they reached the Fourth Division in 1985. In 1988 they escaped plummeting out of the Football League altogether by winning their last match: I heard it on the radio from a Suffolk garden, urging them on as if I were back on the terraces and this were a Cup Final, not a battle for survival.

Burnley still have an impressively strong following, and

I've met fans in the unlikeliest places. But even in the late-sixties, when Burnley were a higher division side, the crowds at Turf Moor had begun to dwindle: the glory of a decade previously was past. In those days I went with Les, a manager at the Barlick Rolls Royce factory, and we'd park his warm, purring saloon a couple of streets away, before taking our place on the empty terraces or in the stand. But in the early 1960s I had travelled to matches with a carpenter named Geoff, in his battered old van, and we'd have to park miles away from the ground and walk; once inside, we'd stand behind the goal where the crowds were sometimes big enough for me to experience that feeling of being carried helplessly downwards, feet off the ground, after some particularly exciting goalmouth incident.

Intimidation, violence and vandalism we took for granted. Whenever I'm tempted to look back on that decade as some innocent age of pre-hooliganism, I remember my brush with a Stoke City fan when I was about thirteen. He was walking ahead of me as (in those unsegregated days) I looked for a place behind the goal. Catching sight of my claret-and-blue scarf, he abruptly stopped and wouldn't budge, so that when I gingerly tried to make my way past his looming bulk he could turn and snarl, 'Who the fuck do you think you're pushing?' He grabbed hold of me, dangled me in the air in front of him, drew his fist back and was about to belt me when a mate of his called him off: 'Leave 'im Mick, it's not worth it, he's nobbut a little 'un.' He put me down: 'Just fucking watch it next time.'

Violence had its own momentum and needed no excuses. I remember the story of a friend beaten up in Skipton bus station.

'Hey, you're t' cunt what's been cleverin' roun' town all evening'.'

'Nay, ah've been in Keighley – ah've just got off t'bus.'

'That's nowt to do wi' it.' Thump.

At the Heysel stadium, and again after Hillsborough, I wondered whether the violence and tragedy that seemed to attend football then might not kill off the pleasure I'd always taken in it. But there's no sign of that. On the contrary, with my sons' fantasies to look after as well as my own, I've renewed my interest. That interest began as a kind of vicarious dream, and it still operates on that level. Listening to Burnley's great escape act the other season, I wasn't thinking how fortunate I was never to have been signed up, or how squalid it would have felt to end my playing days at the bottom of the bottom division. I was wondering why the call from the Burnley manager hadn't come yet, and staying fairly close to the phone in case it did.

Children of the Dales

At first glance, Daniel Procter's bedroom looks pretty much what you'd expect. There are posters of Andy Cole and the fixture list for the football season. There are photos of the England rugby team and a gleaming red Ferrari. There's a globe on the window sill, with a switch to illuminate it. There's a model tank, and a heap of lolly sticks. There aren't many books I can see, but then twelve-year-olds like Daniel are said not to read much any more. What did I think I'd find? The Famous Five?

There is no computer in Daniel's bedroom, but his big brother Thomas has one in his, an Amiga, and there's also a Game Boy in the house somewhere. Daniel's favourite computer games are football games; then what he calls beat-'em-up games, like Mortal Kombat 2, with special moves; then shooting games, like Better Archery. He doesn't have a television in his bedroom yet, but he might when he's older, like Thomas. He doesn't mind because there's one downstairs he can watch. Saturday, he says, is the best night for television.

A few minutes ago, Daniel came home in his school uniform. Now he's wearing blue socks, Bermuda shorts and a red

T-shirt that says BLOGGS/JOE BLOGGS across the chest. His trainers are downstairs, by the back door, ready and waiting for when we're done talking and he can get out on his bicycle.

But I'm lingering in his bedroom, which – now I come to look at it more closely – seems rather less stereotypical. That model tank, for instance: Daniel made it himself, not from an Airfix kit, but at school, in a design and technology class. And those lolly sticks aren't just scattered at random, but form the roof of another model he made, of a house. There are other things Daniel has made here: clay pots, an ugly mug, and a wooden balancing toy. He's more animated talking about them than he is pointing out the sports posters – which are, on examination, oddly dated: the football fixture list is for the 1993–4 season, and that England rugby team goes back to 1991.

I ask Daniel if he reads much. Yes, he says. What sort of thing? At the moment he's reading Robert Louis Stevenson – *Treasure Island* and *Kidnapped*. He used to read Roald Dahl – oh, and all the Famous Five books, when he was younger. Do I know them? he asks. They're by Enid Blyton.

Daniel looks eager to be off outside. He can't show me his chicken run, he says, because it's a bit of a way off, in a small croft, but we could look at his greenhouse, which is right outside. *His* greenhouse? Yes, when he was seven he was given a growing kit, from Toymaster: sunflower seeds, pea seeds, lettuce seeds. It gave him a taste for horticulture: seeing things shoot up like that, from nothing. So for his tenth birthday, he asked for a greenhouse. That bed of potatoes there, where his mother's roses used to be, is also his. You've got to be careful to earth potatoes, he tells me – that means building the earth up over them, because otherwise, if they get above ground, they go green and poisonous. As for the chickens, he incubated them in the house, kept them for a week after they'd hatched under a lamp, then once they'd got a few feathers moved them outside. He feeds them each morning before going to school: he lifts the little hatch and they run out and sometimes jump up on him for bread. Then he collects the dozen or so eggs the hens have laid.

I ask if he gets a weekly comic. No. But he did used to get *Poultry News.*

No childhood is typical. Daniel Procter's is less typical than most, because he lives on a farm. Situated on a hillside close to the Pennine Way, the farm has ninety acres, though half of these are let out and Daniel's father, Howard, since downsizing a few years ago, no longer has a dairy herd, either. The nearest town, half a mile down a track, is a small Lancashire milltown, Earby. But strictly speaking – Daniel's parents had to argue the point with the local education authority – the Procter farm is just inside Yorkshire. Because of this Daniel, like his brothers Thomas and Ben, was able to go to the village primary school in nearby Thornton-in-Craven. Now he goes to the grammar school in Skipton, six miles away. It, too, is in Yorkshire. The Procters feel white rose loyalties, not red.

I have a particular interest in Daniel, because I grew up in the same place, went to the same schools, negotiated the same rift between counties. My parents were doctors, not farmers, and our house, though a little aloof from the village, was not set in such splendid isolation as Daniel's farm. But I walked the same paths, literally – and even had one or two of the same teachers.

Looking at Daniel's upbringing, and comparing it with mine, I wanted to understand some of the obvious ways in which childhood has changed in the past thirty years – and some of the less obvious ways in which it hasn't. In particular I wanted to test the theory that today's kids, wherever and however they're raised, grow up much faster than we did – are rougher, edgier, more knowing and derisive. The recent film *Kids* gave a new piquancy to the theory. But the case has been argued many times over the last few years, usually with reference to the killing of James Bulger and often with a new thesis about who or what's to blame: single mothers, absent fathers, the Pill, the sixties, the education system, the decline of churchgoing, the loss of moral authority.

In a recent article in the *New Yorker*, the film critic David Denby pointed to a different but no less familiar culprit: the influence of television, computers, peer groups and pop culture. Consumed by 'a sense that nothing matters', only instant gratification, the average child, Denby says, 'is rude and surly and sees everything in terms of winning or losing or popularity and becomes insanely interested in clothes and seems far, far from courage and selfhood'. Though Denby is talking about children in the US, any parent in Britain would recognize what he is describing.

Yet there's little in the manner of Daniel, or of his brothers, to suggest Armageddon is at hand: they're bright, responsive, friendly, talkative – even, by all accounts, when not required to put on a show for a stranger like me. When I ask Daniel about his television habits, he says his favourite soaps are *Coronation Street* – 'everyone watches that round here' – and *East Enders*: otherwise games shows like *Take Your Pick*, and *Casualty*, and films, if there's a good one on – something like *Ghostbusters 2*, *Gremlins 2*, the Indiana Jones films, *The Addams Family* and *Addams Family Values*. Nothing too different here from the diet of *Emergency Ward Ten* and *Z Cars* which I consumed at that age.

Does he borrow videos? Occasionally. Or see videos at friends' houses? Yes, he saw one at Laurence Edmonson's, when he slept over there, which he has now done five times. Has he ever seen a 15-certificate film? He seems a bit vague. I explain or remind him about 12s and 15s and 18s and PGs.

'Yes, I think we're seeing one at school at the moment. It's called *Macbeth*, and we're reading the play by William Shakespeare. That's the only one.'

For Daniel the world of play means Amiga, Nintendo, Game Boy, Robocop. In my day, it was Dinky toys, Meccano, Scalextric, Subbuteo and Hornby train sets. A generation or two earlier and it might have been spinning tops, wooden hoops and trolleys knocked together from old pram wheels and orange boxes. It's hard to see that much has been lost. In terms of intellectual stimulus, something may even have been gained.

When I attended Thornton-in-Craven primary school, between 1956 and 1962, I was in a class of eighteen pupils. The class was the whole school; there were just three of us in my year. There was one large room, and one teacher, and though the eleven-year-olds performed some tasks which the five-year-olds didn't, or couldn't, there were also long stretches of the day when we all had to muck in together: for storytime, for milktime, for dinner (delivered in large metal tins by the local authority), for games (no football allowed), for educational broadcasts (all on radio when I started, but later came a television) and for craftwork. Most of the craft-work seemed to involve raffia. Each time we finished craft lessons, and had to pack up, we were told to 'make sure that every last wisp of raffia is tidied away'.

Miss Todd, our teacher until her retirement, was strict. She taught us to read by learning words inscribed on little oblong bits of wood – CAT, DOG, COW, DISH, CAKE. She taught us to write with sticks of chalk on slates, and later, when we were bigger, with nibs dipped in a jar of ink. She read us The Famous Five, and Dr Doolittle and the pushme-pullyou, and Beatrix Potter. (One of Beatrix Potter's stories had a Mr Tod, who was a fox, and when I looked at Miss Todd's long nose and whiskery chin I thought of her as his sister.) Even to us then, the school seemed more like something from the 1850s than the 1950s. Other village schools were closing or merging. We assumed ours would, in time.

But the school has stayed, and isn't spectacularly different today. When Thomas started, in 1984, there were 'twenty-one of us, and just two teachers'. With an increased demand for places, and the erection of a Portakabin classroom, the numbers have now risen to seventy-two – with three full-time teachers, two dinner ladies, a secretary, and three non-teaching assistants, including Daniel's mother, Lynda. These days, the pupils are split into three different classes, or age groups. The school has four computers, and its games activities are enterprisingly diverse: basketball, netball, football, cricket, rounders. But there are still nature study outings up Cam Lane. Hopscotch squares are still marked out on the playground, and the girls use them, when they're not skipping with a rope. There's still 'tig', or catch. Above all, the school still has an intimate, rooted, communal village ethos.

It is easy to be sentimental about that ethos. Villages can be spiteful places; village schools, too. I remember Mrs Hartley, the teacher who succeeded Miss Todd, sitting us on the floor one day, after some misdemeanour, and telling us how she'd taught children in deprived urban areas who were much nicer and better behaved than we were. In truth, our misdemeanours were very mild: the worst we did was steal the school doorknob, which was loose, and easily slipped off, and which we hid in the ivy. But there was a lot of petty feuding and malicious 'leaving out' – in such a small school, to be spurned by two or three children one's own age meant virtual isolation.

The Procter brothers seem to have had a friendlier time of it than I did: more activities, more stimulus, but still the same advantageous teacher–pupil ratio. Daniel remembers doing science from an early age – 'Mrs Butter did that test with us where you put yeast in a bottle and get a balloon to rise'. He remembers doing rubbings with leaves and tree bark. The school dinners don't seem to have improved much. There's lasagne, flapjack and fruit, which we didn't have, but also semolina, mushy peas, lumpy custard and shepherd's pie with onion rings, which we did. They're still delivered by the local authority, to be cooked on site. On some days, says Daniel, the food is 'really gross'.

There are still 'rules': no sweets; no running in the corridor; no shouting or whistling in class; no playing on the grass in winter; no throwing snowballs or making ice-slides. 'Just common sense, really,' says Daniel. He didn't experience much bullying: there was one boy who arrived from another school, and tried it on, but everyone regarded him as thick. It was he who did the worst thing Daniel can remember – stuck pins with Blue-Tak on the door-handle of the supply teacher's car.

Cars are perhaps the main difference between Daniel's experience of school and mine. Then, everyone walked to school; these days even some children from within the village are brought by car. Partly it's convenience: parents can drop them on the way to work. Partly it's the danger: cars, wagons and buses thunder through the village, and there's no pedestrian crossing. Pupils are offered a cycling proficiency course, but the risks of an accident are too great for them to be allowed to cycle alone to school.

There's also the fear – not supported by statistics, but deeply ingrained in most parents now, no matter how small their community – of the strangers who might intercept, molest, abduct or murder any unchaperoned child. Even Lynda Procter feels this up on her farm. 'When the boys used to be brought back by local authority transport from school, I'd always go to meet them at the bottom gate – even though it's just a shortish walk through our fields. And if they're going anywhere, down to the park or even out in the fields here, I always lay the law down, to fix a time they'll be back. I keep tabs on them as best as I can, but you're always aware of the risk, even here, and even though they're boys. We don't go over the top, or spell it out. But they are aware of it. Now if they see anyone strange walking about they come and tell me.'

The message certainly seems to have got through to Daniel, for all his cheerful innocence. And it's more than a matter of wearing a helmet when he cycles to town and back. The other week he went down to the park, and saw a group of teenagers there he didn't know. They had punk hairstyles, and didn't look very friendly, so he cleared off quickly, in case there was trouble. His parents can trust him not to talk to strangers, he says. He's not daft.

This time last year, Daniel began going to Ermysted's grammar school in Skipton. In my day you got to Ermysted's (or, if you were a girl, to Skipton high school) by passing your eleven-plus. Of the three of us who took the eleven-plus from Thornton, Stephen and I passed and Jeffrey failed (which meant a place at the secondary modern in Barnoldswick instead). Before the exam we worked and played together and thought of ourselves as friends and equals; after the results came through, things were not the same: hard for Jeffrey not to resent us; hard for us not to patronize and pity him.

Though Jeffrey, through his hard work, later ended up at the grammar school, I'd seen close-up how divisive selection can be. Two years later, when my sister failed the eleven-plus, it came home to me even more. My parents didn't like Barnoldswick secondary modern, and, since they could afford the fees, decided to send her to boarding school in the Lake District, failing to persuade me that, for equality's sake, I too should go away to school (we looked round Giggleswick, where Russell Harty once taught, but I dug my heels in). My sister had a miserable time of it, and felt punished for her failure. Blaming the eleven-plus for this, not my parents, I looked forward to the arrival of the comprehensive system. It, I felt sure, would put an end to the old divisiveness.

I was wrong. The eleven-plus system is still around, or something like it, under a different name. These days, all pupils in their last year at primary school take tests in verbal and non-verbal reasoning, and those in a 'border-zone' take further tests in English and maths. According to how they do, they're sent to the boys' grammar or girls' high school; to South Craven school, in Crosshills; or to Aireville, in Skipton. The test system isn't as stark and inhumane as it once was. No one talks of 'pass' and 'fail' any more, but of finding the appropriate educational environment. There's an element of continuous assessment. There are teachers' reports and recommendations. There's a procedure for appeals. But there are still winners and losers. And Daniel's family has been divided much as mine was: he and Thomas go to Ermysted's; Ben, the middle brother, to Aireville. It caused a lot of heartache and soul-searching in the Procter family.

Even if Ben had gone to Ermysted's, he wouldn't have been part of one big happy family. The streaming there which I'd assumed would also disappear is still around, again under a different name: Daniel's first-year results mean that he will go into the top stream, 'the Latin form', as Thomas did before him. Ermysted's – founded in 1492, just as the Spanish were discovering South America – has always had the air of a minor public school, but none of the gracelessness. Academic rather than snooty, it ranks near the top of the national league tables for schools, and even those not in the Latin form do well at GCSE. It promises state school students the kind of traditional grammar school education which middle-class parents in London have to look for in the private sector.

Six months before talking to the Procter boys, I went back to Ermysted's for the first time in twenty-six years. On the previous day, the London head teacher Philip Lawrence had been stabbed to death by a teenager outside his school, and on that raw, cold afternoon I was sensitive to signs of change: had this place, too, suffered some violent transformation? But Skipton isn't inner London, and Ermysted's looks remarkably unchanged. There's a splendid new sports hall, and the hundred or so boarders have gone, creating more space. But the temporary classrooms (the 'henhuts') have survived, the ancient canteen and labs are unaltered, there are the same cracks in the corridor floor and (I swear) the same sliding bolt missing from the third lavatory door on the right. The termly *Chronicles* do not, it's true, carry reports of the potholing club's activities suffering disruption because of foot-and-mouth disease, and (with several women now on the staff) no one would get excited about the hiring of a female maths teacher, whereas back in the 1960s there was quite a flutter at the arrival of Mrs Binns. But in other respects, little seems to have altered.

It's a biggish school, with five hundred or so pupils, and to Daniel and Thomas, coming here from Thornton, it was (as for me, before them) both scary and exhilarating. It's less formal now, but not that much. Most teachers still expect to be called 'sir', and many address the boys by their surnames. Inevitably, both Daniel and Thomas have the same nickname, used by teachers and boys alike: 'Procky' or 'Proc'. Listening to Daniel's anecdotes of school, it's as if we might be contemporaries, not a generation apart. Still going on, all of it: the blackboards and bunsen burners; the football in the quad at breaktime; rugby a half-mile walk away, at Sandylands, and cricket, if it's not raining, on 'the Top'; the chemistry teacher giving instruction in how to make a stink bomb ('you could smell it right down the corridor'); the art and design teachers who're 'really daft and let you be cheeky with them'; the endless mimicry, not least of accents – whereas most of Ermysted's pupils come from Skipton and up the Dales, those coming six miles away from Earby and Barnoldswick have a tinge of Lancashire in their voice.

Skipton is a peaceful market town, but back in my day violence was never far away. There was tension between Ermysted's and Aireville, the secondary modern just up the road, and from time to time there'd be a beating-up and rumours of some ultimate gang showdown, with razors and chains and knives. There was the occasional violent teacher, too, like the one who threw board-dusters if you misbehaved, very painful when they cracked you on the head. I got the cane once, not a whack across a naked bottom but several thwacks to a held-out hand. I can't remember now what it was for, only that it seemed a fair cop rather than (as I now think corporal punishment) barbaric. Jack Eastwood, the head, was the reluctant adminstrator of the cane, a man we all mimicked for the way his forefingers made a V-sign whenever he became excited. His predecessor had been the keenly flagellatory Mr Forster, a true Mr Whips, who famously caned a boy on his (the boy's) first day, for the offence of scraping a chair during assembly (forty years on, the boy, Colin Dunn, wrote about it in *Punch*), and infamously ran off with the foreign (and pregnant) family maid. But Jack was a less enthusiastic caner, and there were no real tyrants on the staff. Whereas among the boys . . .

The novelist Saki said, 'You can't expect a boy to be vicious till he's been to a good school', and Ermysted's, being a good school, had its share of viciousness. There was a boy we used to goad called Crowther, a manure-smelling farmboy who if you got him riled enough would go berserk, running amok and screaming like an abattoir. We bullied teachers, too. The geography teacher, Cassie, wasn't only a hunchback but an epileptic, and would sometimes be driven to frothing at the mouth. Being in the top stream, the A-form, made no differ-ence, except perhaps in the cleverness with which we dreamt up new ways to torment. Quiet and sneaky, I was never in the front line, but now that only makes me feel worse: at least some of the others in the class were more straightforward in their torture methods.

These days, things seem more stable. Daniel has seen fights in the playground, but nothing serious: 'If there's a little scrap, no one takes any notice. If there's a big bashing-up, with blood, and everyone standing round in a ring, then the teach-ers break it up.' Pellet-flicking is commonplace; flick knives are not. There are detentions for boys who misbehave or fail to do their work, and he's dimly aware that there are occa-sional suspensions, too – mostly of under-achieving fifth formers who're bored and ready to leave, rather than (as hap-pened at least once when I was there) of sons about to become fathers because their girlfriends had become pregnant. Smoking, he knows, goes on behind the sheds. And some boys occasionally attempt to subvert the dress code – grey or white shirts, grey trousers, blazer, house-colours tie – with boots, for example, rather than shoes, much as we occasionally wore our jumpers back to front, so they were crew-neck rather than V-neck. At his age, I tell him, I was made to wear short trousers. Not any more, he laughs. We wore caps, too, the trick being to balance them as far back on the head as you could (so as to show off your quiff) without them actually falling off. They don't have those now, either – though the regime hasn't slack-ened so far as to admit baseball hats.

Daniel is enthusiastic about big school. He's had fun there so far. He's good at art and design and technology, and Latin, which he is already fluent in the defence of: 'People say there's no point in studying Latin. But it helps you with your English – for instance, you can work out that a word like "dormant" must mean asleep if you can remember the Latin.

I expect it's going to help me with my French, too, which I'm starting next year.' Daniel knows that if he puts the effort in at Ermysted's, he'll get on OK. Work hard and play hard: that's the message he seems to have learned. My fifties father would have been proud of him. His own father is proud of him, too.

Daniel is still only twelve: plenty of time, a cynic would say, to grow out of it, to become cruddy and nihilistic and know-all – just imagine what he'll be like at sixteen. It's a fair point. So I decide to talk to Daniel's brother, Thomas, who *is* sixteen.

By rights he should be slumped in his room, smoking dope and playing loud music. But I disturb him while he's outside, up a ladder, painting a window sill. It's not for show. He's the practical one about the place, he says. Daniel and Ben might help with the odd job, but they're lazy and weedy, compared to him, and his dad, who has back and knee problems, needs the help. He's helped round the place since he was little: learned to drive a tractor at twelve, and knows how to worm sheep ('it's not that difficult, just a matter of shoving a syringe down their gob – but you've still got to hold them'). Like Daniel, he enjoys working with his hands. If he can solve a problem, rather than his parents having to (say) call a plumber in, that's very satisfying.

Thomas doesn't get pocket money, and doesn't think he should: it's wrong, children and teenagers having handouts; the arrangement in his house is that if you really want something (a motorbike aside), and help enough about the place, you'll be bought it. He has more financial independence now, anyway, because he works in a bookshop every Saturday, which is 'a social event really', a chance to meet people. Soon, when he's seventeen and passes his driving test, he'll be freer still. He does sometimes feel a bit isolated, on the farm, with none of his friends living close by. But with a car it'll be easier for them to go out together.

I ask Thomas about girlfriends: he is after all genial, talkative and highly presentable – with his contact lenses and sideburns, he no longer looks the early-teenage swot seen in photographs about the house. Girls? He's not shy about replying, but there's not much activity to report, yet: 'I didn't really look for them until the fourth form. I have a sort of girlfriend, called Tilly, who I met through my aunt. Tilly lives in Bournemouth. We get on really well, like brother and sister. She feels the same as me, that if you go to a single-sex school you don't get the confidence to talk to the opposite sex. The high school in Skipton is very close to our school, but there's not that much intermingling. And for GCSEs we had to work hard. And I can't ever imagine saying, "Sod the work". But when I get the car . . .' Which is his way of saying, apropos sex, that he hasn't, so far.

Thomas, as all this suggests, is studious as well as practical. He has just taken eleven GCSEs, will take five A-levels in two years' time, and was recently accepted as a member of Mensa. Art and design are his strong points. But he quite likes sport, rugby aside (badminton is his favourite game) and especially likes cycling, 'that feeling of your face being blasted by wind'. He doesn't drink in pubs yet (can't, officially), but will have a glass of wine at home, with his parents. The only videos he has are *Forrest Gump* and *Dead Poets' Society*. On television he likes comedy, and most things American, including (of course) *The X Files*, but 'can't be doing with anything Australian'. In music, he again likes most things except heavy metal – Celine Dion, Tina Arena, Louise, Michael Jackson, Phil Collins definitely. He doesn't read that many books, but he can get hold of things fairly easily – whether it's *Jane Eyre* or the latest *X Files* spin-off – thanks to his Saturday job. The other week he went down to Stratford-upon-Avon with his dad, to see a production of *Lord of the Flies*. They do that once a year.

How interested is he in clothes? More than he used to be. In the last year or so he has started to buy his own: 'I prefer casual things – if I can see something with a designer label I can afford, I'd buy it, but I don't care that much.' He isn't much into politics, though if he'd had a vote in the last election he would probably not have voted Labour 'because they wanted to abolish grammar schools'. As a child he went to Sunday school. As a teenager, he doesn't go to a youth club. Nor does he go to church, which would mean getting up early – 'I know that's a bit of a sad excuse, but it's the only day I get for a lie-in'.

What about drugs? He doesn't take them himself, but he knows boys who do. You don't get many drugs at his school, though, so he says. And his account of those who do take drugs suggests nothing more excessive than went on locally when I was his age, the era of pot and purple hearts.

It all seems a bit innocent, much like it used to be, only more so. It's only when I ask Thomas what his ambitions are and he replies, 'I'd like to earn lots of money, obviously' that I feel the eighties open up between us: it wasn't an obvious ambition to me at his age, in 1967, when wanting to earn lots of money (or owning up to wanting to earn lots of money) would have been thought rather crass and conventional, and deeply uncool. He adds, 'That means working hard. And once I start working, I'd like a good job, a house and a wife – though probably not a housewife: I wouldn't be compatible with someone who just stayed at home. And kids. That's all in the future, though.'

Does he feel hopeful about the future generally? 'With technology as it is, things can only get better. There's not much one person can do on his own, but I'd like to see a better standard of life for people in less developed countries. And I think that will happen, in time, because most of us now are aware of the problem of Third World countries. You've got to be an optimist. Around here, most people aren't cynical – and I only know round here.'

*

Thomas 'only knowing round here' has advantages, it's clear: a sense of belonging, a clear set of values, no pining for a half-glimpsed magic somewhere else; not a trace of cruddiness or anomie. But Lynda Procter is aware that her sons' circumscribed upbringing may also have its drawbacks: too much isolation, or insulation. 'I feel quite proud that they seem to be decent and well-balanced lads. But I worry that they're not aware how things are in the big world. How well will they cope when they're subjected to its rigours? Would it be better if they were more streetwise? When I think what I was doing at Thomas's age . . .'

Lynda, I take it, was doing what everyone is vaguely expected to at sixteen: discovering the opposite sex, trying out an intoxicant or two, and generally getting up to no good. (In Howard's case, rebellion meant going off to India, with a backpack and a copy of *The Complete Shakespeare*; he was back within nine months, reconciled to taking over his father's farm.) Now, as Lynda admits, not quite believing it, she has become an icon of stability, whose constant presence about the place the boys rather take for granted. 'I suppose I'm old-fashioned, because I want to be here when they come home from school. We do try to sit round and have a family meal every day, without television on, no matter how cross with each other or silent the boys sometimes are. Parents in full-time work can't do this, I know. Their lives are more stressful. You see them at weekends, dragging their kids around the shops, and the kids getting on their nerves, and them screaming at them and slapping them. I feel we're in a lucky position – all the land and space we have. But it's also partly a choice. We worked hard when we were first married – there was very little leisure time. Now quality of life seems more important than making money.'

In some ways, the Procter family model, like the posters in Daniel's room, does seem strangely dated, a throwback to an earlier era. It's circumscribed, too, and very untravelled. For instance, Daniel tells me he's been to London only once, 'when I was small', and scarcely more often to Manchester, though he did visit the Granada Studios to see the set of *Coronation Street*. Because of the farm, the family can take only a few days off at a time. When they do get away, they prefer to go to a hotel in Scarborough rather than on a foreign package.

But this isn't some mad attempt to turn back the clock. The farmhouse is old, and without central heating, but it's not a hill-billy hermitage. Most of the normal kids' things are here – television, toys, computers, bikes, stereos, videos, CDs. There's no Victorian punishment regime, either (Howard tries to be strict, Lynda considers herself a soft touch, and they have the usual marital spats about inconsistency). Nor, despite the fact that the farm has been in the family for four generations, is there pressure on the boys to follow their father. Howard hopes they'll keep the farmhouse on, to live in. But he likes the idea of them going to university, which he never had the chance to. And he thinks, if they do, they'll have too many qualifications to be interested in farming.

'Well, I'm interested,' Daniel protests. And he is, no doubt of it: how many other twelve-year-olds would take *Poultry World* in preference to the *Beano*? When I ask Daniel to tell me the first thing he would do if he were made prime minister, he pauses, finding the question hard, but then says, with some decisiveness, 'If there's some spare land, a big green area, with good soil, I'd keep it like it is, and not build on it.' Daniel doesn't like cities or congestion. Nor does Thomas. What they want for everyone is what they have themselves: space.

It's difficult to know what general lessons are to be drawn from the case of three farming boys – white, healthy, modestly well off, their parents still together – living half a mile from the nearest road. Their mother would be the first to admit they're not typical. In fact, they're almost too good to be true.

Yet as I leave them on a hot day – the two younger boys, in shorts and wellies, on their bikes; Thomas, older and more watchful – they seem real enough. And I don't feel as if I'm waving goodbye to the 1950s. It's just that they've found a better way of living in the 1990s than most of us – where the gadgetry of childhood is at our service, rather than we being its slaves; where parents have time for their children, and children for their parents; where there's a proper respect for things that grow, whether people or plants or animals. If that makes the Procters an odd lot, then the world needs more oddness in it.

Bloody Students

'You lot were lippy,' laughs John McClelland, leaning back and – very old-style academic, this – reaching for his pipe. I'm sitting with him in his office on the campus of Nottingham University, my alma mater, to which I'm paying a return visit, twenty-five years on. 'Today's students are more like consumers,' says McClelland, lighting up. 'They want the subject served up for them. It wouldn't surprise me if before long some faculties don't set up customer care departments and rename the lecturers "marketing managers". Look at this.'

He hands me a form, a student response to a questionnaire on the teaching of politics at Nottingham University. 'Good until McClelland turned up,' the student has written. And later, under 'Any other comments': 'Everything that McClelland comes out with is incomprehensible, largely irrelevant and a waste of my time.'

McClelland laughs again. He takes a perverse pride in this document. When he got it, he pinned it to the departmental noticeboard, for colleagues to read. It seems pretty lippy, to me; certainly I'd not have had the courage, as an undergraduate, to tell a lecturer he was rubbish at his job, or been quite so sure what was and what wasn't a waste of my time. Back then

I knew John McClelland – 'Mac' – only as a defender in the football team I played for, which consisted mainly of staff from the English department but included me as a token undergraduate. Off the field, there was a bit of an aura around him, as around anyone teaching politics or sociology then: they were fashionable subjects, and Mac's lectures on Marx and Hegel were, I knew, packed to the doors. These days, he says, students aren't interested in radical ideas. What they want is the clear, simple, well-organized lecture with five main points and an overhead projector. They're hard-working but also, in their earnestness, hard work – when Mac recently asked a colleague what his new tutorial group was like he was told, 'I don't know. I didn't see their faces. They all had their heads down.' For all his laughter, and self-mocking old-fogey-ism, Mac sounds genuinely disaffected.

'Yeh, you lot were lippy. But at least you knew you were the pupils and we were the teachers. Now the students sit in judgment on their teachers as much as the other way about. We're not the boss any more. We're supposed to *sell* the subject as well as teach it. We have to wow the weenies. It's the era of customer feedback, and if the punters aren't happy it's *our* fault.'

'You lot' – my lot – went to university a quarter of a century ago. There were some 220,000 British undergraduates then. Twenty-five years later there are 900,000, with Nottingham University's share having more than doubled, to 11,500. In 1969, only one in eight school leavers went on to higher education. Now the figure is nearly one in three – 31 per cent and rising. Student numbers have gone up 70 per cent in ten years. The proportion of first-class degrees awarded has gone up 50 per cent. Until 1992, there were only 46 fully-fledged universities in Britain; now, with former polytechnics renamed and other institutions upgraded, there are 124. The Travelbag

Chair of Tourism at Bournemouth University is not the invention of a campus novelist but a post recently advertised in the *Guardian*.

There have been other changes. In 1969, most degrees were single-track and unified; now – a reflection perhaps of a more atomized society – they are modular, with students pick-and-mixing from a variety of courses, few if any of them compulsory. For us, the academic year was spread over three terms; for them, courses are arranged in two semesters spread over three terms, with two periods of assessment, in January and June. We passed or failed our degrees on the basis of exams at the end of the second and third year, Part Is and part IIs; they pass theirs by accumulating credits through course work and exams – typically, ten credits for each of six courses per semester, 360 credits in all. For us, the staff:student ratio was 1:8; for them it is 1:15. We sat in tutorials of four and lectures of, at most, fifty; they sit in tutorials of six or eight, and for some lectures there are audiences of over a hundred. We did our degree straight through, in three years; most of them will do the same, but the modular structure allows them to take a year out, or even to switch universities. Nearly all of us had come straight from school; 25 per cent of them are 'mature' students, some with spouses and dependents.

Back then, we'd never have predicted such changes. Equally, some of what we did predict hasn't come to pass. In 1969, when every first-year student was offered accommodation on campus, most of Nottingham's thirteen halls of residence, traditionally single-sex, were considering becoming mixed; today, nearly half the halls (three men's and three women's) still retain their single-sex status. In 1969, we assumed that the spaciousness of Nottingham's campus would slowly be eroded by more labs, more libraries, more lecture theatres; today, despite some new building and the doubling of student numbers, the vast green acres are virtually intact.

When I take the long walk round the university lake, old haunt of those nursing hangovers and broken hearts, the only sign of life I come across is a knotted pink condom.

Like any middle-aged person revisiting a site of youth, I'm sensitive to change. The shock at Nottingham is how much has survived. In the Trent Building, with its Georgian windows and clock tower, I turn into the ground-floor corridor that used to house the English department – and, I find, still does. Back in my day the departmental secretary was Esmé Pattison, who by chance had once worked in my parents' surgery and took me under her wing: I'd be asked to Sunday lunch round at her house, and even, once or twice, took out her daughter. Esmé's not here today, but her successors obligingly dig out the current prospectus and some new and old exam papers (also, less obligingly, my admission file, with a photo of me looking about eleven).

There've been lurid headlines lately about worthless or easy-peasy degrees. Kingsley Amis's famous warning about higher education – 'MORE WILL MEAN WORSE' – has been respectfully quoted, even in liberal circles. There's little to justify such a view here, where demanding standards are set even before entry. In 1969, all of us who'd done well at interview were made the giveaway offer of two Es at A-level (E in those days being the lowest pass grade). Today, when there isn't time to interview the 2,000-odd candiates competing for fifty-odd places, the offers, made on the basis of school reports, are for an A, B and C, though in the event the average points achieved at A-level by successful candidates is twenty-eight – two As and a B. On my results I wouldn't have got in.

Despite the much greater presence of gender-related courses throughout the arts faculty ('The Body and Sexuality in Early Medieval Europe' and so on), the academic work is not as different as I'd been led to expect. 'Coping with Revolution', which sounds like something to bring Tory backbenchers scurrying here in search of Marxist propaganda, is the title of a course on the poetry of Carew, Marvell, Waller, Denham and Cowley. 'Discuss Achebe's handling of colonialism in *Things Fall Apart*' is a question from a 1990s exam question, obviously. But 'Malory's handling of the Grail legend is the least original part of his work. Do you agree?' That's also 1990s. Or, 'Write a poem in any style you choose, the subject of which must be the problems of writing a poem in the form you have chosen.' Tricksy stuff from a 1990s creative writing course? No, a question on a 1969 finals paper. 'English Lit., Life and Thought' was the basis of our study then: a solid, traditional, linear degree that took us from Anglo-Saxon through to Auden. But there was room for creativity as well. One piece I remember writing during a finals exam in 1972 was a parody of D.H. Lawrence.

Lawrence's reputation was at its peak then, more because of the film adaptation of *Women in Love* by Ken Russell than the advocacy of F. R. Leavis. I'd have read him wherever I was studying, but he was especially hard to avoid at Nottingham. He had attended the university when it was still an extension college (full university status didn't arrive until 1948), eloped with the wife of one of its professors, and had even written a satirical poem about the donation of land for Nottingham's campus by Sir Jesse Boot, of Boots the Chemist.

In Nottingham, that dismal town,
where I went to school and college,
they've built a new university
for a new dispensation of knowledge.

Built it most grandly and cakeily
out of the noble loot
derived from shrewd cash-chemistry
by good Sir Jesse Boot . . .

From this I learn, though I knew it before,
that culture has her roots
in the deep dung of cash, and lore
is a last offshoot of Boots.

What Lawrence meant is best appreciated on the way into Nottingham by train, if you're approaching from the south: on your left, on a faraway green hill, the university, dominated by the brilliant, white, icing-like stone of the Portland building; on your right, a lowly succession of warehouses, factories and vase-like industrial chimneys. Many universities have this split: gown and town. But whereas in Oxford and Cambridge the university buildings are woven into the city centre, Nottingham's campus lies three miles out, lofty and remote.

This remoteness from town wasn't something that bothered me when I arrived in Nottingham in 1969. I probably didn't even notice it. I'd been driven down from Yorkshire by my father, who'd have gone on ferrying me round until I was forty if I'd let him. I had a large trunk and was wearing the suit I'd been bought for the interview nine months before. My father cried as he left me in the monkish cell in P block in Hugh Stewart Hall. I felt like crying, too. My hair was too short. My clothes were too conventional. I barely knew how to boil a kettle. And everyone looked so much cleverer.

I'd come to Nottingham chiefly to escape home, and I'd come almost by chance. In those days every university south of Birmingham, and some northern ones, too, required those applying to read English to have Latin O-level. I didn't have Latin: I'd had to drop it in the fifth form, on account of a timetable clash, and no one had thought to advise me that this might have implications for later. Halfway through the sixth form, on a casual-seeming walk together round the cricket field, my English teacher suggested I take the Oxford entrance exam after A-levels. But my mind was made up by then. I was impatient and, though I wouldn't have minded picking up Latin again, didn't want to stay on an extra year. Top of my UCCA form among the universities not requiring Latin for an English degree was Leeds, my parents' choice because of its proximity to home. But I didn't like the professor who interviewed me, the Yeats expert Norman Jeffares, and to judge by the difficult offer that came through he didn't like me. Nottingham, my second choice, swiftly became my first, once I'd seen it. Perhaps its conservatism suited my timidity, though I didn't then realize how timid I was. I thought I was bravely off to forge new frontiers. 'The university of life': I liked the sound of that, naively believing that life – sex, drugs and rock 'n' roll – could best be experienced on campus.

Gazing out through the lonely window that first day, I realized I'd made a terrible mistake. Then a student with a Dorset accent from up the corridor stuck his head round the door frame and introduced himself as Pete Norman: he was reading English, too, and the alphabetical arrangement of rooms in Hugh Stewart had put us, by chance, close together. Pete seemed vastly better read than I was – and knew much more about music, too. I felt like running away, but took my suit off and went down with him to supper. By the time I went home for Christmas ten weeks later, happy, wrecked and with a trunkful of dirty washing, my timidity was wearing off. I'd been to concerts with Pete – Roy Ayres, Mott the Hoople, Joe Cocker. I'd smoked pot. I'd sat up all night with a ouija board and a mysteriously moving glass that spelt NIMROD. I hadn't done any work. But nor, it seemed, had anyone else.

Life in Hugh Stewart was cosily, depressingly all-male: cheap beer, French fries, table football. Soon we began to venture into town, which was said to boast the oldest pub and prettiest girls in England. I never found either, but there were record shops, markets and a second-hand shop at which we bought mouldering full-length fur coats. In the second year, I shared a house in Beeston, 236 Queen's Road, a mile from campus. It was supposed to be for six, but to save on rent nine of us moved in and we sneaked in three extra beds, two of them courtesy of my father. It was a big house but not that big, and when, late in the year, I began to spend nights at a girlfriend's the other side of town, in the Meadows, I forfeited my spacious room for a much smaller one, 7' × 4'. Pete liked to cook, and we discovered that if you left it late enough the market in Beeston was good for bargains. On average, we paid 12p each for the nightly communal meal, though for the Christmas blow-out – four courses, brandy and cigars – we had to fork out 37p. Among the other tenants were Clive, with whom I once took LSD, and Ken, a deeply engaging manic-depressive from Bramley whose burden was that he could not persuade his Welsh girlfriend Janet to have sex with him, though they slept in the same bed for over two years. At regular intervals, the wiry next-door neighbour banged on the door to complain about the noise of Cream, Miles Davis and Led Zeppelin, and we'd have to send Mike to answer, a six-foot-six Trotskyist who didn't mind betraying his solidarity with the working class in order to defend our right to freedom of musical expression. Occasionally the landlord would come round, to see about the leaking roof or unpaid rent. When at the end of my two years there, after graduating, I came back with my father in his Dormobile in order to reclaim the extra beds, the landlord was waiting, in a rage, having finally twigged that he'd had fifty per cent more tenants than he realized. He told us he'd sold our beds, in order to pay to clean up the squalor, and that he'd never rent to students again. Pete and another tenant, Phil, had actually been rather house-proud but there was no point in arguing. My father was surprisingly unpunitive, given that he'd lost two perfectly decent beds – even more so since I suspected him of sharing the landlord's view of us all: 'Bloody students.'

Most universities function as finishing schools for the middle class, and Nottingham was – and is – no exception. But twenty-five years ago those of us vaguely pledged to the destruction of the bourgeoisie liked to pretend we came from lower on the social scale. And others, away from home comforts and living on student grants which their parents couldn't or wouldn't top up, genuinely felt themselves to be impoverished proles. Class divisions, we knew, would be eradicated through the revolution we were preparing, and though a major issue for debate were not a cause of conflict in the student body. Other divisions were harder to shift. The biggest of these wasn't so much science versus the arts as work versus leisure, though it came to much the same. Nottingham had a large engineering faculty, and its students were condemned to endless grubbing in labs and lecture halls. Naturally, we in the arts and social sciences, popping in for the occasional lecture, looked down on them. To try hard, and care about exams, was uncool. To think ahead to what job one might have after graduation seemed demeaning. We were above all that, above the common herd.

But all students then were made to feel superior. Streamed since passing our eleven-plus, infused (in the English department at least) with Leavisite notions that higher education is best reserved for a tiny minority, we couldn't help but be elitists. On our first day, wanting to intimidate us into conscientiousness, the then professor of English, James Kinsley told us that thirty-three other people had wanted to sit in the seat we occupied. (Today, despite massive expansion in higher education, the figure is one in forty.) University, we knew, was a meritocracy; you got there if you were clever enough. And only a very few – us lot – were.

In some ways, our politics were elitist, too. We were told that the coming revolution would be led by a Leninist intellectual vanguard, and that part of being at university was to train ourselves for the task. Yet the task itself was socialist and egalitarian. We hoped that increasing numbers of people would go to university, and we believed Harold Wilson and his white-hot technological revolution would bring that about. We were wrong: it wasn't under Labour but in the last years of Thatcherism that the real expansion in higher education came about. But in those days Mrs Thatcher was one of our most hated enemies, the woman who so little esteemed Welfare State measures such as the Butler Education Act of 1944 that she was happy to deprive schoolchildren of their free ration of daily milk.

We protested against Thatcher the milk-snatcher but our most radical protest came in the spring of 1970, within a few months of my arriving at Nottingham, when some three or four hundred of us, following the example of students at several other British universities, voted to occupy the administrative building, over the issue of 'student files' – the files which the fascist university authorities were allegedly keeping on us and which we said posed a threat to human freedom, democracy, the future of civilization, etc. We took this vote at a union meeting which the student union leaders had been clever enough to call late on a Friday evening, when nearly everyone had gone home for the weekend or out drinking on the town. The motion was passed. It wasn't exactly Paris and the barricades, but it felt no less momentous. Yippee, we were going to sit in.

'Taking over the building' required little confrontation: the only fascist bureaucrat we could find was the hapless porter manning the telephone exchange, who, grunting and swearing, was soon overpowered. No other admin workers were due in till Monday morning, so we arranged ourselves, with blankets we'd brought from our halls of residence, for the long weekend ahead on the marble floor of the Trent Building. The mood was excited, heady. Some students had brought beer bottles and I was passed a Newcastle Brown. A woman camped nearby looked disapprovingly, as if by swigging beer we were traitors to the struggle. But beer (and wine and drugs) were part of it. We fancied ourselves to be hedonists as well as revolutionaries. Our leaders might be steely in purpose, but most of us espoused a softer Marxism. It was all a bit of a jape, but at least we were disproving all the jeers about ours being a conservative university: revolution in Berkeley and Paris, students shot at Kent State, at Nottingham one stolen jar of coffee. On the second night, strengthening our position in case armoured vehicles and police with water-cannons should arrive next day, we began moving out from the communal hall into individual offices. I ended up in a room belonging to a philosophy tutor. He had a photo of his family on his desk, and seeing it I felt guilty, a trespasser. Bracing myself, mindful of our solemn cause, I looked through his filing cabinet, in search of incriminating material, but could find only academic journals. A girl I knew turned up, and we spent the night on the floor, discussing Maoism under separate blankets. Sunday was even less eventful than Saturday had been. Society did not yet seem to have been shaken to its core. But we told ourselves we were questioning the structures, and braced ourselves for a bloody struggle next day.

There were no violent scenes on Monday morning – most of the admin staff must have decided or been told not to come in. But on the next day the inevitable union meeting was called, with a motion for the occupiers to withdraw. Many lecturers were sympathetic to our cause, but we were tired and bored and ready for defeat. It was said that all the engineering students, moderates to a man and all men, had been ordered to turn up to vote. A boy in specs stood up and said that it was easy for arts wankers to be high-minded, but he'd exams to pass and a degree to get. We booed and hissed, and I suppressed the thought that if I weren't a first-year I too might have found my loyalties sorely tested – that I could have been him. When it came to the vote, the number wanting to continue occupation was more than double what it had been on Friday night. But it was a large meeting, and the opposition carried the day. Bowed and unbloodied, we emerged, blinking, into the daylight of pragmatism, our blankets round our shoulders. I went back to hall to get some sleep.

That was about as lippy as I got. For the remaining two and a half years at Nottingham, I tried to fade into the background, inconspicuous in my shoulder-length hair, my purple flares with black-tasselled fringes, and my room decorated with photographs of atrocities from the Vietnam War. Others were more flamboyant, including the president of the student union, Nigel Harris, Marxist and Maoist, who once danced naked on a table in the buttery, exposing both radical cheeks. The students' leaders were all men then, though there were women who made coffee or went to bed with them. One of these women was called Mary, and shared a house with my girlfriend in the Meadows. Her bedroom was above ours, and sometime after pub closing she'd come back with a guy from Soc. Soc., rarely the same one. Her bedsprings made it hard for us to sleep. I felt drably monogamous and unradical. My girlfriend said that Mary was being exploited and that student politics had no place for women, except on their backs.

Today's union president at Nottingham is a woman. So is her deputy. So are four of the five full-time 'sabbatical' officers – just the one token man. Madeleine Durie describes herself and her colleagues as 'independents: we're apolitical, though interested in politics'. In the new entrepreneurial spirit, the union runs a shop, print shop, travel service and bar (though, it says greyly, 'a responsible attitude to potential alcohol abuse means a policy of no cut-price alcohol promotions'). All this comes under the umbrella of a limited company, UNU Services Ltd, a 'profit-led' business with a turnover of £2.4 million and a board of directors. It seems a long way from the anti-capitalist euphoria of my day, and the noticeboards down the corridor tell the same story: plenty of happy-clappy Christian Union stuff; clubs for debating, Sega, croquet, Real Ale, role playing, football supporters; not many calls for action. The biggest society here, Madeleine Durie embarrassedly admits, is the Cocktail Society, which offers students cheap cocktails at assorted nightclubs in town. From Soc. Soc. to Cock Soc.: there you have it.

Except that there's also the Community Action group, some 2,000 strong (volunteer work of various kinds, organized by two full-time workers) and a greater sense than we had that the university can't be divorced from the real world. 'We've become more professional since the loopy days of Nigel Harris,' says Madeleine Durie. 'The university listens to us. I have meetings with the vice-chancellor every three weeks: did that happen in 1969? Would it have been amicable? I doubt it. This doesn't mean we won't be a thorn in the side of the university: if it did something outrageous, and it was the last straw, then we would be prepared to demonstrate. But I hate the word "demonstration", and I don't think it does students' reputations any good to kick up a fuss about things that aren't worthwhile. We protest by letter-writing or general negotiating, not by sitting in.'

In 1969 we liked to pretend we didn't care about money. It was easier to do so then: our tuition fees were paid for, local authority grants or the equivalent parental support made it relatively easy to get by, and the graduate job market meant that you'd soon find employment once you'd finished your degree. For students today, the situation is very different. Student grants have shrunk rather than keeping pace with inflation; even a full grant of £2,000 will leave a shortfall. Soon, in any case, grants will be phased out, and the average student will be forced to use a loan scheme. Most have to borrow already – from parents, or from banks. The average debt on graduation is already over £3,000, and when the loan scheme is fully implemented it's expected to be nearer £10,000. If, as seems likely, students are in future charged for their tuition fees (£1,000 a year or more), the figure will rise higher still.

All this inevitably creates a pressure. Several students I spoke to said that it casts a shadow across a phase of life that's supposed to be sunlit and liberating.

'Most people don't think about jobs when they come here. You'll hear them talking vaguely about going into publishing or something. But by the third year they're starting to panic – God, only nine months left.'

'I survive on a grant – or rather I don't. It's lucky I worked for a few years and had something saved. But now I've got an overdraft – and it's not as if I've been spendthrift.'

'I thought everyone would be in the same boat. But they're not, and that causes resentment. There's a huge divide between the working-class kids on grants and loans and the public school or middle-class kids whose parents are paying for them.'

Madeleine Durie is also worried about the effects of the loan system: 'People are coming to university knowing they will leave in debt: how many will it deter?' Graham Chandler, the outgoing university registrar, has his doubts, too. Chandler approves most of the changes he's seen during his thirty-five years in university administration, particularly those that have brought in money to supplement government subsidy: fee-paying overseas students, industrial or private sector funding, 'friend-raising' and fund-raising through US-style lobbying of alumni. But having himself come from a 'fairly humble background' and been supported by a grant, he fears that student loans will deter the lower socio-economic groups and make universities even more middle-class than they have always been.

Nottingham remains a popular university. A 1993 survey of A-level applications found it to be the most sought-after British university. To my eyes, it looks very affluent now, up there on Boot Hill. Research funding has poured in. The halls of residence earn vacation money by hosting conferences and offering 'bed units'. A large chunk of what used to be, in effect, the student building has now been given over to the plushly nineties school of management and finance. Money is the word on everyone's lips: 'It's all we ever talk about,' says John McClelland. But academics, whose teaching hours have got longer while their pay has slipped back, don't see much of this money. Nor, of course, do the students.

It shames me to think how immature I was as an undergraduate. Perhaps youth is always wasted on the young. Perhaps if I'd had a gap year, as many more students do these days, I wouldn't have been so callow. Or perhaps the whole point of university is to have certain awful experiences (mostly predictable: bad drugs, bad sex, bad rock 'n' roll) so you learn never to repeat them. But knowing all this doesn't make the sense of waste any easier to bear. Among the queasier memories is the horror I felt when one of the other students in my first-year tutorial group told me he was thirty-two. Thirty-two! Practically a pensioner. What did he think he was doing? Had he got lost or was he off his trolley or what? Didn't he realize university was for school leavers like me? I steered clear of him thereafter. To pretend to be a bit weird was OK, but true weirdos, as he obviously was, were to be avoided.

But he at least contributed to tutorials. Whereas I in my

immaturity was dumbstruck by shyness, afraid to open my mouth in case I blushed or said something stupid. I'd left school idly assuming I'd no longer have to *make an effort*, that work was behind me. It came as a shock to find that there were exams at the end of each year. Even more of a shock was the discovery that degrees were classified – I'd thought, barring disaster, we all came out with plain BAs or B.Sc.s, not knowing there were firsts and thirds. It may have been I learned this round the time my first-year tutor, George Parfitt, a softly-spoken, kindly Renaissance scholar with red hair down to his shoulders, gave me what must have been the lowest mark he'd ever seriously awarded an undergraduate essay.

I tried a bit harder after that, believing I had to work twice as hard as anyone else just to keep up. But then for my second year I was allocated a different tutor, a large, pale Cambridge man, an expert in Virginia Woolf. There were four of us in his group, and only one – not me – who thought him tolerable. From the start there was an edge, an atmosphere. He found us difficult, he said – taciturn, listless, uncommunicative. We, on our side, resented his casual late arrivals for the weekly tutorial and his failure to stick by or even remember whatever we'd agreed to discuss the previous week. His brilliance inhibited us, while he became paranoid because we didn't respond. In time, his smiles grew more sickly, his humour more limp, while we hardened into sullen silence. At Christmas, he warned he might report us to our local education authorities. It seemed unlikely, given the effort it would take, but a few weeks later I received a letter from Wakefield threatening to withdraw the little financial support I had unless my work improved. I felt indignant: there'd never been any suggestion that our written work was unsatisfactory; the complaint concerned our lack of conversation, something I found hard to start with and all but impossible in the current group. I bucked up none the less, and outwardly there was a kind of truce. Inside I was seething with revenge. I was going to show the bastard. I was going to make him eat his words.

Perhaps the others, who'd had similar letters, felt the same: two of us went on to get Ph.D.s, and a third, my friend Pete Norman, is a poet, songwriter and regular winner of *New Statesman* and *Spectator* parody competitions. In my own case, I was helped by a change of tutor, to Allan Rodway, another member, the most elderly, of our football team, and an enthusiast for modernism. I discovered how to work on my own: the pleasures of long hours in the library (to come out just before it closed at 10 p.m., into the warm spring air, and know there was still an hour's drinking time), and the pleasures of literature. My unexpectedly good degree may also have owed something to football, and a crunch match just before finals in which – it having been impressed on me where my loyalties lay – I turned out for the staff against the students and scored a hat-trick in the 4–3 win. No less surprised was the head of department, James Kinsley, who called me into his room and – making it plain he'd never noticed me before – suggested I might like to think about research. I already had a place for an MA in Canada, I told him. He said it was a pity I felt so jaundiced about Nottingham. Jaundiced? I'd never felt better about the place. If he'd walked in at that moment, I'd even have embraced that gruesome second-year tutor.

Three weeks later, at a campsite somewhere on the way to Morocco, my friends and I lay reviewing our results in our sleeping bags: the agony, the ecstasy, and what it would all mean for our future. The night was silent and we, sprawling outside our tents, were noisy. Suddenly, a voice growled out of the darkness, 'We've all got degrees from British universities. Shut the fuck up and go to sleep.' And so we did, chastened, having heard in that faceless voice that how you do at your degree might not be so momentous after all.

The thought returned a few years later when I read in the

paper that an Eng. Lit. student from my year called Peter Boardman had conquered and then died on Mount Everest. The class of '72 who I'd guessed would go on to fame and immortality were noisy, arty types, the ones who had directed short films, or acted in plays, or run the poetry magazine or student newspaper – things I'd have liked to do myself if I'd had the courage. But Peter Boardman had been quiet, unobtrusive, deeply ordinary. He'd not seemed especially *brave*. He'd not even let on about his interest in mountaineering. I knew there was a moral here, though what exactly I wasn't sure.

We live in a different world now. Going to university used to be the preserve of a minority; now it's a common experience. One sixth-former I talked to put it like this: 'All my friends are going – even the one who wants to be a secretary. Our teachers' jaws would have dropped if we'd said we didn't want to. My parents were working-class and had a sense of making it to university. I think we must be the first generation where it's almost automatic.'

Automatic or not, some of the old divisiveness and exclusivity persist. There is still a two-tier system, a boat race, a scrap between tradition and the new. Perhaps it's always been a boat race, and it's only the names of the crews that change. First it was Oxford versus Cambridge. Then Oxbridge versus red-brick (Nottingham included). Then Oxbridge and red-brick versus the new campus universities (Sussex, Keele, UEA, etc). Now it's Oxbridge, red-brick and campus ('research-led') versus the former polytechnics ('teaching-based'). In time, current divisions and snobberies will disappear. But not quickly. It will be some years before employers accept a 2:1 from the university of Oxford Brookes, say, as being worth the same as a 2:1 from Oxford. Or a Derby degree as the equivalent of one from Nottingham.

A growing number of universities, including of course the

Open University, have made higher learning available to people who used not to have access to it, single parents and early school-leavers included. A growing number of universities see themselves as opportunity centres, not ivory towers. But at safe, old, endearingly middle-of-the-road Nottingham, the evidence is that student life goes on as it always did – a chance to study, drink, take drugs, learn about sex, pursue sporting and leisure interests, and grow up. And surely this is unavoidable – away from all the talk of research, investment, recruitment and business interests, the role of a university is to provide the majority of its students (aged between eighteen and twenty-two) with an interlude between school and work. Even a punitive loan scheme will not deter most of them from seizing the chance.

Before I catch the train back to London, I revisit my old hall of residence. The rooms are as monkish as I remember them – bed, desk, chair, sixty-watt bulb – and the corridors have the same smell of stale sex and burnt toast. At first, the stuff on the notice boards looks unchanged, too: news of sponsored fasts and anti-racism benefit concerts; endless ads for flatshares ('Two normalish blokes required . . . If you are sober, industrious and into Barry Manilow, SOD OFF'); Bad Taste dances tonite (and every night) in one or other hall of residence. But there weren't these affluent For Sale ads then ('Pentax with zoom lens'), nor all the cars parked outside, nor the pittering of laptops behind doors. Most piquant of all is the poster for a sixties disco, with its collage of images from 'way back then' – Mini Minors, miniskirts, moon landings, peace marches. I could fool myself that it looks just like yesterday, but whoever did the artwork must have had to do some research, or ask a parent, to get those images right. I don't want to hear it, but what the poster is trying to tell me, as I take my leave, is that I've said goodbye already, long ago.

South Pacific

The day after my father's funeral I search the storeroom he built under the eaves, his hidey-hole for all the things he couldn't bear to throw away: flagons from his wine-making phase; shoes and slippers he'd impulse-bought, then thought better of, but might always change his mind about again; cigar boxes from before he killed the habit; broken lampshades to repair; racquets in need of restringing; jigsaws whose missing pieces were bound to turn up one day. In a large cardboard box I find his old grey-ribbed cine projector and beside it, in a bag, a snakepile of metal reels. 'Could I take these?' I ask my mother. 'I'd like to watch them again.' In truth, I've another idea: I've seen the ads for places that will make videos out of old 8mm cine films. A memento of the family from thirty years ago: it will make a nice Christmas present for my mother, for my sister, for me.

But for months the cine projector and spools sit untouched in my cold study. I'm too depressed to get them out and see what they've kept of my childhood and my father's middle age. And the present, at least from my mother's point of view, seems a duff idea. If she can't even bear to look at photographs of my father, she won't want to see him in animation.

Summer comes, and autumn. The first anniversary of his death approaches, with Christmas right behind. Finally, one wet November Saturday, I do get the projector out. I'm not mechanical like my father: I have to follow the instructions, and it takes me hours. But at last, miraculously, the bulb lights up, the spools start whirring and clicking, and two figures judder into life – my sister and I on a beach in North Wales burying cousin Kela in the sand. The half-hour it must have taken us to cover her has been edited down to one minute. The cuts and joins make us lurch like puppets. But slowly Kela disappears. There's only her head showing, like Winnie in Beckett's *Happy Days*, when the old withered band turning the spools breaks, the bulb fades, and I'm back in the dark again with nothing to show for my pains.

A drive over the moors, a dark winter's night, a hole in Blackburn, Lancashire.

'This must be it,' my father says, pulling up near a high-lit sign saying ODEON – easy to park, a poor fifties mill-town, just two other cars. 'We'll make it if we hurry. You and Gill get the popcorn. Blake and I'll pay for the seats.'

The popcorn floats palely behind a glass screen. So does the cashier in her sentry box. 'Two adults, two halves,' my father says, as if this were a bus ride. The loop of pink tickets beside the cashier reminds me of a roll of gun caps, or of a spool of film. But our tickets don't come from the cashier: suddenly, of their own accord, they stick their tongue out from the flat metal counter. We're through. We're on our way.

'Bit of a fleapit,' my mother says, over the top of a large scrunchy paper bag.

The corridor is dimly lit, the carpet is fag-holed and Vimto-stained, large patches of flock wallpaper have gone missing from the walls. It gets darker as we go, just a pencil-thin vertical gleam ahead in the distance to tell us we're not lost. The gleam bisects a heavy double door. An usherette stands with a bowl of torchlight in her palms. She takes the tickets and heaves at the door as if it were as weighty as the gates to Thebes, the tomb of Ramses III.

A new world cracks open – loud music, sun floating on sea, an Elastoplast strip of screen. We cling to the lifeline of the usherette's torch as it guides us through the dark, down a thin trail past row after row of smoking heads. Down, down we go, to a clearing at the foot of the giant screen. One, two, three, four seats give way beneath us. *South Pacific* is about to begin.

It's the first time we've ever been to the cinema together as a family, yet I hadn't really wanted to come. My mother bought the LP of the soundtrack some months ago, and has been playing 'Some Enchanted Evening' ever since. The film will mean more of the same, only with pictures. I reach for the popcorn. I prepare to be bored.

My father, next to me, is here on sufferance, too. 'A treat for Mummy,' is how he explains the outing, though I suspect him of having his own reasons. Two weeks ago, he finally acquired the second-hand Mercedes he'd been searching for months for in the pages of *Autocar* and *Exchange & Mart*. It's a particular model he's always craved, a saloon car that also looks sporty, with a top large enough to put a Webasto sunshine roof in. He finally tracked one down – private owner, 27,000 miles on the clock, black leather upholstery – and we had to drive to a pub car park off the A1 in Bedfordshire to inspect it. 'Inspect', I knew, meant purchase and bring home. Tonight's the first time since then he's had the chance for a decent run out: this is why he has come.

Up on the screen a Polynesian woman sings 'Bali Hai'. Bloody Mary is her name, which must be making my father think of pursuits more pleasurable than this. I wait for him to make his excuses – a visit to the gents, a check to see the car's not been stolen, a half-hour disappearance to the pub. Only the mechanics of the film seem to interest him: he swivels his head round to follow the projection beam back to its source.

Each Christmas he does some projecting himself: over turkey sandwiches, mince pies and stewed tea, a small coerced family audience has to endure an hour of his old cine films, with commentary ('Here's Blake and Gill on the beach. And now here's Mummy walking the dog down to the sea. And here are Blake and Gill again . . .'). But to sit watching someone else's film – as we know from experience, and as he is now finding out – is not the same as making or projecting one, even with a storyline, even in colour. It makes my father feel restless. It makes him feel helpless, not in control. His one hope this evening must be that the projectionist will be taken ill and a voice come over the address system: 'Is there a doctor in the house? And someone who knows about film reels?'

Gradually, though, miraculously, my father pays attention to the screen. Blue skies and Pacific breakers behind them, a crowd of American soldiers – or are they sailors? – have begun to sing: 'There is nothing like a dame,/Nothing in the world . . .'. Perhaps it's the setting that has caught my father's fancy: he, too, spent part of the Second World War among islands far from home. I've seen the photographs. The Azores might not have been tropical, but his snaps show the same sort of world: matey, hedonistic, all-boys-together on the beach. *South Pacific* must be bringing it back to him – not just the fun but the boredom, frustration and womanlessness: 'We got nothing to put on a clean white suit for,/What we want is the one thing there ain't no substitute for . . .'. I can't even get my father to pass the popcorn bag, so transfixed is he by the corn on the screen – above all by Mitzi Gaynor, 'corny as Kansas in August' and his sort of woman: small, blonde, optimistic and naive. I'm transfixed, too: when she sings 'I'm going to wash that man right out of my hair', there's the thrill of knowing that behind the swing doors of her shower stall she's wearing no clothes. 'It's so different from Little Rock,' she says. It's so different from Earby, too, and its cramped little world of black and white. Here there's wide-screen technicolour; warmth, light and flesh; polymorphous – or at least Polynesian – perversity. My father is excited. I'm excited too. As I sit there in the dark, I feel the cramped, hushed powerlessness of childhood begin to recede. It looks good up there, in the grown-up frames of kissing. Roll on the adult world.

At last, Christmas and my mother coming, I get the video made. A friend does it, using an ordinary rubber band in place of the one that snapped, and aiming his camcorder at the screen. He hands me the finished product: one VHS tape in place of a dozen reels.

'There's forty minutes' worth,'. he says. 'A bit bumpy, but not bad, considering.'

'How you feeling?' I ask my mother at King's Cross.

'Bit sore, but not bad, considering,' she says.

Three months ago she fell into the stone hearth at home, and broke her upper arm. If they'd operated and pinned it at once, she might have healed by now. But they put it in plaster, and something went wrong, and now she has five long metal spikes sticking into her flesh, holding her crumbling bones together, like a TV aerial, and no knowing when they'll come out. I slip one arm into her good arm and with my free hand wheel her suitcase up the platform.

We've only three stops to go on the Underground, but already I regret not bringing the car: it's rush hour, mayhem and short tempers, and people keep brushing past my mother's aerial. As we approach the automatic ticket barriers, I tell her, 'Just push the ticket in, then collect it and walk through the gates.' But she can't find the slot at first, then she forgets to take the ticket out, and when she does, she steps sideways into the next aisle, the wrong barrier, rather than straight ahead. I'm stuck, too, at the side, with her suitcase, and there's no attendant to be seen.

A crowd is building up behind her, angry, impatient. I'm stranded with the suitcase, unable to get through to her.

'What's up?' someone near me says.

'Dunno, some loopy old dear,' his mate replies.

My mother turns my way, bewildered but trying not to show it. Finally I reach her, and push back through the crowd to the ticket counter, where we find a guard. Through at last, via a special gate, my mother and I wait on the platform, pretending that nothing has happened. Perhaps, in her mind, nothing has.

South Pacific is more than half-way over now, and still my father's paying attention. I'm not used to this, to his art appreciation. I've never known him go to the theatre, or a concert, or a gallery. I have never seen him read a book. Films on television send him straight to sleep. Whereas now – watching Mitzi Gaynor camp it up in front of the lads – he is unmistakably enjoying himself, bobbing his head, clicking his fingers, tapping his feet: 'A hundred and one pounds of fun/That's my little honey bun./Get a load of honey bun tonight.' What is it about *South Pacific*? Not just the wartime island setting, not just the *vive la différence* songs. The point about *South Pacific* is that it's *happy*. Its hero wins the war *and* gets the girl. Its heroine is a smiley, cock-eyed optimist. 'I'm stuck like a dope with a thing called hope/And I can't get it out of my heart . . .'. Song after song seems to express my father's philosophy of life: 'Happy talk, keep talking happy talk, Talk about things you'd like to do'.

'*South Pacific*, written, directed and composed by Arthur Morrison' is what I half-expect to be up on screen as the credits roll. The director, so it says, is Joshua Logan, and the lyrics are by Rodgers and Hammerstein. But when the lights come up, my father wears that look he has after the cine show each Christmas – head down, eyes averted, not wanting any credit, ignoring the applause. As we step over the flattened ice-cream tubs and wooden scoop-spoons, I see him wink at the high window where the projectionist must be. And when we pass out through the foyer, he nods at the manager. It's as if he were everybody involved rolled into one – director, producer, leading actor, manager, projectionist. It's as if it were *his* story.

Outside, in the cold, the Mercedes gleams on the cobbled street. As we pull away, my mother asks my father, 'All right, love? Not bored were you?'

'Bloody marvellous,' my father says. 'We must go again.'

But we never do.

'A little surprise for you, mum,' I say, and press the play button on the VCR, and switch off the lights.

My sister and I lumber into motion, always on beaches – Abersoch, Jersey, Knott End. My mother's there, too, in her frilled fifties swimsuit, on a rug, in a boat. And Granny and Grandpa. And aunts and uncles and cousins.

I keep waiting for my father to walk into the picture, young again, alive, and only slowly do I see how stupid I've been, that he's not going to show, that this is a memento of his absence or invisible presence off-screen. Just as he'd hogged the steering wheel, monopolized the phone, controlled the family finances, so it was he who'd always held the camera: these were *his* films, but he didn't appear in them; this was *his* life, but there's no record of him living it.

I struggle to find a meaning in this – how, if you control things too much, won't trust or delegate or share with others, you can end up with nothing, leave yourself out of what matters most. But perhaps the meaning is simpler, more obvious. I'd hoped the video would bring my father back to life. But

he's not there, he's missing, I've failed. The tape has reached
its ending now: angry hissing dots, a blizzard of nothingness
washing at the glass. I turn towards my mother. I reach for the
stop button and the lights.

2
Public Fictions,
Private Lives

The Woman on the Doorstep

I must tell you that in private life I have no
patience at all with lunatics.
                    SIGMUND FREUD, letter to Oskar Pfister,
                                        June 21st, 1920

A woman stands on the doorstep: tense, greying, fiftyish, tight
lips, green coat. She has read an article about me in the local
paper (a soppy, semi-literate piece about my 'kind brown
eyes'), understands I work for the *Independent* (the Sunday,
used to, but never mind), looked me up this morning in the
telephone book (I've been meaning to go ex-directory) and
has come straight round. She has an article she wants to give
me, for publication. What's it about, I ask? She doesn't want to
go into detail, not out on the step, but she can assure me the
article's good – more than good, sensational. I explain I'm not
at the paper any more, have only ever worked on books pages,
am probably the last person capable of judging what's sensational or not. No matter, she says, that's fine: if I could just
read it, I'll see.

Nervous and resentful, conscious of some line being
crossed, I ask the woman in. We stand just inside the hall, the
door still ajar, the brass lampshade swinging in a gust, and she
hands me a plain brown envelope. Tight-lipped, lines burned
in her brow below the cropped grey hair, she watches as I
take the typescript out. It's long: fifty closely typed pages or
more. I say I'll need some time to get through it, that I can't

read it now, in front of her. All right, she says, as long as I promise not to show it to anyone else, I can keep it overnight. Will I promise? Sure, I promise. Till tomorrow, then. There's her number and address at the bottom of the last page, if I finish it earlier and want to call. I hold the door open. Her feet squeal on the parquet. She nods and walks briskly off, businesslike, turning right up the road, a little stubborn and even angry in posture, but not a sign of author's nerves.

I've work to do. But I can't resist skimming through the piece, and it doesn't take long to grasp the point. It's an essay demonstrating that Iris Murdoch is a Soviet agent. The evidence for this is internal, based chiefly on a reading of the names of Murdoch's characters, which are, it seems, in code. The first clues can be found in *Under the Net*, and are planted in each subsequent novel, culminating in *The Sea, The Sea*. There are long quotes, and tortuous explanations of how the philosophy and necromancy in Murdoch's novels are actually elaborate instructions to Moscow paymasters. The author of the article seems to have read widely in espionage, Soviet history, and the occult. She writes with indignation not so much against Iris Murdoch as the British literary establishment, which is either stupid or, worse, in collusion with Moscow. She very badly wants something done about the scandal. As I read her closing peroration – 'a tissue of lies, conspiracy and cover-up' – I try to think of her face, and to remember small give-away details, like staring eyes or foam-flecked lips. I remember only grey hair and a small, tense mouth.

I go downstairs, to the basement, where the message light is blinking on the answering machine and sheaves have stacked up on the fax. I try to work, but all I can think of is the article in the envelope on the dining table and the woman standing on the step. The piece is mad. But is she? I don't know if she thinks of herself as a writer, but she's not the first person to show me writing that borders on the insane. I ran an evening class once: poetry for beginners. Most of the poetry brought for discussion had begun as therapy; most of it ended as therapy, too, not making it as art, or even sense. I was sniffy: I thought poetry should be shaped, structured, transcendent, should aspire to the impersonal. I banned all biographical pre-ambles: the poems had to work as poems, I said, had to be read cold on the page, without us being told when, why, how, during which life crisis and on what medication they had come. In time, I became less sniffy. There was a man who read a poem with unusual passion. We sat round and discussed in neutral tones why his 'I-I-I' cry of pain failed as rhetoric: how a change of adjective here, a less abstract image there, might have improved it. He fell silent and didn't seem to be paying much attention. I asked him, when we'd done dissecting, if he had anything to add. He said he'd written the poem on the brink of committing suicide: he had the razor out, and the bath running, but sat down and wrote the poem instead. No answer to that. Literary criticism seemed beside the point. Had the world ever known a more important poem? I looked back at my own slim output and saw that I too had written poems as therapy: private lyrics not intended for magazines or composed in the hope of getting on. Some people need to set down words to make life tolerable. There are a lot of us about.

Maybe the woman on the doorstep is like this. Maybe writing about Iris Murdoch has kept her sane, even if the article itself is mad. Maybe she needs me only in order to acknowl-edge or vindicate her, and reading her article, not publishing it, will be enough. Maybe it *is* publishable, and I've missed the point. I go back upstairs and sit with it in the dining room, under the high candle bulbs. It's clean and neatly typed – few typos or misspellings, and no dog-eared page corners to sug-gest it has done the rounds. It doesn't look mad. But it doesn't read any less madly. I flick on through Iris Murdoch's career as a spy in the hope of finding something I can be kind about. I check the tone of the last pages, in case there's something unexpected there, a volte-face of some kind – sudden light-ness – as the author admits the exercise has been a spoof, a satire on a school of literary criticism. Not a chink, not a glimmer. I haven't read all of them, it's true, but the woman seems to mean every word.

Should I have seen she was mad and just told her to fuck off? She could have written, rather than come to my house. I'm not obliged to help. But to refuse even to look at her arti-cle would have been churlish, rude, more unpleasant than she deserved. I look at her address, on the last page. I recognize it. It's local, a quiet residential street, not an institution. I look again: the woman's name isn't there, and this unnerves me. She's a stranger, perhaps unstable enough to do something dangerous. I've let her into my house, but don't even know her name. She made me promise not to show the piece to anyone else, even though she wants it published. What can that mean? How many layers of paranoia are here? Will she be telling me, next, that people are following her, that they wait for her on each corner, their eyes glinting like knives? At that poetry group I ran, there was a man so fearful of showing his work that it was nearly the end of term before he found the nerve. Pale and shaking, he passed round carbon copies, counting them out as he did. The poem was as trite as a greet-ings card: an ode to spring, in nineteenth-century diction, which he read in a quaking voice. His hands quaked too, grip-ping the long table as he spoke of trilling redbreasts and Phoebus peeping 'twixt the boughs. Even down my end, the far end, remote from him, the table shook. We were kind to him, encouraging, feeling his nerves through the wood. I didn't lie that the poem was brilliant, nor resist suggesting that in future he try to write in language such as he would speak. But I was conscious of his vulnerability, and held back criticisms I might have made to someone else. At the end, he demanded his poems back, and counted up twelve copies in case one had been stolen. The images he'd used were original, he said, he'd not had them patented yet, he didn't want people copying them and ruining his chances of publication. Afterwards, a couple of other students complained to me. It wasn't the man's vanity that offended them, but the affront to the gentle, co-operative spirit of the workshop. I worried how to explain to him he needn't be so distrustful of his fellow-writers. I needn't have. He didn't show up again.

I think of him now, stooping over his briefcase, stowing the precious copies away. Is the woman on the doorstep like him, at best deluded, at worst certifiable? But feeling protective of one's work, and worrying that others may steal from it, is nat-ural enough in writers, even more so in freelance journalists trying to make a mark. Nor is holding conspiracy theories – even conspiracy theories about Iris Murdoch – a mark of mad-ness. I've had conspiracy theories, too: about friends, enemies, the British government, about a world invented solely for me to be exposed as its dupe. Which of us can say we're not a bit mad in small ways? Or in big ways? Angels have appeared to me in the small hours, though they looked like the bedroom's hanging lampshade. I've heard voices warning me, and seen foxes sitting at my typewriter. I've done crazy things, even without the excuse of drink.

Has this woman unnerved me because she's facing me with some madness of my own? As a child, I thought the madness was all out there, not within, or close to home. The other kids seemed to think the same. Bananas, barmy, bats, bonkers, crackers, crazy, cuckoo, daft, doolally, dotty, funny, gone, half there, kooky, loco, loony, loopy, mental, nutty, potty, screwy, twisted, weird: we used the words unthinkingly; we used them about each other, with varying degrees of affection and deri-sion. We knew there were others the words must be true of, but not who they were or how they looked. There were institutions for such people, and we had words for those, too: bin, booby-hutch, bughouse, funny farm, loony-bin, nut-house. Suitable places for treatment. Or perhaps unsuitable: bugs are low on the evolutionary scale; farms and hutches are places for animals; bins are where rubbish is thrown away. Not human, then, by the sound of it, let alone humane: how, as kids, were we to know? Menston was our nearest: it lay behind a wall on the way to Leeds. As kids, we taunted each other that we'd end up there, without remotely believing it. Only later, as a teenager, did I begin to see that madness wasn't a walled-off, distant park, that it might begin at home. Auntie Sheila, for instance, my mother's big sister (the only other, of her various siblings, who'd left Ireland to work over here). Sweet-natured, dependable, she'd stayed with us each holiday for as long as I could remember: it was she who'd say, 'Let's go and see the moo-cows' and take me down beyond the bottom of the garden, carefully holding my hand. When I was older I learned she was a teacher in the Midlands, who lived alone – 'a spinster', they said, and I spoke the word aloud to myself, associating it with witchcraft and fairy-tales. Later still, in my teens, I began to notice Sheila's habit of whisper-ing to herself. She talked of going to see the moo-cows still, and was disappointed when I didn't respond. Disappointment seemed to be her thing: she shrank, folded in on herself, became dark and hard to reach. I began to wonder how she coped with classes of thirty children. There were hints she couldn't, that she occasionally took refuge in binges. In time, Sheila's holiday visits dwindled. When she retired from teach-ing, she moved not to a house near us but to Ireland, near her birthplace. My mother said nothing, but I sensed a story involving depression and drugs. I would have liked to hear it. I'd seen the cracks in Sheila years before.

That woman on the doorstep looks a bit like Auntie Sheila. Certainly she doesn't seem a stranger. It must be why I can't get rid of the thought of her – why she bugs me, and why I don't know the right way to respond. I stay up late, under the candle bulbs, not reading her article but imagining the life that brought her to the moment she wrote it from, a life not unlike Sheila's but specific enough, even in invention, to be her own: a loner, and has been for years; went to a small private girls' school (perhaps Catholic, certainly boarding) and did well at O- and A-level; worked for the civil service, as a glorified typist (the best a woman could hope for in those days); loved a man once, who betrayed her, with a so-called friend, since when she's never trusted men, and few women either; began to suffer from depression, off and on; left her full-time job for a less stressful one; left that too; more depression, various forms of treatment (drugs, counselling) but nothing so drastic (e.g., ECT) that she can't say she's not all right; these days, wants to give help rather than receive it; is into causes (anti-bloodsports, anti-EEC), writes letters (never published) to national newspapers; believes passionately what she thinks; has noticed some people are scared by her passion, and move away when they see her coming; has no time for such people; treats them with scorn.

Headlights cross the ceiling, and I lie there inventing her. A fantasy about a woman who has herself invented a fantasy. I imagine her room, the clock on the mantelpiece, the tongues in the gas fire, the tartan rug draped over the cracked leather armchair, the screw-lid plastic bottle with a hundred paracetamols. And there she is herself, at the walnut dining-table-cum-desk, writing in a spiral notebook. If I lean into the picture far enough, I can see the words as she sets them down. They're not an essay this time, but poetry:

The call of bitterns from the sky's throat.
My heart scalded again. The moon like a blade.
The world runs with mascara. I am all mascara.

Black and white, they wait on each corner like elegies.
Their eyes are knives I want to snatch from them
And plunge into their velveteen hearts.

Scrapings of skin from the cherry blossom.
Soon, perhaps, they'll come to take me.
In the hide of Friesians, I watch myself shine and fade.

Death smiles at me and twirls his black moustache.

It's not bad. Maybe she's been to a writing group. Maybe she
came to *my* writing group all those years ago and I've forgotten. Her broken words and stifled cries move me. She's like a
seabird blown off course, weeping out her panic and pain. But
these are words I've only imagined her writing, whereas the
essay is real enough. I check, take it out of the brown envelope
again, weigh it in my hands, as if by doing so I can discover
what's required of me. By chance or premonition, this woman
came to me as someone who'd recognize her, validate her, *vindicate* her. And if I don't, if I can't, if I refuse to acknowledge
her as a kindred spirit – what then? Is she tough enough to go
on if I tell her the essay's mad? Probably: who's to say I'm not
the hundredth person she has dumped it on? But maybe not:
whether I'm the first or hundredth, rejection might hit her
hard. If so, will she turn to that plastic bottle? I'm confused.
Whatever I tell her will be a lie, either kindly-evasive out of
fear, or more sternly-judicial than I feel. I know she's not a
stranger. But I'm too alarmed to think of her as a friend.

The doorbell goes at ten the next morning. There she is,
on the step, a little tenser perhaps, and shorter than I'd
remembered, but otherwise as before. Her solidity reassures
and emboldens me. I lead the way, and she walks through the
hall, under the brass lamp, to the dining room, where I've
left the article on the table. As gently as I can, I tell her that I

don't think it's publishable – that it's much too long, needs cutting and reworking, even then probably wouldn't be accepted, because the evidence for its claims is too slight. Lightly trembling, skittery as a foal on a shale hillside, the muscles flickering in her lower lip, she stands and waits for more. More soothing now, I say I'm willing to pass the article on to the features editor at the *Independent*, would be delighted to, in fact, if that's what she wants, but I suspect, and it's only fair to warn her, that even if I put a good word in, it's very possible this editor would say the same. There is a pause, and silence, and then she takes the article from my hands, sharply, just short of a snatch – but still stands there, as if for more. Unnerved by her silence, afraid I've been too harsh, I say I'm sorry I can't be more helpful, that I'd been interested by the thesis, that the essay is well written, yes certainly the writing itself is not a problem, it's just, well, if only the evidence for the Soviet agent theory were more solid . . . At which point she snaps, and makes a speech, articulate with suppressed contempt, about how, of course, I'm in the same literary mafia as Iris Murdoch, the same lousy establishment, just as all newspapers are part of the same world-conspiracy, and of course it was naive to think I might be interested in the truth, no one in any position of influence is interested in the truth any more, she will have to go on fighting her battle alone, but one day she will win it, no doubt of it, and then I'll be sorry, then my time will be up, and everyone who failed to believe her will be full of shame. She doesn't shout. She doesn't even bang on. It's all said quickly, through tight lips, while she stands in the hall, under the brass lamp, with something important to get out, quaking with anger but unshaken in her beliefs. I show her out, this woman whose name I still don't know. Closing the door, I lean with my back against it, palms and fingers spread on the wood, eyes shut, like someone in a film, the old moviepose that says, Phew, lucky escape.

I see her in the street sometimes: same coat, same hair, same purposeful air, mumbling to herself as she walks. We look away when we pass each other, like strangers, but not before I've registered she has spotted me and not before I've recognized, written in her eyes, a deep and everlasting contempt.

The Two Mrs Eliots

Gregarious. Reclusive. Charming. Obstructive. Vivacious. Defensive. Severe. The adjectives commonly used about Valerie Eliot can't help but arouse curiosity. Can one person possibly be all these things at the same time, or even at different times? It seems unlikely, but in any case they are not the adjectives that come to mind as Valerie Eliot enters the penthouse boardroom of Faber & Faber's offices in Queen Square. Anxious would be nearer the mark, jumpy, apprehensive. Her nerves are bad today: newspapers have been putting her under increasing pressure to talk – 'Speak . . . Why do you never speak? Speak' – and finally, with gentle encouragement from her publishers, she has agreed to an interview. 'I feel sick,' she says, as John Bodley (who, a fellow Faber editor once teasingly wrote, 'earns his salary/by looking after Valerie') ushers her into a seat and pours her a calming glass of red wine.

In her position, who wouldn't feel sick? A film has just appeared which alleges, or has caused journalists to allege, and which will allow large audiences to believe, the following things about her late husband:

1. That he took the credit for writing poetry, notably parts of *The Waste Land*, in fact written by his first wife, Vivienne.
2. That he betrayed his deep love for Vivienne (and his muse) in his crawly eagerness to become a member of the British literary and religious establishments.
3. That he was cold, ruthless, self-absorbed.
4. That he got hold of Vivienne's money by becoming an executor of her father's estate.
5. That he incarcerated Vivienne in a mental institution when she was in sound mental health, cruelly refused to visit her, and – while he went on to enjoy world renown – allowed her to languish there for nine years until, cheated and neglected, she died of heart failure at fifty-eight.

Tom and Viv, claim those who made it, is a 'truly passionate, tragic and wonderful story about an extraordinary couple who found great love but couldn't handle it'. It will, they say, 'enhance' T. S. Eliot's reputation by showing how his art, which he liked to pretend was 'impersonal', grew directly out of his life. Well, they would say that, wouldn't they? But they have been saying other things as well. Michael Hastings, who wrote the original play *Tom and Viv* and co-wrote the screenplay for the film, last week characterized T.S. Eliot for readers of the *Evening Standard* as one of five American 'fascists' who have had a malign influence on modern culture (the others were D.W. Griffith, Walt Disney, Henry Ford and Frank Lloyd Wright). And while Tom is being written off, or written out of literary history, Viv is being instated as 'an exceptional talent, a vivacious and brilliant woman, who . . . was brave enough to put her vision of what a woman's role could be into practice'. That's the view of the film's producer, Harvey Kass. Miranda Richardson, who plays Viv, takes a similar line, describing her as 'a truth-seeker . . . a free spirit who spoke her mind. [She] was a writer herself but nobody noticed. They were too busy lionizing her husband.'

The celebration of the first Mrs Eliot as the real writer in the marriage must leave the second Mrs Eliot feeling very odd. For nearly half a century, Valerie Eliot has devoted herself to the service of T.S.E. As a fourteen-year-old schoolgirl she experienced a 'revelation' on hearing John Gielgud read 'Journey of the Magi'. At eighteen she resolved to work for Eliot. At twenty-two she was taken on as his secretary. At thirty she married him (he was then sixty-eight). At thirty-eight she became his widow and the executor of his estate.

It is Valerie Eliot who edited the marvellous facsimile edition of *The Waste Land*. It is she who is editing his collected letters. It is she who grants or denies permission to quote from his work – a position which has led some to portray her as a dragon guarding a cave of ugly secrets. And now there's this film, based on a play which has already done damage enough to her husband's reputation, threatening to lodge him forever in the public imagination as a mean old bastard who locked up his first wife and didn't even compose his own work.

Despite reports of her 'fury' at the film, the truth is that Valerie Eliot hasn't seen it yet. Some weeks ago I invited her to a press preview, but word came back from Faber that the *Daily Mail* had made the same proposal and that she thought it rather a hack idea: 'A press showing would be too public, anyway,' I was told. 'She'll probably sneak in somewhere incognito.' So far she hasn't. She didn't see the original Michael Hastings play, either, though she did hear it on the radio. Nor has she read Peter Ackroyd's biography. So her alleged anger with the book, the play and the film is not based on an intimate knowledge of them.

Valerie Eliot is tempted to let the brackish waters ebb away and simply get on with her work. She feels that when she does open her mouth to journalists she is always misrepresented or sold short. For example, one diarist quoted her as saying that in editing Eliot's letters she had 'learned rather a lot about my husband I didn't know'. What she actually said, more interestingly, is that she had discovered things *he* didn't know – such as the fact that the last letter he sent to Ezra Pound, which he feared had never reached him, was found in Pound's dressing gown pocket by his daughter two years after old Ez's death.

So Mrs Eliot is wary of dishing out quotes. But silence at present will imply an acceptance of the thesis of *Tom and Viv*. And though she may not have seen the film, she can't escape it. Not even the dentist is safe: when she went there the other day, she was told that he'd just done the teeth of a woman boasting that her daughter had written the film's theme music. There's no getting away from it. It's time to speak. This is why Mrs Eliot is feeling sick.

One of the key scenes in *Tom and Viv* shows a spry and sane Vivienne being asked to solve two difficult logical puzzles. Tom is present during the interrogation. Viv gets one of the answers wrong and is declared insane. A few days later, with his implied consent or acquiescence, she is dragged brutally out of a café (where she had been calmly taking a toast and tea with her friend Louise Purdon) and hauled off in a van to the loony bin.

I describe these incidents to Valerie Eliot, who sits across the table, light blue eyes, royal blue dress, powdery face, golden hair, golden earrings. 'Oh, it's pathetic, isn't it?' she says. 'The whole point of Vivienne going into a nursing home was to be cared for, because she wasn't capable of looking after herself. Tom wasn't even there at the time of the committal – they'd been separated for five years, and he was away in the country. There . . .' she says, fishing in her bag. 'Read that.'

'That' is the photostat of a letter written to Tom by Vivienne's brother, Maurice Haigh–Wood, on July 14th 1938. It seems to blow *Tom and Viv* out of the water.

Dear Tom,

I am very sorry to have to write to you on your holiday but I'm afraid I must.

V. was found wandering in the streets at 5 o'clock this morning and was taken into Marylebone police station . . . The inspector of the police station told me she had talked in a very confused and unintelligible manner and appeared to have various illusions, and if it had not been possible to get hold of me or someone to take charge of her, he would have felt obliged to place her under mental observation.

As soon as I got to the city I rang up Dr Miller . . . He got a reply from Allen & Hanbury's [chemists] this morning in which they said that V. called every day for her medicine, that she appeared to be in a deplorable condition and that they had no idea of her address. Dr Miller was therefore on the point of writing to me because he feels that something must be done without much more delay . . . [He] feels V. must go either to Malmaison [a sanatorium near Paris] or to some home, and I am also inclined to think that, because there is no telling what will happen next.

V. had apparently been wandering about for two nights, afraid to go anywhere. She is full of the most fantastic suspicions and ideas. She asked me if it was true that you had been beheaded. She says she has been in hiding from various mysterious people, and so on.

I have made a provisional appointment with Dr

Miller for 3.15pm tomorrow (this was before I
discovered you were away).

I really don't know whether to suggest your running
up to town tomorrow and returning to Gloucestershire
in the evening, or not. You will be able to decide that
yourself, but I would be grateful if you would send me
a telegram in the morning to say what you decide.

Yours ever,

Maurice

There is also a second letter from Maurice to Tom, dated
August 14th 1938, exactly a month later. This describes how
Vivienne had been taken to see two different doctors, Dr Hart
and Dr Mapother, and the subsequent committal:

Both doctors felt strongly that she should be put into a
home. They handed me their certificates. I then had to
go before a magistrate to obtain his order. I got hold of
one in Hampstead.

I then went to Northumberland House, saw the
doctor there, and arranged for a car to go with two
nurses to Compayne Gardens that evening. The car
went at about 10 p.m. Vivienne went very quietly with
them after a good deal of discussion.

I spoke to the doctor yesterday evening, and was told
that Vivienne had been fairly cheerful, had slept well
and eaten well, and sat out in the garden and read a
certain amount . . .

I gather . . . that Vivienne was in the habit often of
saving up her drugs and then taking an enormous dose
all at once, which I suppose accounts for the periodical
crises.

As soon as you get back I should very much like to
see you . . .

Yrs ever,
Maurice

It is not clear what action Eliot himself took during the
month between these letters, but it is clear that he was not
directly involved in Vivienne's committal.

'The point,' says Valerie Eliot, 'is that if the doctors and
police hadn't acted with the best of intentions, Vivienne would
have had an early grave. She was put there for her own safety,
because the doctors thought she was in need of care and she
wouldn't go voluntarily. Maurice was desperate to have Tom
involved, because he wanted his hand held. But Tom was away,
and separated from Vivienne in any case, so Maurice had to
see to things himself.

'Northumberland House, where Vivienne went, wasn't a
mental hospital as we understand it today, but a glorified nursing home, where degrees of restraint were necessary. It had a
big garden, which Vivienne liked. It was divided into three
houses – Vivienne was in the nicest part, the Villas, where the
patients who needed least watching lived. They only moved
her when she began stealing from and worrying other
patients. She stirred up a lot of havoc in the place, apparently.'

Why didn't Tom visit her?

'Because the doctors had told him he mustn't. He lost his
hair, you know, at one stage earlier, worrying about her. But
he did get regular reports, through his solicitors, on how she
was doing. And because she'd been a ward in chancery, there
was this outside person looking after her interests. I'm quite
sure that if a doctor had said, "She can come out," Tom or
Maurice would have done something about it. Hastings says

that Maurice later regretted keeping her there, but I talked to Maurice for many hours – he used to come and see me to discuss his problems, especially with his son, who was unstable, too, and who eventually committed suicide. I'd pour whisky down him and he'd talk and talk – but he never expressed regret to me. He must have realized it was for her own good. 'In any case Vivienne didn't want to leave. During the War, Tom wondered if she shouldn't be moved to Brighton or somewhere, with a private nurse, in case of being bombed. But she felt safe and protected there.'

To reinforce the point, Valerie Eliot produces another letter from her bag, written by someone who'd been a friend of Tom and Viv when they were married, and who had visited Northumberland House. The letter quotes a remark Vivienne once made – 'I think it must be dreadful to have children, to think that you might pass on something of yourself' – and describes how 'every time she was found a place, she refused to leave. Either she'd become friendly with a nurse, or a doctor, or she said she had won a privilege where she was and didn't want to give it up. Sometimes she would seem fairly normal, though the frightening glare was almost always there.' The 'frightening glare', says Valerie, was something that had also alarmed Ezra Pound's wife Dorothy some years earlier, when she'd been left alone with Vivienne over tea and noticed her eyes fix on a knife on the table.

What does Valerie think of the theory that if Vivienne had lived today, her illness – the hysteria, her almost constant menstruation, her hormonal imbalance – could have been cured?

'It's pure speculation, like the idea that if Keats had been born later he might not have died of TB. You have to remember that Vivienne went to see some of the top doctors of the day in both France and England, and also one in Germany recommended by Ottoline Morrell. Anyone they'd heard was any good, Tom tried – he took every care, I think. She had the best treatment – you can't tell me that all the doctors were half-witted.'

Valerie Eliot takes another sip of red wine and begins to feel less sick. It isn't a pretty or endearing position to be in – having to insist on the madness of your husband's first wife. Still, if clearing Tom's name requires it, it's work she seems quite willing to undertake.

'Tom used to say that Vivienne had one emotion only, and that was fear. He thought she'd been philandered with before he knew her. She was in Paris once, and lay under the bed at the Pounds' house, cowering in terror because there was a storm. When a friend told her about going to a weekend cottage where the electricity was normally turned off, she replied, "How horrible: you could be murdered before the light came on." And she requested in a letter that when she died her body was to be cut open to make sure she really was dead – she was so afraid of being buried alive.

'I think if Tom hadn't taken the job at the bank, the marriage would never have lasted as long as it did. Even there she would ring him up, you know, and ask him to come home to make her hot carrot juice. And he'd have to slip out and get it, while a friend at the bank covered up for him. Whereas Tom would come back from giving an evening WEA lecture, scour the fridge and there'd be nothing there.

'After they separated Vivienne wrote sad letters to him – there's one where she says she'll be in tomorrow evening and will leave the door ajar, but some are incoherent. She went round wearing a hat with *Murder in the Cathedral* on it. Of course, since she could be totally dotty, Tom and Maurice were made executors of the Haigh–Wood estate – one a City man, a stockbroker, the other who'd been a banker. It would have been quite wrong to put her in charge. She was always running up debts – she'd go out and buy a piano or a car, and someone else would have to pay. In the 1930s Tom had to give some lectures at Harvard because he couldn't meet his income-tax bills. She just drained him of money. She couldn't help it, she was ill. But I assure you Tom was scrupulous about money, absolutely scrupulous.'

The film, I point out to her, does acknowledge the eccentric side of Vivienne: there is a scene where, denied access to the Faber office where her husband works, she pours melted chocolate through the letter box in revenge.

'Hastings completely invented that. The doors at Faber were always open, so there was no problem about walking in. But there was a Miss Swan, the telephonist, just inside. Swannee was a wonderful telephonist: you only had to speak to her once, and she'd recognize your voice next time – T. E. Lawrence couldn't get over it. She was also very tactful and kind with Vivienne, and had a certain way of ringing Tom's bell which meant: "Don't come down." She used to say the smell of ether on Vivienne was frightful – it nearly knocked her out.

'So there is no basis for the chocolate story. What Tom did like was a vanilla ice cream with hot chocolate sauce. He was eating it in a restaurant once and a man opposite said: "I can't understand how a poet like you can eat that stuff." Tom, with hardly a pause, said, "Ah, but you're not a poet," and went on eating.'

Was there a time, early on in the marriage, when Vivienne might have been not just a pain and embarrassment but a supportive, even inspiring companion?

'She was obviously very witty and sparky, and talked to him a lot and was a help in that way. But it was really Tom who tried to get her going as a writer, not the other way about. She wanted to be a ballet dancer. She wanted to be a musician. She was restless and had a go at everything – I think with her illness she couldn't focus properly. Tom wrote to Leonard

Woolf, asking how he handled Virginia during her break-
downs and wanting advice. He also sent one of Vivienne's
stories to *The Dial*, and had quite a row with them when they
turned it down. Tom would say to Vivienne, "Why not write
me something for the *Criterion*?" I think he was trying to
steady her with all that.

'I often think of Ted Hughes, and all he's had to go
through. But Vivienne was more like Zelda Fitzgerald than
Sylvia Plath. Tom did tell me that sometimes he'd finish
things which she couldn't finish, so you can't be sure the
things she published are all hers. Her importance is, that she
made him suffer and we got *The Waste Land*. We owe the
poem to her, no question: he wouldn't have written it if she
hadn't given him such hell.'

This is not quite what the film suggests. There Viv says, 'I
am his mind' ('I think that can be disputed,' giggles Valerie),
and it's claimed that she not only gave him the title *The Waste
Land* but wrote parts of it, too.

'I think it was Ezra Pound, if anyone, who gave him the
title,' says Valerie. 'What Vivienne gave him was the title to
his magazine, the *Criterion*. Michael Hastings says you can't
tell the difference between Tom and Vivienne's handwriting
on the manuscript of *The Waste Land*, but I can: you can't
mistake it. Even lines which are in Vivienne's hand, like
"What you get married for if you don't want children?", were
things she and Tom had heard said by their maid, Ellen, and
which they both thought hysterically funny. And when
Vivienne did publish a bit of *The Waste Land* which Ezra had
kicked out, under the initials "F.M." in the *Criterion*, two years
after the poem had appeared, she was simply playing about
with his rejected lines. It was a joke between them.'

Valerie Eliot refrains from making the point that the manuscript of *The Waste Land* is littered with Vivienne's
enthusiastic comments ('Splendid', 'WONDERFUL'),

comments which she'd be unlikely to have made if the words had been her own. But isn't it time for an edition of her work, so that people can judge for themselves which partner in the marriage was the prime mover?

'Vivienne asked that when she died her papers go to the Bodleian. The Bodleian didn't really want them, and for a long time there was no interest in her work, and they sat in a brown paper parcel in the basement. Now anyone who wants to can look – it's a hotchpotch, poems, stories, some rather pathetic diaries. At the moment we can't do much, because I can't break off from the letters to help. But we've someone in mind, to do a selection of her work with a biographical account. She has to be protected from people who are indulging their egos. It has to be scholarly.'

There is a great deal more about *Tom and Viv* which Valerie Eliot wishes to correct. The film depicts Viv's brother, Maurice, as a duffer; he wasn't – she shows me a moving letter he wrote from the trenches, in the spirit of Wilfred Owen or Siegfried Sassoon, on June 17th 1917. Viv's father wasn't a despised philistine; he was a painter, and she was devoted to him. Viv's mother, far from reproaching Tom for his treatment of her daughter, wrote saying she'd like to see him, even after the separation. Viv didn't resist Tom's decision to go into banking; it was through her family that he got in. Viv didn't resent his becoming religious, or batter at the doors during his baptism and confirmation ceremony in 1927. Viv was much less of a poetic mentor than Ezra Pound, who doesn't appear in the film. Viv wasn't even Viv – she was Vivienne, or Vivien (as she liked friends to spell it), or Vivie, but never Viv.

Above all, for understandable reasons, Valerie doesn't accept the idea of Vivienne as the woman Tom loved most passionately and 'for ever'. I mention the disaster of the honeymoon in Eastbourne in 1915, which the film dramatizes with blood-covered sheets and a smashed-up hotel room.

'It's rather awkward to talk about,' she says. 'I don't know if it was to do with sex, or what, but there was nothing wrong with Tom, if that's your implication. I think when Vivienne came his way he decided "I may as well burn my boats", then quickly realized he'd made a mistake. They were just two people who shouldn't have married: each should have married someone else. But Tom tried very hard and for a very long time to make a go of it, and he's never given credit for that, is he?'

No one now is likely to make a film called *Tom and Val*. And Valerie Eliot (née Fletcher) would not welcome it: she is shy about discussing her private life. But the story of her relationship to Tom is as unlikely, and as romantic, as anything in *Tom and Viv*.

She was born in Headingley, Leeds in August 1926, and christened Valerie, though only just: 'I was going to be called Vivien. But my mother's best friend had a daughter twenty-four hours before I was born, and called her Vivien, so my name was changed. Tom had a lucky escape there.' Her father was in insurance, but he wasn't the Bradford millionaire with a silk hat sort, but rather bookish: 'His father had been keen on poets. And Daddy got into trouble in the First World War because of all the poetry he had in his knapsack. There is a wonderful library in Leeds, and he was chairman of its committee. I used to do all my reading there.'

Their family butcher, meanwhile, was a Mr Bennett, and his son, young Alan (born eight years after Valerie), used to do occasional deliveries to the Fletchers. Much later, Mrs Bennett met Mrs Fletcher out walking with her daughter's new husband: 'He did look a nice man. He had a lovely overcoat.' That was T.S. Eliot, Alan told his mother, the most famous poet in England. He'd even won the Nobel Prize for literature. 'I'm not surprised,' said Mrs Bennett, 'it was such a lovely overcoat.'

Valerie grew up in Leeds, but her older brother went off to Repton and she to Queen Anne's School in Caversham. During the war, while her future husband carried out fire-watching duties as an air-raid warden and had a lucky escape when the offices of Faber were bombed, she, too, came under fire: 'One afternoon, walking down the school fields, a plane suddenly came out of the sky and began machine-gunning. We wore long red cloaks, and you couldn't run in them, it was like wearing a blanket. I can still see the face of the pilot now. He was firing and the windows were going in ahead of us. Everybody else was lying down, but it was raining and I thought, "Blow it, I'm not going to get my cloak wet," so I ran for it. We were told later that a store in Reading had a bomb dropped on it, and that a bus going over Caversham Bridge had had its entire top deck machine-gunned.'

She had read *Murder in the Cathedral* even before hearing Gielgud's recording of 'Journey of the Magi', and later sought out the rest of Eliot's work. It was some years before she saw him in person, giving a reading at the Wigmore Hall, but even before she met him 'I felt I knew him as a person, and evidently I did. I even knew a lot of things about Vivienne, I don't really know how.'

A family friend, Colin Brooks, editor of *The Truth*, per-suaded Eliot to send a signed copy of his poems to his young admirer in Leeds. It was to Brooks that Valerie, at eighteen, disclosed her ambition to work for Eliot, and he encour-aged her. Her father wasn't keen on her going to London, since she'd already been away at school and he wanted her at home. But he reluctantly agreed she could take a secretarial course. She found the work boring: 'One afternoon I felt I'd had it, so I went to an agency and asked if they had anyone literary.' They sent her to a man called Paul Capon: 'I told him, "I shall practise on you". I had to play chess with him every lunchtime. He was generous with money when he had it, but often he didn't: he used to pawn the typewriter at weekends.'

When Capon let her go because he couldn't afford to pay her, she worked for another writer, Charles Morgan. But one day Colin Brooks, who belonged to the same club as Eliot, came rushing round to tell her Eliot was looking for a secretary. She walked up and down outside Faber's offices for two hours before finding the courage to apply and be given an appointment: 'I was terrified. In my excitement I'd cut my hand the night before and had a light bandage on it. There were people on the stairs waiting to be interviewed. Tom chatted with me about Herbert and the seventeenth century. At the end he held the door open for me – I can still picture him with his chin against it – and said, "I'm not allowed to say anything, but I hope that hand has healed enough for you to type in ten days' time." I thought, "Well, I'm in the lead at the moment." Two days later I heard I'd got it.'

She was his secretary for eight years before he proposed. It was a friend, Margaret Behrens, who brought them together. 'She had a house on the Italian frontier, in Mentone. She asked me to stay, which I did, twice, and which Tom was frightfully curious about. Then she wrote to him and said, "Look, why don't you come out for the winter. Valerie can stay with me, and you can go to the hotel next door, it'll be fine." Tom wrote back and said, "I can't: I'm in love with her." So Margaret wrote back and said, "Get on with it." And she wrote straight to me, too, and told me, then wrote back to him again and said, "Good heavens, don't you realize she's in love with you?"'

'His friend Hope Mirrlees came to the office once and said to him, "Is Miss Fletcher engaged by any chance? She looks so radiant." Tom wasn't even egotistical enough to think he was the cause of it. He told my mother he hadn't even been sure if I particularly liked him, because, of course, I was trying so hard not to give signals. And he was worried about the age gap: the day he was due to meet my parents, he wrote to a friend saying, "I have an awful feeling I'm going to turn out to be older than her father," which he was. You can see the worry – that it would seem improper.

For a time, to avoid the danger of office gossip, they met in secret: 'We used to go to the Russell Hotel separately, after work, and meet there behind a pillar. There was a nice old waiter we were very fond of who looked just like Rab Butler. When we went back there after we'd been married my father said, "I'm glad you've made an honest waiter of Rab." For a time after I had my engagement ring I wore a finger-stall. And when Tom went to Garrards to buy the wedding rings he said, "I'll pull my hat down so no one will know me." Afterwards, when he went back, he said to the man there, "You know you were very unwise to let a stranger come in and take two rings out." The man burst out laughing, "We knew exactly who you were, sir."'

They married in January 1957, ten years to the month after Vivienne's death: Eliot's penance was over. Tom was sixty-eight, Valerie – at thirty – less than half his age. Many people remarked on his rejuvenation. There are photos of them together which show Tom looking handsome and smiling. He even allowed himself to publish a love poem to her, rather soppy and sensuous, very different from the lines in *The Waste Land* inspired by marriage to Vivienne. He called it 'A Dedication to My Wife',

> *To whom I owe the leaping delight*
> *That quickens my senses in our wakingtime*
> *And the rhythm that governs the repose of our sleepingtime,*
> * The breathing in unison*
>
> *Of lovers whose bodies smell of each other*

Who think the same thoughts without need of speech
And babble the same speech without need of meaning.

No peevish winter wind shall chill
No sullen tropic sun shall wither
The roses in the rose-garden which is ours and ours only.

But this dedication is for others to read:
These are private words addressed to you in public.

'He was made for marriage,' says Valerie, 'he was a natural for it, a loving creature, and great fun, too. We used to stay at home and drink Drambuie and eat cheese and play Scrabble. He loved to win at cards, and I always made a point of losing by the time we went to bed. We had a magnetic set we travelled with. Every time we finished a game, he used to write a message on it for when I opened it next day. When he died . . . Well, I've never opened it to this day: I sometimes think, shall I?'

They travelled, they read, they socialized. One visitor was Groucho Marx, who described Valerie to Gummo as 'a good-looking, middle-aged blonde whose eyes seemed to fill up with adoration every time she looked at her husband.' But Tom's health was declining and the marriage had only eight years left to run. He was plagued by emphysema, and the travelling was mainly to improve his health.

'He loved to lie pretty much naked in the sun, and he swam. But we used to cross off the days till we could go home again. As he said, you get the best climate in the most boring places. When we were in Marrakesh once, the buildings began rattling. Tom said, "It's an earthquake, I recognize this from St Louis." The earthquake was as far away as Agadir, but there was dust in the air and Tom began coughing. The doctor in England said he could have only one cigar a week. Every

Tuesday he'd give me an innocent look and say, "It's my cigar day, isn't it?" and I'd have to say, "No, two more days to go." He had smoked so much, that was the sadness: I think it was because of Vivienne.'

Did they talk about Vivienne?

'If it came up naturally, yes. But he'd gone over the past in his own mind often enough, now he wanted to go forward, and I didn't see much point in lingering on unhappiness. I felt the same when the manuscript of *The Waste Land*, which had been missing for so many years, turned up in the New York Public Library after his death: I was angry at first that he hadn't had the chance to see it again, but once I began work on it I thought, "God knows best, it would have been too painful for him."'

T. S. Eliot died in 1965, at seventy-six. Valerie, then thirty-eight, his literary executor, was left instructions that there should be no biography. Some have described her as difficult to deal with, but she says that she co-operates with genuine scholars: 'Most of the material is there in libraries, for people who want to look. I just write and say, fine.' As for her intransigence towards biographers, she sees this as 'sticking to what Tom said and carrying out his wishes. Peter Ackroyd knew when he set out that Tom had said, "No biography". So to start bleating at the end about not being able to quote from the poetry, when everyone else has had to obey the same rules, is pretty feeble.'

But she granted permission to the makers of *Tom and Viv* to quote from the poetry: isn't this inconsistent?

'Left to myself I wouldn't have given permission – to an honest attempt, maybe, but not to a sensational thing like this. But I was advised by Faber to do so, and the film-makers paid a fee into my charitable trust – it's tainted money, but there's a young man who's an up-and-coming musician who I sent the money to, and it will help him.' Valerie has put a good deal of money towards good causes in recent years, setting up the annual T.S. Eliot Memorial Prize for poetry, donating £50,000 to save the Beckett reliquary for the V.&A. and the nation, and disbursing significant other sums (to relieve illness and hardship) through the Old Possum Trust.

She also accepts that there should eventually be an authorized biography: 'The world has changed since Tom's death, and so much mischief has been made, I shall probably commission somebody one day. Plenty of people volunteer, of course. But I'll only do it when I've found the right person – and after I've done the letters, because there is a lot of information which only I know that's going into footnotes and can later be used.'

Originally her husband was against publishing the letters, too. But he and Valerie were in the habit of reading aloud to each other in the evening, and she began to drop hints by reciting writers' letters during these sessions, and 'one night he just burst out laughing and said, "All right, you win. But if there's going to be an edition, you'll have to do it."'

She has been doing it for thirty years, and the projected four volumes now look as if they'll run to six. There have been some grumbles (and some flutterings within Faber) at the slowness of the enterprise: the first volume appeared six years ago, there is no sign of the second yet, and Mrs Eliot is no longer young. One interpretation is that she's reluctant to complete the task because to do so in effect means letting go of Tom. But she herself speaks persuasively of the vastness of the task (she has a secretary three days a week, but for the rest, 'by the time you tell somebody what to do you could do it yourself'), of the delay caused by the constant surfacing of new material, and of the numerous other problems that postpone its completion.

'When Vivienne typed things for Tom, there were pages missing, the type would go off the page. There's one where he's writing about Shelley which just gives out – I'd love to know what he goes on to say. And then there are letters which I know exist but can't trace. Tom was also very casual about keeping letters. There were some to Middleton Murry, including ones from 1925 where Tom had been asking Murry for advice about Vivienne, because Murry did try to reconcile them. Murry's widow returned them after his death, and Tom burned them in front of me. That's his privilege. They were his letters. But he did tell me he had another bonfire, earlier, destroying lots of letters, and that if he'd known he was going to marry me he wouldn't have.'

After the interview, we go to an Italian restaurant just round the corner from Faber, where Mrs Eliot is greeted effusively and cracks a lot of jokes. For a supposed recluse, she has a remarkably public life, and is often to be found at Faber parties, sometimes wearing a bracelet on which hang silver miniatures of her husband's books with their titles engraved. There is something almost nun-like in her life's devotion to a single cause. And something old-fashioned in a woman choosing to sacrifice herself to a man in this way. But Valerie Eliot doesn't look old-fashioned, or like a nun. Florid and full of appetite, she is the firm's most colourful link with its illustrious past.

Now that past is a biopic, where – in order that (as its makers put it) *Tom and Viv* 'seems a universal experience and not a film about two long-dead literary figures' – truth goes by the board. Michael Hastings's licence with the facts distresses Valerie Eliot. She can't understand what motivates him: is it some grudge against Faber? Was he merely inspired by a throwaway remark by Edith Sitwell, that 'at some point in their marriage Tom went mad and promptly certified his wife'? Hastings claims that Eliot 'Stanlinized' Vivienne. What about Hastings's own *Who's Who* entry, which declines to name his first wife and states baldly: 'one d. by previous m.'? Could it be that Hastings was drawn to the story of Tom and Vivienne by something in his own past?

Valerie Eliot's upset isn't just with Michael Hastings, though, but with the general raking over of the T.S.E. past. Many a widow, many a second wife, would prefer not to know too much about her husband's early life and loves – the bits before he met her. But as Eliot's literary executor, the keeper of his flame, the guardian of his name, it is Valerie's business to know. She has had to face up to his relationship not just with Vivienne but with two other women: Mary Trevelyan ('She was hot on his trail') and Emily Hale ('A woman, now dead, who was a close friend of Emily sought me out specially to say that this theory of Tom's great love for her was all rubbish'). Vivienne, Mary and Emily: she speaks rather tartly of them. But she feels honour-bound, as the editor of his letters, not to suppress the truth.

In the meantime, her greatest distress is the thought of a public who don't know T.S. Eliot's poetry, or who will be turned off it by the film. 'A lot of people come by, taking photographs of my flat, because they know it's where Tom once lived. I keep wondering, now the film's out, am I going to get a brick through the window? The film can't hurt Tom any more, but it's the inaccuracy and dishonesty that make my blood boil. I worry that people will never look at his words but know him only as the author of *Cats* and then see the film and think: what a monster, a monster of depravity, like Macavity the cat.'

Arguments about Eliot's prejudices, and in particular his anti-semitism, do little to counter this impression. But she is heartened by the letters that come, from those who find *The Waste Land* or the *Four Quartets* still speak to them. And she has not given up hope yet that plays of his, such as *The Cocktail Party* and *The Family Reunion*, will be revived on the London stage. One day, too, she knows the letters will be there, complete, on the shelves: her life's work, in effect her autobiography. And then posterity can judge her – not as a muse, but as the woman who made Tom Eliot happy.

Man of Mettle

As the train pulls up at one of the stations towards Exeter, a girl rushes across the platform to greet her parents, her left hand held out in front of her, the fingers spread wide to show off her engagement ring, her fiancé skulking awkwardly behind. Larkin, I think – *his* kind of old-fashioned moment, his kind of poem. But this is Ted Hughes country, the mid-Devon where Hughes has lived for more than thirty years, and that's his kind of river, the Exe, we've been sliding past.

Hughes and Larkin: the twin peaks of modern English poetry; each the creator of, in Seamus Heaney's phrase, an 'England of the mind'. But when people make this comparison, Hughes tends to come out worst. His England isn't ordinary or hospitable: it's wild and mythic, a place of 'empty horror' and stones crying out under the horizons, where 'manners are tearing off heads'. His England, we tell ourselves, is one we recognize only when our minds are disturbed, when we're in extremes of emotional distress. We wonder about its connection with the quotidian country we inhabit. And we wonder what manner of man could create an art of such violent energies.

Some of these doubts – about Hughes's nature poetry, if not about his own nature – are dispelled in a brilliant essay by Tom Paulin in his book *Minotaur*, which argues that 'nature poetry is always a form of disguised social comment', and that to look closely at Hughes's work is to be allowed 'insights into the secret imaginative life of the nation', insights which 'get obscured by the prying attention that is given to his relationship with Sylvia Plath'. Paulin makes connections between the 'entrepreneurial energy and puritan striving' in Hughes's poetry and the eighties Britain of Margaret Thatcher. In the mid-nineties, one might put it differently and say that the ancient feudings and savage indignations of Hughes's verse give the lie to the bland, rootless, at-ease-with-itself Britain conjured by John Major.

As to Hughes's own nature, perhaps the key witness to call is not the critic but the child. Hughes has always been passionate about tending the imagination of children. He has written more books for them than for adults, and his 'adult' poems are set texts in school. While some teachers agonize over his violence, nihilism and Darwinian bleakness, most children have little trouble with *Lupercal*'s fierceness or *Crow*'s cartoon calamities. Hughes's England is more familiar to them than Larkin's. They don't find it stony and inhuman. They'd not suppose that its author is, either.

Ted Hughes's most celebrated book for children is *The Iron Man*, which he published twenty-five years ago. *The Iron Man* tells of a metal-munching giant who appears from nowhere, is feared and ensnared by farmers, but then is freed through his friendship with a boy called Hogarth, and finally saves the planet from the wicked space-bat-angel-dragon. For more than a decade it has been a standard text, adapted for school plays, read aloud to a transfixed audience in class or at bedtime. Some adult readers, if pushed, will admit to preferring it to Hughes's more 'serious' work.

Now Hughes has written a sequel, *The Iron Woman*. In six short chapters, beautifully illustrated (as the second edition of *The Iron Man* was) by Andrew Davidson, it tells of a giantess who rises angrily from the earth, covered in mud. She has risen because of the terrible scream in her ears, the scream of all nature's creatures, who are being poisoned by a waste factory on the banks of a river. The Iron Woman wants to destroy the factory, but if she does so all who work for it will perish. Can nature be saved without humankind having to die? Lucy, the little girl who befriends the Iron Woman and whose father works at the factory, has the bright idea of writing to Hogarth, who in turn summons the Iron Man. Together, the two children and the two giants come up with a solution, a healing miracle.

'*The Iron Man*,' Hughes tells me, 'was about the last of the stories I invented for my children Frieda and Nicholas. I just wrote it out as I told it over two or three nights. I knew it was successful when the next night they asked, "Can we have the Rubber Man now?", and I wish now I'd written down some of the others. *The Iron Man* was like a kit, or blueprint, for putting together a little boy. That's how I used to tell my children stories: I had the feeling that I had their make-up in my hands, and that I should tell them stories that made things possible for them, that allowed them to win. In *The Iron Man* you have the whole mysterious world of technology, the mechanical world, and the boy is brought into relation with it in a friendly way, so he doesn't regard it as hostile, so he feels he can control it. And then you have the terrible, possibly demonic world of what comes up from inside, out of the elements, represented by the creature from space. The boy and the Iron Man are brought into a workable relationship with that, too. In fact it becomes their servant.

'But I always felt a lack in the story of the same thing for a girl. I thought there should be another story, for balance, and over the years schoolchildren would write to me and say, "What about the Iron Woman?". So the pressure built up, and I thought about how one could best do this, and eventually I put together a little girl, and all the elemental power of a woman – her authentic, creative power.

'I began writing the story in the mid-1980s, and at one point I was scared by it and had to back off. The image of that scream in particular alarmed me. I wasn't sure what I was pushing myself into, so I left it alone for a bit and turned to Shakespeare instead while I got used to it. [His massive *Shakespeare and the Goddess of Complete Being* was published last year.]

'I imagine the reader I'm telling the story to as a combination of me and one or two children I know well: it seems a very natural way to write. I still haven't actually read *The Iron Woman* to a child, and I'd be interested to know the reaction. I can remember books I read at eleven that frightened the life out of me, though I can't see why. *The Water Babies* just terrified me, so much so that I didn't want to pick up the book.

'When you're writing for adults you feel you have to smuggle it past a tremendously vigilant defence system – the English are especially vigilant. Perhaps that's what makes English literature so rich – the collision of different streams, the fighting strains: most of the time the suppressive side of the English character is in power, but then a pressure builds up, and when the right moment comes for this conflict to express itself, however briefly, that makes the result more interesting, it's part of the drama. But children you can get through to openly. I certainly felt when I was writing *The Iron Woman* that I was giving things away. I remember a little sequence I wrote for children, *Ffangs the Vampire Bat*, which was sent for review to a poet I know, who wrote to me and said, "How can you expose yourself like that?" He'd put his finger right on it. That's why you write: to feel your secret life leaking out in places. If you're lucky you can make Prospero and Caliban out of it, but failing that you make

Ffangs. When you're writing essays, you're handling a language and manners and intonations that are an amalgam of all the books written in that language: it's like borrowing or translating. In writing for children, you're intimately, intimately giving something away. You're very aware of what's false to you.

'In the end, *The Iron Woman* is an image of the creative act, isn't it? The whole story is a myth about writing a poem.'

Ted Hughes does not give interviews about his work. There has only ever been one, back in 1971, with Egbert Fass in The *London Magazine*, which, he now says, 'made it clear to me how everything you say in an interview is too provisional'. Ted Hughes is obsessively private. So I've been told, and so I remind myself as I sit listening to him in the garden of Court Green, the house in mid-Devon where he's lived on and off since 1961, and where he now lives with his second wife, Carol Orchard. Certainly Hughes is shy – shy of publicity, shy of sudden intrusion (there is a poem of his called 'Do Not Pick Up the Telephone'), and pathologically shy of the camera. He has a creaturely wariness of human motive, and a particular wariness of journalists, most of whom are interested only in asking him questions about Sylvia Plath. He has had to cut down on poetry readings, he says, because of the increasing presence of people who've not come along to hear him read his poetry.

'When a journalist comes up to me at a reading, or some other public event, and asks me about what he or she thinks is newsworthy, nine times out of ten that will be something "controversial", touching on my private life. To them, it's just their job, and they're under pressure. But to me it means being publicly interrogated. It's a funny old situation. And the final judgment will be in the hands of news editors, who

have their own ideas. It's a lesson soon learned. A good deal
of my life is actually fairly public. I like to get involved in
certain things. But I'm averse to that stuffed-shirt side of
public life, that passive sort of parading yourself at events for
no known reason, going through the motions, speech-
making and so on. There's no point getting involved unless
you can be effective. It's a question of priorities. One of the
modern writer's main problems must be – how to have
your say and make yourself clear, yet live without being
watched.'

Hughes, you feel, would like to be able to trust. Here he
is, an allegedly reticent man, speaking volubly on a huge
number of topics. He talks about his enthusiasm for Tony
Buzan, whose programme to expand the brain and improve
memory systems Hughes has supported and which is now
beginning to be adopted in schools. He talks about his
involvement in the Sacred Earth Drama Trust, a body set up
to stimulate the writing of plays with an ecological theme: he
hands me the first Sacred Earth Dramas anthology, with
plays from Thailand, Finland and Switzerland as well as
Britain. He talks about a valley on Dartmoor from which
ravens were fetched to Tower Hill during the war. He talks
about farming in Devon for five or six years in the 1970s, and
the difficulty he had reconciling that work with writing:
'They're two kinds of sensibility: there's a big collision, probably because farming is such a jealous god – it devours
everything.' (But he got a terrific book of poems out of the
experience, *Moortown Diary*.) He talks about a nearby field,
an aerial photograph of which revealed a Celtic circle, bigger
than Stonehenge, probably to the goddess Nymet. He talks
about the possibility of newspapers publishing not just single
poems each day (as the *Independent* does), but a whole page of
poems: 'What you want is to get a feel of the great current
of stuff swimming around. And a relaxed presentation –

maybe the poems could be unsigned – so that you look for a couple of minutes and think "I like this" or "I don't understand that" and then move on. Isn't that how poems ought to be read?' Increasingly, it seems to be how Hughes writes his own poems – they're deeply pondered but ragged and urgent, gleaming with images and insights, but not tidied up.

At sixty-three, Hughes looks a bit older than most of the photographs I've seen: a bad case of shingles, and the effort involved in writing his Shakespeare book, have taken their toll. But he is still a commanding, strong-jawed physical presence (women meeting him for the first time never fail to tell you how attractive he is), and his deep, growling West Yorkshire voice – anyone who has heard him read his work aloud will testify to its power – has softened only a little. Yorkshire is there in his dress, too: he wears a pair of corduroy trousers made by a cousin of his, whose products Hughes sometimes does his bit for, urging fellow-poets and fellow-fishermen to sample their hard-wearing qualities.

This is a side of Hughes that doesn't normally get talked about: it's funny, hard-nosed, down-to-earth, very Yorkshire; it makes jokes; it's generous and even a bit batty in its enthusiasms. You feel he would give this side more room if he hadn't learnt to be so wary. But then again, maybe not. For he also holds an almost mystic belief in the need to protect the trance-like 'poetic self' which, as he puts it, lives its life 'separate and for the most part hidden from the poet's ordinary personality'.

Not that he needs to be coddled – he has suffered enormous tragedy in his life, is a tough survivor – but he finds journalistic or literary-critical attention disruptive. 'For any poet,' he writes in *A Dancer to God*, his tribute to T. S. Eliot, 'the necessary trance is the most fragile piece of the poet's equipment', and loss of it brings 'acute distress'.

The popular view, of course, is not that Hughes has something to protect but something to hide – about his conduct both as Sylvia Plath's husband and, after her suicide in 1963, as executor of her literary estate. The accusations have grown through a series of biographies and critical studies of Plath – by Edward Butscher, Linda Wagner-Martin, Jacqueline Rose, Ronald Hayman and Anne Stevenson – only the last of which, written in collaboration with his sister Olwyn and widely distrusted for that reason, is favourable to Hughes. The most recent contribution to the Plath-Hughes industry, picking over old ground and reflecting on the ethical dilemmas of biography, is Janet Malcolm's three-part, book-length article in the *New Yorker*, 'The Silent Woman'.

'The Silent Woman'! Hughes could be forgiven for finding the title ironic, given how noisy the voices of those claiming to speak for Plath have been. As Malcolm puts it, Hughes has been 'cheated' by the Plath legacy 'of the peace that age brings'. In its sympathy for and understanding of Hughes's position, Malcolm's piece may prove to be a watershed. It notes, for example, that, far from suppressing material about his marriage to Plath, Hughes has allowed some extraordinarily intimate detail into the public domain. It also quotes from published and private letters in which Hughes explains his difficulties. Critics, he writes in one, 'can no longer feel the difference between the living and the dead', and he accuses the poet and editor A. Alvarez of writing of his marriage 'as if we were relics dug up from 10,000 BC'.

For this interview, the understanding was that Sylvia Plath was not to be part of the discussion. It is thirty years since her death, and at a moment when Ted Hughes is publishing a new book, the sequel to a classic, he surely deserves to be treated as an author in his own right, one whose work is worth attending to, not as an adjunct, a walking controversy or a museum piece. Anyone who cares to can look up in various prefaces, articles and published letters his defence of his role as Plath's editor: he is far from being inflexible and self-righteous about that role, is well aware that things might have been done differently. As for his marriage to Plath, one day he may choose to speak about it, but for now – as he once wrote to Anne Stevenson, ruefully acknowledging that there is no right solution – his policy is silence: 'I know . . . [that] my silence seems to confirm every accusation and fantasy. I preferred it, on the whole, to allowing myself to be dragged out into the bullring and teased and pricked and goaded into vomiting up every detail of my life with Sylvia for the higher entertainment of the hundred thousand Eng. Lit. Profs and graduates who – as you know – feel very little in this case beyond curiosity of quite a low order, the ordinary village kind, popular blood sport kind, no matter how they robe their attentions in Lit. Crit., Theology and ethical sanctity.'

One of the things Hughes has never been silent about is the environment, in particular water-pollution. As he reminds me, he published a poem on the subject on election day 1987 – a polemical poem, but not a party-political one. He feels frustrated by the response. 'I received some criticism for the prosody, the absence of commas, but nobody commented on my theme. Most people I talk to seem to defend or rationalize the pollution of water. They think you're defending fish or insects or flowers. But the effects on otters and so on are indicators of what's happening to us. It isn't a problem of looking after the birds and bees, but of how to ferry human beings through the next century. The danger is multiplied through each generation. We don't really know what bomb has already been implanted in the human system. You should read Teddy Goldsmith: he gives us about sixty years.'

Wasn't his starting point, though, particular rivers which he liked to fish?

'You know what West Yorkshire's like: the Calder, and the Don, in Mexborough, they and others were rivers of incredible poison, still are, some of them. So I was aware of that at an early age. And then to see it happen down here to rivers that were once so beautifully clean, and that are only now just pulling out of a state of terrible collapse: there's a big cheese factory by the village here that was pretty wicked for a while. We had a court case recently on the Exe: a friend of mine took the South West Water company to court for polluting his bit of the river, and won. I followed that very closely.'

If anyone else banged on like this, you'd think him an eco-bore. But Hughes has an imaginative and engaging eye for detail.

'Pollution is the whole world's problem, not just England's. Look at those little trees there' – he points across the garden to a pair of spindly birches. 'There are plants now that will no longer grow in Alaska. They used to think the smog over Alaska came from forest fires, but when they analysed it, took a fingerprint of the chemicals, they discovered it was pollution from Poland and Czechoslovakia.

'*The Iron Woman* began by my thinking: how does nature feel about being destroyed? Presumably it's enraged, and the obvious response is an aggressive one, to remove the destroyer. Here there's a happy ending – a single human brainwave. You can't turn back the technology of the world, but you can learn to handle it much faster than we're doing. The day I sent the book off to Faber I read in *New Scientist* that two Japanese scientists have found a way of converting a large range of plastics into some sort of fuel. That's the kind of brainwave I'm indicating.'

He is making it sound a preachy book: poetry that wants to make something happen.

'Well, there is a vague message in *The Iron Man*, too, about peace and war. And I think the message in *The Iron Woman* is a big enough message not to seem partisan. I mean: are the gospels partisan? They're talking about the salvation of souls, and in its own small way my book is talking about the salvation of mankind. But this is just the general pool of concerns that affects the story. What I was really interested in was the goblin of the story, the little demon every story has to have to make the reader keep turning the page. Once you take your attention off that, it's fatal.'

Has the title *The Iron Woman* anything to do with the Iron Lady, Margaret Thatcher?

'No: the image of a woman rising out of a black swamp is one I've always wanted to get into a story. But I did begin to write the book during Maggie's time, and I suppose it must have been a response in some way. My Iron Woman does what the Iron Lady didn't. In fact, during Maggie's time the importation of toxic wastes into England increased by hundreds of times. It became a big industry. Farmers were being encouraged to take on infill as diversification farming: give up a valley, or scrape a hole under your soil, and someone comes and fills it with God knows what. The controls were very lax. So there was that feeling behind the story: why is it that when we had a woman as prime minister – assuming that women are instinctively protectors, of children, of men and of themselves – how is it she didn't do something about it? In *Lysistrata* the women stop the war. Why didn't women get together to stop the destruction of nature?

'In the mid-1980s I read a book called *The Poisoned Womb*, by John Elkington, a survey of the effects of pesticide on human reproductive capacity which showed that the sperm count of Western man fell by 40 per cent between 1940 and 1982. If you mention this statistic to people they tend to laugh and say: well, that'll solve the population problem. But it struck me as shattering. Now the figure is 50 per cent. Imagine the government coming round to each family in

England and saying: OK, today we want one testicle from your husband, or your son. And the woman says: Oh, well, if you say so. In effect that's what happened. But if this little scenario had happened instead – the fathers half-castrated, the sons half-castrated – at what point would women have done what the Iron Woman does and actually stopped it?'

It's not easy, when talking to Hughes, to stay away from the matter of gender. To his detractors, of course, he is an archetypal male oppressor: the scapegoat, or sacrificial bull, which the feminist movement required. But that image is hard to square with his reading habits – during our interview he enthused over *Women Who Run with the Wolves*, an American feminist bestseller – and even harder to square with his new book. In *The Iron Woman*, men are the wicked managers and employees of the waste factory, and for this are punished with a humiliating metamorphosis: they become fish, forced to inhabit the water they have polluted. The women are the goodies: they rise up and control their own destinies by forcing the waste factory to close. I put it to Hughes that if a woman had written the story it would have been called feminist.

'Would it? Men are the perpetrators of the crime, but not necessarily destructive. The male is destructive once he's lost touch with the biological, reproductive powers of woman. That's a break which has historically happened and is now trying to repair itself: that's what feminism is about. But equally a woman needs the little masculine logical element to turn her energies to creative social use. She needs a male component if anything is to be born at all. Men and women are two parts of one system, not two separate systems. I wanted to reach that balance and make sure that nobody was blamed for things going wrong.'

Hughes's way of talking about the balance of 'male' and 'female' qualities reminds me of D. H. Lawrence, and some feminists have used it against him. But he is not saying that particular qualities are confined to one gender, and his book ends in happy union: 'One of my early ideas was that the story would end with a wonderful sacred marriage. I couldn't do it, but there is harmony.'

A reductive Freudian interpretation of *The Iron Woman* would read it as reconfiguration and wishful resolution of aspects of Hughes's life: a woman rises angrily from the ground, intent on destroying the world of men; she is talked down, reasoned with, appeased; in a sunny flower ceremony she is united with the Iron Man. It's possible, too, to link the central image of the scream to the noise Hughes has endured in his own life for more than twenty years. But the main point about the scream is that it's infectious – if one person touches another, the scream is passed on – and another interpretation might be that this contamination by touch is a metaphor for a disease such as Aids.

'Well, I do think everything in the air gets into what you write,' Hughes says. 'I remember a recurrent dream I had in the 1960s, where there'd been an atomic explosion and we were emerging after, but everything and everyone was radio-active – this feeling that you couldn't touch anything or anybody.' All this sounds like heavy matter for a children's book, but Hughes considers his writing for children 'on a par with other things I write', a claim he inadvertently confirms at one point during our interview by referring to *The Iron Woman* as 'a poem'. 'Children's writing must be very simple and immediate, though. You're just playing. I suppose with a lot of adult writing that sense of play goes out and serious responsibilities arrive. Play: maybe that's what all literature is, or should be.'

But hasn't that sense of play been denied him since he became Poet Laureate in 1984 – all those newspaper editors, and public bodies wanting poems for their buildings and

anniversaries, and autograph-hunters? Tennyson and
Wordsworth were similarly besieged, and Hughes denies
being burdened by office. All the same . . .

'It was Tennyson who fouled it up really, writing these
things for every occasion. And so there's been a public expectation that that's what has to be done, and that if you're not
doing it you're somehow failing in the job. But it's not a job.
I don't have to produce anything.

'When Ben Jonson took on the laureateship, it was for
£70, which was the equivalent of the Royal surgeon's salary,
in today's terms £70,000. [Today it is still £70 and the butt of
sack which Ben Jonson also received has become a case of
wine.] And Jonson worked damned hard, putting on court
entertainments and so on. That went on more or less until
the mid-1700s, after which the post became a perk that
politicians offered to friends. Wordsworth was the first laureate after Dryden to whom it was given as an honour. He did
in fact write some poems but he didn't make a great show of
it. When I accepted, I made it very clear that I regarded it as
an honour – though now and then I have felt the public pressure and newspapers have asked me for laureate poems. I've
used the fees from newspapers to raise money for charity. It's
been quite useful in that way. A formal celebratory poem – it
would be wonderful to be able to turn these things out,
but . . .'

The *Private Eye* or parodist's view is that he does turn these
things out, but Hughes felt comfortable enough with his laureate poems to collect them last year in *Rain-Charm for the
Duchy* – not one of his best books, and one much derided at a
time when the monarchy itself was being much derided, but
containing some characteristically rich Hughesian moments.
It's four years since his last 'real' collection, *Wolfwatching*; he's
not been inactive, but 'I needed to get where I wanted to be –
I've been working on something a bit different.' Part of what

he's been working on is literary criticism, of Shakespeare and Coleridge among others.

In the end, Hughes does begin to talk about Sylvia Plath, after all, and about the catharsis of memorializing the dead in books.

'I often wish I'd done that at the time, with Sylvia. It's like not mourning someone; if you don't, it becomes damaging. It's better to try to get control of it. I admire the way Douglas Dunn did it for his dead wife in *Elegies*, painful though it must have been for him to write. It means the world becomes yours – whereas if you don't do it, it drifts away and takes a whole piece of yourself with it, like an amputation. To attack it and attack it and get it under control – it's like taking possession of your own life, isn't it? Otherwise, it means whole areas of your life stand in front of you and stop you.

'Auden says somewhere, "Never write your autobiography, because it's your capital." Perhaps that's exactly what we now find missing from his work. So everything else is a substitute, something slightly synthetic, as if he's gradually being excluded from his own life. Whereas with Tolstoy, the first thing he wrote was just a reinvention of his own life and gave him an enormous grip on himself. What's writing really about? It's trying to take fuller possession of the reality of your life. Unless you do that, you can feel you're just tiptoeing round the edges of yourself.

'My notion was always that it's the one thing you don't do: you don't write about yourself. The shock of Sylvia's writing, when she really began to write, was that she was doing the very opposite of what she would normally have considered a proper thing to write about. I've often wondered how she would have gone on from there. What she'd done was to reclaim her entire psychology. It's almost like a myth in itself, a very pure, clear story. I made a map of it once when I was sitting in court in the States. Everything in the poems is related to this map.

'Where did it come from, that notion of the impersonality of art? Finally, all works of art are just immense confessions of the central thing. It's an illusion to think otherwise, to suppose it's good manners not to talk about yourself.'

So *The Iron Woman* is about Hughes himself?

'It's got to be, hasn't it?'

She Who Must Be Obeyed

Driving north across London, I listen to *Call Nick Ross* on the radio. The subject for discussion is smacking children, and Penelope Leach – for two decades Britain's leading authority on childcare – is the studio guest.

By the standards of most radio phone-ins, this one is mildness itself. Not a single caller rings to say that all kids need is a good leathering; no one demands that the whole lot of them be strung up. On the other hand, there's the man who says that until children understand words, around the age of five, physical chastisement is the only way. There's the chap who recommends dividing things up with one's spouse so that hubby concentrates on the rough stuff. There's the woman who was smacked hard as a kiddie and, see, it never done her no harm . . .

Penelope Leach is keeping her cool, but it must be a little disheartening. Since the publication of *Babyhood* twenty years ago, in *Baby and Child* (1977), *The Parents' A–Z* (1983) and a succession of books, broadcasts and broadsides which have made her the Truby King or Dr Spock of her generation, she has argued against old disciplinarian models of child-rearing. She is deeply involved with Epoch, the campaign to End physical Punishment Of Children. She knows the research. She knows that hitting breeds further hitting, that those who were hit as kids by their parents in turn hit their kids, who in turn . . . And now it's 1994, and still people won't believe her.

While Penelope Leach is fending calls at Broadcasting House, I park near her home in Hampstead. I have *Baby and Child* beside me, a book that has sold millions of copies round the world and been translated into twenty-eight languages, a book which became gospel for a generation of parents, including myself – the bible we kept by the cot to monitor our babies' physical, emotional and intellectual development, and to check if we were doing things right. I have the proofs of her new book beside me, *Children First*, less a bedside manual than a political manifesto for children's rights. And of course I have the Leach folklore – the anecdotes of friends and contemporaries who have spent more time poring over *Baby and Child* than they have over any Booker prizewinner.

Baby and Child may be a bible, but the folklore is decidedly blasphemous. In some young middle-class homes during the eighties, 'that bloody woman' meant not Margaret Thatcher but Penelope Leach. People complain of being enslaved by her advice. They describe the euphoria of chucking *Baby and Child* out of the window or on to the bonfire. They recall swapping Leach horror stories with fellow-sufferers: 'There's the bit where she says toddlers should be allowed to paint their shit all over the walls'; 'She says you shouldn't take kids on holiday because it's dangerous'; 'She says I can't even read while I'm breastfeeding'; 'She says having the radio on retards your child's language development.'

Except that when you turn to the offending passages you find, well, she doesn't say all that, not exactly. Those faeces: yes, it does say 'if you . . are angry when he examines or smears the contents of his pot, you will hurt his feelings', but this is a section not on artistic expression but on potty-training, and it adds that 'you don't have to pretend to share his plea-surable interest.' That ban on holidays: yes, the book does warn that that innocent country cottage may have a bull in the next field, deadly nightshade in the hedge, a well in the garden or a delightful haystack with a pitchfork for him to jump off, which seems a little unlikely given the condition of the English countryside, but this is a section on choosing appro-priate holidays, not avoiding them altogether.

All the same, for the busy parent who believes most chil-dren are hardy, adaptive souls, there's a fair bit to resent here. And not all the anti-*Baby and Child* stories are apocryphal. While I'm in the car, I look up that passage about the radio, and find it to be pretty much as I'd remembered: 'don't have talk as background noise. If you like to have the radio on all day, try to keep it to music.' When parents, or minders, have to question their right to listen to, say, *Call Nick Ross* in their own kitchen, haven't they become slaves to children? And doesn't it make a mockery of Leach's equation of parents' and children's interests, her claim that 'what's fun for him is fun for you'?

Here, perhaps, is the central paradox of the Leach position. She began writing twenty years ago because she wanted to lib-erate parents from the joyless received wisdom about child-rearing: the four-hour feed routines, the crying's-good-for-their-lungs credo, the philosophy of not-spoiling and not-cuddling. Now the complaint is that her philosophy is as joyless and oppressive as the one it replaced. Today's 'quality time' and 'good-enough' parents, and in particular a whole generation of mothers, want to be reassured that it's all right not to spend every waking hour (and sleeping hour) attending to their babies' needs – that it isn't irreparably damaging to leave your child in the care of someone else, or indeed, at exhausted moments, to leave it to cry a while rather than rush-ing to pick it up.

This is why Penelope Leach has come under increasing attack. Women journalists have trooped to her door, drunk her coffee, and gone away and written rather bristling and self-defensive pieces. Most hostile of all was the piece written by a man in the *Independent* Magazine, whose 'merry, energetic, intelligent and worldly wife, . . . a self-confident woman with a distinguished career' had, he said, become demoralized, faltering and guilt-ridden because of *Baby and Child*.

Guilt: this is the word you hear more than any other in relation to Penelope Leach. She makes parenthood seem hard work; she makes us worry that there's more we could be doing for our children; she makes us anxious and neurotic. But above all, she makes us feel guilty.

What kind of woman is it who possesses this unenviable power? The woman leading me down to her basement kitchen, just back from Broadcasting House but with the coffee already made, is lean, brisk, in her mid-fifties. She wears a floral silk blouse, purple slacks, a sort of string-vest cardigan thing, low heels. 'Mumsy' is the last world you'd use to describe her: there's too much fierce attentiveness under the specs, too much cleverness. The woman caricatured as a sloppy liberal is bonily bright and severe.

She is a fluent talker, a bossy advocate of leniency, her sentences full of italic emphasis and exclamations that I've not heard in some time, such as 'goody gumdrops'. Her home, too, for all its sixties furnishings, is austere: lots of pine, cork tiles, no mess or knick-knacks. Her two children, Melissa and Matthew, are grown up now, but this is not a house that can ever have been overrun by child emperors.

Or was it? How permissive a mother was she? Did she never lose her cool and – even just once – smack her kids?

'No, never. It isn't that I'm so bloody virtuous, it's just that smacking wasn't in my tool-kit: it would no more occur to me to hit a child than it would to some parents to, I don't know what, bite them. Of course some do . . but you know what I mean.

'Being anti-smacking doesn't mean I'm anti-discipline. On the contrary, I was quite good at setting limits. But I suppose my children were allowed to do things that were pretty peculiar by other people's standards. For example, we used to have a paved terrace out there in the garden, and they once spent a whole summer cementing the paving stones with sand from the sandpit and water. It did leave me with a lot of sand to sweep up. On the other hand, that's a small amount of work compared to all the time and energy I'd have had to spend thinking up other entertainments for them.'

But there must have been moments when she gave way to anger with her children, when she got fed up with meeting their needs?

'There was once . . . I'd been in hospital for an operation. Matthew was about five or six. It was my first day up, and for some reason there was something we wanted to watch on television during the day, which was very unusual. And Matthew, who had missed me very badly, didn't wish me to watch television: he wished me to pay attention to him, and said so very frankly and put himself in front of the set. I got up and moved him four times. Finally, I said, "If you do not come away from that television, I will put you out." "Do it," said Matthew. So I put him out of the room, and he came back in. Then I put him out of the house. Whereupon he ran round to the back door and I raced to get there first to lock him out. Then I realized it was snowing and that he'd got no shoes on . . .

'That's it, really. But Matthew loves to tell this story and remembers being bitterly hurt: when he was a boy, it was known as "that time you were horrible to me". I hate it, and see it as shameful. It was so predictable, that getting yourself into a head-to-head.'

It's a pretty innocuous memory to have burning a hole in your conscience. *Of course* she behaved like that. This is the kind of story critics use against Leach – they depict her as a pious goody-goody and blame her 'indulgent' parenting methods for the creation of a generation of child hoodlums.

'That's utter nonsense. For every aggressive teenager, there are millions of unnoticed, normal, nice kids out there. Kids don't change in basic ways. This is what was so distressing about the way the Bulger trial was used by the media. Here were those two ten-year-olds who had tortured and killed a child. Ergo, children today must be getting out of hand. Ergo, we should be careful about primary school truants and spoiling tantruming toddlers. Ergo, we should stop picking up our crying children. Ergo, almost, spoil your child and you create a murderer.'

But does it upset her when people make these charges against her?

'In a way I'm quite flattered, just as Ben Spock was [she uses the familiar 'Ben' because they met about eight years ago, and have since become friends] when he was held responsible for the flower-power generation. But really I find the idea that I have influenced a whole generation quite ludicrous. That's a monstrous responsibility, one I'm very reluctant to get assigned to me.'

The compilers of *Who's Who* evidently agree with her: she is not deemed sufficiently important to be granted an entry in its pages. But surely she *has* influenced a whole generation?

'I see what I do as giving people permission or confidence to do what's right for them. Parents really get very little institutional support when you think what's involved in bringing up children. But I'd be surprised if you could find a parent who had planned to do it all quite differently until they read me. That's why I fight you when you say I influenced a generation.'

Since we're fighting, squabbling anyway, I complain that when I read *Baby and Child* on crying babies it made me feel like a very bad parent. It says that 'babies never cry for nothing' and that their crying may even be set off by some tension or unhappiness in the parents which the baby senses through their handling.

'Gosh no, that's fearfully unfair. There is a section on causeless crying. You must have skipped those very careful three pages that say it isn't all your fault and that some babies just do.'

But surely I can't be the first person who's complained to her that *Baby and Child* induces feelings of inadequacy?

'No, I have met the reaction, and it's the one I dislike most, of course, because guilt is such a sterile, useless feeling. But people don't have to buy the damn books and read them. It's not that I sit here knowing all the answers and that every person should do x, y and z. What I have is a much more general mapping – rules such as: the more you push a child away, the more it will cling.'

Do these rules change, though? Her 1988 edition of *Baby and Child* made a number of revisions to the 1977 edition, with post-natal depression, originally relegated to a short note in the index, brought forward into the main text, and more about the dark side of parenting – stress, separation, sexual abuse. But when I put it to her that she has moved with the times, she recoils again.

'I don't think it's worth doing this stuff unless you tell the truth. The thing I most dislike with experts is to see them blowing in the wind. I don't. I never have. If I have a boast at all, it's that. I defy you to find me an example.'

Breastfeeding? Has she back-pedalled on that, given the increase in mothers going back to work and using bottles?

'No, I've never changed on that. Because breastfeeding is directly related to infant health, it's one of the few cases where you couldn't really find a counter-voice.'

Care arrangements, then? And the greater part some fathers play in child-rearing?

'I don't think I've changed my mind about any of it. But fifteen years ago most mothers in Britain were at home, and it was unheard-of for a father to be. The reality now is that a baby's needs may be met by several different people.'

Sensitive to her feminist critics, those who have complained that *Baby and Child* should really have been called *Madonna and Child* because of its sanctifying of motherhood, Leach tells me that she has always been 'at some pains' to stress that the mother–child unit 'need not remain exclusive after the first few months. Baby care is shared all over the world and always has been.'

But even in her new book she continues to venerate the mother, and struggles to grant fathers a role of equal importance. Whatever the social realities of this emphasis, and however much John Bowlby and her own work for the Medical Research Council in the sixties taught her about the importance of the mother–baby bond, it's hard not to suspect that the roots for it lie much deeper, in her own past.

She was born in 1937, the middle of three daughters. Her father was the novelist Nigel Balchin. Her mother, Elisabeth, had been at Newnham College, Cambridge, before marrying Balchin in 1933 and beginning a family the following year. The Balchins lived in Holland Park – until bombs began to fall on London, and Penelope and her older sister Freja were evacuated with the family nanny.

She has always stressed the importance of a child's early years: how much does she remember of her own?

'I'd say I had a happy childhood, as these things go, but there were lots of unexpected bits to it. The war in London was lovely from my point of view. Can you imagine, you're two years old, and the siren goes off, and you're picked out of bed and taken down to the cellar and put in a bunk bed and the adults sit all round you and chat and play cards for the rest of the night. Absolutely perfect. I loved it.

'The first time we were evacuated was with the whole of my nursery school, and eventually we came back from that situation because the nanny didn't like it – we were covered in lice. 'I expect I'd been told we were only going back to London for one night, before being evacuated to my grandparents. But I had failed to understand this, and thought we were going back to Mummy, and there she was and – this I shall never forget – I simply could not believe we had to go away again. Nanny was entirely part of our horizons, but my mother was much missed.'

After the war, the family moved to a farmhouse in Kent and became friendly with the sculptor Michael Ayrton and his wife Joan. Nigel was keen on his being an open marriage; Elisabeth had done her best to oblige him (there had been a disastrous affair in 1941), but felt little enthusiasm. Now, though, after some dutiful partner-swapping, she fell in love and decided she wanted to leave Nigel. By 1949 Elisabeth was spending as much of her time as she could with Michael in London, the farmhouse in Kent was sold up, and family life as Penelope, now twelve, had known it, had come to an end.

But she does not regret what happened. And the parent she vehemently sided with was not her abandoned father but her mother.

'The High Court didn't feel it was appropriate for someone of my age to remain with their mother while she was living in what was then called sin. My little sister, who's seven years younger than me, got away with it, and my older sister escaped to be a drama student at Lamda. But Muggins here was right in the middle, and the courts decided I had to live

with my father. I didn't like my father. I honestly don't know
why, but I think I sensed distance and disapproval. He wasn't
a brute. I just felt he didn't particularly like me. I could put an
adult spin on that and say he really didn't want a second child
unless it could be a son. I know that's true. But it's not unusual
either. I'm sure it's a vicious circle. I expect I drove him nearly
mad because I was nervous of him.

'Bad though those couple of years were, I'm perfectly clear
it was good that my parents broke up. It sounds like a destructive thing to say, but my mother was renewed. And despite all
the aggro you hear about stepfathers, mine meant a great deal
to me. Once I heard my mother laughing, my stepfather
would have had to work very hard to do wrong by me. I
wanted him because she wanted him.

'I hated the day school I was sent to in London: it was full
of very sophisticated, rich children, and I was a country girl
who'd had a pony, who'd never even worn stockings in her life
and had no idea how children in London occupied themselves. I made such a fuss that I got myself sent to boarding
school. I'd no idea what stakes I was playing for.'

So Penelope was parted from her mother during the war,
reunited overnight, re-evacuated, reunited, moved out of
London and back again, made to live with the father she hated
while her mother moved in with another man, and sent away
to boarding school. Finally she was allowed to live with her
mother and her new husband, near Cambridge, where she
attended a day school and eventually, in 1956, went to her
mother's old college, Newnham.

It says something about her closeness to her mother that
their relationship survived these upheavals: 'I suppose we were
unusually close. I can never remember being just children to
her – we were always people.' Here also one can see why the
mother–child relationship acquires an almost mystical importance in her work.

From Cambridge, where she read history and acted ('it was the Peter Cook and John Birt era'), Penelope Leach went on to do a year's social administration course at the London School of Economics, and then worked at the Home Office juvenile crime unit as an assistant on 'the only piece of work I've ever done that was suppressed. It was a statistical survey of recidivism rates in young offenders: the results showed that it didn't make any difference whatsoever whether you spent £60,000 putting these kids through Borstal or £100 on a caution. So we've known for over thirty years that secure units do not help reduce rates of offending, and we're still building them.' After this she began research into parental attitudes to child-rearing, married the science writer and energy specialist Gerald Leach when she was twenty-six, and completed a Ph.D. just as she was having her first child, Melissa, at twenty-eight. Matthew was born three years later.

I'd idly supposed that she must have been a stay-at-home mother when her children were small, but for five years she worked part-time, teaching and researching.

'What I did was to keep a kind of academic presence and my self-respect. I had the usual troubles parents have: I was working part-time for a child development unit, but honestly, it sometimes seemed that people chose to arrange meetings at three on purpose, when they knew I had to be out of the building by 3.15pm. It wasn't easy even then, but it worked fine till I lost my child-minder: I always said that my life would fall apart when she left, and it did. Which is again like everybody else, except that I was lucky enough for a time to have someone wonderful.

'Whether I'd have given up the unequal struggle if Matthew hadn't had meningitis at two, I don't know. He was extremely ill, and could have died: I was in hospital with him for three weeks. For the first week people at work couldn't have been nicer, during the second they were querulous and

children who do it. And what I'd say to any hard-pressed shopkeeper is: Make it a great deal more difficult, then.

'My anger about this sort of thing is as much pragmatic as moral. I really don't know how we can expect children who are treated in this way to turn into involved, participatory citizens. People jabber on about children watching too much television. But many of the kids who are indicted for watching four hours a day aren't being offered any alternative: they would otherwise be bored to death with nothing to do.'

Does she feel a bit of a lone voice, campaigning for children's rights?

'In the UK, maybe; not in the US. And we are miles behind on human rights issues compared to most of continental Europe. There, when something is against the law, like smacking, it isn't done. And it's not only Scandinavia that's ahead of us: in Rome you'd probably get lynched if you hit a child in front of shoppers.'

As she lectures on, I wonder why it is that someone whose ideas I largely accept is none the less difficult to warm to. I remember her on *Desert Island Discs* trying to take her husband as her luxury, being disallowed him, and plumping for a supply of coffee instead. Very narrow, very centred. Not much sense of humour or fun. I try the word 'driven' on her.

'I feel driven by the present political and economic situation. But can I stop thinking about it and go to the movies? Yes. I love to read, I love to cook, I go to art galleries, I read easy fiction to balance difficult academe. It's hard to convey this: we're really rather silly.'

'We' here means Penelope, Gerald, Matthew, Melissa and her husband: a very tight unit. As if on cue, the doorbell rings and it's Melissa, 'just dropping in'. An ungracious part of me is hoping for a junkie, an alcoholic, an airhead, a matricidal basket case. But Melissa is bright, genial, an anthropologist working on gender issues and the environment – 'daughter, friend, colleague and creative critic' as the dedication of Penelope Leach's new book describes her. Matthew is working on pollution problems in Eastern Europe. They get on very well indeed. 'I don't think parents realize how glorious the relationship with grown-up children is,' Penelope Leach says. 'They're adult, but still the people you know best in the world.'

Back home, replaying the tapes of the interview, I notice how indignant she had sounded on that business of my causelessly crying baby: had I skipped the relevant pages? I check it out. It's true that there are, well, two pages on 'Colic' – or rather 'Colic?' as the revised 1988 edition of *Baby and Child* more sceptically puts it. There has been another important change between editions; whereas in 1977, Leach recommended various anti-crying techniques which parents can 'try if all else fails', in 1988 she adds these two guilt-lifting sentences: 'But "try" is the operative word. There may be nothing you can do but your best; you may all have to live through a difficult few weeks.' There you are, mystery solved: I'd not have felt so neurotic a parent if I'd had the later edition.

But maybe guilt and neurosis are a necessary condition of parenthood, or the kind of parenthoods which we offer in the current organization of society. Those of us who have felt angry with Penelope Leach for making us feel bad are missing the point. What we resent is not that she's occasionally wrong, but that she's mostly right: our priorities are wrong, but we don't know how to change them while also remaining active, wage-earning, employed. For Leach, bringing up children is at least as important as any profession and requires that those who pursue it do so with their concentration fully engaged. Whereas most of us pursue the profession on an amateurish, part-time and egocentric basis – with the radio playing if we so choose.

Her stern message is that we could be doing better by our children. And she knows that this is what makes us angriest of all.

'I do meet people who say, "Your book sets standards of parenting which are too high for me". I don't like that, but I can't help it and I can't apologize. I do feel that way. To me not giving it one's best shot would be a bit like getting married to someone and not even planning to be faithful. But I don't expect everyone to succeed. And one of the best things about the design of the human infant is that we don't see the marks of all the fearful things we do, that there is this kind of merciful blanket. We don't have to see our mistakes.'

3
Not Talking about Sex

The Quiet One

She is wearing a hat, that's the first thing I'm unprepared for. She told me only that she'd be in a blue dress, which she is, and a fur coat, 'artificial, in case you'll be wondering'. I'm not wondering, actually: there's too much else to wonder at, or worry about, as she crosses the room to the bar. For instance: is this her at all? It seemed easy enough, over the phone, arranging to meet.

'I'll be wearing a blue dress, and a fur coat – artificial in case you'll be wondering.'

'I'll have a black blazer on – it used to be my Dad's.'

We made it easy for each other, as if we were strangers. But we aren't strangers, or weren't once. I can't pretend I've thought of her every day, or week, or even very often, since last I saw her twenty-odd years ago. But I have an image. It's not the image walking towards me now. Back then, you'd never have caught Christine wearing a hat. Nor would you have caught her being so precise. 'In case you'll be wondering'. That perfect future tense. Or future perfect. Or was it conditional? I'd have known, then, and she wouldn't. Times change.

It wasn't hard to track her down. It was my mother who

started it – ironic, since in the old days she had tried to stop it. When I told her I was going to be up in Leeds, to research an article on changing work patterns in the north of England, she said, 'Of course, one of your old girlfriends lives in Leeds. Christine Phillips she was then, no idea what she's called these days.' I'd no idea, either, so I rang Liz, another old friend, also meanwhile subject to a change of surname or two. 'I have an address. You could try directory enquiries. Stanforth, I think she's called, though the last I heard it was looking like divorce.' It was still Stanforth, in the directory, though the house, what I could hear of it during our short call, didn't sound to be crashing with family. I wanted to ask about her circumstances, but something in her tone discouraged it. And what was the hurry, since we'd broken the silence at last and – this was the good thing – she saw no problem about meeting; if I wanted to see her she'd like to, eight o'clock at the Golden Lion, fine.

Now, here we are, or are we? Is this her? Her first steps into the lounge are bold, full of direction. But halfway down the room she's hesitating.

'Christine . . . ?'

'I wondered if I'd recognize you.'

'Did you?'

'Mm. I think I would have. I do now.'

She takes her hat off, a furry basin, and we stand by the bar stool I've just got down from. What will she have? Only a tomato juice for the moment, she's driving, the police are red-hot round here, maybe something stronger later. I'm trying to talk to her, and to look at her, but it's difficult because I'm also trying to attract the attention of the barman, whose idea of running the bar is to keep his back turned while he reads the evening paper, so that he doesn't have to be bothered with serving drinks. I catch his eye at last, and turn to Christine, mock-exasperated, as she sits at a quiet table. The delay adds to rather than dilutes our embarrassment. It seemed a good idea at the time, to catch up on my past, but now it's the present and I can't think what to say.

Back in the old days, it was me who did the talking. I'd met her at a party, an impromptu one, somebody's parents out for the evening, one of those. She was wearing a black choker and short velvet dress, she held her glass by the stem in front of her breasts, and a single blonde curl dropped onto her forehead like a cup-hook. I knew the girl she was standing next to, and talked to them both, but it was hard getting much out of Christine. The silence was very attractive. The three of us danced, and then at some point only the two. I tried to shout over the music, but Christine's lips were sealed. She avoided looking at me, and I thought she must be bored, but it wasn't as if anything else in the room seemed to interest her either. The unresponsiveness was very seductive: cool, but not *that* cool. She seemed fearful as well, vulnerable, and I wanted to know why. There were no clues at the end of the party, when I walked her home. To my questions she answered 'yes' or 'no' or 'don't know' or 'maybe'. Once I brushed against her, to see how she'd react. She didn't. Outside her door, I asked her if she'd go to the pictures with me, and she didn't say anything, so I suggested the following Saturday, and she said 'all right' and went in. She'd managed about a dozen words all evening.

What was it about Christine? What is it about her now? Here she is with her tomato juice and Lee and Perrins, stirring round the trail of black blood, asking me to tell her why I'm in Leeds. I describe the people I've talked to for the article, how they feel, what they think, whether the old differences between northerners and southerners (economic, social, linguistic) exist any more. I expound my premise: that with the decline of old-fashioned manufacturing (mills, mines, factories), and the rise of service industries, the old values associated with the north – trust, rootedness, a sense of community – are breaking down. She hears me out. We're each in our customary places: talker, listener; watcher, watched. She swims back into focus down the years – the pale skin, the green eyes on the brink of something, the perfect little bow mouth. It was those closed lips, most of all. I thought they meant wisdom, pain, experience, honesty. I wanted to unseal her. I knew she had a story to tell. She needed time and care, that was all.

We started going out. My mother disapproved, and there were rows between us, 'discussions' as she preferred to call them, intimations from her that Christine was unsuitable, protests from me.

'What's your objection to her – that her parents are working-class? That she doesn't live in a big house?'

'Of course not.'

'Some people are better than others because of where they're born – is that what you're saying?'

'No, of course not that.'

'What then?'

'That you're educated and she isn't. That you'll be going to university and she won't. That you're too young to be making commitments yet.'

'I'm not doing.'

'You don't see anyone but her at weekends now. It's serious, just the two of you, not a crowd. She seems a perfectly pleasant girl, but you're still not eighteen, and she's barely sixteen and . . .'

'What about love, mum?'

'Do you love her?'

'I'm making a general point – isn't love the most important thing?'

'Yes, but you mustn't rush into anything. Are you really in love?'

'I'm not in love with anyone. I just don't like what you're saying.'

Which wasn't true: I hated what she was saying because I did love Christine, or had persuaded myself I loved her, or was about to, to spite my mother.

I order another whisky, and this time Christine joins me, a relief: she's only been listening, but listening can be tense, too. Her nails are in her palms. On her left wrist, the muscles are taut under the Nile delta of veins. Her skin has come back to me now. It was white and unblemished when the rest of us had complexions like cheese graters. It still is.

'So how are you?' I ask.

'OK. It feels a bit odd coming here, to be honest.'

'It feels odd to me, too. But I meant: how are you in general?'

'Yes, I meant that too, OK.'

'I heard you were married.'

'Was, past tense, yes. Quite a bit back. Not any more . . .'

It's what I'd hoped she'd say, yet feared she would. Beyond the vain part of me that wants to know that I mean something to her still (if only as a measure of what she felt about me then), there's also guilt at how our relationship ended, and a worry she's been in trouble ever since.

We'd gone out unexcitingly for some weeks – pictures, a walk, a drive in my parents' car (I'd just passed the test), a drink where they wouldn't ask our age, preliminaries, petting, an understanding I'd not get far if I tried it on, all that. It was slow going until one Saturday we were left alone in the house of a friend of hers whose parents were out, and we jumped a few stages – the lock of blonde hair stuck to her brow, the black choker on her pale neck, her white body and me inside it on the nylon carpet. It happened like a silent movie, me braced for the sound of the front door key, Christine her usual mute self. She had no time to make a noise even if she'd wanted to: we were having sex and then (my fault, too excited, gone in a flash) we had had it, past perfect not continuous. We dressed without a word and walked home with even fewer. I felt elated, but suppressed the elation out of gallantry, knowing from her face, grave as the altar, it would be improper to show pleasure. Was she mad with me? She seemed willing enough at the time, I told myself, as boys in those days tended to tell themselves. Christine would have put it differently, later did put it differently: she'd been a virgin, hadn't planned it, went much further than she meant. I'd read in books of girls who would happily shed their virginity, in the right hands – who'd even take the initiative. But Christine wasn't like that. Carried away for a minute, already, in the short walk home, she'd been carried back. Perhaps, anyway, my hands were the wrong hands. Her reproachful silence made me feel like a trickster, as if I'd pulled a fast one. In a gloom of conscience, we passed the fish and chip shop, which was crammed and noisy with men who'd just poured out of closing pubs. We reached her street, one of the terraces clustered round Pickles Mill – Stephen Pickles, whose family started and still owned the mill, was my sister's godfather and one of my father's best friends. Outside her house, a sliver of light through the crack of its net curtains, I hugged Christine to me to convey the solemn irrevocability of what had passed between us (what had passed between us, I could feel and maybe she could feel, was ready to pass between us again). 'Will you call me?' she'd have said, in another time or place, but Christine was Christine, silent as the grave, and this was Barnoldswick, circa 1968, when phones were rare in working-class homes: it was she, we arranged (how else were we to speak?), who would ring me. She put her key in the door and turned with a final tragic stare.

She doesn't look tragic now, cheering up – caution shed –

after a second whisky. But this is how I remember her: like Claude Goretta's lacemaker, deflowered, betrayed and driven mad. Not that I did betray her, straight away; not that, I hope (I'm here partly to find out), she was driven mad. We talked on the phone next evening, or rather I did: it was mostly silences from her. On the Tuesday night, guilty and in love, I sat down and wrote a four-page letter – rhapsodic Lawrentianism, Blakean delight in the senses, summer-of-love stuff. The letter was contrived, sincere, self-justifying and all written to one end: to persuade her that what we'd done was quite OK. Hadn't we both wanted this lovely, life-enhancing thing? In the bright citadel that the young – *our* generation – were building, the old hypocrisies would be swept away and no one need feel guilt any more about making love (except, perhaps, those like me who could make it for only a few seconds). All true and kind, as was telling her I loved her, but I was also careful not to commit myself to anything: just because we'd done it, she wasn't to think she owned me.

Next weekend we drove up the Dales, to assorted country pubs, away from the milling dance halls, the scrunchy heat of the cinema, the sawdust menace of town bars: very middle-class, very courting-couple, me with my pint of bitter, she with her vodka and lime, among dangling horse brasses and couples who, like us, had nothing to say. She was quiet as a mouse, a church, a church mouse. I was quiet, too. There was nothing wrong with it, no point in speaking unless you had something to say. We agreed about this – tacitly of course – and sat on in a kind of worship, a trance-like, reverent conviction that words come easy only to the false in heart. Only this time her silence seemed a different sort of silence, not happily vacant but with bitter words smouldering inside. I waited, and in the car home, suddenly weepy, she told me. Her sisters, who I hadn't met and now decided I never wanted to meet, had discovered the letter I'd written in the jewellery box in her dressing table (or, I suppose, *their*, all three daughters', dressing table). They had been shocked by what it said. They had given her a hard time. They reminded her that they were three and five years older than her; that they were engaged and had their wedding dates fixed for next year; but that they were Saving Themselves. They were shocked at the risk she'd taken, and afraid of what would become of her now that she'd thrown away her – their words – precious jewel.

She cried. I pulled up in a lane near the canal and held her, out of my depth. The fear, the responsibility, the knowledge that if we repeated what we'd done the previous Saturday – as I'd half been hoping we might tonight, in the car – we'd have to think of marriage (the rules of engagement then). I knew all was changed irrevocably. I felt like a cheap exploiter – the millowner's son who'd ruined one of the lasses with his bit of fun. I hated the feeling, the *droit de seigneur* of it, and wanted to show Christine she could trust me. Our relationship couldn't follow the usual teenage pattern, a few weeks of courting then fade-out and goodbye. I would have to stick by her for a decent interval. It mustn't look like a hit and run.

I did stick by her, and even, for a time – the time I'd had that argument with my mother – persuaded myself I loved her and hoped that love would unlock her, make her, if not want me, at least *speak*. There were more drives out to country pubs, and often we'd stop and park on the way back, hot and half-undressed in the car in the lane down by the canal. But she remained in her turret. And became a virgin again. It was 1968, and everyone our age was supposed to be fucking and fellating all over the place, and probably were, if my friends were to be believed, if they weren't just mouth and trousers. It was 1968, adolescence the world over, and all through this I stuck it out with a girl I'd had sex with just the once and who wanted us to suffer for that and who would never, till we wore wedding rings, have sex again.

As the months passed, rather than prising Christine from her silence I surrendered to it. We'd sit for hours in the car watching rain move over a hayfield. We'd walk round the sawdust touchlines of a recreation field. But there was never the moment when one of us said, overwhelmed by the silence of the other's thoughts, 'A penny for them'. I was afraid, perhaps, that her secret wish was to become engaged, just like her sisters – that she was waiting for me to ask. But all I wanted to say was the one thing I couldn't: that our going out together had no point any more, no future, was merely cruel to both of us. I couldn't even say it when I went off to university that autumn, though we did say an intense goodbye. Every week I wrote from my campus cell, assuring her of my love and even meaning it. Her replies were shorter. She came down one weekend in the first term, chastely staying in the guest bedroom of the hall of residence, as perhaps no other girlfriend in the history of British universities had done till then or has done since. I hid her away from my friends most of the weekend, wanting them to notice her beauty but not to engage her in conversation, telling myself she'd be bored, and fearing they'd take her silence (as even I'd begun to) for stupidity. At the bus station, when I saw her off, she dallied in the café, staring deeply into an ashtray and saying she wanted to say something. I waited, but whatever it was didn't come. We walked out through the drizzle to the bus. Mutely, meekly, she went back to Barnoldswick and the letters dwindled and the relationship petered out. At Christmas I didn't contact her. A year had passed since that moment on the nylon carpet. I had done my time.

'So are you working?' I ask, as she pours the ginger ale into her third whisky, well over the limit, flushes of red in her skin and that endearingly skewed top tooth.

'I'm a counsellor.'

'A *counsellor*?'

'Don't sound so surprised.'

'It's just . . .'

'You thought I was a dimbo.'

'Bimbo.'

'Dimbo, bimbo, whichever.'

'No,' I lie, 'just counselling doesn't seem your sort of thing. Who do you counsel?'

'Mainly women with relationship problems.'

'You mean marriage problems?'

'I mean relationships. Many of them aren't married.'

'So you trained.'

'Yes. It all happened very late. I got my degree at twenty-eight . . .'

'Degree?'

'Yes, I realized leaving school early had been a mistake, and I went back to college. Then I got married, and it didn't work out, and I went into therapy. Then I worked with Relate, then more therapy, more training and here I am.'

'It's amazing.'

'No, it isn't. What did you expect I'd be doing?'

'I always imagined you'd marry early and work for a couple of years, then have children and not work again.'

'Almost the opposite. I married at thirty, divorced at thirty-five, and I haven't had kids. But I've worked a lot.'

'Are you sorry about that?'

'No. We shouldn't have married in the first place. He was a good friend, someone I met at college. He should never have been my husband. He's a friend again now, funnily enough, but it's taken a while.'

'I meant, are you sorry you didn't have kids?'

'I still could, in theory, just about. It's bothered me more in the last year or two, since I met Mike. I think if I'd met him earlier I would have. But there's my work, which I'd not miss for the world. And we have each other. That's the main thing.'

'Yes, that's good,' I say, not certain if I think it is good, Christine and Mike having each other. Once I could have had Christine. Once I did have her. Once, maybe, she thought to have me, while I was thinking only how I could decently break it off.

'Have you eaten?' I ask.

'No, but I'm not bothered. I've not got long.'

'Another drink, then?'

'No, only mineral water. I'll watch you. Then I'd better go.'

I look at her hands on the table and remember how I used to argue with her about wearing gloves when we were out walking: I wanted to feel her hands in mine, and promised to keep them warm. Or had I only thought that, and held her leathered fingers, and not had the courage to protest?

'So why did you want to see me?' she asks.

'Just to catch up and things.'

'What things?'

'We were close once, weren't we? I didn't want to lose touch. It feels unnatural letting go of the past.'

'But sometimes it's better to let go.'

'That's what you tell people as a counsellor . . .'

'Sometimes. I'm not being a counsellor now.'

'What are you being?'

'I came here because you asked to see me. I thought there might be something particular, a reason.'

'No. Not that catching up isn't a good reason. But I don't think I know why, exactly.'

'You just rang on the off-chance.'

'No. I've often thought of it. I've often thought of you.'

'What kind of thoughts?'

'Wondering how you were. Thinking back to when we went out. We just sort of faded away. I was never sure why.'

'You didn't want it any more, wasn't that it?'

'Maybe that's true: it's so long ago, I can't remember.'

'You're being disingenuous.'

'Maybe it's guilt, then.'

'What is?'

'I've felt guilty at some level all those years.'

'Why guilty?'

'That I made you unhappy.'

'Did you? I don't think you did. I was a mess, but that wasn't because of you.'

'Who then?'

'Patrick, mostly. Patrick Sheehan. Did you know him? I started going out with him after you went off to university.'

'I didn't know.'

'Yes, it was a big thing.'

'So you were going out with him when you and I were still officially . . . that time you came down to see me . . . ?'

'He was after me then. I was trying to tell you, or get some feeling of whether you cared about me, but I didn't feel anything from you and I thought, what the hell, why not.'

'I'd no idea.'

'It wasn't that serious with him at first. But then I moved in. It lasted about five years. He's the one who broke my heart.'

'Moved in with him?'

'Yes, in Barnoldswick. Huge ructions. My sisters had both been good girls and got married, though one's divorced now. My parents didn't speak to me for about two years. Then it was all right. Then it wasn't all right, because he pissed off with someone else, and I went a bit wild for a couple of years. But I don't regret Patrick. He helped me grow up. Or partly. I still had to go to therapy later. Problems. I could never tell you about them then. Don't look so tortured. Why should you feel guilty? If anyone should feel guilty, it's me.'

And she lays her hand on mine, ungloved. Back then, it was me who'd initiate all physical acts, even the faintest ones, the stroke of a cheek, the latch of a little finger. Back then things were done to her, and she put up with them, mostly in silence. Her body had been a bank-vault at first, then a one-night room, then a beautiful flat where Patrick lived, then an empty house let out to nameless men. I'd thought it was the times – 1968 when I met her, but, this being the small-town North, in effect 1958 – that explained her. Or the religion she'd been brought up with (which? I'd never been clear). Or not feeling loved enough to come out of her belfry. But I'd missed so much of what she was. And miss it now. A lifetime later she puts her hand on mine. I turn it over and clasp her fingers.

'This is daft.'

'Maybe.'

'Sitting here brooding about it when we were just kids at the time. It's always shitty when relationships end. It wasn't so traumatic, was it?'

'Not for me. But I thought you . . .'

'I was OK. And I reckoned you'd be OK.'

'I was. But I worried about you. There was earlier as well. Us having sex, and that making things difficult for you.'

'Did we? Did it? Sorry, I can't remember. Was I under age or something?'

'No, but . . . Aren't you being disingenuous now? Don't you remember?'

'Not really. Sorry. All I can remember was feeling it wasn't like it said it would be in the books. No offence, but teenage sex was crap. Still is, I guess. Even with Patrick it took ages for it to be all right. I liked you, you know – but that side of it, there wasn't the spark really, was there?' She laughs. 'At least I didn't get pregnant.'

'No,' I say, stroking her hand, lost for words.

There's a pause, as if she doesn't know if she should stroke me back, whether anyone walking in and seeing it would get the wrong idea, if it is the wrong idea. Then she says:

'You're very quiet. It's funny, that's what I remember most. You never used to say anything. I never knew what you felt.'

I start to protest, but she takes my hand in both of hers now and shushes me. 'Anyway, enough of being gloomy. I think you got me here under false pretences,' she says, in control and flirty in a way I can't remember. 'You had a free evening, and you wanted to remind yourself what northern lasses are like.'

'There are plenty of northerners in London.'

'But northerners who stay. We're a curiosity to you. That's what this article you're writing is about. I'm a bit of research for you. Admit it.'

'No,' I say, and mean it. 'Stop grilling me. Is this how you counsel people?'

'Counsellors are trained to listen. I heard what you were saying earlier about the north. All of it crap by the way.'

'I'm not knocking most of the changes, but I do think there's been some breakdown in community . . .'

'You're being sentimental. They were pinched and mean, those communities. I wouldn't want them back.'

'No. But I'd like to understand how values have changed. It's to do with my past.'

'But this isn't the past. People still live here. They aren't exotics to gawp at. They aren't bits of film archive. And most of them are a lot better off than they were, especially the women. People in milltowns, they had no power once, no voice except through the union.'

'Now they've no jobs.'

'They've other kinds of job. The mills have closed, and that's sad in some ways, but people have got on and found other work, even if it means moving a bit away, like I've done. You should talk to some of the women I talk to. They may have lousy marriages but they're grateful to be working and not stuck at home like their mothers were. "Service industries": so what's wrong with that, if it means more women have jobs? What's wrong with a job like mine, which didn't even used to exist? Your problem is you've moved away but you haven't moved on. You're still stuck in your adolescence, and that stops you seeing things straight. It's like you're working off some grudge against the north, to justify having left it.'

'Thank you, Dr Phillips. Same time next week?'

'Stanforth. And I don't talk to my clients like this. I'm not judgmental with them.'

'Judge me all you like. Maybe that's why I wanted to see you: to hear your verdict.'

'The verdict's this. I've had a nice time. But now I've got to go.'

Am I imagining it, or does she mean that it's been such a nice time that she has to go now otherwise she won't go at all? Her arm's in mine as we cross the floor, and I can't be imagining it, because in the foyer we veer off, into the lift. We embrace in all its mirrors, then everything happens very fast: the thrust and withdrawal of the card-key in my door, her hat spun like a frisbee towards the bathroom, her blue dress on the floor, her underwear, the white body I thought I'd be trying to remember but which I see now I never really saw. 'We shouldn't be doing this?' Did I say that? Did she? Did she say it then, all that time ago? Or was it only what I thought she must have wanted to say? All that teenage guilt and fumbling, not like the appeasing adult sharpness of it now. The dart of tongues, like birds returning to their nesting boxes. And the words pouring out of her, monosyllabic only, but more than enough.

'I've had a nice time. But now I've got to go.'

No, I must be imagining it, because in the foyer she tugs me right, towards the exit below. There are two flights down, long enough for me to gaze at her earrings, two amber dolphins hanging from the lobes I too once clasped and nibbled at till in a pet she would brush me away. Those lovely ears still, and the intimate tuck of flesh below: it's not too late to stop her leaving, to grab her hand in the revolving door and keep revolving, back up the stairs. But for what? We're strangers now. We'd have to start from scratch. For every old wound healed, a fresh one would open new guilt as well as old. Besides, I can tell from the way she's fishing through her handbag for the car keys that if I tried – tried it on – she'd certainly reject me.

The revolving door spins us out into the night, towards her Astra, her arm hooked neutrally in mine. Her tone is brisk as she describes how Mike will be waiting up for her, brisk enough for me to feel shame, relieved not to have been brought to a pretty pass, or unpretty pass, or impasse. A cold, fruitless moon. Chimes from old clockfaces. The iron tongue of midnight. We shake hands by the car, then I get bold and kiss her on the cheek.

'You have my number,' she says, from the driving seat.

'Yes,' I say, sensing reproach in this, since I haven't given her mine.

'If you're up this way again, come and have a meal with us. Bring the family. I'd like to meet them.'

'Sure, OK, that'd be nice.'

She turns the key in the ignition, and her Astra finds its voice. Full-throated in the urban hush, she pulls out from the kerb and down the street. I stand in the flaky darkness and watch the tail-lights fade away.

Back in my room, I stand at the window, glaring over the roofs towards the orange-lit heights she's gone back to. 'You fucking idiot,' I say aloud, angry at myself for messing with a past that was safer as I'd remembered it, not this gash of humiliation and desire.

I stand there for hours, then sit down at the article on my laptop and tap out the words, changing only her surname and profession. 'But Christine Turner, a 41-year-old solicitor in a Leeds law firm, warmly welcomes these socio-economic changes. "The old structure was class-ridden and patriarchal. Women like me didn't stand a chance. Now we've found a role and a voice . . .".'

Not Talking about Sex

A man I like but don't know very well is speaking in intimate detail about his sex life. Shyly at first, but with growing confidence, he recounts passionate kisses, unbuttoned shirts, fingers probing at waistbands, the squeezing of a nipple, a naked body on top of his. He names names. He gives us the when and where and how. Thoughtfully, without self-aggrandizement, he shares a chapter of his sexual history.

If it sounds an implausible scenario, it is. Men aren't good at talking about sex. Neither priests nor therapists, neither wives nor girlfriends, it seems, can persuade them to open up. And when alcohol does occasionally loosen their tongue, for the benefit of drinking partners, you can't trust and don't want to hear what they say. Only in a bookshop could you hope to find sensitivity and candour – which is where I heard the man in question talking: the writer Tony Gould, reading to an audience an autobiographical piece from the magazine *Granta*. It was a thoroughly endearing performance. But significantly, the events which he recalled not only go back forty years but happened with fellow male boarders at a public school. If the episodes had been more recent, and with women, the effect might have been far less engaging.

Less honest, too, perhaps. Heterosexual men seem to have trouble doing sex scenes these days. Nicholson Baker, writing about voyeurism and phone sex, is a candid exception. So are John Updike and Philip Roth, ageing Americans still prepared to have a go. Otherwise the story is one of growing male inhibition – a belief that some things are better not said. 'I'm not going into all that other stuff, the who-did-what-to-who stuff,' says Rob Fleming, hero of Nick Hornby's *High Fidelity*, in the middle of the novel's biggest sex scene. 'You know "Behind Closed Doors" by Charlie Rich? That's one of my favourite songs.' Salman Rushdie's Moraes Zogoiby feels even greater inhibitions in *The Moor's Last Sigh*: attempting to imagine how his parents first made love he soon breaks off '. . . no, men, I can't do this stuff.' There's a sense such stuff is no longer the right stuff. Even in a novel (where the people are made up) it's an intrusion and can't approximate what sex feels like from the inside. Sex isn't jaded by repetition; the language of sex is. How to convey the ever-pristine tactilities of desire, when so many others have got there first? How to write erotically without being coarse or clichéd? The most erotic moment in Julian Barnes's *A History of the World in 10½ Chapters*, from its parenthesis or half-chapter, is when the narrator describes the nape of his lover's neck. She is asleep and he is trying to be. The writing is sexy in part because the characters are not having sex.

For women novelists, who didn't used to be allowed, writing about sex is an exciting invitation rather than an ancient duty, and some approach the task with appetite. The few collections of women's erotica I've browsed through didn't do much for me, but they weren't supposed to. At least there's a freshness in the writing, even if (the male reader can't help but notice) the sex described is often with other women or items of fruit or domestic furnishings rather than with men. Gay novelists, too, have been energized by the excitement of breaking taboos.

Whereas the heterosexual male writer is weary with the knowledge that it's all been said, and said all too same-ily, before.

But male sexual inhibition isn't just a feature of literary culture. According to a recent survey, it's a national epidemic: we chaps would rather talk about anything else. We bottle things up, especially if we're from the north. If we've a sexual problem, or an emotional one, we pretend it doesn't exist and hope it will go away, taking refuge in sport or television. Holding our tongue, or turning away, we refuse the therapeutic benefits of a talkie culture.

Women, by contrast, think it's good to talk – about their lovers' sexual predilections, and about their own. Their mothers and grandmothers, lying back and thinking of England, may have suffered in silence. But – so the argument goes – young women in the nineties know what they want of men and aren't going to keep mum if they're not getting it. For men it's a perturbing thought: while we clam up, here are women sharing their (and our) most intimate bedroom secrets, telling their friends how adept we are at lovemaking, how long we can keep it up, and how we rate on the all-important matter of size. To which we assume the answers are: useless, briefly and small.

Of course, women who are married or in long relationships are far less likely to spill the beans about their men, unless those marriages or relationships are in trouble. But even they may feel quietly pleased that it's women who are talking dirty these days rather than men. After all, the visceral and physical has always been the natural homeland of women, so it's not simply a matter of taking over enemy territory. The taciturn, paranoid male should console himself with the thought that when women do talk and laugh about our bodies, it's often (so I'm told) affectionately, or at least without malice, even if sexually we've failed them. Lack of love, loyalty or truth are more important failures.

Besides, if men are newly mute and embarrassed, that may be no bad thing: there's still a loudmouth, wolf-whistling history to live down. The talk I heard about sex from other men as a teenager was mostly of a bragging or misogynistic kind. There wouldn't be many details beyond such and such a girl being hot, easy, a real goer, the town bike, all that. Boys then were expected to brag about having sex even if they hadn't, and girls to keep their mouths shut even if they had. Sex was a conning job, to be achieved with the minimum number of words (to her) beforehand and the maximum number (to your mates) afterwards. It was a horrible time. The extraordinary thing, in retrospect, was how quickly we passed from innocence to experience. At twelve, I knew nothing about sex and the first rumours made it sound so ugly and ridiculous that I formed a non-believers' club with a couple of other equally green flat-earthers. Within a few months, as the horrible truth dawned, the club had disbanded. Within a year, we were braying with the best of them.

Later, when longer and closer relationships with women became possible, there was an understanding that the talking had to stop. It would seem caddish, not laddish, to tell a mate, or mates, 'There's this thing she does where she . . .' Why would you want them to know this, about someone you loved or felt protective of or at any rate wanted to keep for yourself? Possessiveness, as well as chivalry, buttoned our lips – and still does. I've had conversations with men friends about their passions but not about positions; we've talked sperm-counts but not Kama Sutra. Maybe it's my age. Maybe I move in the wrong circles, or rather the right ones, away from the noisy conquistadors. But all the men I've asked about this say the same. It would be embarrassing. It would be disloyal. Their women's sexual secrets are safe with them. Stiff upper lip.

There are still a few indiscreet charmers around. The

success of Alan Clark's *Diaries* may have stemmed from its political gossip, but it helped that he was also a blabber of bedtime tales. There are also the men, less famous than Alan Clark, who have shared a sexual past with the Princess of Wales, say, or the Spice Girls – and shared it with us, too, in lucrative publishing deals. The tabloidization of our culture, the use of sexual confessions to sell newspapers or to bump up viewing figures, will prolong the existence of Don Juans – and Fanny Hills – who kiss and tell. Those who think the culture is as sexually obsessed as it can get may find they're mistaken. In all likelihood, for the next generation of biographers, it won't be enough to name, say, Samuel Beckett's lovers; there'll be stuff about the size and texture of his organ; there'll be memoirs that go 'There was this thing he liked to do where he . . .'

Yet candour isn't a relentless forward march. Kathleen Tynan's revelations, ten years ago, that her husband Ken was fond of spanking, sadomasochism and dressing up was neither shocking nor (since he'd advertised this himself) a betrayal of secrets. But the passages J. R. Ackerley wrote in *My Father and Myself* about his own 'sexual incontinence' are still startling thirty years on. For example:

> In truth, her love and beauty when I kissed her, as I
> often did, sometimes stirred me physically; but
> although I had to cope with her own sexual life and the
> frustrations I imposed upon it for some years, the
> thought of attempting to console her myself, even with
> my finger, never seriously entered my head. . . . The
> most I ever did for her was to press my hand against
> the hot swollen vulva she was always pushing at me at
> these times, taking the liquids upon my palm. This
> small easement was, of course, nearer the thing she
> wanted than to have her back, tail and nipples stroked.

Yet looking at her sometimes I used to think that the Ideal Friend, whom I no longer wanted, perhaps never had wanted, should have been an animal-man, the mind of my bitch, for instance, in the body of my sailor. . . .

For a man to write like this about a dog (Ackerley is here describing his Alsatian, Tulip) is risky – and braver than any author would dare to be today.

If heterosexual male authors are reluctant to write about sex, it's partly because candour isn't shocking any more, merely grungy and rather dubious. There's too much bad history in it, too much murk and braggadocio and triumphal swiving – with only men in a speaking part. Most anthologies of erotic verse are depressing, detumescing and solipsistic. However obsessional the author's attachment to his lover, what we end up hearing most about is himself. Boasting is compulsory. A high premium is placed on the theft of virginity. The penis is a pole, arrow or ramrod variously 'rammed', 'shot', 'shoved', 'thrust' and even 'posted' into the vaginal slot. There's also a good deal of conventional male 'wisdom', both nasty and uninformed, along the lines of 'all a woman needs is a good fuck' – as in this nineteenth-century poem, 'Origin of Copulation':

When sorrow torments lovely woman, oh dear,
A mighty good fucking will banish despair;
If her belly but aches, why we all know the trick,
There's nothing can ease it so well as a prick!

   A nice luscious prick!
   A stiff standing prick!
For any young maiden it can do the trick,
Oh, joys there are plenty, but nothing like prick!

Hearty rhythms, beer-swilling choruses and wham-bam attitudes aren't much to do with desire, but they're all that many male poets have left behind. There are honourable exceptions: Robert Herrick extolling the 'fleshy principalities' of his Julia, for example, or Paul Verlaine (wonderfully translated by Alistair Elliott), with his ingenious odes to the vagina – 'the watered silky gap, Mahomet's paradise', 'a soft box of plushy fluff'. But reading even the undeniably successful erotic classics now, it's hard not to be aware of all the silenced women who'd have liked to get out of bed and have their say.

In effect this is what the actress Claire Bloom does in her autobiography *Leaving the Doll's House*, and it makes her an icon for our age: the raw material taking revenge on literature. Having figured, she feels unflatteringly, in a number of novels by her ex-husband Philip Roth, she has decided to redraft the script through her own (non-fictional) account of their relationship. What angers her isn't so much his describing the sex they had but, rather, the sex they didn't have, the sex he (or his protagonist) had with other women. Well, she seems to be saying, two can play that game. She fights back by writing back. And Roth, for all the love she protests for him, comes across not as a charming, priapic Portnoy but as a mean wanker. It's deeply unfair on him: his novels are artifices, alternative versions of reality, not autobiographies. But in a culture which prizes candour, tricksiness is regarded as evasion, fiction as perjury, and an extra-marital sex scene as a confession of adultery. For the moment, despite his stupendous achievements, Roth's moment has passed.

There may be life yet in the tradition of sex-talk which he did his bit to usher in. But for now it's better if women do the talking and men save their breath for the sex.

The Trouble with Porn

The first woman I slept with kept pornography under her bed. The small, mild stack – *Penthouses* and *Playboys*, thrown in among innocuous *Titbits* – had been given to her by an older man who sometimes drove her home, and who hoped that by learning a thing or two about sex she might start fancying him. It didn't work. I doubted she fancied me much, either, but knowing the magazines were there gave my trips to her room an extra frisson: on the bed might be all adolescent fumbling and failure, but underneath lay fleshly perfection.

My inamorata, Sandra, was four years older than me and working as a housekeeper-cum-message-taker for my GP parents. What her attitude to porn was I could never work out. Sometimes she'd mock the mags, and speak cynically of the weakness and predictability of men in finding this sort of stuff *interesting*. But she kept them rather than handing them back to her suitor, and also presumably looked at them in private – as I did, when she wasn't around. Perhaps, male-oriented though they were, they even aroused her. Desire, I grasped, was a mysterious business. There were no rules. Who was to say?

There are still no rules. But there are laws, and some

pundits argue that there should be more. Over the last decade, the fundamentalists who want to ban pornography because it's immoral, or simply embarrassing, have been joined by feminists who regard it as abusive to women. Politics can make strange bedfellows, and this particular two-backed beast – a union of, as it were, Mary Whitehouse and Germaine Greer – is one of the oddest creations of our age.

What drives it is a belief that Man, or man, is an unbridled phallus, a prick on legs – a fallen creature, at his most fallen when erect. He is wily, and harbours dangerous wares. Showing porn to him is like saying 'Kill' to a trained guard dog. Women need protecting from him. Those, like poor Sandra, who have slipped into his clutches and acquired a taste for his porn habits, deserve only contempt. They are his dupes – the sell-outs, Uncle Toms, collaborators, scabs, fellow-travellers, tools, pawns, house niggers, puppets, suckers.

In the U.S., the lobby to restrict sexually expressive material has been more influential than here. Prominent among the 'procensors' are the law professor Catherine MacKinnon, author of *Only Words*, who has said that 'if pornography is part of your sexuality, then you have no right to your sexuality', and the novelist and polemicist Andrea Dworkin, author of *Letters from a War Zone* ('For fun they rape us or have other men or sometimes animals rape us and film the rapes and show the rapes in movie theaters or publish them in magazines'). Under the sway of such arguments, various institutions and state departments in the US have not only confiscated porno mags and videos from shops, but banned sex manuals, removed safe sex posters, withdrawn classical paintings (Goya's *Nude Maja* was one casualty), and suspended professors whose courses have been deemed guilty of having a sexual content. A new age is here, a 'culture of complaint' as Robert Hughes calls it, a tyranny of piety. Big Sister is watching us.

In *Defending Pornography: Free Speech, Sex and the Fight for Women's Rights*, Nadine Strossen passionately attacks the censorship lobby, and offers an indignant liberal defence of threatened freedoms. President of the American Civil Liberties Union, and (like Catherine MacKinnon) a feminist and law professor, she does not believe porn is harmful, sees no evidence that it leads to greater violence against women, and thinks it has been given too high a priority on the feminist agenda while more important battles remain unfought. Her argument – why women should *defend* pornography – may seem a little perverse at first. But historically it makes a kind of sense. Laws against freedom of sexual expression have always been antithetical to women's rights. Censorship is not an answer.

The mistake of the MacDworkinites, as she calls them, has been to treat sex as inherently degrading to women. In their gulag of sanctimony, all men are beasts and all women victims. (Dworkin: 'Intercourse with men as we know them is increasingly impossible.' MacKinnon: 'Compare victims' reports of rape with women's reports of sex. They look a lot alike . . .'.) But sexual expression can't be equated with sexism. Don't women feel desire, too, and doesn't some pornography cater for that? Forty per cent of porn video rentals in the US are now by women. Male strippers have begun to make a living. There is a growing market for erotic novels written by women for women, with an imprint such as Black Lace as much a part of the 1990s as Virago was to the 1970s. If this is what women want, it's condescending to call them dupes, and a patriarchal stereotype to suppose they need protecting from their own desires.

This is an issue, not just about porn, but about equality, or equivalence, of desire. Every Jill must have her Jack, and if that's not possible, she has as much right to jill-off to her material as he has to jack-off to his ('jill-off' is a phrase

Strossen uses: it was new to me). This is also an issue about defining women's sexuality – what they willingly choose, rather than are coerced, to do. If you think women perform fellatio, say, only to please their man, you will be in MacDworkin camp; if you think they can derive their own pleasure from it, in Strossen's.

To Strossen, the MacDworkinite line on gender difference isn't a defence of women but a betrayal of them – a tale of female weakness and male potency. Take the attempt to protect women from harassment in the workplace, by asking employees to refrain from all comment and imagery of a sexual nature. In 1993, for example, the University of Nebraska ordered a graduate teaching assistant to remove from his desk a photograph of his wife in a bathing suit, claiming that this photo created 'hostile-environment sexual harassment of female faculty, students and staff'.

How can measures like this possibly serve the interests of women, Strossen wonders, and she attacks 'the notion that *all* expressions, looks or gestures that recognize a woman's sexuality are somehow antithetical to her personhood'. Equality is one thing; treating women like children, or servants, in front of whom certain words may not be spoken, is another. How are women to reach the upper echelons of businesses and institutions if the men currently in positions of power are made paranoid about how to interact with them – if a climate is created where male and female colleagues can't ever relax, joke or talk dirty without the fear of legal comeback?

The erotophobes have also misunderstood the meaning of sexual images, Strossen believes. Male violence against women, for example, plays little or no part in most porn videos. Even if it did, why assume the incitement of a simplistic monkey-see, monkey-do reaction in the viewer? MacKinnon might equate a description of rape with the act itself, but images are not the same as deeds. What about women who have rape fantasies, or enjoy watching them harmlessly acted out on film: are they in need of a shrink? Or might such fantasies fulfil a healthy function, since the point about dreams of subordination (men have these too) is that they exempt us from the responsibility and pain we might feel in the real circumstances?

The nuances of sexual imagery, Strossen argues, are notoriously difficult to interpret. One person's turn-on is another's detumescence. She gives the example of Lina Wertmuller's 'artistically acclaimed' film, *Swept Away* (it actually sounds terrible), the story of a rich, teasing, haughty socialite on a yacht, who, after being marooned on an island, gets her sexual come-uppance from one of the crew she has previously taunted. Women have reacted very differently to this film: who is to decide for them if it is ideologically sound? And what difference would that make to their response, anyway? Even the crudest erotica raises complex questions of correctness. Take the stereotype of the 'come-shot' – the man ejaculating on to the body or into the face of a woman, who then smears the semen over her skin and licks it. A misogynistic archetype? Or a scenario which empowers women, since the male ejaculation, usually hidden from them, is here forced into the open? An aggressive image? Or one which shows men striving to become like women (the semen as milk, the male as mother to his suckling lover)? Hard to say. And a matter, therefore, on which no one should legislate.

Strossen's biggest argument with her opponents is that they *are* trying to legislate – and to stifle speech. She sees this as a threat to the First Amendment. She does not buy their distinction between 'criminal' and 'civil' suits – if anything, fear of a civil action may be more off-putting to a writer and artist who would like to make sexual expression part of his or her work. She describes the effects of MacDworkinism in Canada, where gay and lesbian bookshops have suffered more at the hands of busybodying customs officials than have the hard porn merchants.

Defending Pornography is a spirited and well-documented book. But it does have weaknesses. The worst of them is that Strossen romanticizes porn. All's rosy in her garden of love. Porn is educational, egalitarian, pluralistic, affirmative, health-giving, the resource of the shy, sad and disabled, the safest form of safe sex. Sex industry workers enjoy conditions 'less dangerous and onerous than those experienced by the women who labor in mills and on assembly lines'. Above all, porn – like high art – challenges establishment values. Every second- or third-rate porn hack who's tried to make a quick buck is welcomed into Strossen's gang of radical artists.

It's hard to reconcile this view of noble rebellion with the kind of bland Euro-porn to be seen on late-night channels or replayed in hotel rooms. Those pumping bums haven't much to do with radical chic. To watch a woman being penetrated both vaginally and anally at once can be diverting, and even educational in a how-do-they-do-that sort of way. But it doesn't get round the basic problem: boredom. The woman is aroused, to judge by her moans. The men are excited, to judge by their erections. But the eyes have a glazed solemnity, the bodies a grungy perfunctoriness, as if this were a work-out, not sexual union, let alone an act of love. And if even the par-ticipants are bored, how can the viewer not be?

Certainly, porn has its uses: like a pet dog, it can console the lonely; like oysters, it can sharpen a lover's appetite; like cocoa, it can get the restless off to sleep. In one form or another, it has been a part of most cultures since time began. But in a world of fake-intimacy, it has lost the power to outrage. Forty years ago, it was furtive – the prerogative of the dirty mac brigade and of men like Philip Larkin, that icon of the 1950s, writing to his chum Robert Conquest: '*Minuit Cinq* has some good rears in now and again, and I've taken out twelve months' sub.' But that age soon passed on to one of would-be Hefner wholesomeness, when mags were still bought mainly to wank to but buying them didn't make you a wanker. Young doctors and lawyers bought them. Students bought them. Men in sports cars bought them. It was healthy and virile. It was OK, at least for blokes.

The rise of feminism promised to destroy all that. To men of my generation, reaching their late teens or early twenties round the time *The Female Eunuch* was published, porn seemed dodgy, even alien. We were curious to see it, if shown, but felt honour-bound not to buy it or keep it around the house. We'd been made aware how it commodified female flesh – to collect it would have been an insult to our girl-friends. Abstention can be a good feeling sometimes, a guard against the development of bad habits. We abstained, and assumed that porn would go away – that it was a bad old Dad thing, soon to pass. We were wrong. It didn't. It simply got bolder. The only shocking thing about porn now, in Europe at least, is that it doesn't shock at all. There is a shrug factor which Nadine Strossen, writing from a transatlantic perspective, doesn't address.

As well as being soft on the soft stuff, she underestimates the nastiness of the hard. Whether Linda Lovelace partici-pated willingly in *Deep Throat* or not, there's no doubt that some women are forced by economic necessity to pose or act in ways that encourage ugly male attitudes to the opposite sex. 'The only thing pornography is known to cause,' Gore Vidal has said, 'is the solitary act of masturbation.' A com-forting thought. But even that solitary act can have a social outcome, as the semen-glued pages of public library books testify. And it seems blind or wilful of Nadine Strossen to deny that porn can sometimes have more serious conse-quences – at the very least, a tendency for some men to see women as objects, to be used with indifference or brutality.

In 1978, in New Cross, south-east London, I had an epiphany. I was running a poetry group at Goldsmiths' College, and the writer D.M. Thomas came along to read his work. Afterwards, we went to the pub – not the regular, where a darts match was going on, but a less salubrious one nearby. The bar was oddly quiet for 9.30 p.m. but music was coming from a back room and a steady stream of punters passed through, beer-glasses in hand. Curious, Thomas and I went to look. The room was bare but for a semicircle of about forty men gathered by the far wall with their backs to us. Wandering across and peering over their shoulders, we saw what they were looking at. A naked woman aged thirty or so lay with her head against the wall and, in time to the music, slowly swivelled her hips along the line of the semicircle, opening and closing her raised legs as she did: *now you look at my cunt, now you look at it, and now you.* After a bit, she stood up and, grabbing a pint glass from one of her audience, poured beer over her pubic hair, smeared it around, then flicked it at the nearest onlooker. A couple of men jeered and *ugh*ed at this, as if to say: *slut, slag.* The woman was contemptuous in return, her gyrations seeming to mock our puny voyeurism, our willingness to pay (there'd been a whip-round, donations of 50p into a pint glass) for a snatch of snatch. I don't know what Thomas got out of the experience (he published *The White Hotel* three years later), but for me it was a lesson in the bleakness of porn, and the mutual antagonism it can encourage. Male stripping is a different matter: it's not about sex but naughtiness; it encourages women to laugh more than to leer. But when women perform for men, fun doesn't come into it.

Catherine MacKinnon wants to ban and outlaw porn because it incites men to rape, murder and child abuse. She quotes the case of Thomas Schiro, whose defence for having sexually assaulted and murdered a woman in Indiana in 1981 was that he would 'get [so] horny from looking at girly books and watching girly shows that I would want to go rape somebody'. Nadine Strossen rightly argues that acceptance of such a defence – 'porn made me do it' – would remove essential notions of culpability and intentionality. She cites counter-evidence to show that in parts of the world where porn has become more freely available – Japan, Scandinavia – the number of violent sex crimes has gone down. She makes her case persuasively: if you ban all ideas and images which might be unsafe, almost nothing worth having will be left. But she doesn't say enough about the undoubted link between child sexual abuse and paedophile porn. And I wish she weren't quite so cheerful about dirty mags and movies, so excitable about the wonderfully infinite variety of the human imagination. A bit of gloomy, post-coital scepticism would have done no harm.

As she battles it out with her two adversaries (though one of her complaints is that in the real world the other two won't meet and debate with her), you begin to appreciate their different strengths. Nadine Strossen has the most command of the relevant information and research. Catherine MacKinnon has the keenest intellect. Andrea Dworkin is the liveliest phrase-maker ('Romance is rape embellished with meaningful looks', 'In seduction the rapist bothers to buy a bottle of wine'). You also hear the echo of other, older, bigger wars in American culture: redskin versus paleface; pioneer versus puritan; individual freedom versus public law. The signs, in the current censorship battle, are that the ground is shifting, and that MacDworkinism has begun to lose the argument. But to the punters with their books, mags, videos, satellite channels and p.c.s, it won't make much difference anyway. Legal or not, under the bed or on the Internet, spiced for nerds or groomed for women, porn is here to stay.

Hymns to Him

'Nothing is more obdurate to artistic treatment than the carnal,' E. M. Forster wrote to Siegfried Sasson in 1920, 'but it has to be got in, I'm sure: everything has to be got in.' Forster himself didn't get the carnal in, not even into *Maurice*, the novel he locked away for fifty years and published only posthumously and post-Wolfenden. But Forster's successors have done a little better. Freed from the laws which forced gay writers into silence or coded 'sensitivity', they've recounted with libidinous candour the love that men can feel for each other's bodies.

Alan Hollinghurst's deeply English but bravely carnal *The Swimming-Pool Library*, in 1988, was some kind of turning-point ('Seeing again how his cock was held in his little blue briefs I was almost sick with love, fondled it and kissed it through the soft sustaining cotton'). But even before that there was Edmund White, with the autobiographical fiction of *A Boy's Own Story* and *The Beautiful Room is Empty*, a sequence that now concludes with *The Farewell Symphony*, a novel both tender and brutal in its honesty: 'I moved easily from one man to the next, my hand sifting through long hair, my lips grazing a soft moustache, my cock engulfed by a hot mouth that like a glass-blower's would make grow and glow through its motion a shape and an urgency.'

A male heterosexual who finds such passages of joy (to use Thom Gunn's phrase) interesting and even enjoyable may start to wonder about himself: so, they were right, I must be poufy after all. But the answer may be more banal, the excitement a literary one. After the limp exhaustion of most contemporary male writing about sex with women, White and Hollinghurst look fresh and energetic.

The energy is partly the elation of breaking new ground. Ten years ago, if not now, a gay novelist could feel uninhibited by precedent. The tradition of Forster and Firbank is eloquent, but it includes very little speaking, plain or otherwise, about the male body – about foreskins and shafts and scrotal sacs, about nipples 'the colour of a drop of blood when it tinctures a basin full of water' and 'balls light and tender as seedless grapes or big and veined like walnuts', about skin as 'warm to the touch as a clay pot left out in the sun'. The territory has always been there, but Edmund White was one of the first novelists to report what it looks and feels like. The image is often flattering, rose-tinted with desire ('basalt-hard' penises, etc.), but not always. 'His mouth tasted slightly sour, like a mildewed washcloth', he writes of one lover. And of another: 'his skin no longer looked like sugar dissolving in a spoon but had taken on the grainy, tobacco-stained hue of old piano keys'. Flab, bad odours, bald patches and excess body-hair are here, too, part of the truth that can't be left out. These hymns to Him are more tactile than anything since the Song of Solomon.

Not everyone can appreciate such writing, even when it avoids the horny clichés and come-on lyricisms of the flesh. There are those who dislike carnal prose in general, and those who'll be turned off by the particular carnalities here described, as well as those (whether women or male heterosexuals),

who can't help but feel excluded. But White isn't only preaching to the inverted. His ideal reader, he says, was until recently
'an imaginary European heterosexual woman', who functioned
for him as a filter, a corrective, someone with whom he could-
n't exchange knowing looks. And even now that Aids and
activism have made him turn for readers to 'other gay men,
young and old', he remains faithful to 'the old ambition of
fiction', to collar strangers and look them sympathetically in
the eye.

To win over strangers, you mustn't be too strange yourself.
Though White depicts himself as uncertain and sometimes
isolated when young, and still deeply conscious of belonging
to a minority, he comes across as gregarious, engaging, good
company. There's a Whitmanesque generosity about him,
both physical and spiritual, and a lack of snobbism, however
refined his aesthetic taste. There are elements in his work of
Proust and Henry James, but he hasn't their physical recoil
and fastidiousness. He's uncertain, too, and not afraid to admit
it, turning his confusion into wise, wistful oxymorons about
love and loss, polygamy and monogamy, Europe and America,
and the vanity of human wishes. Some of the best sections in
The Farewell Symphony narrate, not picaresque adventures in
the flesh trade, but his relationship with his mother, father,
sister, nephew and several women who unwisely fell in love
with him. He's also fascinating on the subject of his literary
ambition. For many years he ached to be published, as if it
were a kind of canonization and only then he'd be redeemed
and vindicated. Once successful, he felt more isolated than
ever and began to write 'out of a mild curiosity about what I'd
invent rather than from a searing need to impose myself on
the world'.

'Happiness writes white', said Montherlant, meaning that
when you're happy you never need put pen to paper. But this
White (who once co-authored *The Joy of Gay Sex*) is very good

at writing happiness, at recapturing sexual delights, delicious meals and funny conversations, always with that elegiac undertow that reminds us they can't last. His metaphors, whether pared or (more usually) lush, suggest a poet *manqué*. And the best of his analogies are reserved for touch: 'warm showers of sparks trailed his hand, as though my flesh were the phosphorescing sea in August.'

White's poetry would get the better of him if he weren't also an astute social commentator, an 'archaeologist of gossip', and an unblinking eyewitness to the changing mores of gay men over the past forty years. In the 1950s, White thought he was the only one; by the late 1960s 'we were everywhere, an army, the coming thing'; in the 1970s, the 'clone' look developed – moustaches and white T-shirts – and White, in love with idiosyncrasy, hated it, though not as much as he hated the 'puritanical disease' that came along in the 1980s. It's all here: the tricking and cruising, the tops and bottoms, the remaking of Fire Island and Manhattan. At one point White describes a club in New York called The Mineshaft, at the centre of which is a wall with saucer-sized holes at waist height – 'glory holes' – through which faceless guys stick their cocks to get sucked off by unseen mouths the other side. To most hets, it's a vision of hell: even at our most perversely polymorphic, we don't come near to this. And yet the rampancy and neediness and addiction are recognizable enough.

White estimates that in thirty years he must have had 3,120 partners, on the basis of three a week. But he is also irresistibly drawn to the notion of the couple. A central theme of *The Farewell Symphony* is the pull towards sensation, novelty and plurality on the one hand and, on the other, a stable relationship with Mr Right ('I wanted to be his wife in the most strait-laced of marriages'). Both, to White, are impossible ideals, which doesn't make them any less worth pursuing. He is an American optimist but also a homosexual pessimist, who knows (and wishes women would, too) that 'of course men betray you, of course love is an illusion dispelled by lust, of course you end up alone'. Promiscuous yet uxorious, his book recalls both the high points of casual sex and the four enduring loves in his (or his narrator's) life: Sean, Kevin, Joshua and Brice.

Brice's death from Aids not only begins and ends the book, but casts a shadow on everything in between. It is, as White puts it, what makes a Gorky comedy about an endless summer house party end up as a terse Greek tragedy. Little is said about the illness. Little needs to be said. Implicit in all the carnal pleasures is the day of their curt removal. As well as Brice's death there are others, briskly catalogued or tearfully mourned. The novel attains a mythic quality, a legend of Paradise and Paradise Lost. For a brief, glorious period, its protagonists dwell in an Edenic community, 'redolent of summer camp', where sex is 'a game of touch-tag'; then comes the Fall. That almost every contemporary gay novel has this story to tell – the growth and decimation of a community based on sexual preference – doesn't make it any less compelling. It is a tale full of love and pathos, and Edmund White is its master chronicler.

4

Canons and
Controversies

The Nobel Cause

Each autumn, on a Thursday morning in Stockholm, a strange ritual takes place. In an elegant eighteenth-century room, around a long table, under a high chandelier, before a bust of King Gustav III, a dozen or so men and women write down a name on a piece of paper. The pieces of paper are then collected in a *stop*, an antique silver tankard or drinking mug, and the names are totted up. At 1 p.m. exactly, the secretary or delegate of these men and women leaves the room, walks through a grand hall (more busts and chandeliers), and arrives in his office, where a number of journalists have gathered. He reads to them the name that has recurred most often on those pieces of paper. In this way, each October, the winner of the Nobel Prize for Literature is delivered to the world.

The stately ceremonials surrounding the announcement of the Nobel Prize are calculated to suggest that the decision in Stockholm is arrived at with diligence, taste, impartiality, wisdom, a deep sense of history and an imperviousness to all outside pressures, especially commercial ones. This is not how the rest of the world always sees it. *Uncommercial?* The value of this year's Nobel Prize will be 7.2 million kronor (some

£700,000), a sum which means that, for the first time, the value of the prize in real terms will be greater than it was on its inauguration in 1901 (and this isn't even to mention the vast ensuing book sales). *Impervious to lobbying?* They don't think so down in Wales, where the Arts Council, the Welsh Academy and the *New Welsh Review* magazine have formed a committee to promote the cause of the poet R. S. Thomas. The committee has written to various professors asking for nominations or support. They hope that the Swedish poets and novelists who recently visited the Hay-on-Wye Literature Festival will have sensed the high regard for Thomas. They even have the support of Thomas himself, who's known to be 'difficult' but is reported to be quietly chuffed.

Impartial? The Nobel committee is often accused of political expediency, and of bias. Wasn't the award to Boris Pasternak in 1958 a diplomatic manoeuvre in the Cold War? Was it just coincidence that the Finnish writer Frans Eemil Sillanpää won in 1939 (when Finland was pluckily resisting the Soviet Union) or that the Polish writer Czeslaw Milosz received the award in 1980 (the year of Solidarity and the shipyard strike in Gdansk)? Wasn't the reason Jorge Luis Borges failed to win the laureateship that he was once photographed shaking hands with General Pinochet? There have been complaints of geographical prejudice, of First Worldism, too. Why were there only two winners from outside Europe and the US in the prize's first forty-five years? Has there been a bias towards French writers (twelve winners from France and Belgium) which is now being over-corrected (only one French winner in the last thirty-five years)? Haven't too many Scandinavians won the prize (seven Swedes, three Norwegians, two Danes, an Icelander and a Finn: fourteen winners in the prize's first seventy-four years) for it to be considered a true reflection of world literature?

And then, aside from the alleged intrusion of extra-literary considerations, there's the matter of literary *taste*, or the lack of it. Question 1: What do Sully Prudhomme, Bjørnstjerne Bjørnson, José Echegaray, Selma Lagerlöf, Carl Spitteler, Władysław Stanisław Reymont, Roger Martin du Gard, Pearl Buck, Halldór Kiljan Laxness, Shmuel Yosef Agnon, Ivo Andrić, Bertrand Russell and Winston Churchill have in common? Answer: they all won the Nobel Prize for Literature. Question 2: What do Tolstoy, Ibsen, Strindberg, Zola, Hardy, Gorky, Freud, Mandelstam, Akhmatova, Joyce, Conrad, D. H. Lawrence, Lorca, Rilke, Stevens, Brecht, Nabokov, Lowell and Calvino have in common? Answer: they all failed to. It's easy to play such name-games, and many commentators over the years have played them unfairly, invoking the omissions of Proust and Kafka, for example, to lambast the inadequacy of the prize, when those writers gained their reputations posthumously and couldn't realistically have been Nobel candidates. All the same, the list of choices since the inception of the Nobel Prize in 1901 inevitably raises a question or two about the choosers. Can they be trusted? How can we tell that all's above board?

The shorter answer is: we can't. The eighteen members of the Swedish Academy – those entrusted with the task of choosing the Nobel Literature laureate – are sworn to secrecy over their deliberations. What goes on in their committee meetings, the nominations, reports, minutes, memos, letters and discussions: all information about this is embargoed for fifty years. A brief citation of the merits of each new Laureate is all the press is given at the time of the award. The bureacracy of decision-making – the when, where and how as well as the why and who – remains largely unknown. The ebb and flow of favoured names, the numbers of votes cast, the identity of those writers who may have just missed out: none of this can be revealed. A bland sentence or two in literary-critical praise of the new laureate, and the rest is gossip or silence.

Frustrating though the policy can be, it's easy to sympathize with the Swedish Academy's pledge of secrecy and its mistrust of the press. Until 1976, the year Saul Bellow won the prize, the Academy had an understanding with the four quality Swedish newspapers that they be tipped off forty-eight hours ahead of the announcement provided they respect the embargo. But that year a television company was somehow leaked the laureate's name, broke the embargo, forced the newspapers to break it in turn, and caused panic and outrage in the Academy. There were also, in the 1970s and 1980s, several indiscretions from one of the Academy's members, Artur Lundkvist, the man widely credited with denying the Nobel to Graham Greene: in various ill-judged interviews, the voluble Lundkvist showed more of the inner sanctum than his colleagues felt appropriate. Since Lundkvist's death, members of the Academy have kept their mouths shut, if only to avoid embarrassments such as that in 1959 of long-time hopeful Alberto Moravia, who, tipped off that the prize was about to go to Italy, threw a party to celebrate his success – only to learn that it had gone to his countryman Salvatore Quasimodo. The story may be apocryphal, but it's part of Nobel legend, which is becoming tarnished by gossip. The danger is that open admission of the Academy's deliberations will reduce media coverage of the Nobel Prize to a bitchy pageant of winners and losers. Besides, how many writers would welcome learning the reasons they were denied the world's highest literary honour? This way at least, there's some gravitas.

All the same, the secrecy sits oddly with Sweden's reputation as a progressive, liberal and open society, and anyone encountering it for the first time, as I did, may be shocked to see how far its ripples spread. Several insiders I wrote to – in

advance of a visit to Stockholm – failed to reply, or replied
only with refusals to speak. The distinguished journalist Bengt
Holvqvist, a seasoned observer of the prize in the Swedish
newspaper *Dagens Nyheter*, declined to meet me 'because of an
incident a few years ago' when his views were misrepresented.
The few sources who were prepared to talk asked that most of
what they said be off the record. Even the Swedish Academy
itself was slow to respond to letters and faxes, and though its
permanent secretary, Sture Allén, eventually proved helpful
and obliging, by the time I met him I'd begun to despair not
so much of penetrating the inner sanctum as of gaining admission to the entrance lobby.

Why was everyone so clandestine? Before I reached
Stockholm I'd been made to suspect that the grave and noble
arbiters of the Nobel Prize for Literature are operating inside
one of the most festering, paranoid, gossip-driven literary
communities in the world. I'd begun to hear what George
Eliot (who died too early to be a Nobel laureate) called 'the
roar that lies the other side of silence'.

Stockholm, in late August, is already autumnal. The middle
classes have returned from their holidays at northern lakes and
archipelagoes. The schools are back, the light has gone by eight,
people wear overcoats against the chill, ice-skates dominate the
windows of sports shops. Built on a range of islands where Lake
Malaren meets the Baltic, a city as dominated by water as
Amsterdam and Copenhagen, Stockholm is quiet, unstressed –
a metropolis to fall asleep in. Three crowns – the emblem of a
nation that has not only kept its king and queen, but, unlike
Britain, allowed them to keep their dignity, too – glow from the
spire of City Hall. Green roofs of patinated copper dominate
the skyline. Cobbled alleys, churches, drinking fountains make
Gamla Stan, the old town, a delight to wander through. The
city is proud of its record of beating pollution: the brochures

boast that you can swim or catch salmon right at its heart (and I did see a man land a perch from a bridge near the royal palace). Stockholm loves to be thought clean, right-minded, above controversy, beyond reproach.

Though the city is generously endowed with statues of its kings, queens, leaders, poets and artists, there's a curious lack of memorials to Alfred Nobel, born here in 1833 and arguably its most famous citizen: no plaque, no museum, not even a monument in the park named after him. Perhaps the lack stems from embarrassment, in a neutral or pacifist nation, that Nobel made most of his money from the invention and production of explosives. It seems unlikely, or unfair if true: as well as the philanthropic use to which he put his profits, Nobel was ahead of his time in providing welfare for his employees, never experienced a strike in any of his factories, and developed nitroglycerine so that it had many benefical social effects. But whatever the reasons, the only legacy of Nobel in Stockholm is a disused factory to the south of the city, a long red-brick building which is plaqueless, barred and boarded-up.

Like other great Scandinavians, Alfred Nobel was a misanthrope. Cosmopolitan, widely read, fluent in five languages, he was always on the move – he had homes in six countries – and over the years his loneliness grew. Despite two close relationships with women, he never married or had children. Which is why, when he died in 1896, he was able to put the major part of his estate, some 31 million Swedish kronor (the equivalent of 1500 million kronor, or £150 million, by today's standards) towards the establishment of five annual prizes awarding those in the fields of physics, chemistry, medicine, literature and 'fraternity among nations' (peace) who 'during the preceding year have conferred the greatest benefit on mankind'. Nobel's heirs contested the will, which he'd drawn up without the help of a lawyer, and it took three years to settle. The prize structure was complex: specialist bodies were empowered to make the choice of laureates, while a Nobel foundation looked after administration and investment. The Swedish Academy, to whom fell the task of choosing the Literature prizewinner, was hesitant about shouldering the burden: some members didn't want to be part of 'a cosmopolitan tribunal'. Even when the first laureate was named in 1901, the then Permanent Secretary, Carl David af Wirsén, felt misgivings enough to recite the following poem at the Nobel banquet:

> *Unwished the task, unsought for, bearing now*
> *so weightily on Swedish backs; it seems*
> *we tremble taking obligation's vow:*
> *henceforth a world will deem how Sweden deems.*

In the event, not even Sweden deemed how Sweden deemed: Sully Prudhomme, the first laureate, was such an obviously poor choice, arrived at because the committee were unduly influenced by a block vote in the nomination from the French Academy, that forty-two Swedish writers wrote an open address to Leo Tolstoy, disassociating themselves from the decision and paying homage to the writer whom they believed should have been laureate. Tolstoy replied that he was 'very glad' not to be given the award: the prize money would have brought 'nothing but evil'. His comment ensured that he would not win the Nobel Prize in any subsequent year, either.

Already, in its inaugural year, a basic pattern in the award and reception of the Literature prize had been established: a debatable choice; attacks on the Swedish Academy, not least from other Swedish writers; rows; a suggestion that the prize can do its recipient more harm than good; petulance on all sides. Ninety-five years on, the essential ingredients have

scarcely altered. Only the Peace prize has shown a similar
power to incite war and strife. In death as well as life, Alfred
Nobel was dynamite.

On the face of it, the procedure for judging the Literature
Prize seems uncontentious enough. It works like this. To be
considered, candidates must be formally nominated, though
any candidate nominating himself (and it does happen) is
automatically disqualified. Nominations, which have to arrive
by February 1st of the relevant year, can come from the following sources: 1. The Swedish Academy or similar national
academies and institutions; 2. Professors of history of literature and language; 3. Nobel laureates in literature; 4.
Presidents of authors' organizations (such as PEN).
Surprisingly, given that rule 2 allows any literature or language professor in the world to suggest a candidate, the
Academy receives only 'several hundred' nominations annually (evidently vast numbers of professors of literature and
language are unaware, or fail to avail themselves of this privilege). Some two hundred names will recur among the several
hundred nominations, and if there are any obvious oversights
and omissions ('Why hasn't Updike's name come in this
year?') the Academy itself can fill the gaps.

A five-man subcommittee of the Academy – the Nobel
committee – then begins to consider the two hundred names.
Very quickly, the list comes down to fifteen. Four or five more
meetings between late February and late May reduce the list
further, until a maximum of six names are presented to a full
session of the Academy. These are debated and sometimes
altered, but a shortlist is arrived at before the summer recess
begins on May 31st. The Swedish Academy does not meet
again until mid-September. The three and a half months'
break – which many members spend away at retreats like
Gotland – allow time for the shortlisted candidates to be read

in depth, which means re-read and *read about*, in literary-critical essays and specialist reports.

On return from their lands of midnight sun, each member of the Nobel committee presents a paper giving his or her choice. Debate follows at each Thursday evening session (5 p.m.–6.30 p.m.), until there seems to be a majority – at which point a morning meeting is called for the following Thursday, in anticipation of a verdict and announcement. The expectation is that this will happen 'in mid-October', but the date is never fixed (and is publicly announced only forty-eight hours ahead), and in theory a decision might not be arrived at until November. If there still isn't a majority verdict, the prize can be held over. In all, the prize has been 'reserved' – deferred to the following year – on six occasions, though the last time this happened was in 1949.

The decision process sounds as dutiful, bureacratic and incorruptible as you'd expect of the Swedes. But what, I wanted to know, of the decision-makers? Who are they exactly? And how heavily do their shoulders sag from the burden of deeming for the world?

Though I have been given an address for the Swedish Academy, in Stockholm's old town, it takes me a little time to find the discreet nameplate to the left of the door. To the right of the door – this partly explains my confusion – is a garish, illuminated screen giving the latest world share prices. I hadn't realized that the Academy's headquarters are situated on a floor of the Swedish Stock Exchange. Art and Mammon sharing the same premises: it's not inappropriate, given that the Nobel Prize, unlike most other literary prizes, brings immense riches to its recipient.

I ring the second-floor bell, which is answered by a neat, handsome man in his mid-sixties, who looks a bit like a genial, tidied-up version of the late Anthony Burgess and whose shoulders don't seem to sag at all. The door opens straight into his cavernous office, large-windowed, late-eighteenth-century in decor, with busts, a ticking clock, and a large desk at the centre. The Swedish Academy, he explains, was founded in 1786, by King Gustav III, who wanted to set up an institution along the lines of the French Academy to preserve and enrich Swedish language and literature. Most of its aims and traditions – as well as the furnishings, it seems – have been faithfully preserved. For instance, King Gustav wished the Academy to give advice on correct linguistic usage, and to this end work began on a dictionary. After two early abortive efforts – one where each academician was allocated a different letter of the alphabet, another which got no further than A – a third dictionary was begun in the 1880s. By 1920, it threatened to swell to such proportions that it would never be finished, and had to be rationalized. Now, it's progressing well, and has reached volume thirty-one, the letter S. Sture Allén smiles wryly. Yes, S for slow: 209 years after its establishment, the Academy still has no dictionary to its name. The Swedes don't like to rush things.

King Gustav also wished the Academy to promote poetry and oratory through competitions, and the Academy still administers a number of prizes, indeed an increasing number of them year by year: The Royal prize, the Bellman prize, the Swedish Language prize, the Drama prize, the Kellgren prize, the Nordic prize, the Finland prize, the Swedish teaching prize. There is a great list of these prizes, over fifty in all. There is even one called the Great prize, not to be confused with that other great prize, the Nobel. The Swedish Academy, I'm made to understand, concerns itself with many different matters. Members are not paid, except for work on subcommittees, but they do traditionally receive a silver coin or plaquette, bearing the motto *Snille och Smak* (Genius and Discretion), each time they attend. Tradition also decrees that meetings may be followed with a meal of pea soup and pancakes at *Den Gyldene Freden* (The Golden Peace), a restaurant donated to the Academy by the artist Anders Zorn. I catch the drift. There is much more to life on the Swedish Academy than the Nobel.

But the Nobel is what it's most famous for, and Sture Allén is happy to answer questions, so long as they don't bear on individual names. We discuss, for example, Nobel's stipulation that the Literature prize go to (as the English translation has it) 'work of an idealistic tendency'. Allén, a linguist, believes that this is a mistranslation, or misreading. The word Nobel used, *idealisk*, is comparatively rare. Early on it was taken to mean spiritually uplifting, even positive, which is why Tolstoy and Ibsen were denied the award. It may be better translated as 'suitable' or 'perfect', or it may suggest 'belonging to the realm of ideas'. Allén is urging the Nobel foundation to consider a better definition. Matters of language like this are regularly pondered by the Academy.

But who exactly *are* the Academicians who decide the Nobel? Sture Allén hands me a list of the eighteen current members. Roughly half are poets or novelists, and half are academics, and a few are a bit of both. Each member is elected for life and is expected, upon taking up office, to pay tribute in a long speech and monograph to his illustrious predecessor, without whose death the opportunity for him to be elected would not have arisen. 'He' is, or was, the operative word. For many years after the war, there were no women members of the Academy, which helps explain why, astonishingly, there was only one female winner, or half-winner, of the Nobel Prize – the Swede Nelly Sachs, who shared it in 1966 with the Israeli Shmuel Yosef Agnon – between 1945 and 1991. Now there are four women members of the Academy, and there have been two female laureates – Nadine Gordimer and Toni Morrison – in the past four years.

Sture Allén busily stresses the qualifications of the members who aren't practising writers: this one is a philologist, that one a sinologist, these two are historians. In the old days, it was common to have a religious man on board – not now, though there is still a lawyer, a former high-court judge. The judge is one of the longer-serving members, but far from the oldest. That honour falls to Johannes Edfelt, a poet and translator, who is ninety. There are two other academicians of eighty-seven and eighty-five, and seven more in their seventies. The average age of the Swedish Academy is 70.5, and was older until the recent appointment of young Katarina Frostensen (b. 1953), whose arrival quietened complaints in the press about senility, sclerosis and ancient (male) members having to be carried into meetings. Sture Allén doesn't think septuagenarianism a disqualification. Election to the Academy has traditionally been an honouring of a writer's lifetime achievement. So, too, is the award of the Nobel Prize for Literature, though ideally it will be given to writers with their best work still ahead of them – Gabriel García Márquez's *Love in the Time of Cholera* was written after his award in 1982. Having older writers do the choosing hasn't meant younger ones aren't chosen: Joseph Brodsky was only forty-seven when he became laureate in 1987.

Sweden is a country where even the less educated speak at least two languages, and where the more educated, like those in the Academy, often read three or four – a great advantage when judging world literature. For writers from less familiar language groups, the Academy calls on specialists, and if a serious candidate hasn't been translated into Swedish it commissions its own translation: an expensive process, but the Nobel foundation has the will and the wallet to make it happen. Sture Allén shows me The Nobel library, across the corridor from his office, which was set up specifically to help the Academy's deliberations. With 200,000 volumes, it now

houses the country's finest collection of world literature –
periodicals and reference books as well as novels and slim volumes and (in the archive) those specially commissioned
translations. Its existence is yet more evidence of how
seriously the Academy takes its role, and of how discreetly it
operates: when a new candidate swims into ken, and the
eighteen members each need to be furnished with the relevant
books, copies have to be obtained from a variety of sources, so
as not to arouse suspicions or raise hopes. 'Our main task is to
be ahead of the game,' librarian Carola Hermelin tells me.
'We try to choose the books that are worth having for the
Academicians. The ideal situation is that we already have
them before they ask.' A good translation of a foreign author
by a talented Swede will carry more weight with the Academy
than any amount of lobbying.

Back in Sture Allén's office, Kjell Espmark has arrived.
Poet, novelist, literary historian, and chairman of the Nobel
Prize committee, he seems a dry man, a bit of a sobersides, but
his own work, by all accounts, shows there's a volcano underneath: his satirical portrait of a newspaper editor in one recent
novel is, I'm assured, 'as vicious as Strindberg'. In 1991,
Espmark published a study of 'the criteria behind the choices'
of the Nobel Prize, an insider's view, an apologia in parts, but
by far the most informative account of the prize ever written.
The book shows how different chairmen over the century
have pushed different tendencies. The early years were disastrous, inclined to honour writers who were religious, royalist
and reactionary. Round the 1914–18 war, the vogue was for
'neutralism'. Between the wars, populist novelists fared better
than modernist poets. After 1945 came the glorious years of
Anders Österling (who honoured pioneers such as Hesse,
Gide, Eliot and Faulkner) and to a lesser extent of Dag
Hammarskjöld, later Secretary-General to the UN, an influential Nobel committee voice. Österling's successor was Lars

Gyllensten (a chairman anxious not to be Eurocentrist), who was in turn succeeded by Espmark (ditto). Between 1985 and 1995 there was only one laureate from Europe, and Nigeria, Egypt, Mexico, St Lucia and Japan were among those to claim the crown. When I put it to him that this is a concerted new policy, Espmark admits:

> Yes, the tendency in recent years has been to broaden the horizon – though on exclusively literary grounds. The Academy didn't have the resources in the past to be genuinely universal. In the last ten years, we've tried very hard to do what should have been done from the beginning. What's most important now is the possibility of directing the attention of the literary world towards writers who would otherwise remain little read. But it must be remembered that the only criterion is literary, not political. And it's still possible for the prize to go to someone like García Márquez, who sells millions.

Both Allén and Espmark deny, even without my making them, the old allegations against the prize committee: that it tries to give each nation its turn; that it's anti-women or (now) pro-women; that its choices can be deadly dull because of fudge and compromise; that it's swayed by politics. 'You have to realize,' says Allén, 'that the Swedish Academy has nothing to do with our government, or with any company or organization – it's completely autonomous.' He's right, of course. But in the past it looked after itself a bit indulgently. There is a photograph, in the Academy's own booklet, of a meeting of its members, all men, in October 1975. They seem a happy group, as well they might be. The previous October, two of them – upper left, Eyvind Johnson, bottom right Harry Martinson – jointly shared the Nobel Prize for Literature.

Though these two wouldn't have been allowed a vote, they were hardly unknown to their colleagues, with whom they'd done weekly Academy business for years. 'Statistically speaking,' Kjell Espmark admits, 'too many Scandinavians have won the prize', which is a way of putting it. Though Sweden now has a deserving candidate, the poet Tomas Tranströmer, he can't hold out much hope.

The clock strikes twelve: time, it's courteously suggested, that I leave. Despite the Academy's reputation for secrecy, there is hardly any question its two representatives have been reluctant to answer. To conclude, Sture Allén takes me to the 'session room' where, one Thursday every October, the Academy casts its vote. The room is quiet, cut off from the world, blissfully free of political or media pressure. I notice only one oddity. Though there are eighteen members of the Academy, there are only fourteen chairs round the table. Not every member attends in person, Allén explains; some cast their votes by post. It seems a bit bizarre, not bothering to put in an appearance when you're a judge of the greatest literary prize in the world and this is its most important meeting. But I let it pass, shake hands, and leave.

It's only later I see the connection between the missing chairs and the one matter Sture Allén has been embarrassed to talk about, the resignation of three members of the Swedish Academy in the late 1980s. After the *fatwa* against Salman Rushdie was issued by Ayatollah Khomeini in February 1989, the Swedish authors and writers' groups, very strong on human rights, put pressure on the Academy to sign a statement to the government in support of Rushdie. The members voted not to: though committed to freedom of excpression, in its two hundred-year history it had never, as a body, made political interventions of that kind; expressions of support for Rushdie were a matter for individual members, it decided, not the Academy as a whole. But two members, the former chairman Lars Gyllensten and the novelist Kerstin Ekman, disagreed with this decision and resigned. And a third member, the poet Werner Aspenstrom, never a man for committees, saw the opportunity to liberate himself and followed suit.

Rushdie himself now says that, 'though grateful for the gesture of support, I'm sad, embarrassed and even rather appalled that because of me the Academy was split. The feeling I got was that the divisions were already there.' There has since been some bridge-building between Rushdie and the Academy: in 1992, he was invited to lecture there, from the same podium where the newly elected Nobel laureate gives his acceptance speech – a rare honour, shared only by Vaclav Havel. But the split in the Academy itself remains, and others in Stockholm confirm Rushdie's hunch that the fatwa row merely exacerbated already existing tensions. When the choleric Gyllensten had stepped down as permanent secretary in 1988, he'd not expected the seemingly mild Sture Allén, 'the first nonentity ever to hold the post', to assume such firm control of the Academy's business, and he deeply resented the usurpation of power. Gyllensten has since venomously attacked Allén in the Swedish press. Though the pretext was linguistics, no one could mistake the bitter personal rivalry.

The problem, as Per Wästberg tells me in his lovely, mid-city flat, is that members of the Swedish Academy *can't* resign. Wästberg, novelist, journalist and vice-president of International PEN, is a writer who'd add lustre to the Academy and is regularly tipped for nomination each time a place falls vacant. There are now three vacancies, in effect, but Sture Allén is sticking to the letter: the Academy is for life, and – perhaps believing in the Stockholm syndrome, the possibility his captors will grow to love him – he won't let the three defectors go free. Though Wästberg thinks it a bad decision – 'Since the Academy plays such a vital role, it's tragic to leave three places empty' – he is reluctant to pronounce on the quarrel. He has a huge admiration for Gyllensten as a poet, but he also thinks the present Academy is more committed, energetic and outgoing than it used to be. Others are not so sure: they worry that, with a passive (and reduced) membership, Allén and Espmark are assuming too much power. What's clear is that the Academy is not the civil, faceless, homogenous body it likes to pretend. Those missing chairs tell a story of power struggles and bitter rivalry.

Nor is the Swedish Academy quite neutral. How could it be, when its members inevitably mix with other authors at home and abroad? In the Gondolen restaurant, with its skyline view of Stockholm, a talented young writer in her thirties – another who asks to remain nameless – expounds her conspiracy theory of why the Nobel Prize never went to Graham Greene. It's well known that Greene had an enemy in Artur Lundkvist, who thought his novels 'too popular' to merit the prize. Less well known is that Greene had an affair with Anita Bjork, the Swedish actress. Bjork was married to the Swedish poet Stig Dagerman, who committed suicide – inhaling car exhaust fumes in his garage – at thirty-one. Lundkvist was an admirer of Dagerman's poetry. Perhaps he was also an admirer of Anita Bjork's body. Or perhaps he blamed Greene in some way for Dagerman's death. There were personal reasons, anyway, for him to resist Greene.

My friend doesn't have the story quite right – Greene met Bjork when she was a widow, not a wife. But Michael Shelden's recent biography of Greene supports her, pointing out that, after the affair with Bjork was over, the particular circumstances of Dagerman's death were used by Greene in his play *The Complaisant Lover*, a tasteless piece of exploitation which caused offence in Stockholm. Shelden is reluctant to believe that merely personal factors could have swayed

Lundkvist. But others in the Academy may have been influenced, too. In many ways, Stockholm (pop. 650,000) is more like a small town than a city, with an everyone-knows-everyone artistic community, and a long memory for bad behaviour. Greene had been a face in town long before Anita Bjork. His novel *England Made Me* (1935) is set in Stockholm, and contains a disturbing portrait of a Swedish business mogul. It's possible that familiarity bred contempt. Not even Swedes are immune to the human factor.

Which is not to say that Swedish Academicians are easily corruptible. Those who have tried to bribe them – like the Iranian poet who shipped over eighteen crates of pistachio nuts, or Indian writers' organizations which have offered free air tickets, hotels and sumptous banquets – have got nowhere, or less than nowhere. Even those with more sophisticated means of lobbying, in the US and Europe, have failed to appreciate how finely tuned the Swedish are to this kind of pressure, and how counter-productive it always proves to be. Just get your nomination in, wait, and let be: that's all a lobbyist can do. It's true that the Swedish Academy, as the history of the Nobel Prize shows, is affected by the intellectual currents of the day; it is currently affected by political correctness. It's also acutely conscious of adverse publicity and of attacks like George Steiner's, who accused it, in 1984, of annually consecrating 'the mediocre and the ephemeral'. But, self-conscious and self-critical, it is also eager to prove its independent-mindedness. It can't be fixed. There's no predicting, in any one year, which way it will swing.

On my last night in Stockholm, I go with a Swedish writer to the City Hall. It's here that the Nobel Banquet takes place each December 10th, with the year's (and previous years') various laureates. First the 1,300 guests dine in the Blue Hall, not blue at all but a vast brick space like an Italian piazza. The statistics are dizzying. Twenty cooks, 210 waiters, 325 bottles of champagne drunk, 505 of wine, 270 litres of coffee. The laying of tables here the previous day takes twenty people five hours, and each waiter covers some five kilometres during the banquet. After the meal, the guests move up to dance in the Golden Hall. Tonight, people are dancing at a different festivity, an international pharmacologists' conference. We gatecrash a while, buy a beer and watch them, then move down to eat in the city hall cellars.

There is more Nobel-ity here. If you book far enough in advance, you can eat – at 710 kroner (£70) a head – any one of the Nobel menus served at the ninety-five annual banquets held since the prize was inaugurated, records of which have all been kept. Because we're last-minute, my friend and I have to settle not for the William Faulkner, 1949 menu, which we'd fancied, but for the Kenzaburo Eo, 1994: roulades of smoked duck breast, mango and chard, mâche salad with pine kernels; fillet of veal with sage and PomPom mushrooms, tomato stuffed with spinach, and fondant potatoes with ginger; Nobel ice cream parfait with spun sugar; plus Moët & Chandon, 1990 Chateau Liversan and 1984 Moulin Touchais. It comes a bit expensive, but you drink from gold-leaf stemmed wine flutes and eat off plates engraved with gold Nobel medallions, and already, by August, so our personalized keepsake menus tell us, 4,835 people have eaten a Nobel meal here this year – 4,000 of them Japanese in tour parties, says the waiter, a bit of a surge since Oe's award.

The Nobel business, one sees, is big business, and could be bigger. Only sloth, integrity or the Nobel Foundation's untold wealth have prevented this happening, but – like the Swedish Academy's dictionary – it is all bound to come: not just meals in the city hall cellars and at The Golden Peace, but Alfred Nobel heritage trails, audio playbacks of acceptance speeches, videos of early dynamite experiments, a Hall of Fame.

Over our meal, the Swedish writer and I play the Nobel Literature quiz game. Two laureates have been called Mistral: true or false? True: Frédéric Mistral of France in 1904 and Gabriela Mistral of Chile – no relation – in 1945. Which winner represented no country? Ivan Bunin, born in Russia, domiciled in France, but stateless. Which writer won posthumously? Erik Axel Karlfeldt of Sweden, who died after the decision had been made. Which country did not win the prize in its first thirty-five years, but has won it, on average, every sixth year since? The United States. Which two writers declined the prize? Sartre, voluntarily, and Pasternak, who was forced to, after having accepted it, by the USSR. Who was the last dramatist to win? Beckett, in 1969.

I change the subject to this year's prize. We know it's no use speculating, we've been told that politics and geography are irrelevant, but what the hell: who is going to win? Germany hasn't won for twenty-three years: how long can Gunter Grass go on being ignored, or has the time come for Christa Wolf or Hans Magnus Enzensberger? What about José Saramago? – there's never been a Portugese winner, and *The Year of the Death of Ricardo Reis* is a great book. China has never won either – maybe Bao Nin, the only name we can think of? – nor Brazil, whose Autran Dourado and Jorge Amado must be possibles. Africa is under-represented (maybe Chinua Achebe, maybe Doris Lessing), so is the Arab world (maybe the poet Adonis), so is Australia (maybe Les Murray). Milan Kundera remains uncrowned. So do R. K. Narayan and (the Swedish Academy have been bravely undiplomatic before) Salman Rushdie – and India has not had a winner for eighty years. Israel hasn't had one for thirty years: is Amos Oz the man to change that? Then there's the Gaelic world, also without a laureate. . . . We argue on past coffee, deciding, firmly, that though the Nobel committee can't be second-guessed year by year, it's a dead cert that over the next few years Saramago,

Kundera, Grass, Narayan or Rushdie, and a writer from China will claim the prize.

Round midnight we wander out, freshly amazed by the reflections off the water. The Nobel Prize process is cumbersome. Its labyrinthine bureaucracy can seem laughable, like something out of Kafka or Borges (neither of whom it honoured). But in which nation's hands would the prize be safer? What else, if not a committee of septuagenarian Swedes? A café of thirty-something French *philosophes*? A pub of British literary critics? A seminar room of American campus celebs? It's no contest.

Larkin and Prejudice

When he first became widely known as a poet in the 1950s, Philip Larkin was talked of as the decent, middling chap next door, polite, taciturn, bicycle-clipped, a bit too ordinary for his own good. Whereas the great modernist poets stood accused of fascistic hauteur and anti-Semitism (T. S. Eliot: 'My house is a decayed house/And the Jew squats on the window sill'), and the thirties poets of a naive public school Marxism, Larkin was a poet for the post-war Welfare State, a man who knew all about respect for others and 'making do', somebody you could trust to avoid extreme prejudice.

Since the publication of Anthony Thwaite's edition of the letters, and of Andrew Motion's biography, Larkin's reputation has undergone a violent transformation. The picture now is of a miser and miserabilist, a misogynist and misanthrope, never nastier than when demeaning women ('Not love you? Dear, I'd pay ten quid for you/Five down, and five when I got rid of you') or insulting those of a different race ('wogs like Salmagundi or whatever his name is' – a reference to Salman Rushdie). Where the adjective 'Larkinesque' once suggested a mild and plangent Englishness, it now denotes rancid bigotry. Already one literature professor, Lisa Jardine, has eagerly pointed out that 'we don't tend to teach Larkin much now in my department of English. The little Englandism he celebrates sits uneasily within our revised curriculum . . .'. Larkin might not have minded too much whether he was studied at university, but he liked the idea of 'ordinary' readers. Now that even these readers have glimpsed what Tom Paulin calls 'the sewer under the national monument', will Larkin's poetry be read by future generations at all?

From time to time, in the controversy, it's been suggested, in a muddled sort of way, that the executors of Larkin's estate are at fault for letting us see so much of him: if we hadn't been told how he sometimes spent his evenings – gin-sodden and masturbating over girlie mags – the poems could be pure and innocent again. This wish to know less stems from a tendency to sentimentalize Larkin as a sort of Betjeman without the teddy, the prickly comic bachelor of Hull. In truth, he was much more and much less than this. The unelevating portrait that's lately emerged is a challenge to how we think and feel about him. But for those who believe that his poetry still offers something, it's a challenge that must be met.

The problem can be simply stated. Can we think the same of Larkin as a poet after reading him write from his home in Hull to a friend: 'Not many niggers round here, I'm happy to say. Except that Paki doctor next door . . .'? And is it possible to shut out awareness of the private doggerel – for example, 'Prison for strikers,/Bring back the cat,/Kick out the niggers,/How about that?' – when we come to read public poems like 'Aubade', 'The Whitsun Weddings' or 'Dockery and Son'?

'How about that?': as the phrase suggests, there was something of the swot-in-specs-talking-dirty about Larkin. He liked to shock. He was bold and memorable in his use of the F-word ('They fuck you up, your mum and dad'), and enjoyed setting off a harsh vernacular (cock, ball, tits, cunt, etc.)

against elegant verse-forms. He adopted the part of mad xeno-phobe (he wouldn't mind going to China, he said, if he could come back the same day) or the reactionary among liberals ('Oh, I adore Mrs Thatcher'). He conceived of his letters as performances – and what could be more entertaining to some-one like Kingsley Amis than to hear his old friend out-Enoching Enoch Powell?

But it is not enough to say that Larkin was merely playing the clown, or that his prejudices were only generational, or that because some of his best friends were jazz records by black musicians ('negroes' as he went on calling them, long after it became a word to avoid), he cannot have been racist 'deep down'. He grew up in a part of England – Coventry, the west Midlands, Powell country – where racial prejudice was rife. He had a father with a soft spot for Hitler. His populism (and he was far more in touch with how people thought and felt than most poets are) helped his poems to be sociable and intelligible; but populism of a more dubious kind was there, too. His work is steeped in Englishness and nostalgia, in a dream of unviolated nationhood ('The shadows, the meadows, the lanes,/The guildhalls, the carved choirs') and a reverence for royalist ceremony.

But how far, if at all, did his views disfigure the poems? Is it really true, as Lisa Jardine alleges, that his poetry 'carries a baggage of attitudes' and 'leaves familiar prejudices intact'? It would certainly be possible to hunt down examples of politi-cal incorrectness in the work: the movement of sympathy in 'Deceptions' towards the rapist rather than the victim; the Donald McGill-like caricatures of a 'cut-price' working class in poems such as 'The Whitsun Weddings' and 'Here'; the squibs against left-wing students, or Labour governments, or (for that matter) eco-hostile businessmen with spectacled grins.

A more striking feature of Larkin's poetry, though, is its

attempt to rise above prejudice. Sometimes, indeed, it dramatizes this very process. 'High Windows' begins by expressing
a grungy middle-aged envy of the sexual freedom of the
young: 'When I see a couple of kids/And guess he's fucking
her . . .'. The speaker then imagines how he, as a young man
unshackled by religious faith, must in turn have been envied
by his parents' generation. But finally he lifts his gaze beyond
the fiddle of ethics and generational bickering and is granted
a vision of eternity – a vision of something (or nothing) vastly
more important than moral wrangling:

And immediately

Rather than words comes the thought of high windows:
The sun-comprehending glass,
And beyond it, the deep blue air, that shows
Nothing, and is nowhere, and is endless.

Such self-transcendence is common in Larkin: for all his
worldliness of tone, he was a Romantic poet drawn towards
Utopian images of silence, light and space – places where all
the noise has stopped, prejudice-free zones.

To be prejudiced, you have to hold firm opinions. In life
Larkin did hold firm opinions, but in art he tried to escape
them. His poems can be argumentative, but the arguments are
always with himself. Hearing an Orange march go past, or visiting a church, he is stirred by the resurgence of deep faiths
and ancient loyalties – but never allows us to forget he is an
agnostic. Ignorance, not knowledge or certainty, is an abiding
theme:

Strange to know nothing, never to be sure
Of what is true or right or real,
But forced to qualify or so I feel,

Or Well, it does seem so:
Someone must know.

Sometimes Larkin fights his way through to an opinion or wise generalization: 'Life is first boredom, then fear . . .'. But before he earns the right to profess knowledge he first confesses the lack of it: 'I don't know' ('Mr Bleaney'), 'Someone would know, I don't' ('Church Going'), 'Much less is known than not' ('Far Out'). His poems are full of hesitations and fallibilities, as if the stammer he had when young had never left him. Rather than offering answers, he asks questions, pressing towards conclusions, checking back, going off on false tracks, correcting himself, analysing his own analyses ('Too subtle that. Too decent too . . .'), warning us not to expect illumination: 'Well,/We shall find out,' concludes 'The Old Fools', but only at the end, when it's too late. Putting himself down, he builds up our confidence: he is tentative, and this seems (or used to seem) trustworthy. What most poets know isn't worth knowing; what Larkin doesn't is.

Prejudice implies confidence and self-esteem. But Larkin thought his mind, or inner self, deeply unattractive. In 'If, My Darling', he warns off anyone wishing to become better acquainted with him: his mind is 'unwholesome', he says, 'looped with the creep of varying light,/Monkey-brown, fish-grey, a string of infected circles/Loitering like bullies, about to coagulate.' This is why Larkin always sounds elated when imagining places where he is absent, where the nasty inner bullies of prejudice can't intrude: 'Such attics cleared of me! Such absences!' Equally exhilarated are those poems where he inhabits someone else's life rather than his own, whether a girl who has just married, a lighthouse keeper or a commercial traveller in 1929.

A great many of the poems Larkin wrote in the 1950s and 1960s are about warding off choice – about not wanting, or not being able, to make up his mind. Nearly all these poems concern marriage: should he or shouldn't he take the plunge, and if so with whom? But beyond the horror of tying that knot is a deeper horror of any sort of commitment, which is seen as stasis and congealment. To choose blocks off all ways but one, 'shuts up that peacock-fan/The future was', with its matchless potential. Against images of blockage, rust, stiffness, stalemate, sediment and hardening habit, Larkin reverently sets images of thaw, dispersal and clean water. Fluidity, rather than iron certainty, is the subtext of his poetry.

He also reveres the little and unnoticed. He was not in any obvious way a nature poet, but he had a simple, almost soppy regard for the tender growths of spring: lambs learning to walk in the snow, trees coming into leaf. One late poem describes his anguish at accidentally killing a hedgehog with his mower. Racists and fascists have been known to be nice to animals, too, but it's a human moral which Larkin draws from the incident, and a gently humane one: 'we should be careful/Of each other, we should be kind/While there is still time.' *Kind* is a word that keeps coming up in Larkin's poetry. He knew that it was hard to find 'words at once true and kind,/Or not untrue and not unkind', but he went on making the effort – in his public art if not in his private life.

Ezra Pound, late in life, regretted the 'stupid suburban prejudice' of his anti-Semitism. There's no evidence that Larkin ever regretted the prejudices he expressed in his letters, or would be apologizing for them if he were alive now. But the poems adopt a very different way of speaking. The crusty old sod who looked forward to seeing the head of miners' leader Arthur Scargill 'grinning down . . . from Tower Hill' also wrote 'The Explosion', a moving poem about a mining disaster. The misogynist who described sex as 'always disappointing and often repulsive, like asking someone else to blow your own nose for you' wrote beautiful poems about love and marriage as well as composing lesbian schoolgirl romances. This is the Larkin paradox. Admirers should not try to explain away his prejudices but examine how his work accommodates, struggles with and floats free of them. Therein lies the secret of his greatness.

Some Books are Better than Others

Paddy Rogers, the Irishman in charge of English at my grammar school, was close to retirement by the time he taught the class I was in. Maybe his elderliness was what made us taunt him, though we did so furtively. He'd be walking down the aisle between our desks reading aloud from Shakespeare, say, and we'd flick ink from our fountain pens at the back of his leather-elbow-patched tweed jacket. He must have known what we were up to but, out of a weary reluctance to confront us, he pretended not to notice. By the end of term, the squares on the back of his jacket had turned from light brown to blue.

He could also be – which makes the memory especially shaming – a great teacher. Even in his sixties, in the face of a misbehaving class, he remained enthusiastic, especially about those early twentieth-century authors whose books, I now realize, he must have bought hot off the press as a young man: Joyce, Yeats, Lawrence, Virginia Woolf, T. S. Eliot, Beckett, Isherwood and Auden. I can't be the only person who thinks Eliot the great poet of the century, Joyce the great novelist, and Beckett the great dramatist, largely because of having been introduced to *The Waste Land*, *Portrait of the Artist as a*

Young Man and *Waiting for Godot* as set texts at school. The books you study in detail in your teens stay with you for the rest of your life. Or they did for me with Paddy Rogers.

Back then, we never questioned the curriculum. There were books we were made to read which we didn't much like, but the principle of having required 'key' texts didn't seem controversial. Now it is controversial, and an otherwise parochial row about the teaching of literature in secondary schools has become a matter of fierce dispute. In itself, there is nothing remarkable about teachers disagreeing over which books should or shouldn't be taught in schools. What is remarkable is that a majority of teachers now apparently reject the very notion of a canon, or core curriculum. That's to say, they disapprove of any kind of author-list or literary consensus.

Privately, most will admit that they have no difficulty working with a list of 'approved' authors. The current stipulation for Key Stage Three pupils – eleven- to fourteen-year-olds – is that they 'should read, but not necessarily study in detail', a minimum of one play by Shakespeare, one work of fiction published before 1900 and one after, poetry by two pre-1900 poets and 'three other significant and influential poets', and some 'non-literary and non-fiction texts'. These aren't very draconian requirements.

So what's the problem? The trouble with a canon, teachers say, is that it makes their task one of heart-sinking duty rather than private passion. They resent being dictated to; they'd like to be free to decide which books are appropriate for the particular pupils or classes they teach; they wish nannying politicians would let them get on with their jobs. And surely they are right to distrust governmental diktats, whether of a nostalgic little-Englander or earnestly multiracial kind. What the canon ought to mean is 'the best that is known and thought in the world'. But what politicians usually want it to mean is the promotion of their own values, which they may have been unable to foster themselves.

Younger teachers, especially, associate the canon with a lost world – with white supremacy, male competitiveness and the guns of Empire. They think the notion of 'great books' springs from the same mentality that creates rigid hierarchies and class divisions – as if the canon were a members' club, open only to an exclusive few. They don't like popular, commercial or 'inferior' books being excluded like naughty pupils. They find that such books (Jeffrey Archer, Jilly Cooper, John Grisham) may be more useful for classroom analysis than 'good books'. They hate the legacy of F. R. Leavis, who believed in minority culture and reduced the great tradition of the English novel to a mere five names (Jane Austen, George Eliot, Henry James, Joseph Conrad and D. H. Lawrence). They cringe at the words 'discrimination' and 'judgement'. They reject the mindset which treats books as if they were competitors, with the passes granted eternal life and the failures doomed to oblivion.

I have sympathy with these arguments. But to declare that some books are better than others is not comparable with racial discrimination, social snobbery or moral disapprobation. All readers, even young children, naturally practise literary judgement ('This book's great', 'This one's rubbish'). And there is nothing sinister about the creation of a canon when it comes out of the shared enthusiasms of teachers and students, rather than from politicians nostalgic for what they were taught in school or eager to use literature as social engineering.

The notion of the canon (from the Greek *kanon*, meaning a straight rod or standard) may once have had mystical or religious overtones, but its sacred texts are simply books which other people have liked. The canon is a list – and everyone likes to make lists, to sort out what they feel and think.

Writers themselves have always made lists of other writers, fantasy leagues of best-evers and all-time greats. 'The reading of Homer and Virgil is counselled by Quintilian as the best way of informing youth and confirming man,' wrote Ben Jonson, who from his own century named as improving authors Thomas More, Walter Raleigh, Thomas Wyatt and Philip Sidney. By the seventeenth century, most middle-class homes had their collection of 'good books' – the Bible, Shakespeare, Chaucer, Milton, Bunyan. Many of us are grateful that the tradition of commendation still exists: time is short, and there are a lot of books in the world to choose from (many more every year), and it's useful to be pushed in the direction of the tried and tested. The canon is no more than this – a happy secular collective, a pool of enthusiasms.

We need a canon of classics, and 'emerging classics', if only so that we can argue about them and replace them year by year. We need them because they provide a common language, a shared area of experience, beyond that of television and newspapers. George Santayana, asked which books young people ought to read, replied that it doesn't matter so long as they read the *same* books. I see his point. Would I ever have been taught *The Waste Land* if appropriateness for a class of sixteen-year-olds in rural Yorkshire had been the criterion?

Ah yes, teachers reply, but there is no common culture any more. The centre has not held. We live and work in a multi-ethnic society. What chance of interesting, say, a class composed largely of Bangladeshi children in L. P. Hartley and H. E. Bates? Very little chance of interesting anyone, I'd say. But that's an argument for changing the canon, not for abolishing it. *Romeo and Juliet*, *Silas Marner*, *Wuthering Heights*, *Animal Farm*, *Lord of the Flies*, *Under Milk Wood* – here are some traditional Eng. Lit. texts which can speak to those whose cultural allegiances are not (or are more than) Anglo-Saxon. The canon, at best, will feed their hunger for learning the language and culture of the country they've newly arrived in, or been born into, or want to feel part of. More than this, great books – canonical texts – transcend national boundaries and ethnic origins, and have something positive to teach us all about humanity, tolerance and mutual respect.

In the United States, canon-formation, canon-revision and canon-busting have been a matter of fierce dispute for some years. In the 1950s, the supremacy of European culture in the humanities faculty was eroded by the growth of American Studies. In the 1960s and 1970s, students demanded greater 'relevance' in what they studied, which meant texts with more contemporaneity and political dissent. In the 1980s, Marxism, feminism and multiculturalism joined forces to denounce the canon as a white imperialist fabrication, a hierarchical mystification promoted by bourgeois institutions to uphold authority and law. At Stanford University, students on a march with Jesse Jackson chanted, 'Hey hey, ho ho, Western culture's gotta go'. Saul Bellow drily replied that he wouldn't mind Western culture going if he knew what would be taking its place: 'Who is the Tolstoy of the Zulus? The Proust of the Papuans? I'd be glad to read him.'

Many suspect, as Bellow does, that canon-busting isn't a positive movement to add authors to reading-lists, but a negative movement, anti-WASP and anti-DWEM, motivated by politics and envy rather than a love of good books. The American critic Harold Bloom has called it a 'School of Resentment' which judges literature on its sincerity, selflessness, justice and 'social energy', which isn't to judge it at all. Bloom's own book *The Western Canon* offers up twenty-six indisputably classic authors and appends a list of 850 must-read others. But his tone is weary and there is an air of defeatism about his enterprise, as if it were closing time in the gardens of the West and all the poor literature teacher can now do is tend the last few fading flowers.

This isn't the spirit in which Paddy Rogers taught me at school. What he believed, passionately, much as his beloved T. S. Eliot did, was that a canon or 'tradition' of some kind was inevitable, but that its shape will constantly change as new authors, or neglected talents, swim into view. More important still, he believed that some books are better than others. I'd be sorry if that provocative conviction were ever to disappear.

Nobs versus Mobs

Clinkety-clink, here they come in handcuffs and leg-irons, the modernist intellectuals, Eliot and Pound, Yeats and Nietzsche, people you find it hard to read, or, if you are Kingsley Amis, gave up reading years ago. Freud and Ortega y Gasset, Woolf and Wyndham Lewis, off to the correction centre, snobs and aesthetes, misogynists and maniacs every one. Wash your mouth out Ezra, less of your lip Virginia, take that sneer off your face Tom.

The modernists have never been short of enemies. Hitler, under whose leadership the books of Mann, Freud, Zola and Proust went up in flames, cleansed German art galleries of degenerates such as Cézanne, Picasso, Matisse and Gauguin. Stalin, with the help of a monster called Zhdanov, stamped out the bourgeois decadence of Akhmatova and Mandelstam. In Britain we have been more lenient: hatred of modernism has been confined to the occasional tetchy outburst – Philip Larkin, for example, identified the 'principal themes' of modern art as 'mystification and outrage'.

In *Nobs versus Mobs: The Intellectuals and the Masses*, John Carey has written the sort of book that Amis, Larkin and the Movement generation would have liked to have written themselves. Witty, passionate, entertaining and deeply wrong, he argues that 'the principle around which modernist literature and culture fashioned themselves was the exclusion of the masses, the defeat of their power, the removal of their literacy, the denial of their humanity'. The realism and logical coherence beloved by the fact-hungry masses were abandoned; irrationality and obscurity, symbolism and ambiguity took their place.

Carey's chief enemy is Nietzsche, who wrote that a 'declaration of war on the masses by higher men is needed' and who encouraged intellectuals everywhere to lord and lady it over the rabble. The newspapers the masses read, the horribly sprawling suburbs they lived in, the tinned food they ate, their sentimental interest in such lowly matters as children, their pathetic efforts to educate themselves or acquire 'culture', their pasty faces and sloping shoulders and stunted physique, their shallow herd belief in 'democracy', the silliness of their women: all these were treated to writerly contempt.

Behind the contempt lay fear, of course. Fantasies of mass annihilation or sterilization, Carey shows, were common in modernist literature. The masses were bacteria, a plague or virus; they were only half-alive; they behaved, in crowds, like savages, like an unruly id. The only way to tolerate them was through a sort of populist pastoral (Pound's equation of a metro crowd with 'petals on a wet, black bough'), or to escape to Italy and India, where the peasants were more colourful. If all else failed, you could always go scaling Alps: up there in the mountains you felt free, and properly superior.

In Carey's anthology of offensive attitudes, few escape the rap. James Joyce almost does, because he treats with loving thoroughness the profoundly ordinary life of Leopold Bloom. On the other hand, Carey points out, 'Bloom himself would never and could never have read *Ulysses*' because of its avant-garde techniques. A revolutionary means of evaluating literature beckons here (is *The Tempest* worthless because Caliban wouldn't have got on with it?), but Carey contents himself with pronouncing Joyce guilty of 'duplicity'. He sniffs out a similar sort of doublethink in Orwell who, whatever his leftist convictions, found the masses both dirty and smelly. Even Mass Observation is seen as a sinister project, because it treated working people as specimens.

In the end only one writer passes muster: Arnold Bennett, 'the hero of this book'. Bennett loves the things other intellectuals detest: seaside crowds, popular journalism, modern bathrooms, advertising. He doesn't feel ashamed of making money from writing. He knows what 'normal people' value, and it's not 'the pastimes intellectuals value – literature, art, philosophy'. Carey, who can be wonderfully sarcastic describing the writers he dislikes, becomes almost lyrical in his sentimentality about his hero: Bennett, he says, 'gives us access to the realities that blaze and coruscate inside dowdy or commonplace bodies'.

The alternative to Bennett, the last chapter suggests, was Hitler. Echoing Donald Davie, who once claimed that the line from imagism in politics to Fascism in politics is clear and unbroken, Carey argues that many of the Führer's beliefs – in natural aristocracy and the divine spark of genius, in the inferiority of women, children and non-Aryans – were rooted in highbrow orthodoxy. (Hitler's hatred of modern art is not alluded to.) So fictional dreams of mass extermination became the Nazi death camps, and empty ideas became hollowed flesh. Thankfully, since the passing of Hitler and the modernist intellectuals, things have begun to look up – Carey finds hope in the lack of obscurity in contemporary poetry, and in a television series such as *Civilisation*. But the old contempt for the masses is still there, he believes, in deconstruction, Roland Barthes, and dread academic theory.

For fifteen years, John Carey has been our leading Sunday

books reviewer – the Archbishop of Wapping, preacher and moral guide, a man who likes to play the part of Joe Public against the snobs of Sissinghurst, the ghouls of Garsington, and all the other dandies, fops and charlatans. This book, too, is empowered by Carey's almost Marxist energy in speaking up (rather as the poems of Tony Harrison do) for the mob against the nobs. His chapter on the suburbs is a triumph of academic research and private indignation. No one, having read it, could ever again use the adjective 'suburban' in casually pejorative fashion.

But Carey, who praises Wells for being in two minds at once and thus saved from 'mere prescription', is too busy hammering the drum of his thesis to allow himself equivalent mental room. He does not seem to have noticed, for example, that in lumping European intellectuals into one mass he is practising the same individuality-denying method he castigates them for; nor that his put-downs of modern writers mimic their own tone of know-better superiority; nor that, in an age when crowds clamour to see Picasso exhibitions, his idea that ordinary people can't appreciate modernism carries its own sort of condescension.

For all his populist protestations, it's obvious Carey would much rather be reading Lawrence and Orwell, Gissing and Wells than Jeffrey Archer, Catherine Cookson and their early twentieth-century equivalents. Whether this doesn't imply the superiority of 'high' art, whether works like *The Waste Land* or *Women in Love* remain undamaged, artistically, by the attitudes underpinning them: these are questions he never faces, just as he never acknowledges the possibility that the 'difficulty' of modernism was a genuine artistic endeavour rather than class warfare – 'an attempt,' as Eliot said, 'to put something into words which could not be said in any other way'. Eliot also wrote that he liked to think his poetry might be 'read and declaimed in the public house, the forecastle and the shipyard', that the 'uneducated' might appreciate it, and that 'the audience for the more highly developed, even for the more esoteric kinds of poetry is recruited from every level': this may have been hopelessly fanciful of Eliot but it doesn't sound like a conspiracy to exclude proles.

Carey is rightly condemning of the snootiness and worse he uncovers, and which a public school and Oxbridge education can still breed. But modernist intellectuals have no monopoly on condescension. You can find hauteur in even so resolute an anti-modernist and anti-intellectual as Philip Larkin, with his 'cut-price crowd' and seamy Whitsun wedding parties. You can find it in Betjeman, too – 'an eight-hour day for all, and more than three/of those are occupied in making tea'.

Towards the end, Carey withdraws from the wilder fringes of his thesis. Looking at the explosion in the world's population, which it is estimated will grow from 5.3 billion in 1990 to 8.6 billion in 2025, he uses a word his despised intellectuals might have used ('no one can tell how the planet will feed and accommodate such hordes') and admits that their predicament is to some extent our predicament, too. He might have added that a fear of the mob (see Shakespeare's *Coriolanus*) has been persistent since ancient times, and that a preference for woods and fields over housing estates still seems pretty widespread, not least among occupants of housing estates. If Carey had allowed himself to ponder such paradoxes he might have written a wise book rather than a merely clever one.

Do Artists Need Statues?

The town of Aldeburgh held its annual carnival last week. There were the usual ingredients of many a fête worse than death: a parade with floats, a smiling gala queen, races, competitions, marching bands, the mayor everywhere in chains. Less usually, at nightfall, hundreds of adults and children walked with Chinese lanterns from the high street to the shingle beach. It was a hot, windless night, and – as fireworks exploded in the sky – occasional lanterns drifted off from the crowd to float eerily by the sea, like brightly coloured, weightless human skulls.

As we stood there next to Crag Path, it was hard not to think of the man who once lived there, Benjamin Britten, founder of the other, more famous Aldeburgh carnival, its annual music festival. Britten did more than anyone – more than even the poet George Crabbe – to put Aldeburgh on the map. Yet the town council has decided not to commission a statue to commemorate him, deciding that a park bench or two, or perhaps a firework display, would be more useful. The national press has been gleeful and indignant. There have been accusations of philistinism, and rumours of posthumous vindictiveness (Britten died twenty years ago), and an impression of churlish ingratitude.

I feel some sympathy for the people of Aldeburgh. They have handled the media naively. They have allowed some nasty prejudices, including homophobia and anti-modernism, to crawl out of the woodwork. They have behaved like landladies of middle-class seaside towns in Britain are supposed to behave, with meanness of spirit. They have surrendered to the yahooism of the yacht club and the golf club.

But, as I say, I feel some sympathy. Aldeburgh doesn't need a statue of Britten. There is a blue plaque on his house in Crag Path. There is the Britten–Pears music school, and the Britten–Pears library at Red House. There is the festival at Snape Maltings, and many concerts and recitals in the area which keep his work alive. In Lowestoft, his birthplace, there's a shopping centre named after him. The whole Suffolk coastal district is a kind of memorial to him.

In Victorian times, the desire of towns and cities to raise statues to their famous was perfectly natural – the public equivalent of family and friends erecting a gravestone. But these days it looks more like a cynical form of twinning, a way of hitching yourself to a celebrity in order to boost local tourism. In their approach towards writers and artists, town councils often resemble the patrons bitterly described by Dr Johnson in his letter to Lord Chesterfield: denying recognition at the time when it was needed, they offer it when it's not.

Often they give the impression of grudgingly succumbing to the pressure exerted by lobbyists and societies – not to mention the press. The 50th anniversary of X's death, the bicentenary of his birth, the 125th year since the composition of his most famous work, and there will be 'calls' for some kind of commemoration. A loose remark from some local spokesman, implying ignorance or indifference, and there's a controversy. Such stories come up regularly now. They're one of the few ways that art makes the headlines, along with rows over prizes, biographies that scandalize friends and family,

and demands that a sexually explicit and/or violent performance or exhibition at the Edinburgh Festival be banned.

But do we need any more statues to stand lonely and
encrusted by pigeon crap (or, at Aldeburgh, seagull crap) in
places that little resemble the places the honoured person
knew and in forms that little resemble his body, either? Last
week-end, there was a report – shock, horror – that the town
of Beaconsfield has no plans yet to celebrate the centenary of
Enid Blyton in 1997. A spokesman said that the town's only
pre-arranged literary efforts next year are for the 200th
anniversary of the death of Edmund Burke, who wrote
Reflections on the Revolution in France while living there. The
rival claims of these two writers are beside the point. What
will come as news to many is that either had important
Beaconsfield connections at all. The fact they do might be an
argument for a guided tour or lecture, pointing out how a
particular street here or incident there might have inspired
Burke's opposition to slavery or Blyton's creation of Noddy or
Big Ears. But it's doubtful how useful this exercise would be.
Burke was born in Dublin, and his mind fed on events in
America and France. Blyton country – the land where the
Famous Five had their adventures, away from their homes
and parents – is a sort of Cornwall of the imagination, not a
bit Home Counties.

To put up a statue is to imply a solid link between the man
(or, less often, woman) and the place where he is standing. But
just as marble and concrete miss the essence of what flesh
feels like, so the statue of an artist (unless perhaps it's Rodin's
'Balzac') can tell us nothing about art. Art may begin in a
place, but it doesn't end there. What we enjoy about music is
its power to transcend: it lifts us beyond the places where we
hear it or where it happens to have been composed. Much
modern painting, too, strives to be universal, abstract,
unpindownable. Even the St Ives School of artists, who were

given a name which ropes them in together by the Cornish sea, have a complex relationship to the landscape – a matter of grain and texture, not simple topography. The casual visitor to the Tate at St Ives, expecting scenic harbours or fishing boats, in the manner of Alfred Wallis, will be disappointed.

This isn't to deny that artists are shaped by the places where they are born or live. Benjamin Britten was when he wrote *Peter Grimes*, *Albert Herring* and *Noye's Fludde* – the Lake Poets were, and Thomas Hardy, and Ted Hughes, and Seamus Heaney, and even the St Ives school. The Scottish poet and novelist George Mackay Brown thought the Orkneys gave him all he needed to know of the world. But some artists merely inhabit places, passing through them or living out of them like suitcases – their real roots lie wider or elsewhere. Is the place that inspired David Hockney's paintings Bradford or Los Angeles? Shakespeare's official residence is Elizabethan Stratford-upon-Avon; his real home is all times and all places.

Perhaps it's a panicky sense that fewer and fewer of us have real roots that's creating our heritage culture, with its requirement that every artist be given a single grid reference on the map. Against the reality of increased mobility, we set these fixed monuments. Against the reality of increased homogeneity – everywhere looking like Milton Keynes – we evoke the spirit of place. But there has never been a straightforward, symbiotic relationship between the heart and the hearth. And not all writers feel sentimental towards their birthplace. I gave a reading recently with a gifted and celebrated poet who was performing for the first time in the city where he'd been born. It should have been a real occasion, a homecoming: special for his hosts, special for him. But it passed off like any other event. There was no extra frisson, no spurious claims on either side. This was only the place he'd happened to grow up in. It hadn't suffused his work.

All writers and artists want permanence – a second life, or

afterlife, to vindicate them. Some, in their eagerness for recognition, accept honours in their lifetime (Benjamin Britten did, becoming a life peer six months before he died), and most would be flattered by the idea of a memorial once they're dead. But the work they leave behind is the only kind of permanence worth having. As for the rest, the marble busts, the blue plaques and the postage stamps, it's as insubstantial as a firework or Chinese lantern.

5
Other Englands

A Fortunate Man

I'll find my own way from Colchester station, I tell Peter Sargeant, but he won't hear of it. He's not decrepit, after all – can still see, hear, walk, drive, do his shopping, look after himself, get about. And it's only a five-mile drive to Boxted, the village – or ribbon development – where he lives.

He's not decrepit, I can see that at once. There he is, standing by his red L-reg Citroën, wearing an open-necked check shirt, blue-ribbed sweater, cravat, sensible brown shoes. His hair is grey, but there's plenty of it. His complexion is ruddy without suggesting high blood pressure. He wears glasses, but can see where he's going, and soon has us back at his trim modern house. Inside, polished wood floors, it's immaculate; outside, a lawn, no less so. Gardening keeps Peter fit, along with regular five-mile walks and a prudent diet. 'I'm not a chocolate biscuit chap,' he says, in his pleasant Essex burr, bringing coffee to the sunny conservatory, 'I couldn't afford new trousers.'

No, Peter Sargeant is not decrepit. But, at seventy-two, he has reached the age when death is not a distant rumour but a noisy alarm bell. Three years ago, his wife Joan died, after a decade or more of health problems. They had been married for forty-seven years. Other friends have also gone, or, with bits missing, are staunchly hanging on. Every Wednesday Peter drives patients to the day centre of a nearby hospice. Seven of those he has chauffeured this year are now dead.

It could get depressing, but age breeds stoicism and Peter has an unusually cheerful disposition. He says many times during our day together how 'fortunate' he is: in his health, in where he lives, in having his two daughters nearby, in the job satisfaction he had from nearly forty years as a primary schoolteacher. He has a habit, whenever he touches on something painful or traumatic, of saying 'Anyway . . .' and moving on to something brighter, as if it would be indecent to linger in shadow. It's not that he's uncomfortable discussing last things, but he's still curious about the world, still learning, not ready for obituaries. He's always been more of a doer than a brooder, and being a septuagenarian isn't going to alter that.

Next year, he plans to move back into the heart of Colchester, and shows me the plans of the flat he has reserved. It's a pragmatic, precautionary, old-person's move: the handy shops, the nearby doctor. But it also completes a circle: Peter was born in Colchester, taught there nearly all his life, and is now, after a spell on the outskirts, returning. His is in many ways an old-fashioned English story, a tale of roots rather than of mobility: how many of us at Peter's age will be able to say that the place where we were born was also where we worked, married, had children and grew old? But Peter doesn't offer his as the *right* way: he thinks a healthy society needs people who move about as well as people who stay – he just happens to be one of the stayers.

He is quick to describe himself as 'a silly old fart', and to point out that he's an acquaintance of one of the England rugby union hierarchs about whom Will Carling famously used the phrase. But though 'an establishment man, a bit to the right of centre, an evolutionist not a revolutionist', he's too thoughtful to be called silly, and too energetic to seem old. He belongs to a generation to which all of us who came after should feel grateful – but a generation which is finding, in old age, how short on memory and gratitude the young can be.

He was born in April 1923, the son of a municipal clerk, and, along with his older brother, went to local council schools before moving on to the Colchester Royal grammar school, where his chief enthusiasm was for games. As a senior clerk, Peter's father would have been on £5 a week, sufficient in the thirties to acquire the semi on a mortgage, and to keep the family comfortable: no fridge or washing machine or hot water system (let alone central heating), but a wireless, a wind-up gramophone, the *Boys' Own Paper*, new cricket bats whenever needed, and plenty of books about (if only borrowed from the library). It was modest but happy. Peter was aware of others at school a good deal less well off.

In 1939 he passed school certificate – 'without much distinction', he says, meaning he'd probably have left school at sixteen even if there hadn't been a war on. He'd already dug an air-raid trench in the garden during the Munich crisis (his father was in ill-health because of *his* war, the First), and was ready to follow his brother into the RAF. But he was keen on Percy F. Westerman's seafaring tales, and in the event, after a spell as an emergency stretcher-bearer, he joined the navy on a special training programme, the 'Y scheme', for seventeen-year-olds. Some time in 1941, never having been further than London before, he sailed out into the North Atlantic, and thereafter spent most of his war on torpedo boats in the Med and Adriatic, rising from midshipman to lieutenant. At the end of hostilities in Europe, he was due to go to the Pacific, 'to fight the Japs', but then came Hiroshima.

Like most men of his generation, Peter has vivid memories of the war, and spends a lot of time talking about them. Until recently, those, like me, who are the children of such men, used to complain of being bored by such talk. Now that we're older, and fewer of these men are left, their reminiscences seem fascinating and our unresponsiveness callow. Peter has two grandsons, aged sixteen and eighteen, at school and university. When he and his brother were that age, they were put in uniform and sent thousands of miles from home. They saw friends killed, and themselves took the lives of others. They learnt about courage, fear, cowardice, death. It's little wonder that for those who served in the Second World War peacetime was in some ways an anti-climax.

As a loyal Englishman, Peter did his best during the war to defeat the enemy, while also believing the Germans were 'perfectly ordinary, likeable chaps like us who probably didn't realize what was happening in Germany'. His worst moment was learning – just before he went on parade one day – of the death of his brother, shot down over the Bay of Biscay in the summer of 1942. Then there was losing his navigator, John Dean, lost overboard one night after an explosion during a confused action in the Adriatic. And Tony, married only a week when he was killed, to a Wren, Liz, a lovely girl, whom he thinks of whenever he hears 'As Time Goes By'. . . .

In recent years, half a century on, Peter has met up again with some of those he served with in the war. There was a chap who called round only the other week, and they went together to Shotley to see the old frigate they'd trained on, the HMS *Ganges*. War service, he says, had a lasting effect on him: the training, tradition, expectations, example. But he doesn't see much point in 'ramming it down the throat' of the young. 'It was a different world then, wasn't it?'

In the new peacetime world of 1945, Peter wasn't sure what to be or do. But a friend suggested teaching, and, quite by chance, and without having trained, he was sent to Boxted school, the village where he now lives. Most teachers, he thinks, hit it off with certain age groups, and he'd always liked kids between eight and eleven. By now he was married, to Joan, a Boxted girl, with whom he'd corresponded during the war. They lived with her parents for a while, then bought their first home before he went off to Eastbourne to do teacher training, a two-year course crammed into fourteen months. One of the exercises he remembers doing with children was drawing a long horizontal line across a blackboard and asking them to say where, in the history of man, they'd place the birth of Christ. Far right, nearly off the edge of the blackboard, was the correct answer. Now, in terms of an average life-span, Peter, too, is close to the edge.

He stayed in primary teaching, in and around Colchester, throughout his career, spending the latter half of it as head of a large primary school which also boasted a unit for the deaf and partially hearing. To start with, he wasn't well paid, and used to supplement his income by doing youth-work: it meant a little extra for Christmas and for the fortnight's summer holiday in Walton-on-Naze, where he still has a beach hut. He was fortunate, he says, counting his blessings again, that his lump sum on retirement went into the Cheltenham and Gloucester building society, which proved a good investment and has kept him comfortable since.

Did he feel under-rewarded as a teacher? Not especially. Though as president of the local branch of the National Union of Teachers he campaigned for better pay conditions (especially for women teachers, who in the 1950s were still getting only four-fifths of a male salary), he doesn't believe quality of teaching has much to do with money or equipment. Eventually he became disenchanted with the NUT ('the militant tail was wagging the moribund dog'), and joined the National Association of Head Teachers. He was a Conservative (still is), after all.

Joan, meanwhile, having spent her early and middle years as a housewife, behind-the-scenes organizer ('flower festivals, bazaars and so on') and 'wonderful wife and mother', got herself a job with the local examinations board. Peter had once been old-fashioned in his views on working mothers, but by this point had changed his mind: 'Having a career was good for Joan, as it is for most women.'

But then she had a couple of coronaries, and a triple bypass. Later, most of her bladder was removed and she became incontinent: 'In all, she was admitted to hospital thirty-nine times. About the only thing she didn't have was cancer. By the end her quality of life had so deteriorated she'd had enough. I remember her saying, "What is there left in life when you're padded up like a baby?"' Though they had often talked about her death, it still came unexpectedly, on a Monday in February 1992.

I ask Peter the obvious question: does he feel lonely without her? 'No. But certain bits of music, like "Nimrod" from Elgar's Enigma Variations, I associate with her. And I do catch myself thinking, I must tell Joan that, or doing something because I know it's what she'd have wanted me to do. After she died, someone said to me, facetiously, "You'll have all the widows chasing you now". I know it was meant to be friendly but somehow it was the worst thing anyone could have said.'

Has her death made him more religious? 'I've no conviction that there's an afterlife, but I do believe that – what's the Rupert Brooke line? – there's "a pulse in the eternal mind". I've learnt to accept there is a mystery, and that I'm not going to find an answer. There's no profit in asking, Why Joan, not me? or Why my brother or John Dean all those years ago, not me?'

Though Peter describes himself as agnostic, he does attend church every Sunday and thinks Christianity important for the intellectual and spiritual framework it provides. 'I don't know why exactly, but there was an extra service last week, and all I can say was that I felt glad afterwards I had been, if only to sit quietly and remember Joan.'

Peter suggests lunch at a pub on the Essex–Suffolk border, and drives us there, slowly – so slowly that we're overtaken by a Citroën 2CV. It's a crisp November day, blue skies, a low sun, cock pheasants in the verges, and I share Peter's sense that he's fortunate to live here. Essex is notoriously flat and dull, but here are all these surprising hills and vistas – a more varied region than you'd think, just like old age.

Peter has a pint of bitter, 'with a handle', and, 'nothing heavy', soup with bread. The pub's friendly and he, too, seems to relax and open up. Though a teacher, he's always considered himself gregarious, not studious or solitary – 'a bit of a committee man', as he puts it, chairman of this and president of that. For twenty-eight years, most Tuesdays, he sat on the bench of Colchester's magistrates court, and can still remember particular faces and cases, like the poll tax defaulters who demanded he declare his interests, and the offender he gave one last chance to who, years later, a reformed character, wrote to thank him.

To be retired from public service when still ambitious and of sound mind can be frustrating, but Peter structures his week so that it isn't a black hole. Monday is domestic chores (washing, cleaning, ironing), then tidying up the churchyard. Tuesday is shopping in town, a drink, a visit to friends. Wednesday is driving patients to the hospice. Thursday and Friday he might call on friends again or drive to the beach hut. Saturday, in summer, means watching county cricket (he played until his fifties). Sunday is church. He watches television most evenings, if only to fall asleep to. His paper is the *Telegraph*.

Now that he's less active, he thinks a lot about how

corporate duty brings a sense of meaning and purpose to individual lives. In our age, he believes, there's too much talk of rights and not enough about responsibilities. He's no philosopher, but Joan's old doctor, now ninety-one, is reading *A History of Western Philosophy*, and they sometimes exchange ideas. He has begun to read one or two men in public life for their insights, including Lord Hailsham, whose book *Values: Collapse and Cure* he shows me, and quotes from, saying that it articulates some of his own thoughts. This is the contemplative phase of life, but it has its spurts and growing-points, too. 'I think we all retain a child in us, and I can see in myself things which I used to tell children off for. But I feel I'm growing up. Each day I learn something new. And the more I know, the more I realize how little I know.'

Driving back, we reach a bit of road that narrows to a single track. A car coming the other way pulls in to wait for us, but another, not seeing us coming or not caring, overtakes it, and we have to brake, no way through. Peter, pleasingly, stands his ground, and the driver of the other car, a young man with a cigarette and earring, curses quietly and noisily reverses to a passing place.

I put it to Peter that being seventy-two is more interesting than he'd have supposed at twenty-two. 'Yes. I'm lucky. Apart from some minor skin cancer I'm having treatment for, I'm in good health. But I went in for a gall bladder operation earlier this year, and suddenly realized there was a faint chance I might never come out again. It didn't worry me at all, but there are still things I'd like to do – trace my family tree, do some research on heraldry, read more. The point is, you never know what's round the next corner.'

What's round the next corner – we stop and park – is the Boxted school, where Peter had his first job, and the church, where he married Joan fifty years ago. He shows me the patched-up medieval church tower, which no one can quite believe is still standing. He shows me the line of gravestones which some builder, having raised, mistakenly put back facing west not east. He shows me a woodworm-infested timber beam that came out during restoration. He shows me the Turkish carpet, by the altar, which he donated in memory of Joan. I can feel tears coming, in my eyes if not in his – all these emblems of mortality, these symbols of the circle of life. But Peter, in his element, helpful guide and good citizen, is eager to get on and show me more.

'One last thing,' he says, and we walk towards an old head-stone with a skull and crossbones – except that close up we see that the crossbones are a torch and spoon. What can they mean? The torch is easy enough, a kindly light leading the soul to heaven. But the spoon? 'Must be a long spoon for supping with the devil if you go to the other place,' suggests Peter, and laughs as we turn into the setting sun.

Bennett's Lug

At one point in his rueful, unfailingly entertaining diaries, Alan Bennett contrasts himself with certain hard-nosed contemporaries who 'get themselves disliked but make money. Whereas I prefer to be liked and thought a nice man. But I'm not. I'm just as bad as the rest of them, only I don't like to show it.'

Few writers can or would want to be accused of niceness. Nice means inoffensive; nice means unprovoking of thought; nice means Betjeman, whose poetry laureateship may have passed to Ted Hughes but whose public mantle – jokes, nostalgia, bicycles, a love of poetry and a profound affection for dear old England – many would like to see worn by Alan Bennett. Except the cloak doesn't fit, Bennett reminds us: he is not as nice as people think.

Nice men are likely to be awkward and self-deprecating, and Bennett certainly looks (or plays) the part, making a success of failure. Dining at Magdalen College, Oxford as the 'most junior of junior lecturers', he catches the sleeves of his gown under the chair leg and is too shy to free them (the food hovers 'tantalizingly out of reach of my pinioned arms'). He goes to Claridge's to meet John Huston and is shown the tradesman's entrance. He pays the £3 weekend supplement to travel first-class on British Rail and is told by the ticket collector, 'You don't belong in here. These are proper first-class people.' He portrays himself as a man of few books and little literary appreciation, and 'the only Western playwright not personally acquainted with the new president of Czechoslovakia'. Later, though, he owns up to having read more books than he likes to let on. And we remember that lecturers in history at Oxford, however, junior, aren't, or aren't usually, daft.

Despite or because of his hapless, bicycle-clipped, rather swotty demeanour, he is imagined to be the kind of writer that mothers like – meaning a certain kind of mother (house-proud, northern, born before 1920), who is fond enough of books but not those written by the writers admired by Bennett (Larkin, Kafka). Bennett's own mother was like this, and if mothers are fond of him perhaps that's because they sense he's fond of them, or at least of her, whose principal reaction when the two of them visited the Brontë parsonage together was horror at the mucky fireplace and curtains ('Too busy writing their books to keep the place up to scratch'). Bennett shares some of his mother's distrust of books, having learnt, during his thirties childhood in Leeds, that they can be treacherous: 'There were owls in hollow trees, so the nature books said, but I saw no owls – and hollow trees were in pretty short supply too.' But books meant education, which Bennett's parents hadn't had and which they wanted him to have, mistakenly thinking it would make him socially confident as well.

Writers who move to London and use their provincial relatives as subject matter are liable to be accused of condescension. They may also be suspected of pandering to an English obsession with class. Alan Bennett is thought to be this kind of writer, but he's not. He describes his background as 'dull', and satirizes those northern writers who overplay the colourful deprivation of their upbringing. When he dramatizes his mam (and dad, aunts, uncles, and so on) he is too much the heir of their social unease to offer it up for easy laughs. Caught between 'being himself' and acquiring 'the necessary accomplishment of saying things one doesn't mean', he can't be sure where his loyalties lie. There is nothing cosy, or merely poignant, in his visits to his mother at a home for the elderly in Weston-super-Mare, one of which culminates in her thanking him for all he's done for her: '. . . it isn't a remark intended to induce guilt. But in a film the next shot would be me looking down at the shaft of a spear protruding from my belly with the head stuck out a foot behind me.'

Guilt – or social obligation – also underlies his protectiveness towards Miss Shepherd, the elderly eccentric who used to park her battered van in his London street, until he allowed her to park it in his garden, hard up against his front step, where it remained for fifteen years, until she died. What's affecting about Bennett's account of Miss Shepherd, *The Lady in the Van*, is that it isn't sentimental; what's winning about it is that it doesn't compete for brownie points. The chief feelings Bennett owns up to are irritation, exasperation and queasiness at the filth accumulating in Miss Shepherd's van – uncharitable feelings, but ones he can afford given his charitableness, which most readers will admit, not even very guiltily, they wouldn't have shown Miss Shepherd themselves.

Miss Shepherd makes Bennett feel a bit of a soft touch. He finds it hard not to be soft, even in his politics, which he describes as 'soft centre', and for a time in the 1980s, as his diary records, he sweetly put up posters for the local Alliance candidate (though Miss Shepherd countered these with her Conservative one). But he is not one to fudge, and around the time of the Falklands war there is the taste of something hard and bitter in his diaries, as Mrs Thatcher, the 'hyena crew of newsmen' and the jingoistic humbug leave him doubtful of the virtues of patriotism: 'Not English I feel now,' he writes in June 1982. 'This is just where I happen to have been put down. No country. No party. No Church. No voice.' Later, he expresses it differently, or has Guy Burgess express it differently in *An Englishman Abroad*: 'I can say I love London. I can say I love England. I can't say I love my country, because I don't know what that means.' It sounds a bit like E.M. Forster's famous remark on patriotism and betrayal, which is appropriate. A sceptical Forsterian liberalism is Bennett's true note, with jokes to boot.

The jokes, delivered in a deadpan Yorkshire accent, are what audiences hear. He could be called an anecdotalist, since he tells good stories; he could be called a master of situation comedy, since he is comic about the situations people find themselves in – including the situation he found himself in when someone wrote for advice about a TV script: 'We sent it to Kenneth Williams and he was extremely enthusiastic about our script but he committed suicide soon after.' There is also, however, a strenuous, though never strained, intellectual wit; a love of *double* (at the very least) *entendre*; and a vein of fantasy – as when he imagines Kafka contemplating the contemporary world. Above all there is his ear (Bennett's Lug, it might be called, to go with *Flaubert's Parrot*, *Foucault's Pendulum* and his own *Kafka's Dick*), in the vicinity of which people hold remarkable conversations. At the home where his mother lives, for example, he hears one lady shout to another, over the noise of the hairdryer: 'I didn't want to be a Trappist nun. My father had Friar's Balsam in the medicine chest but that's as far as it went.'

How compatible making jokes is with being taken seriously is a problem that interests and perhaps vexes Bennett. It comes up with Kafka, a writer with a reputation for high seriousness, about whom he writes brilliantly and who he finds to be funnier and more English than people think – blackly comic enough to have said on his deathbed: 'I think I deserve the Nobel Prize for sputum.' Bennett's is an opposite problem. In this book there are some grandly ringing observations on the human condition: try 'Every family has a secret, and the secret is that it's not like other families.' But it is the jokes people remember.

He wouldn't want the jokes to be forgotten, but he sometimes feels like an imposter. When his play *Getting On*, which he hadn't intended to be funny, or only funny, won an *Evening Standard* award for the best comedy of 1971, he said at the ceremony that it was 'like entering a marrow for the show and being given the cucumber prize'. That was carrying it off gracefully. Elsewhere, the problems which directors, actors and critics have in knowing 'how to take' him give rise to tetchiness, though inevitably it breaks out as humour:

> *Enjoy* now in its second week at Richmond. See it
> tonight, after four days' absence, and find it has turned
> into *A Girl in My Soup*, with the actors hopping from
> laugh to laugh with no thought for what's in between.
> Several people, including Tom Sutcliffe in the
> *Guardian*, describe the play as 'courageous'. Since the
> central character is in drag throughout, this
> presupposes that I spend my evenings idly running my
> fingers along a rack of strapless evening-gowns and
> adjusting my slingbacks. Now it can be told.

It isn't told, because that would be telling. Readers for whom the word 'diaries' is now synonymous with sexual revelations will be disappointed by these, which come from someone who 'can scarcely remove his tie without first having a police cordon thrown round the building'. Though Bennett is not averse to discussing others' sexuality (Larkin's, Auden's), and though he is not wholly guarded about his own (he was tempted to go to Oxford after national service, he says, because of a crush on one of his fellow officer cadets), he evidently feels that this business is no one else's business – perhaps not even the business of Alan Bennett the writer, who has other things to think about.

He must have been strengthened in this conviction by the press's treatment of Russell Harty, a friend who taught him 'that to be silly is not to be foolish' and who is not forgotten here. Harty wasn't forgotten by the tabloids, either, which sent out teams to investigate his life and, as he lay on his deathbed with hepatitis, installed a cameraman in a flat opposite his ward in the hope that he might be dying from a different disease. Bennett feels a fiery indignation against such intrusion, and his diaries offer a salutary alternative. They may have begun in private, and they certainly explore parts of his life that aren't reached by the plays or television, and yet they aren't confessional or even especially gossipy. Mainly, they notice things. It's what he catches, not what he lets slip, that makes his diaries work.

At the end of *Writing Home*, Alan Bennett describes the embarrassing tradition of 'going round' after a play to the dressing room of actor friends to tell them how marvellous they were. Suffering as he does from a tendency to 'discount the praise and remember only the slights', Alan Bennett may be suspicious of the friends who tell him how marvellous his new book is – of the reviewers, too, who will prefer words such as 'irreverent' and 'satirical'. Never mind. All readers need to know is that they won't often come across a more enjoyable book.

Angela's Giggle

From time to time, you'll hear someone asking how come more postgraduate theses are being written about Angela Carter than about any other writer from Britain or perhaps the world. What's her secret? Is she really that good? There are the nine novels, including *Wise Children*, the last she published before her death from cancer, at fifty-one, in 1992. There are several collections of stories, reimaginings of folklore and fairy-tale. There is her brilliantly perverse polemic, *The Sadeian Woman*, which makes out a feminist case for the Marquis de Sade. There are the radio plays, film scripts and other dramatic pieces collected in *The Curious Room*. But for all that something has been missing.

Now we have it, in the shape of *Shaking a Leg*, a six-hundred-page selection of her journalism which explains what makes her a great and indispensable talent.

She came to journalism reluctantly. Her father was a Fleet Street man, a Scot working nights on the news desk, and though she adored him, and tried a brief stint on a local paper at eighteen, she didn't want to follow in the trade. But when she was in her thirties, Paul Barker, to his eternal credit, gave her the platform she needed at *New Society*. The need wasn't for money so much as the chance to test ideas, to find out what she thought and felt. It didn't matter whether the assignment was a book review, a travel piece, a memoir or an academic essay. Whatever Angela Carter wrote, she poured herself into, body and soul.

Body, especially. 'Notes from a Maternity Ward', her account of having her first (and only) baby at forty-three, must be one of the least pious pieces ever written about childbirth, wonderfully dismissive of ideas such as early bonding or of labour as an experience akin to orgasm or transcendental meditation ('colour film would have made souvenir snaps of the finale of my own accouchement look like stills from a Hammer horror film'). Sex, too, was an abiding – indeed *the* abiding – concern. She measured other writers by how they wrote about it: any hint of prudery or prurience, of faint-hearted euphemism or old-style male exploitation, and she'd be on to it. D. H. Lawrence, though 'the greatest English novelist of the century', she sees as a queasy stocking-fetishist. It isn't only men she goes for: affecting to pay tribute to the accomplishments of the porn star Linda Lovelace ('Not every girl can insert a foot inside her vagina'), she denounces her as safe and antiseptic. For Carter, there could be no greater sin of the flesh.

With this intense physical alertness went a tough mind. A 'second-generation grammar school kid', she was brainy without being cerebral: 'I flush hares out of my brain which I then pursue, to the detriment of rational discourse.' Rationalism she saw as an expression of self-confident masculinity, and she wasn't one for sweetly reasoned argument. Rather than slow construction work with blocks of logic, she preferred the task of demolition, 'the demythologizing business'. This isn't to say she was destructive, but she found much of post-war Britain stuffy and hypocritical, a house darkened by brittle lies, and she wanted to let a little light in. If that meant chucking stones, well and good. She had other projectiles, too –

nuggets of truth, pearls of wisdom, even (sometimes) grapes of wrath.

Politicians, especially, made her angry: their lies, their self-importance, their tolerance of nuclear weapons. But rancour wasn't her style. When she put people on trial, for their social attitudes or their art, she didn't solemnly denounce but laughed them out of court. One essay here is called 'Alison's Giggle', a tribute to the heroine of Chaucer's 'The Miller's Tale' for the innocent glee with which she pleases herself and gets the better of her husband, suitor and lover, 'which is more than a girl like her will be able to do again, in fiction, for almost more than half a millennium'. Carter's own giggles aren't so much girly as gently mocking. Her power as a feminist writer is that she's funny, derisive and self-delighting, not earnest at all.

One of her most charming tics is a genteel, heaven-help-us exasperation – expressions like 'dammit', for instance, or 'rum, that' or 'oh dear no' tacked on to the end of a sentence, which are funny because of the stronger words you know must have occurred to her (she was, by her own admission, 'notoriously foul-mouthed'). Yet charm is something she feels uncomfortable with, a family curse, the bit of herself that cloyingly seeks approval, especially from men. She disapproves of the way her early novels 'disarm with charm'. She deplores it in others, too: it's 'what can put you off' the wonderful stories of Grace Paley. Yet Carter can't help but exude charm. It's there in her voice, like the sound of money in Daisy Buchanan's in *The Great Gatsby*. As a teenager she had wanted to be an actress, to captivate and perform. The instinct remained, no matter how she tried to drive it out with something steelier.

If this is one of the great tensions in Carter, the other is the war between northern pragmatism and airy southern caprice. Born in Eastbourne – according to 'the family talent for magical realism', her mother's pregnancy was confirmed the day the Second World War broke out – she spent her first five years in south Yorkshire, where she was brought up mainly by her granny, a 'squat, fierce and black-clad [woman] like the granny in the Giles cartoons in the *Sunday Express*'. It was a social-realist infancy, among miners with hacking coughs. At the end of the war, when the bombs had stopped, Angela and her mother rejoined her dandyish father in south London, and assumed a bohemian lifestyle without rules, punishments or bedtimes. But by then the damage was done. The withering voice of her grandmother resounded in the growing novelist's ear ('Tha bloody fool'), alerting her to all displays of pseudery and affectation, not least her own.

That no-nonsense primal world had also been a matriarchy, however, and gave her 'a sense of my sex's ascendancy in the scheme of things'. This proved inconvenient at home (where her mother set a frailer example) and also when Angela 'was looking for boyfriends in the south in the late fifties', when girls were supposed to be soft and pink. Her adolescent rebelliousness was hampered by having no one to rebel with, her eagerness for sexual experience by a lack of men predatory enough to find her attractive rather than merely threatening. At eighteen, she became anorexic, and went down from fifteen stone to six. Recovering, she married the first man who'd sleep (and go to Godard movies) with her, a man her father thought a 'nitwit'. The marriage didn't last. The feminism did.

Through involvement in the women's movement, and through reading, Carter became aware of herself as 'a new kind of being', luckier than her forbears in being sexually and economically independent. Part of declaring independence was to travel: she lived in Japan for two years, and observed the 'prim lack of inhibition' there (on one occasion she worked as a bar hostess). Other pieces here record her thoughts on Turkey, Arizona, New England, Venice. But even

sturdy British landscapes can look exotic to her: who else but
Carter could see a Bradford sky as having 'the colour and texture of ripe apricots'? Home or abroad, she had a simple
motto: 'The back of beyond is not necessarily the asshole of
the universe.'

Like Bruce Chatwin, she felt torn between being a nomad,
free as a bird, and a homebody, surrounded by pleasing
objects. Lifestyle fascinated her – the Habitat catalogue, the
gentrification of south London where she grew up ('at any
point in history, the one thing you can always be sure of is that
the middle class is always on the rise') . But she never made
the mistake of thinking style an adequate replacement for real
life. It was the same with eating. As her granny might have put
it, Carter liked her food. But she didn't like food fashion or
fetishism. There's a brilliant attack here on the new vegetari-
anism, which she hates for its holier-than-thou sentimentalizing
of 'grain' and 'seed'. The same disabused note (plain Barnsley
common sense) is there when she slices into the vogue for
home-baked bread, or reassesses Elizabeth David and culinary snobbism.

With food, so, I think, with men. Carter has plenty to say
about us behaving (or writing, or thinking) badly. We're sexually predictable, we dominate conversation, we're weak and
hypocritical ('It is a favourite saying among women of my
type that if men could have babies, then abortion would be as
readily available as light ale'). But only a misogynist could
imagine that Carter seriously had it in for men. Her tone is
teasing and affectionate, and not only in 'Sugar Daddy', her
memoir of her father.

Few novelists have written better about clothes than she
does. This isn't because of the influence of Roland Barthes's
semiotics, but because she has been there, worn that, knows
her material, can explain why women (including herself) adopt
a certain look at a certain time. When she writes about the

'bee-sting underlip' in the archetypal sixties face, or analyses the 'wound' of a painted face, or notes how women sometimes choose to be crippled in high heels or shackled by tight skirts, her subject is the *Zeitgeist*, not the catwalk. She admired vulgarity – which was life getting past the taste police. Pornography, pubs, funfairs, wrestling, horror comics, *True Romance*, Judith Krantz, the *Star* and *Sport*, the box ('the essential oddness of television as a medium, the sense of uninvolved participation'): she devoured them with the same voracity as she did surrealism, Frida Kahlo or Peter Greenaway.

Her many literary essays and reviews suggest she felt in good company with her alphabetical near-neighbours on the shelves: on one side Borges, Burgess, Burroughs, Calvino and Peter Carey (whose *Oscar and Lucinda* fills her 'with wild, savage envy, and no novelist could say fairer than that'), on the other Chatwin, Coetzee and Colette. She praises Iain Sinclair and Michael Moorcock for their mythologizing of London. She honours J. G. Ballard for showing that the more imaginative and fantastical fiction is, the better it teaches us the truth about ourselves. If she'd been alive to see it, she'd certainly have stuck up for Cronenberg's *Crash*, and would have pointed out that even in an allegedly 'permissive' society somebody is always appointed to do the permitting.

She once described herself as a 'female black-beetle' – an insect and iconoclast scuttling among the lovely ruins left by dead white European males. The blackness was in her humour, too: 'the only sane existential position to hold', she thought, was 'that at the end of every rainbow, lies not a pot of gold but a crock of shit'. Her cruelly early death suggests she was right about that, as about so much else. But at least for the rest of us there's the gold she left behind in her collected journalism, a treasury of her life and art and thought.

The Great Divide

A couple of years ago, flicking through a book of aerial photographs, I began playing a silly game. From certain angles, bits of the landscape had the look of body parts. Slowly I assembled a human figure. Lulworth Cove, in Dorset, resembled an ear. Orford Ness, in Suffolk, and Spurn Head, where the River Humber enters the sea, provided a pair of arms. Silbury Hill looked like a nipple. Striding Edge, in the Lake District, served as a spine. Teeth came courtesy of the Needles, off the Isle of Wight. Numerous ancient burial sites competed for the role of navel. Keep the game up long enough and I knew I could end up with something like the Cerne Abbas giant, a figure of mythic potency, a sleeping giant, one body, one nation.

Since Labour's 1997 election landslide, the image of Britain as unified body seems much less whimsical than it did in the years of Thatcher and Major. One of the key moments of the 1997 campaign was Tony Blair's speech about Labour as the 'one nation' party, 'behind which people from all walks of life, all classes, all parts of Britain can unite . . . a Britain with shared values and purpose . . . where no one is cast out'. It's true that to win the hearts of middle England (wherever that is) Blair had to change Labour's hue: there's a rinse of blue through the old red, making the colour purple. It's also true the map of Britain still has mottled patches, not least those liberal bruises of yellow. Still, the dream of unity seems closer to reality now than it has done for many years.

Or does it? There remains an embarrassing obstacle to national oneness: the North–South divide.

No one is sure exactly where to locate this divide. Does it run in a line from the Humber to the Mersey, or from the Wash to Chester? Does passport control lie further down, closer to Birmingham, or even as far south as Watford Gap? Is the divide really a diagonal from the Exe to the Tees, separating the upland north-west from the lowland south-east? And how about Scotland, Ireland and Wales: should they be included in the equation, or – since they have their own north–south differences, just as Italy and France do – is it best to think of the divide as an English, not British phenomenon? The topography of the North–South divide is complex. But most people understand easily enough what's meant by it: not just that northerners are different from southerners, but that they're economically worse off.

Few people these days like to mention the divide. Northern mayors, full of civic pride, are as reluctant to speak of it as are plummy metropolitan power-brokers. Least likely of all to acknowledge it, for obvious reasons, are parties in government. In the 1980s, Margaret Thatcher vigorously denied its existence several times. Kenneth Clarke said it was 'a ridiculous simplification'. Lord King, chairman of British Airways, said it existed only in our minds, and that we should get rid of the complex. Most brazenly of all, Lord Young, in 1987, proclaimed that 'until seventy years ago the north was always the richest part of the country', so it was only right and proper if 'now some of [the wealth] is in the south. It's our turn, that's all.'

Lord Young was historically inaccurate: even at the height of Mancunian prosperity in the nineteenth century, only a third of millionaires came from the north. Mrs Thatcher, too, was disingenuous: her Cabinet in the late 1980s had only one minister out of twenty-two from the north: his name was Cecil Parkinson. As for the business community, the fact that ninety of the top one hundred companies in Britain at the end of the 1980s were based in London and the south-east gives the lie to the idea of a wide cascade and equal spread of wealth. The vast majority of private swimming pools, and of *Who's Who* entries, are concentrated inside the M25. Surveys show that there are bigger wages there, higher house prices, longer lifespans, more dishwashers, less smoking and alcohol consumption, less sex, less baldness, fewer burglaries and less heart disease, too. For some years now, the population of England has been drifting southwards – a bottom-heavy redistribution, with the population of the Milton Keynes district growing by 42 per cent. Aptly, the zone which grew most (both economically and geographically) in the 1980s, along the south coast and up through the Home Counties, had the shape of the £ sign.

But while the divide may have widened in the 1980s, as the Conservative Party strengthened London and the south-east as a power base, it was created a long way further back. Historians of the phenomenon – including Graham Turner in *The North Country* (1967), David Smith in *North and South: Britain's Growing Divide* (1989), Frank Musgrove in *The North of England* (1990) and Helen M. Jewell in *The North-South Divide* (1994) – emphasize its roots in the ancient past. Indeed, the more you read about it, the more it begins to seem a matter of landscape and human temperament than of mere economics. All in the head? No, it's as solid as Hadrian's Wall.

I grew up on the Lancashire–Yorkshire border. The first divide I knew was a local one: on one side, the Yorkshire

Dales – sheep, limestone outcrops, drystone walls; on the other, a valley of industry, Lancashire and its cotton mills. The divide was even audible in our voices: the local grammar school had a catchment area of only a few miles, but we all spoke in slightly different accents, according to which county, town or village we came from.

So I never thought the north homogenous. But what united adults and children alike was a sense of belonging on one side of a much larger divide. Over the hills somewhere lay the Home Counties, 'Them'; which made Us the away team, proud of where we lived but marginalized. Southerners don't have much a sense of themselves as southerners, unless they venture north. But northerners are always deeply aware of being northerners, wherever they are.

Growing up where I did, I resented the fact that the image which southerners seemed to have of the north was uniformly urban: street after street of terraced back-to-backs – whether Sheffield, or Manchester, or Liverpool, or Leeds, or Newcastle. From L. S. Lowry to *Coronation Street*, from Charles Dickens to Richard Hoggart, the story was the same: the north as poor, urban, and – a few millowners aside – exclusively working-class. Factories, foundries and fish and chip shops. In the gaps between the houses, slag heaps, cindery recreation fields and men in flat caps out walking whippets.

But of course my view of the south was no less of a cliché. The south meant London, the Big Smoke. Or if not London, a ridiculously posh and prettified village: thatched cottages, neat gardens, a church with its spire, a gentle river, unstrenuous hills, sunshine, a pub with the name of an English king, oaks and chestnuts, a cricket field, the vicar on his bicycle, mildness in the air, the elements tamed. Something a bit cutesy and picture postcard-like. A place not so much lived in as passed through by tourists. A picture of middle-class affluence and affectation. There are villages in the Yorkshire

Dales which don't look so different. Never mind. That was the stereotype.

When did the divisive stereotypes begin? Most people would say in the nineteenth century, with industrialization. In 1854, Elizabeth Gaskell published her novel *North and South*, about a southern family uprooted to a town called Milton-Northern (Manchester), in the county of Darkshire. The heroine Margaret's first impressions are ominous: a deep, lead-coloured cloud hanging over the horizon; long straight hopeless streets of small redbrick houses; 'the ceaseless roar and mighty beat and dizzying whirl of machinery'. For his part, John Thornton, the millowner who pursues Margaret, has similarly sharp prejudices against the south – a society of ease and affluence, decadent and purposeless, a land of fops and idlers, 'clogged with honey and unable to rise and fly'.

Engels, Dickens, Ruskin – all added to the picture. Alexis de Tocqueville, another visitor to Manchester, wrote of the stream of industry flowing out through 'this foul drain' to fertilize the world: 'Here humanity attains its most complete development and its most brutish; here civilization makes its miracles, and civilized man is turned almost back into a savage.' In the era of carboniferous capitalism, of iron and steel, coal and cotton, canals and railways, it was the north which had the energy and owned the resources. Middlesbrough, on the Tees, was a single farmhouse in 1830; by 1880, it had a population of 50,000.

But the rift between north and south is much older than a hundred or a hundred and fifty years. Halifax, for instance, which in Dean Clough (built in the 1840s) once boasted the largest carpet factory in the world, has a wool industry that goes back to the fourteenth century. And the reports of two great travel writers visiting Halifax circa 1700, Daniel Defoe and Celia Fiennes, suggest that images of an incalcitrant and barbarous north pre-date industrialism by some way. As Macaulay put it, 'No traveller ventured into that country without making his will. [The people] are scarcely less savage than the Indians of California.' A long line of English kings proved noticeably reluctant to visit the north, passing through by necessity rather than choice. Only Richard III had any real feeling for the region – and no monarch has a worse reputation. Further back, there'd been the harrying of the north, by William the Conqueror, to punish the area for its Danish sympathies. Many people were killed, and villages destroyed. Northumbria, an economically disadvantaged area to start with, was ruthlessly laid waste. It was centuries before the region could begin to recover.

Such were the tensions between northerners and southerners at Oxford University in 1252 that twelve peacemakers were appointed from each side. Chaucer, putting together 'The Reeve's Tale' in the late fourteenth century, made differing speech patterns and dialect an integral part of the story: the two Cambridge students who outwit the unscrupulous Trumpington miller are from Northumberland, and their broad vowels (Chaucer would have heard such speech while serving as a page to the Duchess of Clarence, in Yorkshire) convey a canniness that enables them to turn the tables on their enemy. The North–South divide has left its mark on ecclesiastical history as well as linguistic. The Church of England has been divided into two provinces, one in Canterbury, one in York, since the eighth century – and still is today.

There's not much record of northern counties in the Domesday book of 1086, itself a symptom of neglect. But we know this was a less populated region, one reputedly 'lurking with wild beasts and robbers'. We know also a north–south division had already opened up before the eleventh century, between the kingdoms of Mercia and Northumbria. King Alfred refers to the divide, when he complains that very few men 'this side of the Humber' could translate a single letter from Latin into English. A sense was developing of northerners as truculent, or uncultured, or proudly independent, depending on where you're standing. Even the learning and influence of Bede, in eighth-century Northumbria, did little to dispel this impression.

Earlier, the Romans had divided their outpost of empire into Britannia Superior and Britannia Inferior, and never felt so secure in the north as in the more easily subdued south. Tacitus, describing Britain in the first century, compared the shape of the country to a double-headed axe, and reminded his Roman readers, 'One must remember we are dealing with barbarians'. Even the potter's wheel took longer to reach the north – the region lagging behind southern fashions, as always.

You could say that whereas the south has been shaped by Roman and Norman influence, the north, because of Norse or Viking settlement, has a more Scandinavian character. There are people in Newcastle-upon-Tyne today who claim to feel more affinity with Sweden and Denmark and Norway than with London. They imagine building a Geordie nation state which is 'very like Scandinavia' and speak of 'a broad northern arc where the Channel Tunnel is left to a congested south, while Geordies break free for trade routes their forbears knew – out of Ireland, and Scotland, and across into Scandinavia, the Baltic, Russia' (quotes from Robert Colls and Bill Lancaster's book of essays *Geordies*). It's in the same provoking, northern-separatist spirit that the millowner's son in the classic comedy *Hindle Wakes* looks upon London as 'the place where rich Lancashire men go for a spree if they have not time to go to Monte Carlo or Paris'.

What all this suggests is that the great divide is as old as the hills. Literally. Lack of hills in the south-east meant the region was best suited to arable farming; an abundance of hills in the north-west meant pastoral farming and, later, industry. In the Lake District can be found the oldest rocks in England: they're hard and ancient, pre-Cambrian, some 4,000 million years old, and naturally attractive, in their alpine grandeur, to Romantic poets. The chalk downs of the south-east are younger and softer.

Rocks and hills affect human temperament as well as human activity. 'Our soul is, above half of it, earth and stone in its affections and distempers,' said Jeremy Taylor. Since the Pennines are often called 'the backbone of England' it's no wonder if those who live close to them like to think of themselves as gritty and tough, and look down on southerners as soft-bellied, spineless and effete – the lounge lizards of the Home Counties. They think of them as flatter, too, less colourful, less jaggedly individualistic, since to a northern eye the landscapes of the south-east look drear and monotone, which can't help but affect their inhabitants.

These myths may be simplistic, but that doesn't make them any less pervasive. You can point out to a northerner that vast tracts of the south – Cornwall and Devon, East Anglia and the Fens – are physically, morally and economically remote from the charmed circle of the M25. You can point out to a southerner that blunt speaking (that famous northern trait) does not mean absence of intelligence or sophistication. But the old prejudices are deeply rooted. There are still northerners who believe (as Eddie Waring pretended to) that people in the Home Counties eat with their gloves on, and there are still southerners who share the feelings of Beau Brummel, in the late eighteenth century, who on being told that his regiment was being sent from Brighton to Manchester said he hadn't bargained on foreign service when he joined up. On both sides there's long been a feeling of: sod the other half. Why not saw the country in two, so London can join Brussels while

Manchester, Newcastle, etc. are towed out into the North Sea?

'With the skyscrapers coming,' said the painter L. S. Lowry in his eighties, 'everything will be the same fifty years from now.' George Orwell and J. B. Priestley made similar predictions in the 1930s. Their prophecies haven't been realized – the great divide still runs deep – but superficially Britain does *look* much more homogenized than it used to. You can go to any medium-sized town anywhere in the country now and find the same: the pedestrianized high street, the out-of-town super-store, the light-industrial estate with corrugated sheds, and all these places called centres – the leisure centre, the garden centre, the shopping centre – which don't really have a centre, only a cash register. This is where most of us live now, in a place vaguely resembling Milton Keynes. In a northern city like Sheffield, you no longer see smoke blooming from the old industrial vases. J. B. Priestley, looking at such a cityscape in the 1930s, described it as 'a hideous muddle, where industry has had a dirty meal and done no washing up'. Now the cups and plates are gleaming, and the bricks have lost their grime. The mills and factories have turned into heritage centres, restaurants and art galleries. Even the hills beyond look different. There are new white windmills on them, like rotorblades, farming the prevailing westerlies.

Lowry would have hated it, but if we are – outwardly – becoming more homogenized it may be no bad thing. To bury our differences feels decent and grown-up. Regional identity is a deeply Old Labour idea, the ticket on which Neil Kinnock fought the 1992 election when he lost to the 'man from nowhere', or Huntingdon, John Major. To speak in a regional accent seems Old Labour, too, now that Estuary English is the norm. Loyalty to the ground we come from seems narrow and sometimes dangerous. Rootsiness is discredited and out-of-date. Most of us are exiles these days, living away from the place we grew up, our feet in one place, our heart in another. It's a common condition of late-twentieth-century life, not something to bleat on about. My having been born in the north of England, or you in London, don't seem matters of great import now the globe has shrunk. Travel broadens the mind, and road, rail and air links help eliminate local prejudice and superstition. We're all citizens of the world.

But homogenization is a damaging myth, when used by politicians to paper over cracks. Disraeli once spoke of Britain as two nations, 'as ignorant of each other's thoughts and feelings as if we were inhabitants of different planets', and economically, almost every survey suggests, we are still two nations. People in the north have long lived on the wrong side of the money divide. A fairer spread of power, wealth and health must remain the task of any responsible government. It's to be hoped that Tony Blair, as the first northern prime minister since Harold Wilson, will confront the great divide, rather than argue as Mrs Thatcher did that it's 'all in the head'. There are cracks in the nation's fabric that can and should be closed up.

But there are also cracks we can celebrate, divisions that belong to history, geology and culture – even, perhaps, to human temperament. Flying over the country last year, by plane and helicopter, it struck me how rich and varied the English landscape still looks. However flattened out from 4,000 feet, and however softened by genial summer sunlight, sharp differences kept poking up. The human differences they give rise to, in how we talk and think and feel, are ones that will never disappear. A good thing, too. They're the differences we're richer for.

A Tourist in My Own Backyard

You didn't get many hikers in the winter months, but round Easter they'd start slogging through, their backpacks heaped under the village tree as they disappeared inside the post office, our one shop, in search of ginger beer or Kendal Mint Cake (no chance). It was usually windy as well as raining, and I couldn't understand the attraction. I knew the next mile or so of the route – up School Lane, past the quarry, down across the fields, by the marsh, over the hill to the lonely white farmhouse by the beck, up and down another hill, on to the canal bank and round by towpath to East Marton. I'd done the walk many times with my parents and cousins, always ending with crisps and lemonade at the Cross Keys. But I can't say I envied the walkers their route. It was cold. The light was pale as primrose. You'd not catch me dead trekking the April fields in heavy boots.

Partly it was just that it was home, by definition boring: you can't be a smiling tourist in your own backyard. And though the Pennine Way ran through, our village – Thornton-in-Craven – wasn't that pretty: publess, straggling, and bisected by a busy main road, it was too near the Lancashire border to

be a proper Dales village. When I did start doing some walk-
ing, in my late teens, I chose the Lake District, or the
Pyrenees. I was thirty before I tackled a section of the Pennine
Way.

By this point, having moved south, I'd come to understand
that Thornton has its charms, that nearby Skipton is an
unusually pretty market town, and that beyond in all direc-
tions lie beauty spots that people will drive hundred of miles
to visit. All for free on my doorstep. But I'd been too blind,
indolent or moodily adolescent to see.

My father *had* seen it, choosing the nearby mill-town of
Earby to set up in medical practice with my mother partly
because of its proximity to the Dales. On his rare days off, he
could think of nothing better than a drive to Malham Tarn or
Burnsall or the White Scar Cave near Ingleton. But he was my
boring old dad, and as we negotiated the Pennine switchbacks
the main feeling my sister and I had from the back seat of the
car wasn't *joie de vivre* such as he felt but that he'd better wind
the window down or we'd throw up.

Now my father is dead, but my mother and sister still live in
Thornton. A tripper to childhood sources, I go back several
times a year, often driving my own children to the same places
to which I was driven thirty years ago. Bolton Abbey and the
Strid, for instance, where you can park near the Cavendish
Pavilion and walk down to the twelfth-century priory, a ruin
which Ruskin once praised for its 'sweet peace and tender
decay', and which has more recently featured in one of David
Hockney's photographic collages. Across from the priory are
stepping stones, always good for a wet plimsoll or two, and in
summer, trout leap from the slow brown water. A walk on
either side of the Wharfe will take you back up to the Strid,
where, whatever the season, white water swirls in the narrow
ravine between two sets of rocks. The name, I was always
told, comes from the bare *stride* it takes to get from one side to

the other. If you're foolhardy enough. For centuries this has proved too giant a step for many a man, and once you're in the black water you don't come up again, not alive. Wordsworth commemorated an early casualty in a poem written circa 1808:

> *And hither is young Romilly come,*
> *And what may now forbid*
> *That he, perhaps for the hundredth time,*
> *Shall bound across the Strid?*
>
> *He sprang in glee – for what cared he*
> *That the river was strong and the rocks were steep,*
> *But the greyhound in the leash hung back,*
> *And checked him in his leap.*
>
> *The boy is in the arms of Wharf,*
> *And strangled by a merciless force.*
> *For never more was young Romilly seen*
> *Till he rose a lifeless corpse.*

If you've not made Romilly's mistake, you can follow the Wharfe up past the aqueduct south of Barden Bridge. Further on lies Burnsall, and beyond are Grassington, Linton and Threshfield, all delightful villages in my day though Grassington now gets very busy. Crowded or not, Wharfedale remains one of the most beautiful landscapes in the country. It was after seeing it that Turner painted 'Hannibal Crossing the Alps'. Alps would be pushing it, but high up on an April day, watching the hills roll away to infinity, you can feel you are breathing mountain air.

The other outing we regularly used to make was to Malham and Gordale Scar. From a distance, the climb (to the left of the Scar) looks difficult, even dangerous, but it is not.

The walk round Malham Tarn takes you past a house at which Charles Kingsley once stayed – *The Water Babies* is supposed to have been set here. Most exciting of all were – and are – the rocks above Malham Cove (that extraordinary 250-feet stone curtain). I wasn't good enough at geography to understand the explanations of why they look as they do – i.e., that they'd been 'created when glacial melt waters ran down the steep hillside produced by the fault and eroded back, cutting into the edge of the limestone bed'. But I knew what I liked, which was scrambling and leaping about. By June, martins would have arrived to build nests in the great rock overhang.

The Craven area – my bit of the Dales – is notable for its limestone: the stream-carved brightness, the sculpted white-ness, so different from harsh granite and coarse grey millstone grit. It was a special moment at school when I discovered Auden's 'In Praise of Limestone', the first poem I'd read in which I recognized bits of the world I knew. What Auden admires in limestone seems much like his love of wearing slip-pers and going to bed at nine – a comfiness:

> . . . *when I try to imagine a faultless love*
> *Or the life to come, what I hear is the murmur*
> *Of underground streams, what I see is a limestone landscape.*

From a distance, it's sometimes impossible to work out which bits of a facing hillside are limestone outcrops and which bits sheep – sheep being the other dominant feature of the land-scape. Being middle-class incomers, we were moved by the annual dramas of sheep-rearing: the lambs mewing patheti-cally for their mothers, the silly ewes and tups getting their heads stuck in wire fences, the rituals of dipping and shear-ing – including that moment when the bewildered, upended sheep would be set back on its feet and run off in relief, little red nicks in its new nakedness. The farmers were less sentimental, measuring dead lambs in lost income, not tears, and warning that any dog found worrying sheep would be shot on sight. These farmers were famous for their curt tongues and tight wallets. I grew up afraid of them.

There were other places we must have visited on days off: Gaping Gill, Simon's Seat, the Valley of Desolation, Kilnsey Crag (where you park and try to pick out the fluorescent-bright climbers on the rock face). But looking back, I'm conscious of all I failed to see and do. I explored Ingleborough Cave, learning there (and promptly forgetting) the difference between stalagmites and stalactites, but this was on a guided tour – unlike some of my schoolfriends, I wasn't hardy enough to take up potholing. I climbed Pen-y-Ghent, but not the other two summits of the Three Peaks (the challenge was to do all three in twelve hours). I only once visited Skipton Castle, home of the Clifford family – Lord Clifford being made famous, in Shakespeare, for fighting on the wrong (Lancaster) side in the Wars of the Roses. I never took the Settle–Carlisle railway, one of the great achievements of civil engineering (seventy-two miles of track, twelve tunnels and fifteen viaducts through an area of high fells and deep valleys). I even turned down the chance to board at Giggleswick school, preferring to be a state day boy in Skipton.

There was always the feeling that the real action must be elsewhere. One summer's day in the late 1960s, I drove a friend to a remote Dales farmhouse, where, he'd assured me, a guy he'd met at a party would be waiting to give us two tabs of LSD: the idea was to drop them there, in beautiful sur-roundings and where no one would see if we behaved weirdly. The farm was deserted. The wind sang emptily around. We walked off, came back, hung about and nothing happened. So it goes, said my friend, several hours later, and so we went. In London or even Manchester, I was sure, there must be more to life. Rural adolescence was one non-event after another. Postponement – which the rainy weather contributed to – was its essence. I even wrote a poem about it.

Everything I look forward to gets rained off:
the fêtes, the football, the summer dances.
When I'm dead, they'll put, as my epitaph:
'Cancelled, due to unforeseen circumstances.'

But the place had its pleasures, home-grown (gooseberries and broad beans), home-made (crumbling towers of Wensleydale cheese) and home-brewed (Theakstons ale from Masham). There were also the pheasant and grouse which friends or patients would bring my father, and which he'd hang for a week in the outhouse – a bit too reminiscent of the dead crows which Pennine farmers string up to discourage other carrion, but we consumed them, with breadcrumbs, none the less. One August, no doubt with paternal instructions to smuggle a brace back with me, I took part in a grouse-beat on the Duke of Devonshire's land, as one of a large group of (male) adolescents. We were driven up on to the moors in the back of lorries and Land Rovers, dropped at hundred-yard intervals, and then – at a signal – set off in line swishing and shouting at the heather. The little birds skirled off ahead. We could hear guns popping in the distance, though by the time we reached the spot the lordly, tweedy, booted, deerstalker-and-four-plus-clad gunmen would be lounging on tartan rugs drinking champagne. No rest for us: it would be straight on to the next beat – there were six in a day, and needed to be, if the aristos were to bag enough braces. I became a socialist that August – though a vegetarian and anti-blood sports campaigner might have been as appropriate. We were paid 12s. 6d. a day, as I recall, not as good a rate as they paid on other estates. When one of my friends asked for a pay rise, and – refused – tried to persuade the rest of us to go on strike, he was told never to show his face again. Footsore, I didn't show again either.

My school exercise books from a few years earlier display a complete indifference to moorland birds such as grouse, but are full of excited descriptions – mostly (I suspect) copied from the *Observer Book of Birds* – of birds seen about the garden: mistle thrushes, rooks, jackdaws, redstarts, long-tailed tits, pied wagtails, wheatears. Many species didn't come till summer, but in April there were already curlews to be heard in their plaintive crescendos, and lapwings to be seen hurling themselves about (a performance, I was told, intended to lead would-be intruders away from the nest). Hares sat up on hillocks (their ears twin peaks) then rocketed away. The becks ran fast, and snow hung on in shady gullies.

It gives me a chill just to think of it. Global warming or not, the climate of the Dales hasn't changed much in quarter of a century. Flowers are still scarce in April: snowdrop, primrose, celandine. The swallows, too, come late. And the fields by the Aire, or by Thornton beck, are often under water. But when the sun shines on their plate glass, or a curlew cries, or I stoop to restore a fallen piece to a drystone wall, I feel a different kind of chill: the hair standing up, shiver down the spine kind. I wouldn't want to live there all the time – not now, not yet – but it's where I think home must be.

Nature Comes to Town

While I sit here in my basement trying to write, a fox jumps over the small brown hedge. Upstairs, a sparrow flies in through the kitchen door to pick up breakfast crumbs. Grey squirrels skip across the grass. Canada geese parade like sentries round the nearby lake. Jays and magpies bustle in the trees. Herons have been sighted circling ponds. There's probably even a questing vole somewhere, feather-footing it through a plashy fen.

These aren't supposed to be nature notes, and if all I've described were happening in the countryside it wouldn't be worth mentioning. But it's happening in an inner-London borough, six miles from Leicester Square. Those foxes have their earth in a suburban garden. Those geese are nesting in a council estate. Welcome to the peaceable new kingdom, the rural metropolis.

As a child in a Yorkshire village, I used to pore over guidebooks to British birds and mammals. It was my ambition to spot the rarer species – pine martens, polecats, hoopoes – and if their habitat was remote and mountainous, as it usually seemed to be, there was always the hope I'd spot them from the car on holidays. I didn't get very far: plenty of tits and finches, but nothing more exotic than the occasional redstart or hedgehog. At school I read Ted Hughes's poem, 'The Thought Fox', which imagined 'the sharp, hot stink of fox'. It wasn't a smell I knew; thought was as close as I got to foxes. On Boxing Day, the local hunt gathered, red in face and coat, with such excited hounds and in such numbers it seemed certain there must be foxes about the place somewhere. I never saw one. Now I see them every day.

I'm not sentimental about having nature close by. Herons carry off goldfish. Squirrels are just rats with bushy tails. As for foxes, they rip open plastic rubbish bags, burst plastic balls, sick up heaps of red berries, steal any clothing or gardening gloves left out overnight, dig up plants, and keep us awake with their unearthly mating cries (not that they only do it at night: there's a good deal of shameless daylight rutting and knotting too). The children, brought up on tales of foxy cunning and dreaming them as big as wolves, are prone to nightmares. Above all, or rather under all, there's the shit on the lawn. It may have come from a wild animal rather than a pet, but fox shit is no more pleasant to step in than dog shit.

It's no idyll. Foxes can be pigs. Yet there's an uneasy mutual respect. They have their territory and we have ours. We chuck them discarded bones, and they let us watch their cubs at play. Some canter off over the garden wall if we get too near, but others – older, bolder, lolling in long grass or sunbathing on sheds – don't even bother to get up if we approach. One even walked into our kitchen.

Darwin, in the Galapagos in 1835, marvelled at the tameness of the birds there, which would perch on human shoulders. But he also felt frustrated with their stupidity, their failure to acquire a proper terror of mankind. Twentieth-century fox, by contrast, is clever enough to know such terror is inappropriate. Since 1945, the emigration into cities has been relentless, and there are now twice as many foxes in

London as in the outlying rural south-east. The pickings are richer here, square meals easier to come by: the women who might once have worn foxes round their necks now feed them bread and meat. Cars are a hazard: 50 per cent of urban foxes are run over, and whereas foxes in captivity can live up to fourteen years on London's streets their life expectancy is a mere fourteen months. But they breed in such numbers their population is steadily growing, and it seems they feel safer away from the guns, insecticides and open spaces. We townies speak more nicely to foxes than our country cousins do: we don't make them feel like vermin.

Fifty years ago no one would have predicted that the fox would return to the human fold, nor that so many other species – pipistrelle bats, badgers, sparrowhawks, short-eared owls – would prosper in an urban environment. Some species are flourishing almost too well: grey squirrels, for example, with their nasty habit of bark-stripping and nipping out the ends of acorns, and Canada geese, which raze the grass and are driving out native breeds.

This countrification of the city, or urbanizing of nature, overthrows many inherited assumptions. Traditionally, the city has been thought the enemy of all creatures except man. Only the nastiest vermin, it seemed, could survive here (rats, cockroaches), and the authorities took due measure to eradicate them: the Pied Piper of Hamelin was a precursor of Rentokil. Domestic pets were allowed a place, on a lead or on a sofa, but for wild animals – fear of whom was one of the motives for building cities in the first place – the only niche was in a cage or at the zoo. For any faintly succulent breed, the commonest fate was to be served up at the table.

Now, there's a desire to readmit the wild, and the city is home to a variety of creatures. Some are opportunists (like the fox) or arrive out of the blue: a few years back there was a documentary about a family of kestrels which, outdoing King

Kong, colonized the Empire State Building. Other species have to be encouraged, in specially cleared or constructed nature reserves. The London Wildlife Trust, for example, has fifty-seven sites across the capital, and has shown that there's more to nature in the city than wallabies in Battersea Park or kiddie farms with rabbits, sheep and goats. Such 'management' is artificial, but it's one of the insights of the conservationist movement that nature can't be just left to go hang. In the eighteenth century, civilization, the antonym of nature, meant pet monkeys and dancing bears. Now civilization lets the buffalo roam in theme parks just outside the capital, while birds, bats, badgers and butterflies are invited in.

Meanwhile, the pest control agencies, ecologically wised up, are redefining what pests are. Nuisance to humans isn't enough of a criterion. One man's vermin may be another's deep communion with mother nature. When bees swarmed against my kitchen wall a few years ago, then crawled inside in hundreds up the waste pipe, no agency would touch them: though they can sting no less than wasps, bees are not classified as a pest. Exasperated but oddly grateful, I had to find a bee-keeper, who in turn had to find the queen.

Conservationists rightly insist that we still have a long way to go: one swallow nesting in the eaves of a computer firm doesn't make a summer. But the proliferation of urban species does seem to defy the rhetoric of those environmentalists who argue that an industrial or post-industrial society is necessarily hostile to nature. More, the resilience of the urban fox, or of those species whose habitat is now the motorway verge, reinstates something tough and Darwinian into ecological debate. Nature isn't always a helpless victim: it can adapt and prosper. And we humans may be less aggressive than we give ourselves credit for: those Canada geese on the council estate have not yet had their necks slit by bored teenagers or ended in the poor man's pot.

If nothing else, those foxes down the garden are an excuse to deny the kids a family pet: why this big need for a dog when there's so much doggy behaviour (barks, puppy-fights, leg-cocking) available just outside? At best, they inspire the hope that the world is slowly being put to rights, allowing us a modern Eden where we live and work in cities while also staying close to other species. Close but not too close: there's no better cure for soulful pantheism than a sole full of fox shit.

Two Wheels Good

Nearly, we can do it . . . harder. Harder . . . almost there . . . keep going . . . that's it . . . so near, oh yes . . . one last push, oh God, yes, yes . . . there . . . made it . . . Jesus . . . bliss.

Is there a more ecstatic experience than cycling to the top of a small hill in coastal Suffolk and seeing spread out, as if on a vast screen, what you've spent the last few miles heading towards: the North Sea? Climbing a mountain would probably give you more sense of achievement. Looking down at a craggy cove on the west coast of Ireland might be more uplifting. Oysters, peaches, Chablis, silk shirts, French kissing, the fur of Labradors, the cry of Manx shearwaters, a sunset at Key West, a delicate drop shot at tennis – all have their rival sensual charms. But still: to dismount from the saddle and stand there a moment, a light dew of effort on your forehead, the bike tipped at an angle on its stand, the wheels stilled so you hear the gulls and terns weeping . . . and the distant shoosh of the waves trying and trying again to make something of themselves . . . and the whiff of brine competing with other scents – sage and thyme, heather-blooms from the bracken, campion, foxgloves . . . and then to unclip the drinks bottle from the frame and take a swig of water, slightly warm maybe and with a tang of heavy plastic, but at this moment, under the sun's heat and in your own heat, miraculous as the wine at Canaa. Here is my nirvana, my Garden of Eden, my G-spot.

I first got to know the Suffolk coastline about fifteen years ago – which was also when I first learned to ride a bike. The two, for me, are inseparable. You'd not catch me dead cycling in London, where I live: too frenetic, too dangerous. I wouldn't dream of cycling in the other places I've visited when on holiday, like Cornwall or the Lake District or the Pyrenees: too many hills, too much like hard work. No, give me empty lanes, and gentle dips and rises, and dry weather, and a breeze of elderflowers, and the skirr and plink of the spokes, and the freewheeling, no-particular-hurry of it all. I don't want to have to think about what I'm doing. I don't want to have to worry. This is the point: it's an entirely sensuous, hedonistic, self-forgetful experience.

Because I'm not a Lycra-clad cycling buff, let alone an eco-militant. 'Two wheels good' is a slogan I'll happily lend my name to, but not if it carries the rider 'Four wheels bad'. I approve the idea of a nationwide web of cycling paths, but I'm not a campaigner. I've no special feelings of fraternity with fellow enthusiasts. I don't know about carbon fibre or fillet brazing or derailleur gears or all the other boysy gadgets. I don't attempt tricks, or marathon distances. I'll have a go at mending a puncture, in an emergency, but I prefer to rely on Obie Baggott, the one-eyed octogenarian living nearby who's taken up bike repairs since his retirement and will solve any problem you have for a quid or so, so long as you'll wait a while in his shed, among the discarded frames and twisted wheels and handlebars like rams' horns and white dusted inner tubes and rusting pumps. I've had to visit Obie a lot. I ride an old, squeaky, five-gear racing bike made by a company I've never heard of somewhere in Poland. Puch, it says on the frame; maybe that's pronounced Puck. The bike is certainly puckish in its unreliability. Thanks to Obie, though, it and I are still magically intact fifteen years on.

It's no surprise we've had our ups and downs, since I've developed the habit, on my excursions, of starting out on roads and then quitting them for footpaths and bridle paths instead – beginning smoothly a few miles inland and roughing it at the end to the beach at Dunwich, or Walberswick, or Southwold. You set off down the most minor of B-roads, or C-roads, or maybe it's even a G-road, pheasants rattling away unseen in the hedges or sometimes scuttling out of ditches with their long, erect, brown tails. You wind past pink, thatched cottages and lonely, moated farms, past pigs in their metal Nissen huts and meadows boiling with wheat and barley. You twist and turn as far as the lanes will take you, then strike off on to paths through woods, the route lumpy now with tree roots and gravel, the saddle juddering under your bum, and with the risk, in a dry season, of sudden stretches of sand that can bunker or topple you. You keep going somehow, even where the path's narrow and strewn with ferns, and then at last you're out, and up on to the common, a different landscape again, bracken and gorse and purple heather, and it's here you get the first view of the sea. And if you stop a moment and run your fingers through your hair, you'll find something odd's happened: your hair feels silky, the vibrations of the handlebars have sensitized your hands just as the handle of a motor mower does, softening the fingertips, so that your hair's become like someone else's, the girl in the shampoo advert, a miracle of silk. Feeling good about yourself, the last half mile is easy, path and road and then the sand and shingle of the shore, where you sprawl with the bike that got you here, at rest now, upside down with its wheels in the air, the sliced cliffs with martins nesting in them behind you, the swell of the sea in front of you in tune with the swell in your heart.

Do I make it sound a pastoral idyll, a marine dream? Perhaps I should mention the less utopian aspects: saddle sores or tender tendons; the midge lodging in the corner of an eye; your hands oily from where you had to put the loose chain back on for the nth time; the cross-hatching of scratches between knee and ankle, where in one of many moments of carelessness your foot slipped from the pedal, which rapped and shinned you in reply. But these sores are minor irritants. If there's pain, it's of the pleasure-enhancing kind, a little frisson of blood and sharpness, nothing too masochistic.

Yet I can't pretend my pleasure in cycling is altogether wholesome. On the contrary, I'm probably about the only person in the country for whom it has the thrill of something dangerous and forbidden.

As a child in rural Yorkshire, I wasn't allowed a proper bike – nothing bigger than the trike, the three-wheeler I'd been given at the age of six. A fast road ran through our village, and my parents, knowing they could hardly confine my bicycling to the garden, feared what might be done to me by a passing car. I argued, I pleaded. I endured the humiliations of pedalling hunchbacked around the house on three wheels while friends, several years younger, performed stunts on two. Alone on holiday with my cousins in Manchester, at the age of ten, I secretly began trying to teach myself to ride – but it felt wobbly, and unnatural, and a nasty high-speed fall left me wondering if my parents might not have a point. Then my best friend Simon was knocked off his bike, just outside the village, and I knew they were right. There weren't helmets for cyclists in those days, and Simon suffered serious head injuries. I took fruit to his bedside and watched his silent pallid face, his hair turbaned with a white bandage. For a long time he didn't speak at all, and when he did speak it was in the voice of someone else. He came back to school some months later, but was never the same. I'd lost a friend. And all because of cycling.

I gave up arguing with my parents after that. 'Easy as learning to ride a bike,' people would say about such-and-such a task, but the analogy was lost on me. In time, my not having learnt to ride a bike became my darkest secret. Throughout my teens, at grammar school and university, I hid it from friends, as shameful as dyslexia or an undescended testicle. There were other things I couldn't do either: take throw-ins, though I played football; dive, though I could swim. But being afraid to ride a bike was the deepest humiliation.

And then one day in my late twenties, I arrived for a back-pack holiday in Corfu, and mopeds seemed the only sensible way to get about the island: taking my life in my hands, I shook and teetered, but I didn't fall off. Emboldened, I came home, hired a bicycle in East Anglia, and I was away, the last taboo broken twenty years on. I still feel vaguely defiant in the saddle, as if I'm cheeking my parents, or showing my friends – 'Look, two wheels' – that I'm normal, just like them.

As I said earlier, I'm not a propagandist for bikes, but a sensualist. I don't mind if no one else discovers the bike routes I've grown fond of these last ten years; to be honest, I'd be happy for visitors to Suffolk to stick to the main roads in their cars. Hedonism is selfish like that. Still, I do confess to feeling smug that the consumer product which gave me most pleasure in the early eighties, when Thatcherism was at full pelt, wasn't a BMW or a bottle of Bollinger but a humble bike. And I like the idea that here's a truly democratic pleasure, open to rich and poor alike. Sceptics might say it's a form of nostalgia, a yearning for the days of simpler transport. But I don't think so. I still drive a car. And when I do ride my bicycle down a country lane I don't feel myself to be living mistily in the past but intensely, for the moment, this moment, now.

Better than sex? No, nothing is, only more sex, or different sex. But perhaps all those leering jokes about being 'in the saddle' have a point. I'm not thinking of the fact that it's the genitals that come into closest contact with the bike. Nor do I look on the bike itself as a love object: if my bike were a love object I'd surely have swopped it years ago for a lighter, younger and more elegant partner. Nor is this fetishism – the perfect, fetishistic hymn to bicycles was written some twenty years ago by the Irish playwright Stuart Parker. I remember seeing his play, *Spokesong*, being performed in London, and enjoying it – but it didn't inspire me, any more than Norman Tebbit did, to get on a bike.

No, what connects sex and bicyling is that they offer a kind of self-transcendence. They are a union between you and another; they require physical exertion and co-ordination and a sort of trust. But at the pitch of pleasure you're on your own. Indeed there's hardly even you there: it's pure sensation, pure tactility, a moment of such refinement of space and time that, paradoxically, the where and when fall quite away.

Try telling that to the postman on his round. Try telling it to the population of Peking. Try telling it to Obie Baggott. All right, I don't want to be precious. This isn't Zen and the art of bicycling. But put it this way. What you get from riding a bicycle is, at its best, a pleasure you can't find anywhere else – something between action and indolence, freedom and control, mental vacancy and sensual super-alertness, self-transcendence and self-confirmation.

And you can always stop – much easier than in a car. Stopping and looking is important: being the sole unbusy thing while the world rushes about its serious business. Just pause a minute, or freewheel for a few yards, and look at all the work going on around you: electric pylons trudging towards Sizewell, shouldering their heavy load; delivery lorries with bread and tins and clinking crates of lemonade bottles hurrying to the last few village shops; horses in fields, heads down deep in thought; kingfishers flashing up reed-beds, herons cranking themselves aloft from marshes, innumerable bees and wasps wafting themselves round blackthorn and wild rose. And just you, alone in a country lane, engineless, idling, your mind gently ticking over as the spokes beneath you also tick, your hands steering but at rest in front of you, the sun above and a cool breeze in your face. Who could beat it?